PLASTICITY

SLOANE CARTER

*****

PROLOGUE

Los Angeles... the City of Angels or a city of devils? Liv, a beautiful, unassuming UCLA coed from a quiet small town, finds herself questioning not only that, but everything else. Led into a posh maze of wealth, sex and absolute privilege, will Liv's virtue be enough to keep her safe? Or will she realize a little too late that Los Angeles is full of devils masquerading as angels, and that the most notorious one of all is the one she just accidentally fell for. It won't matter in the end though. Nothing could ever have prepared her for the confidence within the ocean blue eyes set like gemstones in Chase Swanson's face; her best friend Michelle's dangerously enchanting older brother. Arrogant and used to getting anything he wants, Chase is clearly trouble, but he's also a twelve in a city filled with tens. He's the worst thing for her... and the only one she wants.

PLASTICITY

Bel Air Brats

"Liv! Stay with me this summer at my parent's house in Bel Air! It will be so fucking fun!" Michelle shrieks from somewhere near my knees. She's upside down at the moment, suspended above a keg by two lanky fraternity boys; a third is busy trying to stuff a hose full of beer into her mouth. She yells something about swallowing, which elicits a loud chorus of cheers, and then proceeds to suck a mythological amount of beer down her throat. This produces an enthusiastic roar from the stacks of males surrounding her, apart from a handful of extra drunk underclassmen who are stunned to silence by the glory of what they've just witnessed. Michelle has that kind of effect on males. It's the end of Spring semester at UCLA and a beautiful evening in Los Angeles. It's a time tested recipe for wild, out of control house parties. Ordinarily I'd already be plotting my escape route, but I'm so astonished by what just came out of my best friend's gorgeous

3

mouth that I hardly notice the chaos. And besides, Michelle never takes no for an answer. Her family is Hollywood royalty and she's used to getting exactly what she wants. Her father is the most successful music producer in the world and her mother was a famous supermodel. They're the definition of A-listers and everything they do is over the top. Spending the summer with the Swanson's means I'll be undressing every evening in the most lavish mansion in Los Angeles, and waking up to a full service staff and the most Lux lifestyle imaginable. It might sound cliche, but it's literally a dream come true.

"Wow!... Michelle!" I stammer. I'm still beaming, too dumbfounded by her offer to say much of anything. "That is so nice of you!" Becoming friends with Michelle Swanson is definitely the craziest thing that has ever happened to me. I'm from a tiny Midwestern town that barely made the map. I wasn't exactly wild in high school, but compared to these L.A. girls I might as well have been raised Amish. She just grins and glides away gracefully into the haze on sky high wedges that I can barely stand in. As I follow her, I can't help but be impressed, for the millionth time, by her long defined legs, tiny waist, and large perfect tits. It's all explicitly displayed right now in a skintight Versace dress. Her hair dances mesmerizingly in shimmering blonde waves as she struts and suddenly, I feel insecure. She's absurdly, breathtakingly beautiful. A naughty Barbie doll with an exotic twist. If you were to Google 'California dream girl,' her picture would probably appear.

I make a mental note to do it later to see if I'm right. I watch her as she applies nude gloss to her lips. She has the kind of impossible lips that women pay thousands of dollars and endure painful injections to attain... only that's not how she got them. No one believes me, but I've seen pictures of her as a child and they were just as impossible then. She stops abruptly and spins around, her blue eyes glinting with mischief.

"Livvie, let's be Bel Air brats this summer!" she squeals, doing a playful twirl. All eyes are on her as she does it, as they are pretty much all the time. The boys stare lustfully and the girls glare and secretly die a little on the inside. It's nothing new, she's been a showstopper her entire life.

I grew up in the Midwest, in Illinois, but not in Chicago like everyone always assumes. The population in my hometown is only 488, which is about how many students were in my first class here at UCLA. I remember walking into the auditorium feeling overwhelmed and out of place. It must have shown because a stunning blonde took pity on me and invited me to sit next to her. She laughed when I told her that my entire town could fit in the auditorium.

"Where are you from?" she asked, studying me curiously.

"Um.. a small town in Illinois," I replied, looking down at the floor. I felt like a brown paper wrapped shoebox next to a real Christmas present sitting next to her. My eyes were drawn to her Prada pumps and how much they contrasted with my beat up

Converse. "You've probably never heard of it. It's called Kaneville," I added.

"Small town girl..." Michelle whispered to no one in particular and then casually leaned forward and snatched a water bottle out of a random girl's hand to use as a microphone. She hopped up on her chair like it was a tiny stage and began belting out "Don't Stop Believin'" by Journey in a very outdoor volume. She ignored all of the judgmental looks from the other students and simply sang even louder. I giggled, wide eyed and genuinely fascinated by the confidence of this vivacious girl.

When she finally sat back down, she grinned and said, "I'm Michelle. Michelle Swanson."

"I'm Olivia. Nice to meet you! Wow! Thank you for that performance!" I was still nearly in shock but also touched by the gesture.

"No big deal! I've won karaoke contests singing that song!" she said airily. "Olivia..." She put her finger to her mouth as if in deep thought. "That's a long ass name. How about if I call you Liv from now on?" She flashed me a million dollar smile, which I later learned was a billion dollar smile. I think Michelle found it refreshing that I didn't fawn all over her because she's a Swanson. Apparently most people do. I actually had no idea how important her family was, or even who they were, until later when I really got to know her.

I snap back to the present. Michelle is retrieving a large heart-shaped sunglass case from her pink crocodile Hermès Birkin bag. She flips the case open, revealing a gold 'W' crest and pulls out a pair of round, white sunglasses and puts them on. I grin at the sight of her in these adorable frames. They make my posh yet intimidating friend appear instantly more playful and approachable. I've seen her in Gucci, Prada, Versace, Tom Ford, etc., but never in sunglasses like these. They say *Bel Air* on the top and *Wildfox* on the bottom, and in reversed order on the other side. She purses her lips at me.

"Say yes, Liv! I mean, come on! It's fucking BEL AIR! You don't really want to stay with Kevin in that cramped little apartment do you?" she asks, rolling her eyes. Before Michelle's invite, I was planning on living with my friend Kevin this summer in a studio near campus. His usual roommate Hunter won't be around, and by not around, I mean he's currently in jail and then heading straight to rehab.

"Hunter probably left his cum everywhere!" Michelle shouts as she crinkles her nose in disgust. "Dude, you could get an STD from just sitting on the couch!! Considering how my only encounter with Hunter went, she might have a point.

Fucked Up Southern Prince

I met Kevin Taylor first semester in a Women's Studies class. The female professor picked on him mercilessly. He was one of the only males in the class and I guess she wanted to make an example of the "enemy." The enemy being white over-privileged American males. Yes, Kevin is a white male in America, but over-privileged and cocky? Not a bit. He's from rural Michigan and grew up in a small town just like I did. I came to his rescue one day when the professor was being particularly cruel to him and we've been friends ever since. Kevin's roommate on the other hand, is the spoiled rotten son of a Texas oil tycoon and exactly the kind of over-privileged white male she'd been railing against. The first and only time I met him was certainly memorable.

It was a balmy October evening and I had walked over to Kevin's apartment to study for an exam. I knocked on the door, but instead of Kevin like I expected, an unfamiliar and very Southern male voice yelled, "it's open!" I entered the apartment hesitantly and was greeted by the sight of a naked man sitting on the couch, watching porn and stroking a very oversized erection. I froze. I assumed he would be horrified and possibly mumble an apology as he bolted for a bedroom, but no, he just looked over and winked at me without missing a beat. Pun intended.

"Hi! I'm Hunter!" he declared in a charming Southern drawl, as he flashed me a toothy grin.

I composed myself, sort of, and attempted a deadpan expression.

"Um... hi.... I'm Liv," I mumbled, trying not to stare. Just then, Kevin emerged from his room and just stood there for a moment, suspended in disbelief. He quickly recovered and turned crimson with anger.

"Hunter!! What *the fuck* dude!?!"

"Oh hey Kev! You bring her for *me*?" Hunter asked him. "Hell yeah, you're a fucking rock star!" He lowered a rolled up bill to the powder that was arranged in white lines on the coffee table.

"No, I absolutely did not!" Kevin retorted with both hands over his face, clearly dying of embarrassment. Hunter ignored him as he wiped white powder from under his nose. He summoned me with a quick whistle.

"Hey, Kevin's friend, do you want to help me finish?" he asked, pointing sincerely to his erection. "I'll share this here blow with you and you can keep the C-note! I don't give a single fuck!" He picked up a stack of bills that was sitting on the coffee table next to a large pistol and the rail yard of cocaine. "I can wipe my ass with the Benjamins 'cuz I'm rich as hell! Making it rain, baby!" he yelled while flicking dollar bills all over the apartment. I had never seen anyone so brazen, so uninhibited, or so shameless in all my life. I bit my lip and looked away.

9

"Um, that's okay. We have to study," I said and quickly followed Kevin into his bedroom. When I sat down on Kevin's bed, he looked at me and shook his head.

"I'm so sorry you had to witness that," he said softly. It was a predictably chivalrous response; a Kevin response. "He's such a dirt bag!" he groaned with his head in his hands.

"I mean, yeah, that was pretty crazy, but it's okay Kev, Michelle Swanson is one of my best friends, I'm used to this kind of stuff by now!" I said cheerfully and smiled at him.

"Yeah? Well maybe we should set them up!" he said and managed a smirk, despite visibly blushing at the symphony of porn and his roommate yelling enthusiastically at his own penis.

"Hell yes girl!! You spit that little baby dick out an' come chew on the pride of North Dallas you hot, dirty slut! That's right, let Daddy show you why everything's bigger in Texas!" Hunter hollered at the screen. I put my hand over my mouth to muffle my laughter. At this point I found the situation hilarious, instead of horrifying like I guess I should have. Kevin let out a sigh of relief when the living room went silent.

"Finally!" he exclaimed. But our relief from the madness was short lived. Kevin's bedroom door abruptly flew open and we both screamed as it slammed into the wall. Surprise instantly turned to astonishment, and I tried not to burst out laughing when I saw Hunter standing naked in the doorway, his once proud erection now drooping and sad.

"Last chance, Kevin's sexy friend. I might have coke dick right now, but you're hot enough to finish me off," he drawled, pointing proudly at his manhood.

Hunter, the fucked up Southern Prince Charming who comes bearing gifts of cocaine and cash to entice the princesses.

"Sorry, you're on your own there," I said, trying not to smile.

"Fuck it then, off to the strip club on Sunset. Hope ya'lls studying goes well!" he said as he winked at me and strutted off naked down the hallway.

Hunter made it almost a whole year at UCLA, living life to the fullest and getting away with his brand of debauchery; at least until about two weeks ago. As the story goes, he saw an empty police car parked at a convenience store and decided it would be fun to do a line of cocaine off of the hood for an Instagram post. When the officer spotted him, Hunter proceeded to steal the police car, after which a high speed chase ensued. A fraternity house threw a "Free Hunter!" party on the spot. That's one odd thing about Los Angelenos, if there's a high speed chase going on, they will drop whatever they are doing to watch it. We were all riveted to the 90" plasma, cheering for Hunter from the basement of the fraternity house as we watched him driving as fast as he could in the cop car towards West Hollywood.

"Hunter, get on the 2, bro!" one guy yelled frantically at the TV.

"No dude, stay on Sunset!" another screamed.

Hunter only made it to Hollywood Boulevard before he crashed into a storefront. We all watched in horror as he climbed out of the police car and tried to run before being tackled on top of a star on the Hollywood Walk of Fame. There are rumors that it was James Dean's star, others that it was Marilyn Monroe's. Regardless, the aftermath of his arrest was pure pandemonium. Some party attendees threw shoes at the television in protest, but the bolder ones took their objections to the streets. There were angry students jumping on top of cars, drunken frat boys trying to light beer soaked couches on fire, and groups of gleeful rioters pushing parked cars over onto their sides. I left just before the LAPD S.W.A.T team arrived. Michelle stayed and got tear gassed. She was temporarily blinded by the effects of it, but still scoffing at the suggestion of being caught when she ran headfirst into a tree. I can still see remnants of the bruise on her forehead.

After that disastrous event, Hunter's dad decided enough was enough. When he finally gets out of jail, there's a spot waiting for the fucked up Southern Prince at a drug and alcohol rehabilitation center in Malibu.

Wildfox Bel Air Shades

"Liv!" Michelle yells as she claps in my face, snapping me out of my memory lane tour of Hunter. "Babes! We will give you a car so you can get to your summer classes or whatever!" I think about my recently stolen beach cruiser, which was my main mode of transportation over the last year, and realize I'd be crazy to turn down Michelle's offer. I make up my mind on the spot.

"Yes! My answer is hell yes Michelle! Thank you so much!!" I say excitedly.

"Aieeeee! So stoked!" she squeals. "We are going to have so much fun Liv! You're already like fam and my parents adore you!!" She strokes my face sloppily, filled with sudden adoration.

"Um... do you guys want me to pay rent... or anything?" I ask, just in case.

"Adorable!" she giggles, removing her sunglasses. "No, no rent silly!" She puts her glasses on my face. "Here, wear these. They are yours now! Liv, the *fresh* Princess of Bel Air!" I'm so happy, I can't stop smiling.

"Thank you, Michelle!" I declare as I kiss her cheek. "I will never take them off!" She gives me a thousand watt smile.

Suddenly, a tan, good looking fraternity boy sneaks up behind Michelle and wraps his arms around her. I've seen him on campus; I think his name is Brad. He is tall and athletic with the kind of L.A. looks and charm that can get away with murder. The boys at UCLA are all cut from the same cloth; cocky and handsome, with devilish grins that appear mischievous even in the rare moments when they're behaving. Brad is wearing a fraternity shirt that is currently covered in beer, and snug fitting American flag board shorts.

"Michelle, lets go upstairs, baby! I've missed you!!" he booms while sloppily grabbing her large silicone filled breasts. They were a gift from her parents on her 16th birthday. "Oh hey, what's up Liz? You're looking hot in that sundress," he says and smiles slyly at me while giving Michelle's perfect booty a firm slap. I roll my eyes but secretly I'm flattered. Michelle spins around to face him.

"A. Her name is *Liv*, not Liz, and B. She's not interested Brad and neither am I! You haven't called me in like a week!" She feigns a pouty expression. Brad kisses her bottom lip which is sticking out.

"Baby, I'm sorry. Let me make it up to you! I'll go down on you again! You fucking loved that shit last time!" he slurs and winks. Before she can answer, he leans in to grab her and throws her over his broad muscular shoulder. She lets out an exaggerated squeal.

"BRAD! NO!!" she yells and pounds on his back, but I know she isn't actually mad because there's a very naughty smile on her face. After all, Brad is one of her boy toys, and she wouldn't dare pass up a fun fling for the evening. I watch her long legs dangle down his chest as he drunkenly yet effortlessly carries the *real* Princess of Bel Air up the staircase.

"Hey Trey, play 'Versace On the Floor,'" Brad instructs a boy standing near the sound system. The pledge nods dutifully.

Michelle yells to me over Brad's shoulder, "Liv, my dad's people will take care of everything, have all of your stuff packed and ready to go tomorrow! Byeeee!! Love you!!"

Bruno Mars fills my ears as the song blares from a pair of huge speakers. Well played Brad. Knowing your designers and your music is a non-negotiable for Michelle. It doesn't matter though, she'll hypnotize him with her magical bedroom eyes before her dress ever hits the floor. I sigh, wishing that I could be as effortlessly confident as she is and have a boy toy of my own.

I look around for anyone I might know, but all I see are half naked coeds and fraternity boys yelling and wrestling. I know Michelle isn't going to be back anytime soon, and I'm not in the mood to get hit on by boys that I know will never call, so I push my way through the sea of testosterone towards a side door.

It feels amazing to step into the calm evening, away from the chaos. I make my way down the rickety wooden staircase to begin the trek back to my dorm room, weaving in and out of drunk college kids on the sidewalk. There are other house parties in full swing and the larger ones are already spilling into the street. My

15

mind is filled with possibilities as the sun fades slowly into the edge of the crimson sky.

A girl playing beer pong in a driveway yells, "I love your sunglasses bro!"

"Thanks!" I reply. The girl gives me the hang loose symbol and I give her a thumbs up, and immediately feel like a nerd. I put my fingers on the sides of the Wildfox sunglasses. "Bel Air...." I whisper to no one as I look up at a palm tree. I close my eyes and smile as I let it all sink in. "I'm moving to Bel Air, Mr. Palm Tree!" I say out loud. I must be a little tipsy, but I really do love these California palm trees. Actually, I love all the other quirky Dr. Seuss looking trees too, and all the crazy Pacific Coast plant life that you only ever see here. I love the warm coastal air on my skin. I love all of it. Nothing here ever dies; everything is always alive and welcoming and free.

I pop my earbuds in and turn on some music. I walk past bougainvillea and let my fingertips graze the petals as I inhale the scent. I wave at the the Bruins bear; he looks like the one on the California flag atop the pole next to him. The bear will always reign here.

The City of Angels has so much sparkle, so much glitz and glamour. It has been an adjustment for sure but I'm getting the hang of it. Thanks to Michelle's disgust with anything last season and her insatiable appetite for shopping, my dorm room closet is always overflowing with her gilded rejects. She frequently brings

16

over trash bags filled with tens of thousands of dollars in designer everything. She says it's all stuff she just 'can't stand looking at anymore.'

"Liv, EW!! Those are so last season!" she scolded as I stared longingly at a pair of discarded Louboutin's. I didn't care, I thought they were amazing.

Trustafarian

I hope my hippie roommate Becky has already gone home to Telluride for the summer. We never really hit it off, despite my best efforts to be friendly. I think... well actually I know, that it had a lot to do with my friendship with Michelle. I naively assumed that we would all just get along, but then Michelle met her and instantly nicknamed her "Rainbow Bud." And I don't mean she called her that behind her back. It was more like 'I don't know why you keep saying your name is Becky, Rainbow Bud.' It's obvious why Becky hates Michelle, since Michelle is always mean to her, but I'm not sure why Michelle has so much disdain for Becky. Maybe it's because she has dreadlocks and likes to hula hoop for fun, but I honestly have no idea.

"Who the fuck hula hoops for fun? What a douche!" Michelle said loudly one day as my roommate grabbed her hula hoop from behind the door. "I bet your drum circle is going off right now! Don't get too turnt!" she taunted as Becky fled the room, clutching the hula hoop tightly against her body.

Becky usually tried to ignore Michelle's rude remarks, but one day she made the fatal error of actually engaging her. It happened months ago but I remember it like it was yesterday. It started with Michelle barging into our room out of the blue.

18

"Livvie, I've been seriously thinking, and I don't want to be mean or whatever, but your hair straight up sucks!" I flinched a little at her casual cruelty but Becky's jaw nearly hit the floor.

"You need some serious highlights! I can't take it anymore! Your hair is just so... brown! And boring!" She walked over to me and placed a concerned hand on my shoulder. "These are my people and they are going to help you," she explained condescendingly as two stylists made their way into the room.

A man walked in after them, pushing a glass cart. Sitting on top of the cart was a gold bucket of champagne on ice, half a dozen champagne glasses, some of which were filled with candy, and four cute black and white striped porcelain jars labeled Uppers, Ganja, Secrets and White Lies. She squealed with delight when she saw them.

"Yes! I fucking love these pills!" As she was shoving her hand into the jar that said Uppers, I remember thinking that it was so strange that Michelle was able to pull this off in a dorm room. Did she pay someone off to get away with this, or did she really just roll the dice? I glanced apprehensively at my roommate who was by now visibly pained.

"Are you SERIOUS right now? Can't you guys do Olivia's hair somewhere ELSE?!?" Becky erupted, pointing dramatically at her computer screen for effect. "I have a really big test later that I need to study for!" Michelle turned around slowly and glared at her.

"First of all, Rainbow Bud, her name is Liv, not *O-liv-i-a*," Michelle snapped, exaggerating each syllable of my name.

"And no, *we* won't. I wouldn't expect you to understand this, since you have stinky, gross dreadlocks, but this is a hair emergency! If you don't like it, then *you* get the fuck out!" she shouted, and then calmly flicked an orange pill into her mouth.

Rainbow Bud managed to compose herself just enough to mumble "bitch" under her breath. I heard it clearly, and I cringed when I realized Michelle had heard it too. Big mistake Becky. From the eerie silence that followed, I could tell verbal attack mode was over and physical attack mode had been engaged. Michelle gave me a disarming wink, and then calmly removed the champagne from the bucket, aimed it at Becky's face and pushed the cork out with her thumb. Becky gasped as the little projectile slammed into the wall next to her ear.

"Poppin' bottles, BITCH!" Michelle yelled wildly. She picked up the bucket of ice and sauntered over to Becky with it. I watched, mouth hanging open, as Michelle dumped it on my terrified roommate's head, drenching her and her computer, equally. The strangest part was that the stylists in the room didn't flinch at any of it, not even when Becky began to sob.

"Ew. Your crying is super distracting," Michelle said while chewing a handful of white pills.

"I just had to pop some bars because you are literally so annoying. I was planning on having an upper day, but you just

20

ruined it by being a dumb asshole. No one wants to hear that shit. Go be an emotional hippy somewhere else." She made a shoo away motion with her hand and a distraught Becky sprang up to run out of the room.

"Oh and Rainbow Bud,..." Michelle said in an ice cold tone, as she rolled a pill casually between her fingertips. Becky stiffened and froze. "If you tell anyone about this, I *will* kill you." The hair on my arms instantly stood on end. Michelle glanced over at me and then giggled charmingly and flipped her hair off her shoulder. "I'm kidding!" she said while flicking her wrist flamboyantly. "But, I will absolutely make your life a fucking hell," she said and winked. Rainbow Bud bolted from the room, running as fast as one reasonably could run while wearing Birkenstocks. I could hear her sobbing all the way down the hallway. Then, as if nothing had happened, Michelle turned to the stylists.

"So anyways, I was thinking you guys could do a combination of highlights and lowlights. Give her a natural, sun-kissed I was just at the beach, look!" she suggested airily.

"Oh Michelle, you are so sophisticated!" gushed one stylist.

"You are amazing, Michelle! Like hella great idea!" squealed the other.

I was still reeling at what I just witnessed as they brushed blue paste and wrapped section after section of my hair in foil. Michelle plopped down next to me on the bed with a champagne flute in her hand. She made a fake gun with her other hand and aimed it at my roommate's desk.

"Bang bang, bitch!" she yelled and giggled as her big blue eyes flashed with naughty delight. She reminded me of the deranged DC Comic book character Harley Quinn, and I suddenly realized that I needed to tread very lightly around Michelle and *never* get on her bad side. She rolled her eyes and took a delicate sip of champagne.

"Liv, your roommate's the fucking worst! Do you want my dad to pull some strings? Get you out of this mess?" she asked.

"I guess so..." I replied, still dazed.

Michelle called me a week later and was furious...

"Dude, fucking Rainbow Bud? She's like filthy rich!!" she screamed into the phone. "She has a big fat trust fund and is just a hippie because she sucks! She's a fucking trustafarian! Ugh! Sorry girl, my dad tried to take her down, but she has too much money protecting her." She groaned in defeat. "Oh well, just make sure you steal her Colorado weed. They do it better in the mountains, and I really need to fill up my Ganja jar!"

From then on, Michelle changed Becky's nickname from "Rainbow Bud" to "Trustafarian Bud." Needless to say, it was an awkward rest of the school year living with Trustafarian Bud.

Damaged Doll

I unlock the door to my dorm room and breathe a sigh of relief when I see that Becky's side is completely empty. I quickly get into my pajamas, brush my teeth and use a wipe to get my makeup off. I'm way too exhausted to actually wash my face. I have never been more eager to get under the blankets in my narrow little bed. I'm so tired I can barely keep my eyes open. I look around at all my stuff in boxes as I pull the covers up.

"You did it Olivia, one year as a Bruin down, ten more to go," I say out loud. "I mean, good job *Liv*," I correct myself, as if people can hear me and might ridicule my real name. "You're going to make a great psychologist someday. The long nights studying will all be worth it." I close my eyes and snuggle in, but just as I'm starting to dream, my phone begins vibrating excitedly on the nightstand. I groan and roll over to answer it. The screen has a 213 area code number that I don't recognize.

"Hello?" I mumble.

"Good evening, Miss Walker. Emma here, Mr. Swanson's personal assistant. Michelle informed me that you will need your things picked up. We will send the movers tomorrow. She also informed me that you will require a vehicle for the summer. Is this all correct Miss Walker?" Emma's accent is an odd blend of L.A.

23

and Sweden. I've met her many times, but I guess she's forgotten, or maybe she simply doesn't care.

"Hello, Emma! Yes, and oh my gosh a car would be fantastic!" I reply enthusiastically.

"We will send a Mini Cooper. Will this be to your liking, Miss Walker?" she asks. I have so many butterflies in my stomach.

"Um, yes, that would be great! Thank you so much!" I respond, glad she can't see my cheesy grin through the phone. "Oh. My. God..." I mouth silently to the ceiling.

"I trust you know how to get to the Swanson's estate...." she probes.

"Yeah, I've been there many times. Don't you remember me?" I ask, genuinely confused.

"Great! We will see you soon. Goodnight," Emma says curtly, ignoring the question.

"OK thanks...er... bye," I stammer, momentarily confused by the silence because she hung up without saying goodbye. Typical. I'm still getting used to the fact that the people in this town always seem to be in a rush. Emma is no exception.

I text Kevin to break the news. I forgot to do that earlier.

"Hi Kev! I'm actually going to stay with Michelle for the summer! Sorry! Thanks so much for the offer though, I hope you can find someone to take Hunter's place!" I write.
My phone dings almost immediately.

"No prob! I'm sure I'll find someone, but not someone as great as you!" he writes, following it up with the sad face and the wink emoticons. I smile thinking about how sweet Kevin is. He is a breath of fresh air in this dog eat dog city.

"At least it's not Hunter. Lol. Goodnight Kev." I write and press send. I pass out with my phone still in my hand.

I wake with a jolt after what seems like a moment of sleep, to my phone vibrating incessantly next to me. I roll over and fumble with it, squinting at it through sleepy eyes. "Michelle Swanson" is flashing over and over again on the screen so I press the green talk button.

"Hey Shells..." I say sheepishly, knowing that she has probably called at least ten times and I slept through all of it. She likes to do that. If she can't get you the first time, she just keeps trying. Michelle prefers phone calls or FaceTime to text messaging or social media. I kid you not, I once received a hand written letter from her, and she actually mailed it to my dorm room with a stamp. The letter was just about what she did that day. It was so strange that I never even mentioned it.

"Hey bitch! Oh my God! I have been calling you for hours! Why are you not awake yet? Emma is sending someone with the car in thirty minutes! I am already at my parent's house!" she yells impatiently through the phone. "Just leave your shit, the moving dudes will take care of it. Pack an overnight bag for now. I miss you, Liv. You need to come now! I have to tell you about my night!

Brad was insanely good in bed! I rode his dick all night long and I came like four times in a row! Then we drank so much Cristal! I got super fucked up and had to do like so much blow to sober up!" She starts giggling and I wonder if cocaine really sobers people up. "I've been eating chillies like all morning to kick this stupid champagne hangover!" she exclaims and then groans dramatically. "Chillies" are what Michelle calls anti-anxiety meds and pain killers, like Xanax, Percocet and Vicodin. I think I hear her chewing one now. "Anyways, love you babe! See you soon! Byyeee." She hangs up before I can even say a word. Classic Michelle.

    I stretch out, throw the covers off, and stumble to the bathroom. I hope I made the right decision to spend the summer with her. Michelle is a bit unstable, and truth be told, I'm kind of scared of her. She has high highs and low lows. I've cared for her through it all though. I look in the mirror and think about the 'incident.' A horrible evening that I will never forget. Michelle was already pretty messed up when I got to her place to go out, and it only got worse from there. We made a few stops at 'friend's houses,' which I'm pretty sure were really her drug dealers and then ended up at a party at Justin Bieber's place. Twenty minutes in, she fell in the pool and nearly drowned, then proceeded to throw up on not one but *both* of the Franco brothers. She tried to make a beeline for the exit but face planted instead and had to be carried out of the party because she couldn't stand, much less walk on her own. My last image of Michelle that evening was of her being carried off, hanging limply over a security guard's shoulder, still wearing a vomit soaked pastel dress and vintage 1970's square sunglasses that covered almost her entire face. She looked so... rock and roll.

The 'Incident'

It was a little after midnight when I left the party. Struggling through bleary eyes, I called an Uber to take me to Michelle's place so I could check on her after the disastrous evening. She lives by herself in a beautiful penthouse apartment near campus. Michelle didn't have to suffer through dorm room hell like the rest of us; another one of the many perks of being a Swanson. When I arrived at her place, I rang the doorbell and knocked, over and over, and then called her at least a dozen times on the phone. I suddenly remembered the key she had given me to her place to let myself in. 'Use only in case of emergency,' she had said with a wink.

"Michelle?" I called tentatively as I walked softly down the hallway toward her bedroom. As I got closer to her door, my stomach dropped. Her dress was in a pile on the floor and there was vomit everywhere. I followed the trail of puke into her bedroom and found her lying on her bed, naked and face down. She looked like an ice sculpture; a mangled Sleeping Beauty. "Michelle? Oh my God... are you okay!?!" I heard myself asking, my voice unsteady and panic stricken. I shook her, praying she would open her eyes and wake up. Her body felt cold and clammy against my hand. Her smooth tan skin was somehow pale now, with hints of blue. "Michelle?!" I shrieked as I shook her again, this time more forcefully. She was completely unresponsive. I rolled her over. "Fuck! Oh no! Oh God.... Michelle!!!" I screamed, as dread shot through my body. She was unconscious, her perfect mouth framed in a strange foamy vomit. "Michelle!! Wake up!!" I shouted at her motionless body. I was positive she was dead. Remembering my CPR classes, I placed my fingers on her neck and felt nothing. Sobbing, I kept trying and trying, until I found the faintest pulse. I fumbled with my phone to call 911. The dispatcher just kept asking for her name. "Michelle! Michelle Swanson!! Please hurry!!" I yelled into the phone.

"Hang on," the dispatcher said, too calmly for comfort. I paced back and forth for what seemed like an eternity, waiting for the sound of a siren, but the sound never came. Minutes later, there was a firm knock at the door and I ran to open it. Instead of the paramedics I was expecting, a doctor and two nurses pushed their way past me, followed by a man wheeling an I.V. stand and carrying a bag of medical supplies. Mr. Swanson and his assistant Emma trailed behind the medical team, looking irritated and put out by the inconvenience. Emma glared at me and told me to leave the room. I complied and waited anxiously just outside the door. Moments later, Emma and Mr. Swanson stepped back into the hallway.

"How is she?" I asked them urgently. Mr. Swanson bent down to my level and put his face uncomfortably close to mine.

"Young lady, you are *never* to call 911 when Michelle has these episodes," he hissed at me through clenched teeth, "you are to call Emma. We got lucky this time. This could have been very detrimental to her and to my family's name! I've done a great job of protecting her from the media jackals for nineteen years. Now that she is on her own, the risk of her getting noticed has grown exponentially! I will not have my daughter followed and stalked by those paparazzi vultures!" He glared at me, the veins bulging in his muscular neck. Why was he so angry with me? I just saved his daughter's life, you would think he would be praising and thanking me. I drunkenly stared at him through my wet eyelashes, hardly believing what I just heard.

"An episode?!? Sir, with all due respect, that was an overdose! Michelle almost died!" I could feel the tears beginning to stream. Emma handed me a clipboard with a piece of paper on it.

"It's a confidentiality agreement," she explained clinically, "we can sue you and your family if you tell anyone about what happened here tonight. You wouldn't want your dad to lose his farm, now would you?" she asked coldly as she handed me a pen. I was baffled and sick to my stomach. How could these people be this heartless?

"I wasn't going to tell anyone..." I mumbled, my voice and hands trembling, barely able to sign. Emma snatched it out of my hands when I was done. I assumed they would stay to make sure Michelle made it through the night, but they didn't. T.J. and Emma

30

turned around and began walking hastily down the hall towards the front door.

"Mr. Swanson!" I shouted. "Where are you going?!" Emma's Christian Louboutins glowed red like the devil with each step. I stood and ran after them. I grabbed the back of her crisp white shirt and attempted to pull her back towards the bedroom.

"Don't touch me!" she barked. Stunned, I let go and watched as they stormed away, slamming the door behind them as they left. It was one of the worst feelings I had ever known. I walked, disgusted and disillusioned, back into Michelle's bedroom. My heart broke at the sight of my best friend hooked up to an I.V.. It made me think of my mom on her death bed. With trembling hands and tears streaming down my face, I picked Michelle's phone up off of the nightstand. I wanted to call her mom, or almost anyone really, just so she wouldn't feel so alone; so unloved. I tried all kinds of password combinations and finally surrendered in defeat as her iPhone denied me again and again. I placed it back on the nightstand, crushed and overcome with sadness. My head still spinning, I pushed a large chair over to the bed. I held her hand and sobbed softly in the dark for hours. At some point in the early hours of morning I felt a sudden squeeze from her hand and her blue eyes shot open. She looked terrified. I squeezed her hand back and told her I was there and her face softened. She licked her dry lips and looked at me, smiling sweetly. I leaned over and kissed her forehead. She touched my face, whispered, 'thank you,' and fell back asleep almost immediately

I woke up in the chair around noon. Michelle was not in bed. I looked around the room. There were no traces of the night before. All of the vomit and all of the medical equipment was gone. It was as if nothing had even happened. I heard the sound of Frank Sinatra soulfully crooning "Drinking Again" through the pristine walls of the penthouse. I followed the song to the balcony, where I found her staring blankly into the distance.

"Hi babe," she said quietly without looking at me, her voice scratchy and strained. "Amelia made coffee, if you want some." Amelia is her maid, who sometimes acts as the punching bag for Michelle's outbursts. She is the most patient and loving woman I have ever met. "Amelia!" Michelle attempted to yell, but her voice was still too hoarse from having her stomach pumped the night before.

"That's okay, I can get it," I said softly. As I was walking back to the balcony with the coffee mug in hand, I felt an overwhelming sense of compassion at the sight of her. Michelle Swanson, always animated and larger than life, right now seemed so small and fragile, as if her patio chair and sweatshirt might swallow her whole. She was wearing large dark sunglasses, with tears rolling slowly down her face beneath them. Each one left a little wet line that glistened for a moment under the California sun.

I recognized her sweats. They were a gift from me. I went to Fred Segal in Santa Monica to find them for her. Sundry is her favorite brand of lounging clothes, but I didn't realize that sweats from the South of France cost a small fortune and I had to dip into my savings account to buy them. She was so happy when she opened them on her birthday that it was worth it. Michelle was holding her coffee mug close to her chest with both hands, like it held the antidote to all of her problems. I felt so much love and understanding for her in that moment. Under all that bravado, wild-child behavior, and abrasiveness, is just a confused little girl who doesn't feel loved. I mean, how could she? Her dad treats her as if she is a nuisance, her mom is always MIA, and Michelle doesn't talk to either of her siblings. In fact, I've not only never met either one of them, I've barely even heard anything about them. She really only spends time with me.

"Can I join you?" I asked her cautiously. She nodded and lifted her sunglasses, wiping her eyes, embarrassed. I snuggled in next to her on the oversized chair and rested my head on her shoulder. She grabbed hold of my hand. I gave her hand a gentle, reassuring squeeze. The Vitamin String Quartet's haunting version of Queen's "Bohemian Rhapsody" was filling the quiet, sad air.

"Shells.... Remember in *Wayne's World* when they were singing 'Bohemian Rhapsody' in the car?" I asked her as a way to lighten the mood and cheer her up. I know she loves that movie. I triumphed on the inside when I saw a small smile start to form on her face. "Did you know that Aurora, Illinois, where Wayne and Garth are from, is near my hood? I will take you sometime," I said and nudged her gently with my shoulder. That made her smile widen enough to see teeth.

"I would like that," she said to me in her still very hoarse voice.

"We can drive around Illinois and blast this song, but the real version by Queen," I suggested engagingly. "I'll buy you a Chicago Blackhawks jersey, and then maybe we can be Wayne and Garth for Halloween!"

"I want to be Garth because I just got a pair of really cute eyeglasses from Chanel. They are super nerdy chic," she replied, suddenly looking a whole lot bubblier. When the faster transition in the song arrived, I started to head bang just like in the movie. She grinned heartily and tried to join me.

"Oh God..." she groaned, holding her head in pain.

"Maybe no head banging just yet," I said, which made her giggle a little. "I can do it for the both of us!" I continued to sing while exaggeratedly flailing my hair to the beat of the song. She clapped in delight.

"Thanks Liv. I love you babe," she whispered, and I couldn't tell if she was thanking me for cheering her up or for saving her life.

"I love you too," I said earnestly, feeling grateful that I had just saved the life of someone I care so much about. I kissed her head at the end of the song and whispered the last lyric into her hair. She smiled and snuggled into me.

I still don't know if her overdose was on purpose or an accident and I never asked. I replay this story a lot in my head though; probably too much.

International Playboy

I finish shoving clothes from a box into an overnight bag and make my way to the bathroom to get ready for the day. I start by brushing my long blondish brown hair. The highlights have faded a bit, but at least my hair isn't boring anymore. My eyes look extra amber contrasted against the black eye makeup I just put on. I inherited gold colored eyes from my mother. My mom had the warmest, most vivid eyes. Her beautiful face flashes intensely in my mind like a painting that has been restored. Wow, she really was beautiful.... she even looked pretty when she was bald and near death. I blink away the tears that are trying to form; I'm tormented by the way my thoughts always seem to go there, pretty much every time I think of her.

"Not today, Liv," I say bravely to the girl staring back at me from the mirror. "You just put on your Dior Blackout mascara... it's expensive!" I scold myself as I push the memory aside and vow not to cry.

I study my sun kissed face with its light dusting of freckles and apply some rouge blush from a pot to my cheeks. I swipe a brush doused in highlighter across my relatively high cheekbones. My lips are now receiving their favorite treatment of luscious, sticky lip gloss from the wand. Michelle gave me a tube of MAC Cthru 'Lipglass' at the beginning of the school year, and not a day goes by when I don't wear it. I think it's become a nervous habit at this point. I'm constantly applying and reapplying it every time I think it's fading from my mouth. I've gone through ten tubes this year, like some sort of obsessive weirdo. I like the way it looks on my face, but mainly, I love the way it feels when I rub my lips together. It's soothing, like a thick, protective silicone barrier. Michelle refers to my endlessly glossed lips as DSL's, or 'Dick Sucking Lips.'

"Good enough," I say to my reflection as I grab my new Wildfox Bel Air sunglasses from the vanity and slip them onto my head. As I'm packing my toiletries, my phone rings again.

"Michelle is so damn needy!" I complain to the empty room through gritted teeth. I glance at the phone and tilt my head. "Kelly Rose" is flashing on the screen. I barely know her. Why on earth would the daughter of the famous rock star Lexxi Rose be calling *me*?

"Hello..." I answer hesitantly.

"I heard you're staying with Michelle Swanson for the summer," Kelly says, her voice quick and low, with threatening undertones.

"Wow, word travels fast! Yep, that's true," I say. I'm pretty confused right now.

"Oh my God!" she squeals. "Girl, you are so lucky! I hate you right now! Like seriously hate you! Grrr!"

"Yeah, the Swanson's Bel Air house is super cool. I'm really excited!" I reply earnestly.

"Whoa, hold up, you really have no idea?" Kelly asks and I can hear the triumph of a know-it-all brat creeping into her voice. "Michelle didn't tell you?"

"No..." I answer tentatively.

"So you don't know that Chase Swanson is on his way home *right now*?" she asks. "Oh! This is *too* good!" she shrieks, with gossipy trouble maker dripping from her voice.

"What? Her brother? Where has he been?" I ask, stunned. My stomach flutters as I think about how many times I've stared at framed photos of Michelle's gorgeous older brother.

"Liv! Hold on a sec! It's Cara Delevingne on the other line! I have to take this, she probably just heard about Chase! Don't go anywhere!" Kelly announces bossily and the line goes silent.

I'm sitting still in a quiet room, but my mind and heart are racing. A sharp electrical current runs down my spine at the thought of him; at the thought of us. I'm going to wake up every morning, all summer long, in the same mansion as the most beautiful mystery in California. I've fantasized about him a hundred times, probably more if I'm being honest, but other than the photos, I don't really know anything about him. I asked Michelle if he was coming home anytime soon. She said it was a sensitive subject and that I was never to bring it up again. I never asked again as I don't want to pry, or worst of all, upset her. I find it strange that no one ever talks about him. I've heard his parents talk about Michelle's older sister Blaire, the pride and joy of the family, the perfect, overachieving 21 year old who attends Stanford University, but never about Chase. As far as I know, he has never come home to visit, even for the holidays. Michelle completely refuses to speak of him.

The photos that line the walls of their mansion are mostly displayed in black and white. Only the ones of Mr. and Mrs. Swanson are in color; any pictures of their children are not... which is actually really strange now that I think about it. But who am I to judge? The Swanson children look stunning, even in black and white. It's obvious from the photos that Chase and Blaire are equally if not more attractive than Michelle. My favorite photograph is displayed in the smoking room, a swanky, upscale lounge in the center of the estate that always smells like marijuana or expensive cigar smoke. Michelle affectionately refers to it as 'the man cave.'

When I saw the room for the first time, I was transfixed by a floor to ceiling black and white mural of James Dean, or so I thought. As I got closer to it however, I realized it wasn't the real rebel without a cause. It was a far more stunning 17-year-old Chase Swanson, captured in the classic James Dean-esque pose. My entire body tingled at the realization that my best friend's older brother is much, much hotter than James Dean. He might be the most enchanting man on Earth. I've stared at that mural every time I've been to their house. Like literally made excuses to leave the room to go stare at it. Ok, maybe I'm obsessed with it. Once when I was really high, I kissed it as soon as Michelle left the room. Omg I'm so embarrassing! I can't help it though, he's so gorgeous it's ridiculous. My other favorite is a framed photograph of Michelle and Chase that's on display in a different wing of the library. They're dressed in matching togas and they're both flipping off the camera.

"Liv?" I hear Kelly's voice. "I'm back! Oh my God! Chase is hot as hell! If I lived there, I wouldn't be able to keep my hands off of him! He's delicious!" she purrs in my ear. "We went to the same high school. I had the biggest crush on him, but he was way out of my league. Chase was a notorious womanizer... he was a total bad boy! Liv, he was so bad that he got sent away during his senior year! I don't know what he did! No one does! He just didn't show up for school one day! Kids used to disappear all the time to go to rehab, but Mr. Swanson doesn't believe in rehab so it couldn't have been that!"

"Oh, wow!" I chime in weakly.

Kelly talks over me, "I kind of forgot about Chase, until my dad brought him up the other day. My dad is super good friends with T.J. and Daddy told me that Chase is going to be working at the studio starting Monday. He will probably even take over the business! I think T.J. is like soo over it and is dying to retire! Anyways, I was curious about what the hell Chase Swanson has been doing for the past seven years so I hired the best private investigator in the biz. Turns out Chase has been living in Europe, but he's always yachting, skiing, traveling and partying! He never sits still, Liv. He's always in like Vegas, Ibiza, Marbella, Miami, Aspen, Chicago, New York... the list goes on and on! But, here's the weirdest part... he hasn't made a single trip to Los Angeles. Not one! Not even a flight to John Wayne or SFO..."

"Oh," I say, trying to hide my trepidation. Something really bad must have happened if he hasn't set foot in California since he got sent away as a senior in high school.

"I couldn't uncover anything about why he left... it was highly classified. But at least we know he's still a super hot playboy! Well, an international playboy now!" she giggles lustfully. "Anyways, you should be careful, Liv," Kelly warns me disingenuously, "like, he might be crazy or something! He's bad news!" Suddenly, there is a loud bang at my door.

"LIV!!" someone yells my name from the out in hallway and I nearly fall off the bed.

"Liv? What was that?" I hear Kelly's panic stricken voice ask through the phone. I cautiously approach the door and look through the peep hole only to find a giggling Michelle standing there. I roll my eyes at her immature antics.

"Sorry, Kelly! It was just Michelle trying to scare me!" I unlock the door and Michelle barges in. She is still giggling hysterically and her nose is scrunching in that cute way it does when she's super entertained by something. Almost every one of her expressions radiates mischief.

"So... um.. I should probably go. Thanks for calling," I say to Kelly politely.

"Make sure you keep me posted on Chase. I want to do dirty, dirty things to that boy," she practically growls.

"Bye Kelly." She hangs up without a word. I roll my eyes. I don't know if Kelly Rose will ever grasp the concept of hello and goodbye during a conversation. Her spoiled rich kid manners are atrocious.

Beautiful Disaster and The $38M 'Rari

Michelle jumps up and hugs me like a spider money. She wraps her long legs around my waist, nearly causing me to topple over.

"I missed you, baby doll!" she says breathlessly in a fake little girl voice as she kisses me on the lips, her energetic smooch leaving traces of fruity lip gloss on my mouth and chin. "I told the guys who were going to bring your car over here to fuck off! I wanted to do it! We have to drive to Hermosa and meet my pill dude. I only have like three of my white pills left!" she sighs as she hops off of me and tosses her purse on my bed. She raises an accusatory eyebrow at the phone in my hand.

"Liv, were you just talking to Kelly Rose?" she asks, staring at the phone as if it was on fire.

"Yes..." I answer, with hesitation in my voice.

"That nosy bitch," she hisses. A look of realization splays across her face, and her large eyes widen even further. Michelle's eyes are so big and blue, sometimes I wonder if she has her own sky within them. "Kelly told you about Chase, didn't she?" she asks as her gaze frosts over and turns to ice. I nod warily, taking into account that admitting this will place Kelly into freezing waters with the ruthless Ice Princess; Michelle's eyes could freeze the

43

whole world right now. "Kelly Rose is a stupid, chubby, gossipy cunt! She's lucky her skanky drug whore dad is signed with Swanson Music Group or else I would beat the shit out of her myself!" She's so worked up I half expect cartoon smoke to start coming out of her ears. She finally gets herself under control, barely, and sighs. "I wanted to be the one to tell you! I've been putting it off because I thought you would say no to living with me this summer." She plops down on my bed, crossing her long legs elegantly as she pats the mattress and motions for me to sit next to her. Michelle is flaunting her svelte figure today with short shorts and a Guns N' Roses crop top that exposes just enough of the right kind of skin to drive her legions of male admirers crazy. I can see the underside of the round silicone mounds that sit above her fit tummy with each movement of her body. The barely there rock and roll shirt is paired with long platinum blonde hair that has been flat ironed to perfection and parted down the middle. She looks more like the daughter of a rock star than the daughter of the man who owns and controls the rock gods. Music royalty and chic California bombshell pulse intertwined through her veins, every moment of every day.

"So, yes, Chase will be home today," she announces, somewhat solemnly. "Now you can finally see what he looks like in person!" She smirks and runs her fingers through her shimmering hair.

"Wait? What do you mean?" I ask, trying to sound casual even though I know I've been totally busted.

"Oh come on, Liv! Don't play dumb with me! I've seen you stare longingly at pictures of my brother, and don't think I didn't see that time you fucking kissed the mural of him in the smoking room!" she says giggling as I turn crimson. "It's all good! I totally get it! I mean, Chase is the *boy* version of me! But he doesn't have this blonde mane like I do," she says and arrogantly flips her perfect hair off her shoulder. It's too bad you've never seen his face in color, his eyes are super cool, like very electric! I must admit, he's a handsome devil!" I raise my eyebrow skeptically at her. "Don't look at me like that!" She giggles. "We aren't like a family of incestuous hillbillies! We are the fucking Swansons for God's sake, Hollywood's finest! I'm not saying that because I want to fuck him, I'm saying that because he's drop dead gorgeous as a person! Don't you think?"

"Yeah, he's pretty cute," I answer nonchalantly. But what I really want to tell her is that I think he's the hottest guy I've ever seen in my life, and that I have crazy butterflies in my stomach right now, but I wouldn't dare admit that.

"Oh, and by the way, sorry you never made it to his room the other day," Michelle says and playfully shoves me. I feel the heat from my face spread down my body as I think about the last time I was at the Swanson's estate. How does she know all of these things? Privacy is nonexistent in Swanson World.

In their Bel Air estate, at the top of the curved staircase that leads up to the massive children's wing, is Michelle's bedroom. Blaire's is in the middle directly across from the elevator and Chase's is the farthest one, tucked into its own corner. The doors are always shut, but on that particular day Chase's happened to be open. As I walked past it, intrigue got the best of me and I stopped to peer inside. His room is different than Michelle's - still ultra posh like hers, except so very deliciously male. There were artifacts of a lifestyle so affluent that only the cream of the crop could imagine it, but also hints that he didn't care all that much. It spoke of a rich kid, confident to the point of arrogance, but free of the delusions that thrust lesser men across that line. The décor was very collegiate, with all of the requisite car, band and half naked girl posters. There were trophies tucked in every nook and cranny. The maid who was cleaning his room saw me looking and scowled as she shut the door in my face. I still don't know what those trophies were for.

Michelle's bedroom by contrast, is much larger. She has her own living area and a kitchenette next to the sleeping quarters, which is attached to an elegant bathroom and the kind of walk-in closet that little girls and grown women alike dream of.

Later that night, while we were hanging out in her living area, I couldn't get Chase's bedroom out of my head. I saw pictures in there that weren't in black and white and I desperately wanted to take a closer look. Michelle finally fell asleep... and by asleep, I mean she passed out on the floor with a bong in her hand while rap music blared through the B&W sound system in the ceiling. Liquid courage was whispering to me to explore Chase Swanson's room once and for all, so I decided to do it. I gently tapped Michelle on the shoulder; she mumbled something unintelligible and rolled onto her stomach. Satisfied that she was sound asleep, I covered her with a blanket and snuck away like a thief. I was elated when I actually made it to his room.

"Excuse me Miss Walker," a security guard boomed, intercepting my late night snoop mission. "You need to return to Michelle's bedroom, please." My newfound elation dropped like a broken elevator and I reluctantly removed my hand from the door handle.

"I'm sorry..." I muttered. The guard put his walkie-talkie to his mouth.

"Friend of child number three is en route to the bedroom now, Don," the guard announced to the control center. I might as well have been wearing an orange jumpsuit and shackles as I shuffled in front of the security guard back to Michelle's bedroom. "Sorry Miss, just following protocol," he said as he closed the door, leaving me alone with my humiliation.

Michelle, somehow awake, grabbed my leg and gave it a squeeze, thankfully rescuing me from my memory walk of shame.

"Liv... I'm pretty nervous about seeing him." She bit her lip and looked away. "We used to be really close, but... I don't know how he's going to feel about me now." She looked down at her hands, which were tightly pressed together in her lap. "We were so bad together, like always in trouble! He's been a little shit since he was a child! My parents always said that Chase was the perfect name for him, because they were always having to chase him around and clean up his messes. Well actually, the team of nannies were,... but whatever, we put up with his shit for so long! And we all tried to make it work. The final straw was the night of the party in Miami." She looks as if she might cry. "Chase beat the shit out of one of my dad's biggest clients. Someone very important to my father's career." She paused for an uncharacteristically long time. "And someone very important to me..." Her voice caught a little, which surprised me. "Chase stormed out of the party and snatched the keys to my dad's Ferrari 250 GTO from the valet stand. I ran after him and jumped in the car to try and help him cool off, but he started driving like a maniac. I tried to get him to stop, to slow down, anything, but he was so angry. He wasn't hearing me. He pulled into our driveway so fast... way too fast. We shot through the garage door, through the back wall and into the living room! It was scary as fuck!" In the midst of my astonishment at this crazy story, I realize that Michelle's eyes have closed and her bottom lip has begun to quiver. "'Beautiful Disaster' by 311 was playing as he crashed it... he definitely did it on purpose." I place my hand over my mouth to hold in a gasp.

"Dude! I know! My dad was fucking pissed! He literally bought that 'Rari two days before at an auction for like thirty eight million dollars! That's the reason we were in Florida in the first place! We got so lucky, we could have died or killed someone!" She turns her attention towards me and I can tell she is trying to gauge my reaction. Surely, she must know that I'm wary. As comforting as it will be to live in the same mansion as my friend's reckless, possibly crazy, but absolutely gorgeous older brother,... it could also be the worst decision I've ever made. I swallow my jitters away.

"Holy shit!" I finally manage to react.

"I know, right?" she says, in nearly a whisper. "Anyways, since it happened at our place in Miami and not here, my dad was able to keep that one on the low low." She moves her hand up and down to demonstrate 'low low.' I chuckle nervously.

"Thank God!" I don't know what else to say. She absently runs her fingers up and down her legs and takes a deep breath. A sense of dread appears to wash over her and I brace myself for what's to come.

Crowd Pleaser

"So fast forward like two days later. We're back in Bel Air. I woke up to my dad and Chase yelling at each other in the hallway outside my bedroom. I could hear Blaire crying and begging them to stop arguing. I just froze. I pulled the blankets over my head like a weak ass bitch." She frowns and squints. "I heard a car pulling into the courtyard and I ran to the window. My brother was walking towards a blacked out SUV, carrying a tan duffle bag and nothing else. He looked so pissed! His beautiful hair had been completely buzzed off and his jaw was clenched so tightly. I opened the door to my balcony and screamed 'Chase!' but he wouldn't even look at me. My mom was sobbing by the fountain. He walked right past her. He looked so defeated and upset Liv. I'd never seen him like that before, ever. I watched, horrified, as the SUV drove away down the driveway. I kept willing him to look back at me, but he didn't." She paused for a moment. "I haven't spoken to him since," she said softly.

"My dad sent him to military school for the rest of his senior year of high school. He told Chase he never wanted to see or speak to him again. Basically, Chase got bought out. He still has access to the family money and to all of our homes... except the one in Bel

Air. My father said he would kick his ass if he ever set foot in Bel Air again."

I am sitting across from Michelle on the bed, feeling especially nervous. Her legs are perfectly crossed, while I could be a commercial for restless leg syndrome. My hair twirling feels obsessive and repetitive so I tuck some strands of it behind my ear and finally muster enough courage to ask her a question.

"But why after all these years... is your dad reaching out?" I rush through the words, faster than I want to. She puts her matte black painted fingernail to her lips as if this is the first time she has ever thought about it.

"Maybe it's because my dad has been working a lot more on himself lately. He brought a spiritual healer onto his team. Dante. He's amazing..." she says and smiles dreamily, "I'm guessing it was Dante who talked him into a reconciliation. I mean, it was so quick! It was like, Chase and my dad met at a café in Paris, and then, BOOM!" She claps her hands and I jump, surprised. "Just like that, he's back! I have a brother again!" She bites her lip. "Yay!" she says, but I'm not convinced. She jumps off the bed, and her body language is back to being boisterous and wild.

"Enough of this depressing shit!" she says as she reaches into her purse. "Let's go meet your new car!" I don't even try to contain the grin that spreads across my face as she holds up the key fob to a Mini Cooper. We run down the stairs to the first floor and then outside, where I find the handsome little car parked in

51

the dorm room parking lot. A fresh from the showroom, white Mini Cooper convertible with red interior. Its top is down and teasing me, tempting me to hop in. The car is so gorgeous and sporty. It has red stitching on the steering wheel and and matching stitching on the edges of the leather seats. There are two black stripes across the hood, making it look like it just came from the race track. Michelle even had the Union Jack flags put on the side mirrors because she knows I love everything British. I place my hands over my heart, overwhelmed with gratitude and admiration.

"Michelle, this car is amazing!! I can't believe you guys are letting me borrow it for the summer! Thank you so much!" I squeal, practically bouncing up and down.

"Borrow? Who told you that?" she scoffs. "It's all yours! This is a gift!" I slide the Bel Air sunglasses off of my face, making no attempt to cover the stars in my eyes as I stare at my little red and white starry surprise on four wheels.

"Michelle... seriously?" I whisper, trying to take in what she just said. "This is mine?" She nods affirmatively with a brilliant grin on her face. I feel my eyes starting to well up at her response and it makes me so happy I could burst! But it feels so wrong at the same time. I've never been given such a lavish and expensive gift before. "It's too much, Michelle..." I declare with resolve, "I can't accept this."

"Oh, yes you can! These are just fun little toys! Daddy sometimes gives Mini Coopers out as party favors. We just love

Minis!" she giggles, petting the convertible as if it were a small adorable dog. Did she just say what I think she said? $30,000 cars are considered party favors? Mr. Swanson must be sitting on a pile of money so high that he has his head in the clouds. Is her dad Oprah or something? That's insane!

I notice that the Mini has been hastily parallel parked across two handicapped spots. I laugh and shake my head at Michelle's terrible parking job.

"Really Shells?" I tease her and point.

"I'm more of a valet girl. Everyone knows parking is for poor people!" she says airily as she tosses my overnight bag in the back seat. "Besides, it looks exactly like when the valet guys leave it out front!" She giggles with rich kid ease and slips her long stems under the steering wheel as the most enviable butt in Bel Air drops gracefully into the driver's seat. I inhale sharply. Shit... Michelle is driving. She is the scariest driver in the world. I take a deep breath and climb into the passenger seat. She doesn't appear to notice my hesitation as she checks her phone and rolls her eyes.

"Ugh! Nooo! Sigalert on the 405!" she groans. "Well, at least we can use the carpool lane!" She grabs my thigh. "Buckle up, Liv, this is going to be the ride of your life!" I can't tell if she means the drive or spending the summer with her...

Michelle treats the 405 like her own personal race course. We're already going 120 mph and she is weaving in and out of traffic like a maniac. I am dreading the inevitable traffic snarl that will force us to come to a sudden and possibly fatal stop.

"Michelle! Slow down! You're going to kill us!" I shout over the music, the rush of the wind and the other vehicles.

"Oh, relax! These brakes are legit. Plus, my dad made me do this driving school thing on a track. I went with the Jenner's," she says casually.

"Jenners? As in Kylie and Kendall?" I ask, amazed that I'm actually having this conversation.

"Duh, who else would I be talking about?" she asks sarcastically and laughs. She turns the radio up. The stereo is blasting a remix of that summertime song by Sublime. Michelle is rapping along as she pretends to take a puff off of a joint. "See what I did there? I changed the 101 to 405 in that lyric!" she says and runs her fingers through her hair as if she is the shrewdest person to ever exist. "You know, because we aren't on the 101!"

"Very clever, Michelle!" I fake flatter and secretly roll my eyes under my glasses. I glance at the screen and take note of the song so I can download it later: "Doin' Time" by Sublime (Marshall Arts Remix). It will be a perfect addition to my California playlist. Suddenly, right around Culver City, I see the impending traffic jam and look over at the speedometer. Michelle is still going way too fast.

"Shit!" I mumble, rubbing my nervous, sweating palms along my skirt. I shut my eyes tightly and grip the seat in anticipation of a crash, but as promised, she slams on the brakes with perfect timing. The car screeches to a halt, barely avoiding the SUV in front of us. I exhale sharply.

"See! I told you I was an expert!" she brags as she flips her platinum hair towards me, sending the scent of very expensive shampoo and conditioner along with it. Michelle Swanson might be the only girl in the world whose hair stays perfect in a top down convertible. It's still mink shiny and doesn't have a single tangle in it. Me, not so much. I pull a clump of hair that has gotten stuck to my lip gloss away from my face for the fifth time and frantically comb through it with my fingertips, trying not to jump every time I hear a motorcycle whizzing by. I've lived in California for a year now, and I still cannot get used to the fact that motorcycles are allowed to ride in between lanes. It just seems so wrong and dangerous.

The next song that comes on is "Crazy" by Aerosmith. Michelle's playlists are always super entertaining. I've never met someone with such eclectic taste in music, but I guess if you are the daughter of a famous music producer and your last name is attached to one of the biggest production companies in the world, it kind of makes sense. She is singing the Aerosmith song very seductively to me as we inch our way down the freeway. We are at a complete stop when I notice a lifted truck full of men staring at us, but mainly at her.

The driver rolls down the windows and they all crowd over to one side of the truck's cab, whistling and cheering. To my surprise, Michelle throws the car into park and stands up on her seat. With a confidence I could only dream of having, she begins dancing seductively and singing into an imaginary microphone. Her abs are glistening in the sun as she runs her hands up and down her body. Her sparkly, tan skin is luxuriously silky. I'm looking up at her with a mix of shock and admiration when I hear the men in the truck go even wilder. Michelle has lifted up her crop top, giving them and everyone else around us a view of her perfect boobs. She squeezes them and throws her head back, her eyes electric from the attention. She arches her back, sending her golden hair cascading down her ass. Sexuality is dripping from her soul and I am just as mesmerized by her glamour and audacity as the men in the truck are.

"Michelle! This could be a music video!" I yell, basically star struck. She is in the zone and totally ignores me. The traffic starts to move again, and I join the men in a round of applause. She does a little bow, still standing on her seat.

"Thank you. Thank you very much!" she says and blows them a kiss. The car behind us lays on the horn. She flips off the person who dared honk at her and plops back down in the seat, taking her sweet time to put the car into drive, just to punish their insolence to the queen.

"I will be in their spank bank forever!" she proclaims self-assuredly as she waves to the cheering men in the rearview mirror as we exit at the 105 and head towards PCH. Michelle Swanson, always the shameless crowd pleaser.

Hermosa Beach

As we drive down the ramp to the 1, I see row after row of exquisite private jets parked on the tarmac below us. Driving near the airport in a convertible is the only thing louder and more intimidating than the passing motorcycles and the incessant honking on the 405. The runways are so close to the highway that it feels like I could touch the planes as they are descending. I'm fascinated by a commercial jet taxiing over the bridge above the highway, when suddenly, a very unique and special plane catches my eye. The sun glints brightly off of its underbelly as it descends. I stare at it with wide eyes. Is the bottom of that airplane gold? I'm captivated as I watch the graceful aircraft touch down on the runway and then turn off into the private jet stables. The long wingspan gives it such a regal presence. I take a closer look and realize it isn't my imagination, the bottom of the plane is in fact gold. Michelle's hands have visibly tightened on the steering wheel.

"Gold bottom," she whispers, "that's our Gulfstream." I squint and make out 'Swanson' painted in black on the side of it. "Chase is in there. He's here. In that plane. He's in L.A.," she says, with an anxiety in her voice I've never heard before. I gulp and clear my throat.

"Should we pick him up?" I ask and instantly feel stupid. I'm sure he already has a luxury car waiting for him on the tarmac.

"No..." she snaps. The symphony of honking, the faint music from the Mini's stereo, and the wind should be filling the static air, but my best friend has gone into silent mode and I can't really hear anything either. She finally turns the music up, piercing the silence. Amy Winehouse's soulful voice is crooning, "Back to Black" through the speakers. Michelle is gripping the steering wheel so hard that the veins are popping out of her forearms.

"Amy Winehouse is my spirit animal," she announces flatly. "We will be partying together soon enough!" The casual yet creepy way in which she just spoke those words makes my mouth go dry and my stomach drop. The image of Michelle's naked, pale, and unresponsive body during 'the incident' flashes uninvited in my mind.

"Michelle, Amy Winehouse is dead... please don't say that. You're scaring me." I beg her, my voice betraying my dread.

"Sorry, babe," she says and twists her mouth slightly.

"It's okay..." I reply. I quickly go into diversion mode to pull her out of her angst. "Shells, why are all these buildings starting to look like Taco Bells?" I ask as I outline the curves of a terra cotta rooftop on a bank with my eyes. "Is Hacienda style required or something in this section of PCH?" She doesn't reply. I turn my head to look at her and notice that her bottom lip is trembling.

"Liv, I loved him," she whispers as she changes lanes quickly to avoid a parked car that has somehow appeared in our lane. I furrow my brow.

"Who?" I probe.

"But, he was married," she mumbles, "things always work out that way, don't they?" she asks no one in particular.

"Who, Michelle?" I ask again. She ignores me a second time. The song appears to have put her in a trance as she turns onto Pier Avenue. I know she isn't going to answer my question. When Michelle goes into silent mode, there is no coaxing her out of it.

I bite my lip as I take in all of the young, beautiful, care-free people walking along the glittering streets of Hermosa Beach. Some are carrying surfboards under their arms, others are jogging. They seem exceedingly content and far more friendly than the people of Los Angeles. There are multiple surf shops and cute boutiques on my right. The beach scene on my left looks like a magical fairytale land of tan, light-hearted people playing volleyball and socializing. It looks so fun. I wish I could be with them and not trapped in this uncomfortable situation. Finally, Michelle pulls into the driveway of a beach house along the Strand. Stacks of hundred dollar bills in rubber bands are practically spilling out of her Gucci bag.

"This will only take a minute," she says, "watch this to entertain yourself." She presses something on her phone and the

60

music video for "Crazy" by Aerosmith starts playing on the screen in the Mini Cooper.

"You can watch music videos inside of the car?" I ask, amazed. Michelle gives me a sexy, polished smile in return.

"Pay attention, Liv..." she says as she walks over to the passenger door and places her palm lightly against my cheek. I press the button to put the top up so I can watch the video. With the glare gone, I can clearly see Liv Tyler and Alicia Silverstone in a convertible looking effortlessly confident, cool, and gorgeous while rocking out to "Crazy." As I watch, it dawns on me that Michelle reminds me of Alicia Silverstone, especially as Cher in the movie "Clueless." Except, she frequently transforms into Margot Robbie as Harley Quinn from "Suicide Squad" before my very eyes. It's a constant cycle of poised, well put together Bel Air stunner transforms to beautiful psychopath disaster and back again. Repeat at will.

"Damn..." I whisper to the video, as I feel a rush of admiration for Liv Tyler. She is dancing on stage and singing like a goddess from the screen. I wish I was Liv Tyler, daughter of a rock star, not Liv Walker, farmer's daughter from middle America. I snap out of my wistful thinking when I see a slightly happier version of Michelle approaching the car. I quickly put the top back down so she doesn't get mad at me for changing things, but she doesn't appear to notice, she just presses the Start button without saying a word and turns the car back towards Los Angeles. There is no

61

conversation between us, only music and the Mini Cooper's cute but persistent beeping reminding Michelle to put her seatbelt on, as we languish in bumper to bumper traffic on the 405 North. Michelle is pensive and preoccupied with something. She perks up a little bit when we turn onto Sunset Boulevard.

"Those fuckers better not take a picture of us!" Michelle says haughtily and from out of left field. She rummages around in her purse for a hat, swerving as she does it. It dawns on me that 'those fuckers' are the celeb crazed tourists posing for photos in front of the Beverly Hills sign. They're looking in every direction, hoping to catch a glimpse of a star; or better yet, to get one to join them in a picture. She pulls out a Dodgers cap, and pulls it down low on her her face as we drive past them. They don't even look at us and I immediately start thinking about how Michelle always takes Beverly Glen to get to Bel Air when I'm with her, because she knows how much I love the palm trees. They are tall and stunning and the perfect backdrop for all the elegant Beverly Hills estates.

The Military Compound

Michelle groans. "Ugh! It's one of those fucking Hollywood tour buses!" She lays on the horn impertinently. "You're never going to find Spielberg's house!" she yells, disdain dripping from her voice. I feel sort of bad for the tourists because Michelle is right, they will never actually see the homes of the ultra rich and glamorously famous, because their estates are always hidden from view. The higher up you go in the Hills, the more hidden the homes become, with large walls and gates blocking the high-profile mansions from view. Michelle's estate is so well hidden it might as well be behind a magic curtain; you can't see it at all. And of course, it comes with more security gadgets than a military compound. Sometimes I think the Swanson's essentially built themselves a beautiful prison.

You can see pictures of their home online, all taken from a helicopter, but that's about it. I've learned over time that Bel Air is for the extremely wealthy and the super famous, and that Beverly Hills is for the entry level royals - at least according to Michelle. I had no idea there was such a discrepancy between them until I saw Michelle freak out on someone who made the mistake of suggesting she was from Beverly Hills.

We drive up and up a twisty road until she finally turns onto her street. The inconspicuous white gate in front of us is the only indication of the Swanson's estate. The walls that surround the gate are overgrown and covered in ivy. It gives the impression that whatever is within will be unkempt and dreadful, but it's merely an illusion to ensure that prying eyes remain uninterested. Michelle places her left hand on a well camouflaged scanner and the gate slowly opens for us. We drive through it and begin the gradual climb up the cobblestone driveway, which feels like it's a mile long... because it is.

Security cameras glare at us like sentinels from either side of the drive, turning to follow our movement, while miniature drones buzz ominously overhead. The first sign of life is a robotic dog straight out of a sci-fi movie. It is laying down in front of a second gate, which is far more ornate and elegant than the first. This gate is brilliantly gleaming gold with a large 'S' at the center of it. As Michelle stops the car, the robot dog stands at attention and marches mechanically towards us. Robotic noises fill my ears as it shuffles up to my door. The "dog" has a sticker on it that says 'Mastiff,' which is actually kind of odd if you think about it. I can't help but close my eyes as 'Mastiff' keenly observes me, its camera head twisting and turning as it does. It stands almost as tall as the Mini Cooper. Don, the head of security, is controlling the robot spy dog right now from a desk in the rather unattractive utilitarian building to the right of us. The dog finally decides it likes me and trots away on its metal legs. I breathe an inadvertent sigh of relief as the golden gate swings slowly open. Two security guards wave to us as we pass. Michelle smiles and blows them a kiss.

There are multiple golf carts parked near the staff parking lot. We continue on past it and a second lot for guest overflow, which is currently empty, and eventually make our way to and around the fountain. I can see the ridiculously oversized pool and the guest chalet where I will be staying this summer. The chalet is bigger than the house I grew up in, but I know that I won't be spending much time there. Most of the summer will be spent with Princess Michelle in the castle that she calls a home. As we are pulling into the underground parking garage, Michelle glances over at me.

"You're lucky my dad is letting you park down here, usually guests have to park upstairs." She pulls the car into a spot next to another Mini Cooper. "This is your parking spot, number 123. Do not forget! My dad hates it when the cars are not in their proper spots!"

"Got it!" I reply as I stare in awe at the hundreds of luxury cars surrounding me. The emblems on them scream sophistication, performance and pleasure for the ones lucky enough to wrap their fingers around the finely stitched steering wheels. Each one is designed to please its master.

Starboy

The parking garage makes my jaw drop every time. It is filled with more luxury cars than I have ever seen in my life. Endless rows of Ferraris, Bentleys, Porsches, Maseratis, Lamborghinis, etc. They are stacked one above another on lifts and sorted by brand. I am transfixed by an elegant Rolls Royce convertible that is spinning slowly round and round on a large turntable made for cars. Michelle says a Bugatti is usually displayed there, but Mr. Swanson recently sent it to The Circuit of the Americas in Austin. The turntable adjacent to it teases the eyes with a yellow McLaren P1. Her father has a lot of older cars too. I recognize the emblems on most of them, but I have no idea what they are or how much they are worth. A short, overweight man is detailing an older red car that looks like it could be in a James Bond movie.

"What is that?" I ask Michelle as we approach it. "Is that the 007 car?" The man stops what he's doing and smirks at my ineptness. Michelle laughs pompously in my blushing face.

"No, silly! James Bond drove an Aston Martin! Those are over there." She points to a row of handsome sports cars. "This is a 1955 Mercedes Gullwing. My dad went up against Jay Leno for it and won!" she says proudly. I am still confused. It looks old and what does she mean went up against him? Did they get in a fist fight? It must have been an amusing sight to see T.J. and Jay Leno fighting over an old car.

"So, did your dad get in trouble for beating up Jay Leno?" I ask earnestly. Michelle and the man who looks like Mario from Nintendo burst out laughing. I feel my face turning crimson.

"Livvie, no!!" Michelle exclaims. "Him and Leno are tight! He outbid him at Barrett-Jackson!" I nod, even though I have no idea what any of this means.

"It's an auction for cars, miss!" the Mario man clarifies as if reading my mind. Michelle runs her fingers along the man's back.

"Oscar, isn't Liv cute?" she asks flirtatiously.

"Yes, Miss Michelle..." he mutters, looking down. I can see him struggling not to make eye contact.

"The car looks great!" she purrs. "Maybe I can take it for a spin later?"

"Maybe..." he mumbles, glancing up at us. Michelle bends over seductively to press the gold elevator button. She flashes him bedroom eyes as she does it. He turns bright red. I catch him adjusting his pants as the doors close. As soon as it starts moving, I scrunch my nose.

"Ew!" Michelle, he totally loves you! I think he had a boner! I can't believe you just flirted with him like that!"

"Duh!" she says and rolls her eyes. "How else am I going to get full access to the fleet? Think about it, if I blow Oscar, head of cars, and Don, head of security, then I can drive *anything* I want without my dad knowing!" she boasts as she pretends to smoke a cigarette. I shake my head. Michelle never ceases to amaze me.

"Gross!" I squeal. "That's crazy!" She gives me a carefree shrug.

"Whatever. They know they would never have a chance with me in the real world and it kind of turns me on to make their wet dreams come true!" She smiles wickedly as she rationalizes the vulgar acts.

"Nooo! Michelle! You are unbelievable!" I chastise her through playful giggles.

"Thanks, Liv!" she says and puts her hand over her heart as if it was a genuine compliment. She purses her snobby lips at me. "Girl, Come ON! If you were in my position, you would do the same thing!" I stare at the elevator's gold tiles. Would I? I wonder as we make our way up to the common floor.

There are four stories and two separate wings in this colossal, modern-day palace. I have gotten lost numerous times in the Swanson's estate; one time I got lost outside in the garden, for hours. A security guard had to come rescue me in a golf cart over by the helicopter pad. I almost died of embarrassment. Michelle says their home looks like a European castle because of the time her parents went to France for the summer. As the story goes, after less than a week on holiday, Mr. and Mrs. Swanson summoned their architects and interior designers to Paris and said, "we are bringing Paris to Bel Air! Build us the Palace of Versailles and decorate it with the Louvre!"

Everything in their home is extraordinarily ornate and lavish. Opulence abounds. The hallways and living areas are dripping with Austrian crystal chandeliers, Italian marble statues, and French furniture fit for a king. The elevator doors open to 18 karat European rose gold Roman columns that would look at home in the original Caesar's palace. I stubbed my toe on one of them once. I've also crashed and burned on the slick black and white checkered floor that Michelle's mother is floating towards us on right now in sky high heels.

"Girls!" she squeals as she hugs me sloppily, nearly pushing me over with her embrace. I can smell the liquor on her breath. She reaches for her daughter next, but Michelle pushes her away.

"Mom, you look awful! Go put on some lipstick or something," she says rudely, but her mother doesn't appear to notice or care about her daughter's animosity towards her. Michelle always acts like a bitchy teenage girl when she's home, and Mrs. Swanson couldn't look awful if she tried. She is just as gorgeous as she was when she was strutting down international runways and gracing the covers of glamour magazines. She looks about half her real age thanks to her svelte figure, flawless complexion and gifted plastic surgeons. I might mistake her for Michelle's older sister if I didn't already know her.

"Would you girls like a drink?" she asks enthusiastically. "What do you want? Wine? Mimosas? Or should we go straight to the harder stuff... whiskey?! I'm a whiskey girl myself!" she slurs in her half California, half Louisiana accent. I glance at my phone; it's 3pm. How is she this drunk already?

"Um, I will just have water, Mrs. Swanson, thank you though," I reply shyly.

"Nonsense!" she says, waving her hand dismissively. "Vi!" she calls out. Vi is the Swanson's main maid. I don't know what Vi's actual name is, and I kind of think Michelle's mother just calls people whatever she wants. With her looks, she can get away with murder. Of all of Mrs. Swanson's striking features, her eyes are the most memorable. Those blue-green irises that as of late, encircle perpetually dilated pupils, have been captured by camera lenses tens of thousands of times. Her eyes are mesmerizing and change color with her emotions. When she is sad, upset, or anxious, they are green; when she is content, they are blue. Today they are absolutely glowing green, which signals trouble.

We follow her as she struts off down the hallway in thigh high snakeskin Cavalli heels. Michelle's mother is poised, beautiful and graceful, but most notably, never arrogant. It always baffles me that she could be married to someone like T.J., who as far as I can tell, is as cold as ice.

I spot Vi dusting pictures next to a zebra head which has recently been mounted above the mantel. The maid is wearing her

70

signature uniform, which looks oddly like safari apparel. It honestly could've been pulled from a shelf in the 'sexy costume' section at a Halloween store and I can't help but wonder if Michelle's mother ordered Vi to go on an African safari in her ironic outfit to hunt down the latest addition to the Swanson's collection of taxidermy animals. I try not to laugh out loud at the preposterous thought of a scantily clad Vi sniping majestic beasts in the heart of the Serengeti. I accidentally make eye contact with the most recent victim and a feeling of sadness washes over me. My heart is now breaking for the once regal black and white striped beauty staring back at me. I wonder if it knows that it died in vain for one of the wealthiest families in America's viewing pleasure. That poor baby hanging above the fireplace has joined the herd of other dead zoo animals in this American castle. Mr. Zebra was killed for the same reason that the stuffed giraffe who towers over me in the smoking room was killed, or the baby elephant that pleads for its life through devastated eyes in the barbershop, or the angry monkey that glares at me in the theater room. They were killed because they were pleasing to the eye.

"I'm sorry..." I mouth to the dead zebra, even though I had nothing to do with its untimely demise.

"Vi! There you are, my scrumptious little cup of fine British tea!" Samantha purrs to her pretty young maid from across the room. "Would you please get these girls some mimosas and me a couple Valiums while you're at it?"

71

"But of course, Mrs. Swanson!" Vi replies in her enthusiastic British accent.

"Oh!" Michelle's mom calls out as if remembering something important. "You should use the Dom Perignon that Snoop Dogg brought over the other day for the mimosas dear. It's shit champagne, perfect for college students!" she slurs, smiling sincerely.

"Brilliant idea, Mrs. Swanson! I will be right back with those!"

"Thank you, Vi!" Michelle's mom says. I watch Vi hurry away in her racy safari uniform. That outfit choice is so odd. Come to think of it, all of the Swanson's staff wear bizarre uniforms. The car maintenance team is required to wear race suits, except apparently for Oscar, who I just met; he was wearing an Adidas tracksuit. I think he might be a bit too fat to wear the required outfit. Even Mr. Swanson's assistant Emma is in uniform. Always a crisp white blouse, black pencil skirt, and five inch Louboutin heels. I kid you not, I once saw her wearing those sky high red bottoms in the middle of the night, plugging away on that iPad with the red cover that she always has with her. I'm starting to wonder if the shoes are glued to her feet.

Roses in Bel Air

Mrs. Swanson's silicone enhanced breasts are spilling out of her blouse as she bends over to pour more whiskey into her Baccarat crystal lowball. Her jet black, mink shiny hair bounces like an astronaut in space with each movement her body makes. I feel like I'm watching the classic L'Oréal Paris commercial that she appeared in; the one I've watched on YouTube dozens of times. I've always wanted to touch her hair to see if it feels like it looks. It's too glossy and luxurious to have been grown from a human head. She sits down with drink in hand on the black leather couch beneath the zebra and gracefully crosses her long, tan legs.

"Oh my heavens! You girls are too cute!" she coos. "So, how's school? How were finals? Happy to have you here this summer, Liv! You are so pretty and just sweet as a peach! Have you lost weight?" she asks. She is speaking so fast and slurring so much that I'm having trouble following along. She smiles brightly, yet vacantly and takes another swig of her drink. Michelle crosses her arms and gives her mom an icy glare. Vi is back with the mimosas. As she sets them on the side table, I hear a beep and then the muffled voice of a man from the walkie-talkie that is attached to her safari belt.

"Child number one is now entering the premises," the mysterious voice announces.

Vi removes the walkie-talkie from her belt.

"Roger. His room is ready to go," she says into it. The walkie-talkie beeps again.

"Oscar reporting... Mr. Chase's cars are ready. Over and out." My stomach fills with an entire pavilion full of butterflies. The Prince of Bel Air has returned to his kingdom. I glance at Mrs. Swanson. She is frozen in place on the couch. Her hand is gripping her whiskey glass so tightly that her fingers are turning white.

"Chase. My baby..." she says to no one in particular.

"There, there. It will be alright Mrs. Swanson," Vi purrs soothingly while handing Michelle's mom two little blue pills. "It will be quite lovely to have him home." Samantha nods absently as she puts the pills in her mouth and washes them down with more whiskey. Her hand is shaking as she sets her glass down on the coffee table. I hear heavy footsteps in the hallway, and Michelle's imposing to the point of intimidating father enters the room. I cower subconsciously in his presence.

"Come Samantha, let's go greet our son," he commands as he snatches his wife's trembling hand from the couch and lifts her to her feet. She stumbles out of the room, using her husband's arm for balance. Michelle is seated next to me on the couch, frozen and silent, staring blankly ahead. I place my hand gently on top of hers.

"Shells, are you okay?" I whisper. She nods bravely, but I know she's not. I have never seen her this nervous before. We hear the front door open and someone entering the foyer.

"Hello son," Mr. Swanson says calmly and evenly.

I can hear Mrs. Swanson crying and saying, "I'm so sorry, baby. I love you, I love you," over and over again.

A deep, penetrating voice fills the room.

"It's okay, Mom. I love you too. It's nice to be home." I hear the footsteps moving closer and my breath quickens. Finally, he turns the corner and I see him for the first time... and suddenly I can't even breathe. Oh. My. God... I knew he was going to be good looking, but nothing could prepare me for the photographs turned three-dimensional. He is so attractive it's surreal. Standing before me is the tall, tan, smooth, handsome, stunningly drop-dead gorgeous, Chase Swanson, my best friend's long lost older brother.

He's wearing a black v-neck t-shirt that is just tight enough to display his chest muscles. I stare, still speechless, as he flips the baseball cap he is wearing around on his head, a mess of dark brown hair gliding through his fingers as he does it. The backwards hat mixes with the perfect amount of stubble, making him look manly and rugged. He has magically transformed from the smoking room teenaged version of Chase Swanson into the man version standing across the living room from me right now. Oh fuck... he's so hot... so insanely hot. Kelly Rose was right... how am I going to keep my hands off of him?

Chase has a natural athletic build like his father's, muscular but not in an overly constructed way like that of a vain gym rat. His muscles look like they serve a purpose other than as a mere display for my viewing pleasure. His stride is effortlessly agile, all of his movements are athletic and purposeful. He looks like he could play any sport he wanted and be the MVP, and with a gorgeous face like that and those striking features, he could be a male model if the professional athlete thing didn't work out. I hear something hit the ground, and I realize that Vi has dropped her duster.

"Right.. um... sorry," she mumbles, visibly flustered as she picks it up. I can tell she is equally as enchanted by Chase Swanson as I am. Just then, Emma marches confidently into the room.

"How you doing, kid?" she asks. She looks tiny standing in front of him, even in her sky high heels.

"Emma! What's up, gorgeous?" Chase flirts with ease as he kisses her on the cheek. Her eyes sparkle as she pulls him in for a hug.

"Wow! You sure have grown!" she says admiringly and squeezes him tighter.

"And you haven't grown at all, Emma," he quips. "You're still a little spinner, just like I like you!" He winks and she giggles and touches his arm. Jealousy pulses through my body. I hate Emma right now. I watch the veins in his athletic neck pop when his eyes finally land on his sister.

"Hey," he says to her, pokerfaced. My pulse quickens as he glances at me. Our eyes lock for a moment, and then he is back to being focused on Michelle. I anxiously follow his gaze and start to panic when I realize that she is terrified.

"Chase. I'm..." Michelle tries to speak, and her eyes well up with tears. His face softens in a protective, older brother kind of way.

"Hey! Don't cry!" he says sweetly. "We're good." She looks up at him as if to ask, 'are you sure?' He shrugs, a small smile splaying across his face, and her body melts with relief. His half smile morphs into a full fledged grin that is dangerously charming; it promises endless mischief and fun. Michelle meets his grin and runs to him. She hugs him like I've never seen her hug anyone before.

"Chase!... I've missed you... so much!" she chokes out between sobs as they hug. He rubs her back reassuringly. Michelle wipes her eyes as she pulls away from him.

"I missed you too, you histrionic little freak." He delivers the insult with love and compassion in his voice, and it somehow comes across as a charming compliment. Michelle giggles like a school girl with a crush in response to it. "So... my adorable little sister... what's new in your world of make believe? Are you still a pill popping nymphomaniac?" he asks her. I stiffen. Except, she doesn't fly into a rage. She continues to giggle and gives him a playful shove. What on... how did he do that? Ordinarily, Michelle would lose her mind on anyone who dared to speak insulting words like that to her.

"Do you still fuck anything that walks as long as it has an IQ of 7 or below?" Michelle asks him, continuing their odd brother sister banter.

"You know I only fuck 10s and above, an 8 if I'm super drunk," he says smoothly, winking like he just won a bet. I glance apprehensively at Mr. and Mrs. Swanson, but they are completely unfazed by their children's explicit exchange. I try to compose a deadpan expression as it dawns on me that Chase Swanson might be more brazen and unapologetic than his sister.

Michelle goes off to the kitchen, leaving me sitting awkwardly on the couch with my legs tightly crossed. Chase notices me and his eyes flicker with curiosity. When I finally look up to meet his stare, I am met with the most electric eyes I have ever seen. The kind of eyes that women get lost in. They are so pretty... like sapphires and emeralds in the sun, only with slightly dilated pupils. I wonder if they change color with his emotions like his mother's mood ring eyes do. I look away, but despite my best efforts, I feel myself look up and take Chase Swanson in again. 'Wow...' I almost say out loud. I can't take my eyes off of him... he's devastating. I sit up straighter when I realize that his full attention is now on me, because he just busted me staring at him. I feel electricity moving slowly down my spine...

Breathless

"Who are you?" he asks me, and I flinch at the cutting way he just spoke to me.

"Me?"

"Yeah, you. Unless there's another pretty girl sitting on my couch right now," he says, with the easy charm of a natural womanizer. He drips sarcasm and wit; his body language is self-assured to the point of cocky.

"I'm Olivia – er - um, Liv... I'm Michelle's friend," I stumble over my words.

"I'm Chase. Michelle's brother," he says and puts his hand out to shake mine. I stand up from the couch and feel like my legs might give out. I walk towards him feeling like Cupid is piercing me with a thousand arrows.

"Nice to meet you," I say breathlessly as I just barely manage to shake his hand. Electricity shoots through me again as soon as our fingers touch. It feels like someone just hit me with me a stun gun and suddenly, I'm frozen in place, enchanted by his magnetic eyes. He gives me the deal sealing smile. Omg his mouth is amazing. Chase Swanson is literally dripping with sex appeal and yet somehow it's completely effortless. I smile back at him in a daze. He's the most exquisite work of art. My inner monologue is telling me to get it together, to stop acting like a lovesick puppy. I turn my face to stone and look away, trying to avoid his mesmerizing oceanic gaze. Michelle returns from the kitchen and puts her arm around me in a friendly, reassuring way.

"Chase, this is Liv, my best friend from school. We decided yesterday that she's going to live here until the Fall semester because she has summer classes or some nerdy shit like that. She's a sweetheart and way out of your league, so don't even think about trying to bone her while she's here!" Michelle warns him, leaving me feeling completely shocked and flattered all at the same time. Did she just say that *I'm* out of *his* league? She is out of *her* mind!

"Does she speak?" Chase asks his sister as though I'm not standing there. It sounds like he is asking her about a sex doll or fem bot that she got him as a gift. "Just curious... is she your run of the mill, prissy L.A. hottie or is she just painfully shy? Because I can't really tell." He cocks his head towards me and I turn crimson. I've never felt more embarrassed, awkward, or flattered in my entire life. Chase Swanson has no filter and gives zero fucks if he offends me. Besides Hunter, the fucked up Southern Prince, I don't think I've ever been around a man who could literally care less if he makes me mad. It's refreshing yet infuriating at the same time.

"Olivia is a smart girl, son. She's a good influence on your sister," I hear Mr. Swanson boom from behind me. "We felt it would

80

be wise to have her around this summer to care for Michelle, so Dante can focus on me and my needs. I don't really want to hire two spiritual healers." T.J. Swanson is the only one in the family who calls me by my full name and Michelle has never corrected him, she wouldn't dare. He checks his Patek Philippe 'Sky Moon' watch aloofly and yawns. "Listen, Chase, I would love to catch up with you some more, but I have a conference call in ten minutes and I need to finish eating my peanuts," he says as he pompously shoves a handful of peanuts into his mouth from a crocodile shaped tray on the coffee table. Wow... T.J. hasn't seen his son in like eight years, and he is just going to dismiss him like that? It makes me want to throw the peanuts in his face. No wonder Michelle needs her relaxation pills, AKA her 'chillies.' They help her to not freak out on her asshole father. Just then Emma clears her throat and opens up the iPad.

"Mr. Swanson, we canceled the conference call with Bob Iger to make time for a family reunion, per Dante's suggestion," Emma says professionally, while showing him his schedule on the iPad. He rolls his eyes and checks his watch again.

"Alright! We will give you all twenty minutes!" T.J. says with self-importance coming out every inch of his 6'3" frame.

I nervously clear my throat. "I can go to my room and let you guys catch up, if you want," I say while staring at the ground. Michelle grabs my hand and gives me a pleading look.

"No, stay!" she begs. I can't resist my best friend's imploring eyes so I regretfully oblige.

We all find our seats in the family gathering room once Mr. Swanson finishes his peanuts. It's hard for me not to roll my eyes as he takes his precious time to eat them, while we all awkwardly stand there watching him. Mrs. Swanson is happily drinking more whiskey and stroking her son's arm on the next couch over, as if on another planet. Chase is sitting across from me looking regal and perfect in a chair that looks like it once belonged to King Louis XIV. Why does he have to be sitting in that ridiculous royal chair? He looks absurd on that outlandish piece of old world furniture. I try not to smile. Emma and Dante are sitting dutifully next to Mr. Swanson on a crocodile leather chaise. Michelle is sitting next to me, and staring into space with a detached look on her face.

"Well, let's get down to business," Mr. Swanson begins. This family reunion feels more like a board meeting on Wall Street. "Chase, sitting here with you is something I said would never happen. I once told Don Henley that a reconciliation with my son would happen when hell freezes over!" He laughs pretentiously. "This reconciliation is going to take my memoir to a new level, everyone will love the plot twist!" He unexpectedly turns his attention to me and I try to disappear into the couch. "Listen, Olivia... I don't know if you know this about me, but I might be the most interesting man that has ever lived who isn't famous," he boasts. "Except that I *am* famous!" He chortles enthusiastically at his terrible joke.

"That reminds me…" he says. "Emma!" he barks even though she is sitting right next to him.

"Yes, Mr. Swanson," she replies, sitting at attention like a devoted puppy whose only purpose in life is to serve its master.

"Call my ghost writer after this and fill him in on the most attention-grabbing parts of this family reunion," T.J. commands his assistant. "But only the moments that make me look like a perfect father and a family man, okay?"

"Absolutely, sir!" Emma says with eager adoration in her voice. Chase crosses his arms on his chest.

"Glad I could be of service to make your memoir more interesting, Dad," he says evenly, but I can hear hints of disgust and sarcasm in his voice. I can tell that he is doing his best to play nice, but is fighting the urge to punch his egotistical father.

"Son, I hated you with all the hate my black heart had to give after your disgusting and vile acts, and the disrespectful way in which you treated everyone in this family. You're lucky I'm giving you a second chance young man! Don't you dare cross me again!" he cautions.

"I would never do that, father," Chase says unenthusiastically, trying his best to hide his disdain. Mr. Swanson laces his hands behind his head and leans back.

"Did everyone see the spread they did about me in Vanity Fair?" he asks us. Panic sets in as I realize I somehow missed that article. Everyone mumbles 'yes' and I do too even though I'm lying! Shit! I hope he doesn't quiz me! I nervously uncross my legs and cross them again. I can feel Chase's eyes on me and I avoid his gaze. I sit up a little straighter. A shiver washes over me from the air conditioner hitting my skin. This house is always so cold. I cross my arms in an attempt to hide my nipples, or maybe I'm just trying to shield myself from his obvious scrutiny. Curiosity is getting the best of me, and I finally look at him. I am met with a flirtatious, mischievous grin. I roll my eyes. I will not play his game, especially after the disrespectful way he treated me. I adjust my top and run my fingers through my hair. His eyes linger on me for a beat too long. I know what he is doing, or perhaps I am picking up on signals that aren't really there. I have been warned about his womanizing ways, but why would he waste his charms on me? My stomach twists into a tingling knot of butterflies at the thought of my biggest crush in the world trying to seduce me. Why? What on earth would be the point? Chase Swanson could literally have any woman he wants. I make eye contact with him again and he gives me a covert wink that registers in my mind like two crystal champagne flutes clinking together. I rub my glossed lips against each other and accidentally bite down on my bottom lip while staring at him. My heavily mascara'd lashes flutter as I twirl a lock of hair with my fingertips, pulling down on it until it is next to my mouth. His eyes flicker with lust, and my stomach tingles uncontrollably.

Mr. Swanson continues stroking his own ego and name dropping like it's his job, pulling Chase and I from our subtly seductive exchange, "...right before the article was written, I had lunch with Elon Musk at The Ivy. He wanted me to include a Tesla in the photo Vanity Fair took of me with my cars. I told him that I didn't want a $100,000 golf cart ruining my photo! Real men don't drive electric cars!" He laughs heartily at his own joke.

"Honey, Teslas are actually $101,500," Mrs. Swanson quietly chimes in. "I just bought one for myself the other day. Electric cars are a really great thing for the environment, you should consider owning at least one. I've loved all of mine!"

"Samantha! Shut up!! Shut up, Samantha!" Mr. Swanson berates his beautiful wife. I wince, but she doesn't seem at all fazed by it as she takes another sip of her whiskey and reapplies her crimson Chanel red lipstick, smirking in amusement.

"Are you blind?" Mr. Swanson shouts at her. "Have you not seen my P1 spinning for weeks on the turntable? That car *is* a hybrid! Do you not know *anything* about my collection?!" Michelle groans heavily beside me.

"Dad, you can only drive like 6 miles with the P1 in electric mode. It's a hybrid to make it launch, not to like, help with the environment," Michelle says, and I'm astonished by how much she knows about cars. It's odd when my super girly best friend goes into tomboy mode. "Mom is just saying that you would like the Tesla because it drives itself. Omg, you could tell Emma what to text us, from the drivers seat!" She turns her mouth up on one corner. "That would be perfect for you!" she declares sarcastically. I am trying to disappear into the couch. This is so awkward, I could die.

"No one asked for your opinion, little girl! This is between me and your mother! Stay out of this and stay out of my P1! Don't you dare touch it, ever!!" he shouts at her.

I'm so confused as to how a fight even got started. Is Mr. Swanson so volatile that his wife's lighthearted suggestion that he should own an electric car made him fly into a rage?

"And might I remind you that I'm doing far more for the environment than all of you, by owning hundreds of vehicles!" he yells and looks around the room. "Because guess what? They are parked and *not being driven*!"

"T.J., stop with these hurtful words..." Dante finally rescues us from Mr. Swanson's wrath. I love the way Dante says 'these,' it sounds like 'tease' in his Jamaican accent. "You must think in your mind, how your anger affects the people you love. It's not a nice way to speak to your wife and daughter. It did not feel good to their souls," he chastises in his soothing accent. "Take a few deep and cleansing breaths with me..." Mr. Swanson reluctantly closes his eyes. "Ready... one... two..." Dante begins to assist him in

86

meditation. Emma types something in her iPad and Bob Marley starts playing loudly in the room.

"Excuse me," an irritated Chase announces, as he stands and walks away. I hate that he is leaving me alone in this uncomfortable situation. I want to go with him. The fluttering in my stomach entangles me as I watch his calf muscles flex with each stride as he walks out of the room. His cavalier gait is as royal as the chair he was just sitting on. I would do anything to go with him.

Tiffany-Tangled

Mrs. Swanson tried to move the reunion to the theater room to watch a movie as a family, but Mr. Swanson yelled at her and told her he needed to get back to work, so it's back to business as usual at the Swanson household. Michelle and I are out by the pool drinking champagne and smoking weed with Dante, the famous spiritual healer. He keeps looking at Michelle with lust in his eyes, and I can't help but feel a pang of jealousy. Not because I have a crush on Dante, but because I wish a guy would look at me that way. Don't get me wrong, Dante is a very good looking dude in a hippie mountain man kind of way. He's tall with a lean and muscular frame and has perfectly shaped Bob Marley dreadlocks. His chiseled jaw and big lips make him look like the Rastafarian version of Tyson Beckford, except that instead of wearing fashionable clothing, he is clad in beads and a loose hemp tunic - most likely, his required uniform. His walkie-talkie erupts in sound.

"Dante! You are needed in the office by Mr. Swanson," Emma's muffled voice announces through the device.

"On my way," he says back to her. Dante gets up and kisses Michelle on the cheek.

"Take care, my loves," he says and heads inside to deal with whatever neurotic problem Mr. Swanson is battling at the moment.

I wonder if Dante is even his real name, or if Mr. Swanson named him that. I push him from my mind and direct my attention towards my best friend. She seems to be on another planet as she stares into the L.A. night sky and absently strokes her champagne flute. I wonder if she is still upset about her brother or if this is about her parent's ridiculous fight over electric cars.

"What's wrong Michelle?" I ask, probing gently. I know I should tread lightly when it comes to topics that upset her.

"Nothing... I'm fine," she snaps and then frowns. She swallows more champagne, takes a deep breath, and just like that, her body language transforms from melancholy to cheerful, like a robot who has been switched into 'fake it' mode. I guess the bubbly brought the bubbly back into her beautifully sad doll face. "I'm just super baked and drunk!" she giggles.

"Me too!" I say and take another sip from my flute. I can feel the excitement building in my stomach as my mind drifts to Chase. Just the fact that he is inside the house right now has put my body on high alert.

"Liv, I'm bored..." Michelle pouts and sticks her bottom lip out like a little girl who didn't get her way at the carnival.

"Do you want to go bowling?" I suggest lightly, hoping for another chance to catch a glimpse of her brother.

"Oh my God, yes! That is like the best idea you've ever had!" she squeals, sounding drunk, stoned and overzealous. She takes me by the hand and we giggle over nothing as we stumble through a sliding glass door and into the house. I scan the common floor for any sign of Chase, but I don't see him. We make our way to the East wing, the entertainment side of the mansion, and take the elevator down to the basement. As we walk past the arcade, Michelle stops abruptly, like a zombie that found a lifeline. She takes me by the hand and I groan. I hate when she wants to hang out in the game room. She inevitably morphs into a little kid that won 1,000 tickets but can't pick a prize. I feel like the bored-to-tears babysitter every time this happens.

"Livvie, play me in air hockey!" she demands and leads me by the hand to the brightly lit table that blows air in my face.

"Do I have to?" I whine in vain... but, of course I have to; it's her world and I'm just living in it. She's already placed the puck on the table and is stretching her arm out as if she is a serious athlete about to play a professional hockey game. I let the contraption in my hand purposely fail me each time she shoots the puck towards me.

"Damn! I will never beat you!" I declare as convincingly as I can. She does a little victory dance in front of the table and skips away, headed straight for the vintage Pac-Man game. I need a diversion tactic before I get stuck here all night. "Hey Michelle," I call out to her, hoping I can manipulate her short attention span. "Remember when we ate out of that giant sized carton of ice cream in the catering room?" I ask. She flips around, her mouth in an exaggerated O... she looks just like a kid on Christmas morning.

"Yes!" she squeals, jumping up and down in her vintage Adidas shoes. "Oh my God! Liv! Let's go get it!"

"And then, how about that bowling game?" I ask casually, as we walk to the kitchen staff's preparation room, holding hands.

"Yeah, totally, that, whatever," she mumbles dismissively.

"Shhh!" She puts her finger to my lips when we get to the door. She pushes it open and we tiptoe inside. I pull out the ice cream and she pulls the whipped cream from the fridge. She inhales a whippet from it. Drool comes out of her mouth and she giggles hysterically. "You want one?" she shouts in what I think was intended to be a whisper, as she offers me the can. I push the nozzle to the side but only to get the cream in my mouth, I don't want to do whatever it was she just did to get high off of it. We take off running with the goods like first time thieves. Michelle keeps taking more whippets as we run. "Run Livvie! Run!" she yells, with a mouth full of whipped cream. I giggle and run faster.

"What are you little weirdo's doing?" I hear as we run past the basketball court. The deep voice stops me in my tracks. My eyes grow wide and then I see Chase standing there. He looks more delicious than the ice cream in my hands, or anything else I think I've ever seen. He's wearing athletic shorts and a black sweatshirt with the hood pulled up over a black baseball cap. He's holding a basketball, looking athletic and perfect. He removes the hood, revealing a Ferrari emblem on the front of his hat. When he casually flips the hat around backwards, I am driven crazy with

91

desire. It looks like he just finished a Polo match for Ralph Lauren himself and is about to be chauffeured in a Rolls Drophead to QB his Friday night lights football game.

Michelle lets out a little squeal... "Chase! You scared the shit out of me! I'm not used to dudes being down here!" Chase chuckles and continues to dribble the ball.

"Did you save any ice cream for me? Or did Liv eat it all?" he asks as he passes the ball between his legs with an athlete's ease and shoots a perfect 3-pointer. I can't believe he remembered my name. I laugh out loud, praying he can't hear the butterflies in my voice.

"No... I haven't had any yet. We were just on our way to the bowling alley with it," I say, full of guilt, but not sure why. Michelle hands her brother the whipped cream. He takes it out of her hand while looking at me.

"You can come, if you want," she says to her brother, superficially. I bite my lower lip, anxiously awaiting his response. He continues to stare at me while he takes a whippet from the can. I feel my face grow hot. My heart is beating out of my chest, and my palms are wet.

"Yeah, let's go *bowling*," he says and directs the words at me with a hint of playful banter. I am feeling flustered and anxious as I shuffle behind Michelle and her brother towards the bowling alley. His calf muscles flex and ripple with every step, and his perfect butt, muscular back and imposing swagger are intoxicating.

I can't stop staring. Chase's larger than life charisma makes me question how someone can be so intimidating yet so charming at the same time; it's a dangerous magic.

Welcome to The Doll House

"Blaire picked me up from the airport today," Chase says offhandedly to his sister as we pass the twenty-five seat theater room. I can see the taxidermy monkey glaring at me from within. I quickly look away. I don't want to have to apologize to it right now.

"That snooty bitch..." Michelle says under her breath. "Why didn't she come inside?" I can feel the frost in her coldblooded Ice Princess voice.

"She isn't ready to see you," he replies with mediatingly cool composure.

"Blaire is a cunt!!" Michelle blurts out.

"Come on!" Chase reprimands, "she's your sister!"

"I don't give a fuck!" Michelle yells, full of attitude as she flings open the door to the bowling alley. "Lets get this fucking party started!" she hoots as she sprints to the control center to turn on the music. Chase rolls his eyes.

"Fuck... back at the doll house!" he says to me. I do my best to smile at him without blushing.

"Yep..." I reply as cordially as I can. "Summer Time Beach House" by Doc Hollywood & Ya Boy is now blasting through the multi-colored bowling alley. Michelle is moving her hips to the

94

music as she turns on the disco lights above the lane that we are about to use. I feel Chase's eyes linger on me as I slip into a pair of bowling shoes. He is sitting across from me with his hands laced behind his head and his legs splayed out like he owns the place, which I guess he kind of does. I look up at him warily, and he gives me the Swanson smile. I've seen this heart melter before from Michelle. It's designed to disarm and bewitch... and it works like a charm.

"Relax." he says. Despite his softly spoken command, I feel myself stiffening as he walks over towards me and takes a seat. He sits a little too close for someone I barely know, but I don't mind, the excitement is delicious. My stomach tingles as I inhale his scent. It's a mix of fine cologne and a hint of something masculine that I've never experienced before. I don't know what it is exactly, but it's quietly driving me wild. "You're terrified of me, aren't you?" he asks with a hint of satisfaction in his eyes.

"No. I'm not..." I object. My lie causes my heart to skip a beat.

"Good." He gives me a friendly nudge with his shoulder. His touch sends a current of electricity into my body. "So, are you ready to dazzle me with your bowling skills?" he asks, a sarcastic smile dangling on the corner of his lips.

"I will have you know, I am an excellent bowler!" I protest, and instantly hate myself for reacting too defensively.

"So you *do* speak!" Chase marvels. I blush as I think about what a shy dork I was earlier. "The sex bot has finally opened her mouth!" he announces to no one in particular. I shrug my shoulders and giggle. "Cool shoes by the way," he says with the sexiest half grin I've ever seen. He points to my feet and I try and hide the shoes under the bench, but there's nowhere to hide my blushing face. "Are you going to wear fins when we go to the pool too?" I continue to giggle and cross my legs. He squares an ankle over one knee with his hands still laced behind his head. His foot is almost touching my leg that's crossed towards him. I place my hands on my knee and look up at him like an enchanted Disney princess.

"When are we going swimming?" I ask him, more earnestly than intended.

"Why? Do you need to go put on your one-piece and swim cap?" he teases.

I shove him playfully. His grin grows in perfect sync with the twinkle in his naughty eyes.

"I don't wear a one-piece! Or a swim cap!" I protest through giggles.

"Just checking," he says and chuckles. "I look forward to seeing you in a bikini then." He traces my body with eyes that have somehow transformed from a vivid blue to an electric green, and an unfamiliar sensation of heat washes over me. Ah, so he did inherit his mother's legendary eyes. I thought they were Tiffany blue flecked with hints of green and amber, but right now they would make the 16th hole at Pebble Beach envious, they are so luminously green. Chase has the kind of eyes that make women forget what they're doing. They distract everyone when he walks into a room, and then his presence takes over, making him unforgettable. Maybe eyes really are the windows to the soul. I hear Michelle singing and quickly come to. I disengage from my emerald green hypnosis and glance at her. She is oblivious to our flirtatious exchange, still dancing around and twirling while picking out her bowling ball. Unable to stop myself, I turn my attention back to Chase.

"Are you ready to get your ass kicked in bowling by a girl?" I ask him and bite my lip.

"We'll see about that..." he taunts. He gives me a flirty wink, and my lip bite turns into a full fledged grin as the butterflies inside of me flutter with reckless abandon. I look into Chase's eyes one last time to imprint the memory, and I can practically hear the waves crashing along the shoreline. They are magically back to ocean blue. I look away and realize that Michelle is back and holding two sparkly pink bowling balls.

"Here you go, Liv," she says and hands one to me. "Chase, you can get your own ball!" He rolls his eyes and stands up.

When Chase is out of sight, Michelle whispers, "Was he being nice to you?" I nod, struggling to hide my bewitched grin. "Okay, good! I will kick his ass if he's ever a dick to you!" she says and flexes her little bicep. She opens a giant carton of mint ice cream and scoops up a bite on her spoon to feed to me.

"Thank you!" I manage through a full mouth. The game commences and much to the ultra competitive Swanson siblings surprise, I win. This might be the only time I am grateful for growing up in a small town with nothing to do.

"Well played," Chase compliments me, as I'm taking off the nerdy bowling shoes that I wish I hadn't worn. I beam with pride.

"I told you I would win!" I can't hide the flirty undertones in my voice.

"You got lucky."

"Chase! You're such a sore loser!" Michelle yells, the irritation evident in her voice. "You can't be the best at everything, brother!" She glares at him, her playful mood from before is rapidly shifting to something darker. The hair stands up on my arms from her sinister energy.

"So, Chase..." she says, her eyes flickering with spite. "How's your truth journal going?" Chase looks uncomfortable with the question. My eyes dart from Michelle to Chase and back to Michelle. I can't quite read what is going on.

"What's a truth journal?" I ask them. They ignore me. Chase scowls at his sister.

"Shut the fuck up, Michelle..." he says. I flinch at his sharp tone but Michelle looks smugly vindicated at his response.

"Okay," she says, and it's more of a threat than a reply.

Champagne Tub

"Brrr! That ice cream made me so cold!" Michelle declares between shivers. She turns off the disco lights and the music in the bowling alley. "I need to take a bath! Come on, Liv!" She grabs my hand assertively. "Sorry, Chase! Girl stuff! You're not invited! Can you put the ice cream and shit away?" she asks him sarcastically from the door. He flashes her the middle finger in response.

"Goodnight, Liv," I think I hear him say, but Michelle has already led me out of the bowling alley and away from him. I walk behind her in a daze as I think about the flirtatious exchange I just had with her brother. I have this wild urge to spend more time with him, even to do something naughty, like sneak into his bedroom. My heart skips a beat at the thought of being alone in his bedroom with him. I wonder if he would kiss me... or would he think I was a fool. My face falls. I feel wretched at the thought of him rejecting me. Oh no, am I delusional or was there actual chemistry between us? I am starting to lose my breath thinking about it, and I can't tell if it's because of the stairs I just climbed, or because of him.

"Michelle! Why didn't we take the elevator?!" I ask as I lean on the railing exaggeratedly.

"Because we have to burn off that ice cream!" Michelle responds flippantly. "We can't get fat, Liv!" I groan and follow her

99

up the curved staircase that seems to go on for eternity. I rejoice when we finally get to her bedroom door and our inadvertent workout through 40,000 square feet is over. Michelle's house is equivalent to sixteen of mine. The guest house alone is the size of at least two Kaneville homes.

We walk through her living room, past the kitchenette, through her bedroom and into her extravagant bathroom. The centerpiece of the room is her champagne tub. When she first told me about it, I pictured her bathing in champagne. Ridiculous, I know, but you never know what is normal and what is not in Swanson world. Water cascades luxuriously down from the waterfall fixture protruding from the marble, filling the oversized tub. She messes with her phone and a song begins playing from a speaker above. It is sad and haunting, filled with dramatic melodies.

"What is this?" I ask. I close my eyes and let the melancholy symphony fill my mind. "It's so pretty..."

"It's a Metallica song. 'Nothing Else Matters,' played on cellos. The band Apocalyptica did this one," she purrs as she pours velvety bubble bath soap into the oversized tub. "My dad loves to hear how songs translate into instrumental form. He says it shows him the true quality of the writing. Daddy loves bands like Metallica and like, all metal, because their songs sound so badass like this. He calls them the modern day Bach and Beethoven's of Los Angeles," she says as she kicks off her shoes. "But lately, he

100

likes pop music..." She sighs as she removes her shorts and panties. "Just whatever will make him the most money." She pulls the Guns N' Roses shirt off over her head, revealing her perfect breasts. The room is filling with steam, and the scents of vanilla and cherry blossom are dancing in the air. She presses a button on a remote control and the water stops flowing. Another button causes jets and bubbles to bring the tub to life. I watch her slip gracefully into the water. Her body is elegant and poised, like a ballerina's. I wonder if she did ballet growing up. I think about the music box my mom gave me when I was a child. It had a beautiful little ballerina that would twirl and twirl to a song from 'The Nutcracker.'

"Michelle, were you a ballerina?" I ask. She giggles guiltily.

"Of course I was! Weren't all of us Bel Air and Beverly Hills brats?" she asks rhetorically as she blows bubbles into the air off of her hands. "Liv, get in!" She pats the water.

"Okay..." I mumble. I am working on being more carefree and open. Los Angeles has subscribed to the free love philosophy for decades. So this must be normal, right? Best friends taking a bubble bath together is not a big deal, I reassure myself. I undress shyly and slip into the water across from her. Michelle is staring into space as she takes a hit of weed off her custom neon pink pipe. It looks like an accessory in 'Ganja Barbie's' dream house.

"Liv, I want to live a life of adventure..." she says as she blows the smoke sensually out of her mouth. The room fills with her wistful mood and the scent of marijuana. "I want to travel the world! I want to do cocaine in Peru with the locals, I want to smoke the best weed in Jamaica with new friends while we listen to Bob Marley on the beach. I want my passport to be so full, they will have to add extra pages!" She shrugs her tan shoulders dreamily. "This life is lonely. I don't know who truly loves me. I don't even think my own parents love me," she says, as a pained look spreads across her beautiful face. Her expression is one of deep hurt and dejection. I stare at her with compassion in my eyes.

"I love you, Michelle," I say and give her leg a comforting squeeze.

"I know you do," she responds and smiles sweetly. "It's lonely at the top, Liv. Will you stay at the top with me?" She hands me the pipe.

"Yeah, I can do that," I say as I take a hit. I blow the smoke into the steamy air.

Suddenly, Michelle gets up onto her knees causing water and bubbles to splash everywhere. She seems overly excited about something.

"Dude! We should try and get this bath to overflow with bubbles!" She's full of naughtiness and giggles as she reaches for more soap. She pours more in and messes with the remote. We stare mesmerized as the bubbles come alive. I know I am stoned, but this might be the coolest moment of my life. Michelle is on her knees facing away from me, flinging and blowing bubbles all over the bathroom as if she is throwing confetti. Her long blonde hair is lying wet against her back, and the bubbles are outlining the curvature of her body, all the way down to her perfect bubble butt. She looks like a mythical creature, too beautiful to be real, just like her brother.

"I wish I was as pretty as you…" I blurt out. She flips around urgently; water splashes me in the face and I wipe it off. Michelle sensually wipes away the bubbles that are covering her firm nipples.

"Liv, you are beautiful, so very beautiful. Plus, you have inner beauty, I don't have that. My soul is ugly. You don't want to be me." She sulks and furrows her brow. "I go to dark places…" she whispers. She somehow shakes the angst away and her face softens as our eyes meet. "You were always pretty, Olivia Jean Walker, I just helped tune you up a little bit, and now you are one of us! You are *Liv from Bel Air*!" She playfully throws more bubbles into the air and snorts. "Oh God, Liv. Remember those awful pants you had?" she asks with a cruel laugh. I smile halfheartedly at the memory. She had a look of horror in her eyes when I showed up to her place in the Carhartts that I used to wear when I helped my dad work on the farm. She burned them in her fireplace. It actually made me kind of sad, but I went along with it to appease her. I'm always appeasing her.

"Those wouldn't even fit you now," she says. I feel her big blue eyes fixate on me intently. She moves slowly towards me, but not in a predatory way, rather, in a gentle and curious way. "I liked molding you," she whispers, her voice sultry and low. She is now kneeling in between my legs, her face so close to mine that I can feel her hot breath on my skin as her wet blonde hair brushes against me. Her hands find the top of my thighs and glide slowly up my body, pausing on my tits. She gives them a firm squeeze as if I am a science experiment. I jump slightly. "Hard to believe these are real," she says flatly, "they won't be perky forever, though. We should get some implants in them sooner rather than later." She grabs my hands and places them on her tits. "Give them a squeeze!" she urges. I squeeze gently. "They feel real, right? These implants are called gummy bears." She places her hands on top of mine.

"Yeah, very realistic," I respond quietly. I swallow. My nerves are really jumping. I try and calm them by listening closely to the song that is playing. I feel like the rhythm is moving through me. It works and I begin to relax. I close my eyes. I feel Michelle's gentle touch on my body. She is covering me with bubbles as if she is washing me and I feel my back starting to arch.

Her delicate fingertips are softly tracing circles on my skin. Much to my surprise, I feel my nipples harden. As if on cue, Michelle slides her manicured fingernails to the inside of my thighs and begins to walk them slowly upwards. I open my eyes to her seductive blue eyes penetrating deeply into mine. My breath is quickening now. She bites her cherry red bottom lip with perfect white teeth and looks up at me through long black eyelashes. I've seen her work this magic many times; it drives men *and* women crazy. And now I understand why. Michelle has virtuoso bedroom eyes. It's a master class in raw, unadulterated sexuality. She moves her lips closer and I close my eyes and purse my lips in anticipation of a kiss...

Sexual Deviance

But the kiss never comes. Her lips land softly on my neck. She licks and sucks my skin and then runs her tongue slowly up towards my ear. I can feel her warm breath and smell her Coco Chanel as she moans softly, yet lustfully.

"Am I turning you on right now Liv?" she whispers, as she continues to absently trace circles around my belly button with her fingertips. My lips part but I can't find words yet. The slow circles begin to move lower and lower. The tone of her voice is vibrating my body. The weed, the music, and her touch are taking me on a journey towards an escape I so desperately want. I've never been with a girl, but this is making me feel things I have never felt before.

"Yes," I finally whisper, shocked by my answer. She presses her body against me, her nipples hard against mine, she breathes heavily into my ear, and I can't help but let out a little moan.

"Oh yeah?" she says tauntingly. "Let's see about that..." I gasp as she sticks her finger inside me. "Liv! You're wet!" she says, delighted. "Maybe you have a little lipstick lesbian in you after all! The body doesn't lie!" She slides back over to her side of the tub, looking quite pleased with herself. I'm too stunned to know how to react but I'm more than a little turned on, if I'm being honest. I stare at her with a confused expression. "Don't worry, good girl. Nothing is going to happen. I just wanted to see if I could do it," she says, taking another hit of weed. "Just a game." She holds the smoke in her lungs for a moment. "But, I would be down to experiment if you ever want to. I go both ways," she says, the smoke still in her lungs. She lays her head back against the edge of the tub and closes her eyes as she blows it all out. It fills the air around her perfect, dream girl face. "I love the cock, but there is nothing quite like the sensual touch of a woman. I much prefer a woman to go down on me," she says and starts to touch herself, "they are so much better at it than men. Soft lips and no stubble, you know?"

"Ahhh..." She moans and licks her lips as she pushes her hips into her fingers and begins to swivel them slowly. Her voice sounds strained by the pleasure she is giving herself. I nod even though I don't actually know if girls really are better at it, considering I have never had a man go down on me or even make love to me, much less a woman. "Orgasms when you are high are so much better!" She moans louder as she fingers herself. I'm not going to lie, it is really turning me on watching Michelle, the sex kitten stunner, masturbating confidently right in front of me.

"Trust me, you're going to want to do this too..." she says to me. I have a desperate ache for a release. The desire is so deep it's making my body physically hurt. I've never been this horny before. That flirtatious exchange with Chase is on my mind. His scent, his wink, his delicious face and body. I start to explore myself as I think about him. I've tried this before, but I never really knew what to do or exactly where to touch. Michelle's eyes are glowing as she watches me intently now.

"No, up a little higher. Swirl your index and middle finger at the same time," she instructs. "It's that spot near top that will set you free. You'll know when you find it." I move my fingers a little higher and just like Michelle said, I find the magic button. My head leans back and my mouth opens as I moan with newfound pleasure.

"Oh. Oh my.. oh... SHIT!" I practically scream. "It feels so fucking good!!"

"Haha, you found it!" Michelle laughs, her eyes sparkling excitedly. "That's your clit Liv, you're going to want to touch it all the time now!" she squeals, "I always cum the hardest when I rub my clit and finger myself at the same time... it's almost as good as having a really talented escort go down on me!" Michelle's eyes flash electric blue as she bites down on the tip of her finger, "Do it right now Liv! I want to watch you have your first orgasm, it's so fucking hot!" I obey immediately and start to circle my fingers around the spot Michelle showed me. My legs begin to tremble as the slick wetness intensifies the sensation a thousand times over.

"Now your finger Liv," Michelle whispers as she drags her fingertips lightly across her wet, erect nipples.

As soon as I penetrate myself, I begin to go over the edge. An edge I didn't even know existed. I no longer have any sense of time or place, only of a singular purpose. Pleasure. It is the most intense, decadent sensation I have ever felt. The vibrations are pulsing through me in quick bursts, each better than the last. It feels like lightning is striking every cell in my body. Michelle announces that she has cum after a series of moans and "oh fucks!" but I barely hear her. My legs are shaking and my back is arching as I struggle to control my moans.

"You feel it building, right?" Michelle asks, but it sounds like she is speaking to me through a dream.

"Yes..." I whisper.

"Circle your clit slowly now, it will be more intense," she instructs. I do as she says and I'm rewarded with a wave of pleasure rippling through every inch of my body. My hips are now moving rhythmically and instinctively. I spread my legs and finger myself more deeply. I realize I would rather die than pull my hands away. I feel a surge of wetness and sense that something unforgettable is about to happen, like a rollercoaster's first big drop. My back arches sharply and I bite down hard on my bottom lip, my eyes flutter to a close, and I lose all control as my first orgasm hits me like a tidal wave. My body is the puppet, and my fingers, the puppeteer. A second series of waves roll through me and it's so intense I can't even breathe, and I don't care.

"Oh fuck! This is so hot to watch!" Michelle screams. She has a second orgasm just from watching me. Our moaning peaks, drowning out the jets and filling the spacious bathroom with a symphony of sexual release and gratification. When it finally ends, we sit a few moments, breathing heavily across from each other in the lux champagne tub. I look around at all of the bubbles. They are on our clothes, touching the shower, some have even started to make their way onto the carpet of her bedroom. Michelle turns off the jets with the remote. There is now silence between us except for the music.

"Wow..." I finally say.

"You're welcome," she says arrogantly as she makes her way out of the tub. "You poor thing! I can't believe you didn't know how to do that!" She hands me a towel. I inhale sharply.

"Michelle, I have to tell you something..." I say as I start to dry myself off.

She interrupts me, "let me guess, you're a virgin...." she says flatly.

"Yes!" I admit and bury my face in my hands.

"No shit, Liv!" she says and I laugh, relieved. "Have you ever even given a blow job?" she asks and smirks.

"Yes, I have done that!" I say feeling some pride when I think about the time I gave that fraternity boy a blow job at a party, but then frown when I think about how he never called me.

"I just worked so hard in school..." I say quietly, "I never really had time for boys."

"I'll give you some pointers!" Michelle proclaims as I follow her out of the bathroom. She slides under her purple Egyptian cotton sheets, naked. "I'm the blow job queen!" I giggle as I slip into a pair of star covered grey pajamas from her dresser. I pull the impossibly soft sheets back and get into bed with her.

I listen to some of Michelle's kinky stories and conclude that she is the most sexually adventurous person in the world. Then we watch porn on her computer so she can show me examples of how to fuck like a porn star.

"Wait for it... wait for it.... Yeah!! The money shot!" she yells as a guy shoots his load all over a girl's face. Next, she takes me to her living room to blast sultry music from the sound system. It is so loud that I wonder if Chase can hear it. I hope he knows that his sister is training me and that I want him to use me for his pleasure. Michelle teaches me how how to perform a striptease, about the magic behind bedroom eyes, and then gives me a Vegas stripper worthy lap dance to "Electric" (feat Khalid) by Alina Baraz. Next she goes to her dresser and pulls out the most realistic dildo I've ever seen. Well actually it's the only dildo I've ever seen in person. And its larger than I even knew penises got. After waving it around and chastising it for not calling her, she gets a wicked look in her eyes and comes over to where I'm sitting wide eyed on the couch. She drops to her knees in front of me and proceeds to demonstrate, in depth, the proper way to give an earth shattering blow job. I can't stop giggling as she licks it slowly up and down while fondling its imaginary balls. She then slips her mouth over the top and slides it all the way down her throat. I start to stand,

111

panicked that she might choke on it, but she just winks at me and slides it slowly right back out. I sit back down, embarrassed at my inexperience. After like a 5 minute lesson on how to use your hand to complement your mouth while blowing and how its important to not only make eye contact but to make it sound a little sloppy, I realize that this is the luckiest fake penis on the planet. I take mental notes to do every last thing she's showing me... to her brother. The final lesson for the evening is about S&M and sex toys. She pulls out her "box of pleasure and pain" as she calls it, and tosses me various whips and chains and some odd contraption she calls a cock cage.

"Michelle... is this stuff for S&M? Do boys use these things on you?" I ask, shocked.

"No way! I don't let boys abuse me! I am a dominatrix, Liv, I abuse them!" she explains with a wicked grin. "My brother used to be like the boy version of a dominatrix. He was into the traditional S&M shit... but, he has control issues." I can't help but perk up at the mention of Chase, even if it's to hear something disconcerting like this.

"Your brother is a sadist?" I whisper. She ignores the question and stares at me intently. Her eyes flicker with an emotion I can't read. The silence between us is deafening.

"Be careful there," she says. She cautions me as if I'm holding a fully loaded revolver and it's my turn in Russian roulette. Dread fills my belly. "Chase will charm your dress off and then leave you high and dry. You will never be the same afterwards. My brother is bad news."

"Oh..." I say sadly and roll over to my other side, away from her. I protectively rest my cheek in my hands. "Good night, Michelle," I say, fighting away tears.

I dream about her bad boy brother. He is kissing me everywhere and using my body as he pleases as he spanks my ass and dominates me. I wake up before Michelle, to wetness on my thighs and an aching desire to do what I did last night. My clit is begging me to touch it again; I feel the release beginning the moment my finger makes contact. A moment later I orgasm, quickly, silently, and intensely as I pray Michelle is still sleeping.

Live Fast, Die Young

Michelle leaves early for a modeling shoot in Santa Monica, and I'm looking forward to finally having a day to myself. I've been craving time in my favorite place in this loveless castle that I now call home; the Swanson library. It reminds me of the library in my hometown, except it's three times bigger and about a hundred times more impressive. The one at home doesn't have elegant sliding ladders, probably because it also doesn't have ornate wooden shelves that reach nearly to the ceiling. It also doesn't have beautiful burled mahogany desks or quilted leather couches interspersed throughout. It blows my mind that Michelle has zero interest in her family's library. It looks like *The Beauty and the Beast* library for God's sake! How could she not be completely in love with it like I am?

"Ugh, you just go," she said dismissively when I asked her once if she wanted to come with me. "That's so boring, Liv! I don't know what your fascination is with those stupid books!" She clearly hasn't spent much time there... their library has so much more than just books. The shelves are overflowing with original movie manuscripts from famous films of the last 75 years, super rare comic books, hand written lyrics by some of the greatest artists of yesterday, and my favorite section - the classics and first editions.

I'm too timid to actually borrow a book. There isn't a librarian like at home and I certainly wasn't given a library card, so instead, I spend hours wrapped in cashmere blankets on the supple white leather couches, escaping into magical paper fantasy worlds.

"Bye, Liv!" Michelle whispers as she kisses my cheek. "Have a good day!" I pretend to be asleep and roll over dramatically. Once I know she's gone, I throw the covers off and jump out of bed. I fetch my backpack, the one the maid hung on the coat rack, and scamper away in my silk pajamas and cashmere lined slippers to the West wing. A sense of satisfaction washes over me when I arrive at the lux French doors. As I push them open, I'm greeted by the heat from the L.A. sunshine penetrating the glass. The twenty-foot tall wine colored velvet curtains have been pulled back this morning, revealing floor to ceiling glass and a bird's eye view of the grounds surrounding the fountains behind the house. I close my eyes for a moment to adjust to the bright light. With the glass dome above me, it feels like I am in a planetarium. I used to love the one in Chicago.

"Hi tigers!" I say to the statues at the entryway and place my hand on one of their solid gold heads. "It is so bright today, isn't it?!" There are no stuffed zoo animals in the library to apologize to, just a pair of 24-karat gold tigers that I converse with like a fool. I place my iPod on a dock near a photo of Chase and Michelle and pick one of my favorite playlists. "All You Need is Love" is the first song that comes on.

"Yay! I hope you like The Beatles, Mr. Tigers!" I say to them as I peruse the books in the psychology section of the library. As I sing along to the song, I feel a pang of sadness at the thought of my dad; he absolutely loves The Beatles. I pull my phone out of my backpack and dial his number. It goes straight to voicemail, like it usually does.

"Hi Daddy! Guess what I'm listening to in the library at my friend Michelle's house?" I hold the phone up to a speaker. "Just made me think of you. I miss you. Call me, I love you," I say softly and hang up. I sigh as I place my phone back in my backpack.

I climb the ladder to retrieve the book I want but as I pull it out, a stack of folders falls to the ground. Papers scatter in disarray on the floor.

"Oh my God! I'm so fucking clumsy!" I mumble, seriously annoyed with myself as I make my way back down the ladder. I pick a folder up that says *Child 3* on the cover. A paper that has fallen out of it catches my eye.

Michelle Swanson. The Bacchus. Indulgence. Her astrological chart and a description of her personality are below. As I quickly skim it, words and phrases like *quick to anger, needy* and *paranoid*, jump out at me from the page. I really shouldn't be looking at this stuff, and I feel like someone is spying on me. The library is empty but I can't shake the feeling. Maybe it's me that is being paranoid I think... and then I see the *Child 1* folder. I open it as covertly as possible.

116

"*Chase Swanson. Deity. Live Fast, Die Young.*" I furrow my brow, feeling super perplexed over these folders. What the heck is this stuff? Was this written by a psychologist or an astrologer? What a peculiar thing to have in the family library. Regardless, a hand written description of him now has my undivided attention.

'*Be wary of the Scorpion's sting. Chase's mood swings can be a bit disturbing. He is independent, fearless, ambitious, adventurous, and lustful. He loves women and craves their attention, will frequently use the phrase, "the best I've ever had" after sex. Manipulation is his favorite game... uses his good looks and charm to get his way. Chase is intensely loyal to his family and friends. He has a dark sense of humor and is very quick witted, frequently uses sarcasm to cover up his emotions. May appear to be aloof and distant, but underneath is a warm hearted and caring person.*'

I quickly shut it and sigh. Great, the quintessential bad boy... my kryptonite. Chase Swanson is the guy that every girl falls for, hoping they can be the one to finally tame him. I climb the ladder glumly and replace the folders back on the shelf. Not me, I won't be the next victim of Chase Swanson, I think. I carefully climb down and head to my favorite couch with the book clutched to my chest. My normal sense of relaxation in the library has abandoned me today. I can't focus at all, as visions of Chase dance in my mind. Butterflies and knots occupy my belly simultaneously; I can think of nothing but him.

"I'll bring the book back after class!" I announce loudly just in case anyone is actually watching me. "Bye tigers! See you later!" I say and pet a gold head on the way out. With my head spinning, I get ready for class in Michelle's room. Ten minutes later, I step aboard the elevator and try to focus my thoughts on driving my new car. Anxiety sets in when I realize that I don't remember my parking spot number or even where the Mini Coopers are located in the garage. I take a deep breath, open the doors and look around.

"Oh no..." I whisper as I take in the overwhelming number of vehicles before me.

"Here is a bottle of water for the road, Miss Olivia," a man with a Spanish accent says. I scream and jump away from the mysterious voice.

"Holy shit!" I squeak. "Oscar! You scared the crap out of me!" I hold my hand to my heart. He lets out a little chuckle.

"Lo sienta, chica!" he apologizes in his native language and smiles kindly. I respond in Spanish. "You speak Spanish?" he asks, surprised.

"I do... I'm fluent in Spanish and French," I reply. "My mother spoke Spanish with me when I was little and I learned French recently. I plan to study abroad next year....so...." I abruptly stop talking and feel my face turning red. It sounds like I'm bragging or something.

"Wow! Gorgeous and smart! I bet the boys go loco for you!" he says. I giggle over his silly and predictable compliment. He suddenly reminds me more of George Lopez than Mario from Nintendo.

"Oh, stop!" I say, genuinely charmed.

"I'm sure Mr. Chase could not believe his lucky stars!" Oscar gushes. A lightning bolt of hope races through my body. Did he just say 'Mr. Chase,' as in Chase Swanson?

"Chase?" I ask, dumbfounded.

"Yes, of course Chase! He is probably losing his mind thinking about you!" Oscar says enthusiastically.

"Oh..." I say, surprised. "I highly doubt that! I'm not really his type..." I shuffle my feet and stare at the ground.

"You are exactly his type," he says sincerely. I look at him with wide eyes as I nearly drop the key fob.

"Would you like me to get the car for you, Miss Olivia?" he asks, breaking the spell.

"No, that's okay. I can get it," I manage, and look around again. Okay, there is the P1 on the turntable and that's British so maybe it's near that? Wait... the Rolls Royce is on the other side and that's also British. Oh no...

"Mini Coopers are over there," says Oscar, gallantly rescuing me from becoming lost in the parking garage maze.

"Thanks Oscar!" I respond, relief evident in my voice. I walk swiftly to the Minis and identify my little car, but my hands fumble with the key fob as I attempt to unlock it. The spare key falls out of the fob and onto the ground, making a loud metallic noise against the concrete.

"Shit," I mumble. The sound echoes through the parking garage and I quickly reach down to pick the key up. As I do, my backpack slides over my head and smacks me in the face.

I groan. "Olivia, you are so out of your league here," I scold myself as I stand. Feeling slightly defeated, I open the door and drop into the lipstick red leather drivers seat. I take a deep and cleansing breath as I put the top down, then I throw the car into gear and drive carefully up the ramp. I make my way through the courtyard and down the long, dramatic driveway. The robot dog doesn't even acknowledge me as I leave. 'Mastiff' just lays motionless off to the side of the golden gate. The cameras and drones don't seem nearly as menacing this time around. I continue down the lane and the grip of the Swanson spell loosens little by little until finally, I watch the massive white gate closing behind me in the rearview mirror of the Mini Cooper... which I still can't believe is mine, despite having named her Victoria after my favorite Spice girl, Posh Spice.

As I'm driving down Stone Canyon towards UCLA, my iPod surprises me with the classic Christmas song "Rockin' Around the Christmas Tree." I really don't have the heart to change it despite it being summertime and nowhere near the holiday season. Instead, I giggle gleefully and turn it up. As I sing along loudly, I think about the movie *Home Alone*. My mind drifts to Illinois where the movie took place and then naturally, I think of my dad. I feel like I could cry thinking about how I didn't go home for Christmas. In fact, I haven't been home at all. I spent Christmas with Michelle in Los Angeles.

Orphan Christmas Party

Michelle's parents went to their Aspen home for the holidays but Michelle was disinvited for reasons that were never disclosed to me. We threw an 'Orphan Christmas Party' at their Bel Air mansion on Christmas Eve. We even had carolers and snow making machines brought in. The Bel Air castle looked picturesque with a light dusting of snow around it, even if it was wasn't real. I felt very nostalgic as I picked up some fake Hollywood snow and formed a snowball to throw at Michelle during the 'Orphan Snowball Fight.' She's startlingly athletic and dodged it with ease of course. I remember all the lonely rich kids, smiling weakly and throwing fake snowballs at each other; all the 'orphans, the 'misfits,' i.e. the ones who weren't invited on whatever ultra luxurious vacation their parents went on because they are the trouble makers and the oddballs.

The next morning, the misfit orphans and I battled through our hangovers and shuffled downstairs to open our extra large mink Christmas stockings, which were hung on the mantle above the fireplace. The stockings were all filled with the same gifts: three organic jumbo lollipops, a platinum Rolex Day-Date, an absurdly oversized joint, a silver bullet of cocaine and 5 grand wrapped in rubber bands drug dealer style, inside of a bright blue YSL clutch. To top it off, Michelle was dressed in a sexy Santa costume.

"Holy shit, Michelle! This is amazing!" I said as I hugged her. "Thank you so much!"

"Stop it!" She pushed me away. "Vi put these together, not me," she said indifferently. As she reapplied her juicy red lip gloss, she reached for an envelope resting on the end table next to the couch. "But... I did get you this." She handed it to me. I pulled out two VIP tickets to Coachella. "It will be fun," she said and shrugged. We ended up not going because she went to London for a modeling shoot the weekend of Coachella. She didn't even remember that she had gotten me the tickets. I am pulled from the memory when I notice some onlookers from a Hollywood tour bus eyeing me curiously. I must look insane, blasting a Christmas song in a convertible in the middle of June. Embarrassed, I turn the music down and avoid their eyes.

Whiskey on Ice

I park in the nearest student lot and make my way to class. I attempt to focus on what my professor is saying, but I can't stop thinking about Chase. In fact, I can't get myself to think of anything but him. The memories of his devastating smile and sparkling eyes, and our flirtatious exchange in the bowling alley, play in endless loops in my mind. I wonder what color his eyes are right now. Deep sapphire blue or brilliant emerald green? Is he wearing his hat backwards? I think about the strength everyone notices in his neck and his tanned capable hands, his perfect mouth and how badly I want to feel those soft lips upon my skin.

After class, I pull back into the parking garage at the Swanson's estate and make sure to park in my designated spot. I do *not* want to piss off Mr. Swanson. Oscar is detailing a gorgeous black Porsche as I approach.

"That's a pretty car!" I say cheerfully to Oscar while waiting for the elevator.

"It is Mr. Chase's practice car. She's bonita, isn't she?" He stands back and lets out a low whistle as he stares admiringly at the glossy sports car.

"Yes, very!" I reply as I step inside the elevator. "Be good, Oscar." I wave as the doors shut.

"Adios!" he responds.

I get off on the common floor and walk swiftly towards the West wing. I am guilt ridden about the book I borrowed and I have to get it back to the library before anyone notices. My flip flops stop dead in their tracks when I hear the sound of a girl's laughter mixing with Chase's smooth deep voice. Self control evades me and I rush to investigate the noises. My sandals flip and flop rapidly against the pristine black and white checkered floor, keeping in perfect time with my heart. I move almost magnetically towards the entertainment wing. My nostrils fill with the intertwining aromas of cigar smoke and expensive perfume. Stealth now entirely forgotten, I follow the terrible sounds through the partially closed door. Chase is in the smoking room, reclined in a black crocodile leather chair in front of the mural of himself, and being straddled by a beautiful half naked girl. Her long black hair reaches her bubble butt as she grinds her body into his to the beat of a rap song. Thankfully, Chase is still fully clothed in a black button down polo and dark khaki pants.

He takes a long pull from his thick cigar, holds it in for a moment and then exhales slowly like some kind of beautiful dragon, looking the girl in the eyes the entire time. He sets it down on an onyx ashtray, next to a crystal tumbler of expensive whiskey, on the mahogany side table. Disgust and jealousy pulse unchecked through my body as I watch him evaluate the raven haired beauty with lust and approval in his eyes. His attention is

125

focused only on her and I desperately want his attention on me, although perhaps not just right now. Certainly not on her though, she doesn't deserve any of it. His hands are all over her perfectly sculpted body. She presses her oversized fake boobs against his face, and he awards her with a brilliant Cheshire cat smile for the slutty move. The sight is sickening but I can't look away. He spanks her toned bottom with a casual authority and I cringe imperceptibly. He detects the movement like an apex predator and turns to look right at me. I look away quickly but it's far too late.

"Would you like to join us?" he asks coolly, flashing a mischievous grin. My face turns crimson. The girl flips around and glares at me. I recognize her immediately. Sierra Villa, pop star and model.

"Sorry..." I mumble and scamper away.

"Who was that?" I hear her ask rudely, but I am already too far away to hear Chase's response. I am running as fast as I can towards the sliding glass doors. I open them frantically and almost fall when my feet touch the pavement. I rush into the guest house and dive onto my tightly made bed, my mind aflame. Does Chase like her? Sierra Villa? He's a notorious womanizer, I know this, so why is what I just witnessed irking me so much? I shouldn't care what he does or who he likes. I lay on top of the comforter and try and stare mindlessly at the ceiling. The sun is shining through the window, and when I go to close the blinds I see the glare on the vast swimming pool. I can't just stay inside and mope, it's summertime in Bel Air.

I grab my sunglasses and my book and step into the luscious Southern California sunshine. I pull my maxi dress up, sit down at the edge of the pool, and dangle my feet in the water. The warm liquid is more inviting with each movement of my legs, and the heat from the sun feels exquisite on my bare shoulders. I wonder what Chase is doing right now. I want him out here with me and not with stupid Sierra Villa. Chase Swanson sparkles brighter than anyone I've ever met. He is an enigma I can't solve; a perfect balance of mystery, shameless confidence and soulful, pragmatic protector. I have never met anyone like him.

Olivia... stop, I scold myself. Stop being a stupid girl, it's not going to happen with him. I must be logical. I must guard my heart. Having my heart shattered by a man like Chase Swanson would be devastating. I mentally write a book full of resolve but the words on the paper are gibberish to me; they read as thoughts of him and I together. I wonder how it would feel to touch Chase's flawless skin, to give him pleasure, to submit to his desires. Would he still want me tomorrow? Probably not. My silly crush on him is just that, silly. It can't be based in reality, can it? I need to forget about him and move on. Who was I kidding? Girls like Sierra will always win.

Country music starts to play on the outdoor speakers. It's such a moving and soulful song that it makes me want to cry. This must be Michelle's Southern mother's doing. I look around to find her, to thank her for putting on music for me, but she's not out here. My eyes land regrettably on the scene in the courtyard. Chase is in front of the fountain kissing Sierra goodbye. His preppy outfit from before has been replaced with a black Metallica t-shirt and board shorts with Porsches on them. His new clothing choice makes him look like a rebellious teenage boy.

"Bye baby," I hear him say as he spanks her on the butt. The wings on her Robin's jeans fit perfectly against her perky bottom. She giggles as he lifts her effortlessly into the driver's seat of her white Range Rover. I look away and stare broken heartedly into the pool. I could never compete with her. She's a cover girl, a performer. I am just... nobody. I look down at my book, feeling tormented. I hear Sierra's car leave the driveway, and my heart begins to race as out of the corner of my eye, I see Chase walking towards me. I will myself to be oblivious to his presence. Of course I don't notice Chase Swanson, I am too enthralled by this psychology book. I refuse to look at him even though he is now standing right over me.

"Hey nerd," he says evenly, "Can I join you or are you too busy geeking out on whatever kind of nerd shit it is you like to do?" He doesn't wait for me to say yes or no, he just sits down next to me. His feet are now moving in unison with mine in the warm pool water. I ignore him and pretend to be absorbed in my book. I sense his curious blue-green eyes on me, but I don't care. He pulls a joint out of the pocket of his board shorts. "I thought you said you would wear a bikini when we went to the pool," he says with a smirk on his face. I reminisce about our seductive exchange in the bowling alley for the hundredth time. I shrug shyly, and his smirk dissolves. "It's okay, I like this too," he says and points to my strapless dress.

"By the way. I saw you in the library this morning. I saw you take that book." He points to the book in my hands and lights his joint. My nerves jump and twist. I wish I could be transported to anywhere but here.

"I'm sorry, I hope that's okay," I say, my voice filled with shame, "I swear, I was planning on bringing it back!" I stare at him earnestly. He coughs and chokes on the smoke that he just inhaled as he throws his head back in laughter.

"Don't worry! Your secret is safe with me. I would hate for you to get arrested by the book police!" he teases and continues to laugh heartily. "I'm sure they really miss that 'Social Psychology' book!" My body relaxes, and I meet his gaze with my best attempt at a cool and nonchalant smile. He takes another drag off of his joint. "I would offer you some but you don't seem like the type," he says as he inhales more of the smoke into his lungs.

"Actually, I would love some," I say confidently as I reach for it. He hands it to me with a bemused expression and looks even more surprised as I take a long drag and blow the smoke in his face.

"You were on the way to the library earlier, weren't you?" he asks.

"I was," I reply and avoid his eyes, "sorry I interrupted."

"Not your fault. I should have closed the door," he dismisses me. Before I can stop myself, it just comes out.

"Is she your girlfriend?" I ask and immediately feel foolish.

"No," he says firmly. "Notice how I just sent her home? She's fun to look at but not much in here." He lightly taps his fingertips against my head. "She's not interesting." He shrugs and stares contemplatively into the pool. "She was boring the shit out of me, actually."

"Chase?" I say, eager to change the subject. "Did you turn on this music?"

"Yeah. I thought you would like to have music on while you studied," he replies, still focused on the water. My eyelashes flutter under my sunglasses.

"Thank you, I really like these songs... who is the artist?" I say, trying to hide the fact that I want to squeal over him paying attention to me.

"Chris Stapleton. The first song was 'Traveller' and this one is called 'Tennessee Whiskey.' He's good, isn't he?" Chase asks.

"Yes, very..." I whisper.

I am finally feeling the calming effects of the THC. I close my eyes and sway my head to the music. My body comes to life when I feel a tap from Chase's foot on my leg. I inhale sharply and my stomach fills with butterflies. Is Chase Swanson playing footsie with me? He answers my silent question by slowly sliding his foot along my calf. I again fight the urge to squeal and instead, rest my toes on the back of his ankle for a moment and then slowly trace my foot along his perfectly sculpted calf. He wraps his leg around mine and they gently intertwine in the water. It's as if I am being slowly struck by lightning. Our bodies fit together perfectly, like a puzzle. I open my eyes and am met with a seductive smile. More lightning strikes go through me as he leans in and places his full lips to my ear. The pleasure of his mouth on my skin is intoxicating. The music has now been replaced with his breath. He lingers on my ear for a beat. His electric touch is setting my body on fire. My breath is quickening, my heart rate is climbing; I can't think straight.

"We should probably get that rogue book back," he whispers as he runs his careless fingers along the book and then on my hand that is holding it.

"Yeah..." I reply softly and then wonder if I actually said it. He tosses his joint into the pool, stands up and extends his hand. Enchanted, I take it and let him help me up. My legs feel wobbly as I walk in front of him towards the house. When we get into the foyer, he places his hand on the small of my back as if I belong to him.

"I love the library," I say, to fill the silence between us.

"I can tell," he responds and gives me a knowing grin. "You're a hot little nerd, you know that?" He tugs on my ponytail flirtatiously, and I think I might die of happiness. Chase Swanson thinks I'm hot?? I follow him up the majestic staircase that twists at the top. "Oh and Liv, I'm a Beatles fan myself, but I don't know if the tigers are," he says playfully. I am so glad that he's in front of me on the staircase and can't see my crimson, blushing face.

"Wait! What? You were watching me this morning?" I ask, stunned. "Why didn't you say anything?"

"Because I liked watching you," he smirks coolly. He pushes open the doors to the beautifully posh library that always makes me feel like I've been transported to old world London or Paris. "By the way, the tiger's names are Dixie and Roxy. I named them when I was a kid because we never had any pets growing up." He puts his hand on one of their heads.

"Hi Dixie! Hi Roxy!" I say jokingly to the tigers and pet the one opposite him. I take in his response to my silly gesture and realize he is smiling at me... I've seen him smile before, but this one is different, he is *genuinely* smiling. It is probably one of the most authentic, magnetic smiles I have ever seen. A little devilish yet friendly. I didn't know that a grin could convey a thousand promises and a thousand lies. I can't help but think about all the women that have gone weak in the knees over the boyish twinkle in his blue-green eyes. Oh no. I shift nervously on my feet and bat my eyelashes to try and hide the fact that I am becoming increasingly spellbound. Another victim of Chase Swanson's magic. He looks amused at the effect he is having on me. He knows damn well that he's charming. I wonder if he just likes to play the game like his sister. How could he possibly be interested in me? There's no way I'm anything more than a tool to stroke his ego in this moment.

"So, Liv," I flinch at the assertive way he says my name. "I know that you are drawn to the classics and the first edition section of the library," he says casually. My mouth goes dry.

"How did you..." I start to ask.

"There are cameras everywhere," he says, waving to one of them, "they record everything you do in here." My head drops and I feel an instant surge of shame.

"I wasn't trying to steal any of them..."

"I know," he says, pointing to my favorite couch with the light blue cashmere blanket. "That's your spot, isn't it?" My eyes widen. I have never felt so violated. He leans into me and I shrink a little, afraid that I'm in trouble. "I know a place with no cameras that we can go sometime," he whispers, his lips almost touching my skin. The way his breath feels against my neck, and his inflection when he says, "I know a place," sends a shiver down my spine. "Come with me," he says, and I happily obey. We walk without speaking over to the first editions section. Chase begins to root through the books on the shelf with a careless abandon. The first edition of *Alice's Adventure in Wonderland* hits the floor. He doesn't seem to notice or care that a $20,000 book just fell off the shelf.

"I've been meaning to ask you," he says, glancing at me with a twinkle in his eyes. "Where is that *adorable* Midwest accent from?"

"Oh God, you noticed that?" He laughs and turns his attention back to the books.

"Liv, it's cute! I like it!" he declares, still laughing.

"Omg, stop! I'm from a small town in Illinois. Kaneville. You've probably never even heard of it." I look away shyly.

"Nope, never been there. We have a penthouse in Chicago though," he explains. He continues sifting through the books. They are steadily falling to the floor. I cringe as at least $100,000 of first editions piles up at his feet.

"I love Chicago..." I say reflectively as I pick up the original *Harry Potter* and put it back on the shelf, "I miss it." I sigh. "I miss my dad." I wish I would stop opening up to this man I barely know. He pauses from throwing priceless literary works everywhere, and looks me in the eyes.

"If you want to see your dad this summer, I can set that up for you. I haven't been to Chicago in a while, and I'm definitely due for a trip. We could share the Gulfstream out there. No point in making it go on two separate trips," he says. My body comes to life at his suggestion that we share a private jet to Chicago.

"I would love that, Chase," I say and bend down to pick up another book from the floor.

"Ah, found it!" He strides effortlessly in front of me like the dark angel that he is. "Close your eyes," he instructs while holding the book to his chest to hide it from me. I look at him skeptically. "Trust me," he says. Something in his expression forces me to surrender and I obediently shut my eyes. He places the book in my hands. "Don't open your eyes yet. I have to tell you a story first."

"Okay," I whisper, hypnotized.

"My mom made a special trip to Chicago to purchase this book. I went with her. I was little at the time, ten maybe. We had a great day. She didn't send me away with a nanny that day... she took me to Navy Pier, bought me a Bull's jersey and then we went to the museum," he says in a soft tone. "She even rode the Ferris Wheel with me." I take in the timbre in Chase's voice, knowing that it will echo in my mind later. "My old man, Michelle and Blaire were in London, and my mom and I had to meet them there. When we boarded our jet, I got in trouble with the pilots for pressing buttons. I loved the cockpit, I couldn't help myself. My dad would have freaked, but my mom didn't care. She let me cuddle with her on the couch up front. I usually had to sit with a nanny in the back of the plane. She read me this book the entire flight and played with my hair, something she rarely ever did... she wasn't really the touchy feely type. She wasn't the warm person you know now..." he says and I can pick up on a little bit of pain in his voice as he talks about his mom. "I remembering loving the story but not really understanding it. My mom said I would when I was older, and she was right, I get it now. Anyways, I want you to have it... open your eyes."

I blink a few times to get my eyes to adjust to the light. It takes me a moment to process what I'm seeing. I gasp. The first edition of *Great Expectations* by Charles Dickens from 1863 is staring back at me.

"Chase..." I whisper. "This is the original... it probably costs a fortune, plus it has significant meaning to you! I can't accept this!" I'm beyond flattered but also completely stupefied as I try and hand it back to him.

"Liv, it's not a big deal. I would love for you to have it," he responds sincerely, "please, take it." He pushes it lightly into my chest.

"But..." I start to object again. He places a finger assertively on my lips.

"Shhh. This isn't up for discussion," he says. I look down at the book warily.

"Chase... I don't think I can...." I stammer.

"Are you always this bad at accepting gifts?" he asks teasingly. "Just take the fucking thing!" He winks and gives me a million-watt smile. I beam back at him. My smile is as bright as when Pip is told he's going to move to London to become a gentleman, or when he sees the beautiful Estella for the first time. I squeal in delight.

"Thank you so much! I love this book! It's one of my favorites!" He gives the camera a thumbs up.

"She loves it! Thanks for the tip my man!" he praises the mystery man behind the camera. This delights me even more. Maybe being spied on isn't so bad after all. I practically jump on him when I hug him.

"Seriously, thank you!" I say in his ear and squeeze him tightly. He returns my warm embrace.

"No big deal." His deep voice vibrates through me. After a moment, the mood of the embrace turns into something different. The platonic playfulness is fading like my inhibitions, as I smell his neck and feel his body pressing against mine. He smells so good I can almost taste him. I am utterly breathless as he lightly strokes my back with his hands. He runs his fingertips slowly up my body, pausing with his hands on the sides of my boobs. Before I can stop myself, my lips are on his. He laces his fingertips into my hair and pulls me into him. When I open my eyes, I'm looking directly into his. His irises are the most exotic, mesmerizing shade of ocean blue. I've never seen anything so enchanting. I bat my lashes and try and catch my breath. But suddenly, it feels so wrong, so very wrong. I push him away.

"We can't," I whisper. "We really can't," I say more assertively. "It will never work! You are my best friend's brother!"

137

"So," he says coldly, "she's not your warden." I push myself away from him.

"Chase. You were just with Sierra," I say with frost on my voice. "You're a womanizer." He scowls, and I back away from him even further. "Thank you again for the book," I say standoffishly to eyes that have somehow transformed from blue to a glowing green. I feel like crying for some reason as I make my way out of the library and down the staircase.

Creep

I have been purposely avoiding Chase for a week now. It is getting more difficult by the day to fight off my ever increasing feelings for him. I was unprepared for the butterflies that begin to collide inside of me when I think about him. My longing desire to explore the undeniable sparks between us; it makes me physically ache. I have never felt this way about anyone. I remember that scene in the movie *Sixteen Candles* where the main character is talking to her dad about the guy she likes; ironically, the rich, popular, good looking guy who drives a Porsche. Her dad explains why they call them crushes, and how they would call them something else if they were easy. I finally understand what that line means. I literally feel crushed when I think about him and his smile. Specifically the smile he gave me in the library, the magnetic, authentic one that I know was meant just for me.

On the nights when I sleep in Michelle's room, I curl up in a ball of sadness, tormented by the fact that he is so close yet so far. I wonder if he is thinking about me as well. Two near strangers with an undeniable attraction for one another, separated by concrete walls. The other night, I heard footsteps and a woman's voice in the hallway. I must have a masochistic side because I peeked my head out of Michelle's bedroom door, only to find Chase

139

playing cat and mouse with a scantily clad blonde in a tight black dress. They walked past me hand in hand, and my heart shattered when his ordinarily intoxicating eyes stared impassively through me. I sat on the couch in Michelle's room that night, angry and awake, hating the walls. Not the concrete ones; I was glad they were there so I wouldn't have to see him with another woman. Rather, I hated the metaphorical walls. The walls of social class, the walls that people like him put up as barrier against love.

I thought about *Great Expectations*. I have been fixated on it lately. Why did he give it to me? Was it to warn me to stay away from him because, like Estella, he is incapable of love? If he is Estella, does that make me Pip? A simpleton climbing the social ladder on the way to becoming one of them? One of the lucky ones? More likely, he gave it to me because he gives lavish and thoughtful gifts to all of his conquests. He wants to corrupt me and use me for his own twisted pleasures. Maybe nosy Kelly was right, he is bad news.

I toss and turn, these thoughts swirling unchecked in my mind. I finally fall asleep, only to wake - it feels like minutes later - to the sound of Michelle rummaging loudly through her dresser drawers. Then I remember; she has a music video shoot this morning in Laguna and I have to do the pool party preparations on my own. We are throwing an extravagant, over-the-top pool soiree, catering to the young, rich and famous this afternoon at her Bel Air home.

"Hey, you're awake! I'm going to be on set until around noon and then I'll be back. I can trust you with the preparations for the party, right?" she asks, in a volume slightly below train horn.

"Yeah..." I mumble, pulling the blankets over my head.

"OK BYEEE!" she yells from the door before she slams it. I flip over and immediately fall back asleep. I dream of him. We are in the pool on an inflatable golden swan, laughing and kissing. He is stroking my hair and holding my hand. I wake to the sound of my alarm a few hours later.

"No!" I groan and slap at everything on the nightstand in an effort to stop the incessant beeping. I desperately want to go back to Chase dreamland. I eventually succeed and summon the will power to get out of bed. I make myself a latte with the Nespresso in Michelle's kitchenette and pull out my sparkly blue Beach Bunny bikini.

As I'm putting the bottoms on, his comment keeps repeating in my mind, 'I look forward to seeing you in your bikini.' I sigh and think about the way he jokes around with me. Could someone that adorable, hilarious, and charming really be bad news? I miss our banter. I miss his smile. I miss his eyes. I miss... him. I hope he comes to the party today, but even if he doesn't, at least Kevin will be there. I'm excited about seeing a familiar face. I desperately need some sort of grounding in reality to pull me out of my funk.

Michelle leaving me in charge of the party preparations basically means that it's my job to boss around the staff, which isn't something I'm comfortable with, much less good at. I stand awkwardly near a group of employees. They are blowing up a flock of giant inflatable gold swans for the party guests to lounge on in the pool. I feel like I should be doing something too, so I pick one up and start blowing. As I do, I unintentionally make eye contact with a man sitting across from me who is red in the face from inflating them all morning. His eyes widen in horror.

"No, Miss!" he says anxiously, "you could get hurt!" He hurries over to pull the swan away from me.

"Oh.. um ... I'm sorry," I stammer, "I was just trying to help!" He shakes his head disapprovingly. I can feel my cheeks starting to flush, so I adjust my beach wrap and walk away from the pool and from the awkward situation. I step into the house and my body instantly connects with cool air. I have been baking in the intense California sun all morning, and the air conditioning feels delectable against my hot skin. My wedges make click clack sounds on the black and white checkered floor as I walk past the smoking room, cringing at the memory of Chase and Sierra as I pass. A faint tingle from somewhere in the back of my mind slows my pace. Something is off... I spin around and rush back to the doorway.

"Where is the mural?" I whisper in shock to the empty room. The onyx chessboard is in complete disarray. Everything in this house is always immaculate; the maids would never allow an

142

expensive board game to become disheveled like that. I pick one of the pieces up and gasp when I see that the wall with Chase's mural is facing in the complete opposite direction, as though the wall has been rotated. Michelle once told me that her house is full of secret passageways and hidden rooms, but she's never actually shown me any of them, so I assumed they only existed in her imagination.

I'm looking down a hallway straight out of a fairytale, or maybe *The Wizard of Oz.* It is narrow and lined with brick. There is a pathway of yellow stone on the floor, and some kind of door at the far end of it. Curiosity gets the best of me and I step inside. I begin walking softly and cautiously, my arms brushing lightly against the ivy that is clinging to the brick. I reach a heavy copper door and slowly push it open, and then I hear the music. Very precise notes are being picked on an acoustic guitar, and I can almost feel the guitarist's fingers sliding expertly along the neck. I push the door open fully and it hits me... I'm standing in the entrance to the Swanson's secret music lounge. A singer's voice suddenly pierces the room, and I feel goose bumps from head to toe. The timbre and gravel in the voice... Chase. It has to be him, so I step inside. There is a swanky lounge and a dance floor with a crystal chandelier above it. Both are completely empty. Everything is dark except for the lights above the stage which are shining down on Chase.

I tiptoe inside and take a seat in the very back on a red leather couch to watch the sexiest man living perform his rendition of "Creep" by Radiohead. There are thick red velvet curtains on either side of him, and he is sitting on a chair with a black acoustic guitar in his lap. His singing voice is incredible; deep and smoky, with just the right amount of grit. I had no idea he was so musically endowed. As he transitions seamlessly into the chorus, tears well up in my eyes. I'm watching him pour his heart into a performance meant for no one at all. He is so vulnerable and passionate right now, and I can't help but wonder if he is thinking about me as he sings this song. The lyrics are decidedly self-loathing and describe feeling unworthy of receiving love from a special someone. His face darkens and his angst is almost palpable when he sings about the girl leaving him. When he finally notices that he has an audience of one, he stops abruptly. The silence is deafening. I am met with glowing green eyes and a burning gaze. I nervously bite my lip as I take in his intense stare.

"What do you want?" he asks coldly through the microphone. His tone strikes me like an arrow through the heart.

"Um, I just heard you playing and it was... you have an amazing voice," I stumble over my words as I walk closer to the stage. He places the guitar back on the stand.

"Thanks," he snaps.

"I love that song..." I say, desperate to soften his callous mood. He is still ignoring me but I proceed anyways. "I have

144

something to play for you. Do you mind?" I ask warily. A long moment passes but he doesn't reply, so I press on.

"I can't play any instruments and I can barely sing, but I have a song that I want to play you, from my phone," I say as I try to control my red, burning face. I anxiously look around for the iPod dock that is in every room of the mansion, but I can't find it. Just as my courage begins to abandon me, he tosses me a cord to plug into my phone. It might as well be a lifeline.

"No iPod dock in here, princess," he says coolly. My heart is stumbling over every beat as I fumble with the cord. I find the song, press play, and anxiously await his response. He is staring dispassionately into space as he sits down on a Steinway & Sons white piano bench on the stage. He closes his eyes and listens intently, as if really dissecting it.

"The girl rendition of 'Creep,'" I explain.

"Karen Souza?" he asks. I nod. I cautiously take a seat next to him on the piano bench.

"I love these lyrics," I say, as I stare deeply and inquisitively into his angry emerald eyes. "I think that everyone feels like this at one point or another."

"Not you, you're perfect," he says, disdain dripping from his voice.

"Actually, I've felt this way before..." I admit in a whisper. The distrust in his glare softens and begins to fade into a reluctant compassion. He opens the lid of the piano, and I notice it has been signed by John Lennon. 'Dreamer' is also etched on the inside of the lid. "This piano is incredible!" I stammer, filling with admiration. I think about the "Imagine" music video with John Lennon and Yoko Ono, when they sit at the white piano bench together. It is a beautifully simple yet powerful music video. It didn't need anything fancy, the message of the song in and of itself was enough.

"'Imagine' is my favorite song," I say, more confidently now, as I trace my fingers along the engraving.

"Mine too," he says. He stares at the piano intently. "Some people... their light shines too bright. They leave the world too soon... you know?" He glances at me and I nod, trying to fight away tears as I think about my mom. "But, they leave starlight behind. John Lennon was one of those. He left the world with some powerful music. 'Imagine' was a work of art. I think the dude might have been a prophet," he says as he effortlessly plays the chords to "Imagine" on the piano over the song that is still playing. Of course he can play multiple instruments. What can't he do? "Imagine" on the piano paired with the jazzy version of "Creep" sounds like a mashup that a quirky club DJ might create, mixing two contradictory messages that somehow fit together perfectly, like two lost pieces of the same puzzle.

Moonlight Dreamer

I stand up and glide over to my phone. I hit play and our favorite song by John Lennon fills this enchanted room. He watches me curiously as I dance back to him.

"Liv..." he says, as I'm standing under the stage lights.

"Yes, Chase," I say quietly. He closes his eyes, furrows his brow and rubs the stubble on his chiseled jaw.

"You're amazing," he finally declares. The long pause broken at last, and he is filled with passion and earnest admiration towards me. I feel weak in the knees over his words as I land softly next to him on the piano bench. My body is filling with starlight. I hope he doesn't notice the goose bumps on my skin as he takes me in. We stare into each others eyes for a moment. His eyes are as blue as the summer sky and I wonder how many stars come out at night behind them. I can't help myself... I gently stroke his cheek and let his stubble wind its way across my hand. He closes his eyes as pleasure spreads slowly over his beautiful face.

"Dance with me, babe," he says, as he grabs my hand and pulls me up off the piano bench. He leads me to the dance floor, and with the magical chandelier above us, we dance to *our* favorite song. The light from the chandelier creates a sparkling moonlight meant only for us. Time stands still. I take in his smell. I

147

take in the way his hand feels as it encircles mine. I nuzzle my face into his neck. His body is intoxicating and I'm definitely drunk on it. It's a rare but refined cocktail that has me transfixed: one part desperate ache and two parts giddy excitement. I look up at him, and he gently brushes a strand of hair off my face.

"Thanks," I whisper. I run my hand along his back and he pulls me closer. We dance with our bodies pressed tightly together like this for almost the whole song. He sings the last lyrics softly into my ear and the goose bumps again cover my aching body from head to toe. When the song is over, he lightly presses his lips against my forehead.

"What the fuck are you doing?" I jump when I hear Michelle's jarring voice. She slithers through the door, and strides towards us, an uncomfortable malice growing with each and every step. I quickly pull away from her brother.

"Just dancing..." I say and shrug my shoulders while staring at the ground. She places her hands on her hips and stands as imposingly as possible in front of Chase. He is still much taller than her, even with her sky high heels.

"Chase, isn't Liv pretty?" she asks him. The tone in her voice is dry ice cold. I can practically see the steam coming from her curled lips, which are full of icy contempt. "You should love her, love her, love her, love her," she says over and over again, menacingly, like she's reciting a witch's spell. My blood runs cold. It's a line from *Great Expectations*. Does Michelle know about the library? About the gift? She stares at him as if she is going to turn him to stone with her gaze. "Do you even know what love means, Chase?" Michelle asks her brother cruelly. He ignores her. "That's what I thought," she taunts.

"Oh and Liv," she says. I flinch when she turns her angered attention towards me. "The party fucking started already, and you were nowhere to be found! Get your shit together! When I ask you to help me plan a party, I expect you to actually do it, not just fuck around and flirt with my brother!" She glares at me for a moment and then storms out of the room. My mouth is dry before the copper door even slams, and my heart is pounding out of my chest. Chase on the other hand, appears unmoved by his sister's words and tantrum. I turn my attention to him.

"Did you tell Michelle about the gift you gave me?" I ask him and cross my arms. "About the book..."

"No," he snaps. He turns his back to me and pulls a joint and a lighter out of his pocket.

"Oh, then how did she..." My brow knits in confusion.

"Liv, don't worry about it," he interrupts me, "just go have fun at the party." He lights the joint and walks up the steps to the stage.

"Okay," I say softly, and my heart shatters over his sudden change in mood. "Chase?" I ask. He flips around.

"What?" he responds impatiently, and my heart now hurts with a physical pain.

"Are you coming?" I ask quietly. "I mean, to the party."

"No Liv, I'm not," he responds in a casually cruel manner.

"Why not?"

"It's a party for kids." He picks up a guitar from the stand. The joint is hanging loosely in his mouth as he starts strumming chords. I can tell I've lost him again. That temporary glimpse of vulnerability I witnessed is gone. I hastily unplug my phone and make my escape. Chase doesn't even say goodbye to me when I get to the door. My wedges click clack quickly against the yellow brick hallway that doesn't feel as magical this time around.

"Why do you have to be such a jerk?" I ask his James Dean-esque mural like a fool. I glare at it, and the face that I may have accidentally fallen in love with, stares back at me, unfazed. "I like you way more than I should..." I whisper, and then sulk away. I grab my Bel Air sunglasses from the kitchen, put on a fresh layer of lip gloss, open the sliding glass doors, and step into the warm, welcoming lap of luxury.

The transformation that has taken place while I was inside is startling. The glitzy pool party is in full swing; I feel like I teleported from Bel Air to Las Vegas. The workers basically turned Michelle's backyard into the Rehab Beach Club at the Hard Rock. She really went all out with the party planning! Three stunning bikini clad girls in oversized sunglasses are dancing as suggestively as possible next to the DJ. He is spinning a remix of "West Coast" by Lana Del Rey, while occasionally throwing in beats from Dr. Dre's

2001 album. Michelle is lounging in a large white cabana with a group of friends. She looks every bit the svelte, spoiled model in her sparkly gold bikini and 24k Tom Ford sunglasses. Vixen attitude is in full force as she purses her heavily glossed lips for a photo with the son of a famous actor. A stunning brunette in a barely there black two piece shakes her perfect bubble butt in front of Michelle. She giggles and spanks the girl's ass. At least her sour mood has disappeared. I breathe a deep sigh of relief. The palm trees that surround the patio are swaying lightly in the breeze, flirting with the infinity pool beneath them which is filled with golden inflatable plastic swans. Gorgeous Hollywood royals with flawless beach bodies are lounging on them, sipping drinks and admiring one another.

I can hear Emma Watson's elegant British accent distinguish itself from the general din as she greets Michelle and graciously thanks her for the invite. Maybe I will work up enough courage to tell her about the first edition of *Harry Potter* that I saw in the Swanson's library. She walks past me and smiles kindly. I try and open my mouth but only a squeak comes out; I am far too star struck by her to speak. Kill me now, that was so embarrassing. I turn my blushing face towards the diving board and water slides. A guy with washboard abs is jumping off the high dive with flawless precision. When his head emerges from the water, I recognize him and wave. He waves back with a charming grin. We had a class together last semester. Now that I think about it, it was probably Cordell that brought over the Dom Pérignon champagne.

"Hey Cordell!" I say to the fellow Bruin. "Did you come over the other day with your dad?" I ask.

"Yeah! How'd you know?" he asks. I shrug. "You missed a funny moment... Michelle's mom kept trying to rap 'Gin and Juice' while drinking her martini and got it wrong every single time and then argued with my dad about the lyrics." I giggle and face palm.

"Arguing with Snoop Dogg about his own song, sounds about right! She's lucky she's so gorgeous, she can get away with her antics!"

"Haha for sure, good to see you, Liv!" he says as he athletically boards a swan.

"You too, Cordell! Don't be a stranger this summer!" I blow him a kiss and then smile brightly when I see Kevin being escorted in by a security guard.

"He belongs here, I promise!" I say to the guard and giggle. "Kevin!" I squeal as we embrace. He looks genuinely excited to see me and it's nice to feel wanted for once.

"Liv!" He gives me a big kiss on the cheek.

"Well, shall we go catch up on a swan?" I ask. "Definitely big enough for the both of us!"

"When in Rome!" he says, sounding like a total nerd. We jump in the pool like little kids. I grab an empty swan and hold it for Kevin so he can get on first but he can't manage. He tries to hold it for me. I also flail and slip back into the water. It's a disaster and it makes us both belly laugh.

"Did they not teach you guys to swim in the Midwest?" Michelle asks haughtily as she floats past us. She looks like a princess in her sparkling gold bikini that matches her golden plastic swan. The Princess of Bel Air herself, Michelle Swanson, upon her floating throne.

La La Land

Kevin and I finally get our swan to cooperate. We are sitting across from each other, sipping champagne and catching up. Michelle and the pretty girl in the black bikini from the cabana are also sharing a swan and have started making out. A stud with black hair and chiseled features slides onto their swan and now it's a three-way makeout. I recognize him - he's an Italian model from Milan. The three of them climb out of the pool and into the hot tub next to it. Black bikini girl is removing Michelle's top while kissing and grinding on hot male model guy. Now they are stumbling hand in hand towards the pool house. Kevin looks uncomfortable. I know he feels out of his element around these people; it took a lot of convincing to even get him here.

"Liv, I'm so sorry, but I forgot that I was supposed to feed my friend's dog today," he says. I can tell he's lying. "My friend Beck... he's umm... out of town, he has a dog named Ranger, he's a... golden retriever." I sigh heavily. With both him and Michelle missing in action, I don't know who I'm going to talk to. Kevin hugs me goodbye on the swan, because he knows that if I get off of it, I will never be able to get back on.

"Be good!" he yells over the music and chatter, from the edge of the pool.

"Bye, Kev!" I shout back, blowing him a kiss. A security guard escorts him out of the party. Kendall Jenner is valeting her Ferrari in the courtyard and Kevin walks right past her at the fountain without so much as a glance. My nerdy friend had no idea he was just in the presence of Hollywood royalty. I giggle at his lack of coolness and down the rest of my champagne.

"Excuse me, sir, may I please have another?" I ask the bartender at the pool bar. I'm going to need it to fake my way through all the vapid conversations that are about to take place. My cheeks always hurt after these parties from the perma-smile on my face. I always hope I will charm one of the A or B list-r's and get them to actually speak to me, but it never happens. And it's certainly not going to happen today, as all of the super elites are in their own cabanas surrounded by security guards. It is just me and the C to Z list-r's left in the pool. The Kardashian/Jenner crew and the Hadid sisters cabana has like ten security guys in front of it. They have their personal body guards with them plus two of the Swanson's. If I'm lucky enough to get past the guards at any of these cabanas today, I still have their entourage to deal with.

When Michelle is with me, I'm allowed into the heavily guarded VIP tents , but I don't ever speak with the royalty. I always end up ensnared in small talk with some rich kid from a celebrity's entourage. The conversation is always painfully predictable.

"So where are you from?"

155

"Illinois," I reply, only because I wouldn't dare name the small town I'm actually from.

"Oh, Chicago!" As if that's the only acceptable mark on the map in a ghastly flyover state like Illinois.

I'll then be informed that their parents have a place in Chicago. "My parents have a penthouse in Chicago!" they'll declare airily. Occasionally, one of the more cocaine fueled male celebrities will briefly engage me.

"You're Michelle Swanson's friend, right?" they'll ask, and then immediately glaze over and move on to someone more interesting.

I wish I could say something amazing like, 'Oh hi, I'm Liv, Steven Tyler's daughter!' In reality, my dad, who is the farthest thing from a rock star, would be horrified if he knew I let everyone here change my name from Olivia to Liv.

Speaking of the daughter of a rock star, nosy Kelly Rose is eagerly paddling her swan towards me. I know she doesn't want to actually have a conversation with me, she just wants to talk about Chase. As her swan bumps into mine, she tosses back an impressive amount of bubbly from her plastic champagne flute, spilling it all over her black one-piece in the process.

"I was hoping Chase was going to be here," she says, pouting. Per usual, she has abandoned all standard conversation starters. There is no, 'Hi Liv, how are you?' She doesn't care about being polite or about how I'm doing; I'm simply a vessel for the information that she wants right now.

"Hello, Kelly. How are you?" I blurt out sarcastically, hoping she will understand basic pleasantries someday. She ignores my unsubtle hint.

"So, do you talk to him, or is he still like, all aloof and distant?"

"I talk to him, sometimes...." I concede.

"Girl, come on, you can't hold out on me! I want to know everything!" she pleads. A rail thin topless girl floats up to us on her swan.

"Kelly, did you try a pink pill from the pharm bowl in Michelle's room? I am seriously like on another fucking planet. It's so lit bro! Michelle's parties are the illest!!" Shockingly, she notices that she has interrupted a conversation and actually acknowledges me. "You're pretty! What's your name?" she asks as she floats a little closer to me.

"I'm Liv. Nice to meet you," I respond shyly. She is almost on my swan as she strokes my hair.

"You are so pretty!" she says. I laugh nervously at her complete lack of personal space.

"Thank you. So are you!" I return the compliment. She purrs like a kitten and places her hand gently against my cheek.

"I'm Kara. I like you Liz!" she slurs, "there's some shit going down in the pool house in like twenty. I want to see you there!"

157

She takes a sip of champagne, loses her balance and falls off her swan into the water. When her head emerges, she yells, "I'm OK! In case anyone was worried!" She looks down at her topless self in horror as if noticing for the first time. "Oh my God! What happened to my fucking swimsuit top? Someone stole my swimsuit top! It's Dolce and super rare!" she shouts as she makes her way to the edge of the pool to find the imaginary perpetrator. Kelly laughs snootily.

"And that's the daughter of a famous golfer! You can't buy class!" she says with an arrogant smirk. "Welcome to La La Land!" She holds her flute towards me to clink for a cheers. I press mine into hers and fake a laugh, even though I don't think her mean girl comment was funny. I really just think that Kelly Rose is awful.

From the outside, you would think I was having a blast, laughing, drinking and socializing at this fabulous party amongst Hollywood elites. A mere mortal, lucky enough to be invited into their world. I know I should feel fortunate, but I can't shake this sense of apathy. My smile is as fake as the plastic swan I am sitting on. I desperately crave someone with substance.

As I look around at all of these beautiful plastic people floating on their plastic pool toys, all I can think about is how much I wish Chase was here. I want him on this swan with me. I want to nuzzle into his neck. I want his strong arms wrapped around me. I want to find comfort in him. The DJ is spinning a sultry remix of Britney Spear's "Make Me..." featuring G-Eazy. I

158

can't focus on what Kelly is saying. It's like Britney is talking over her and coaxing me to go explore what I might have with Chase. The hook of the song sounds like the resolution to a long term problem; it echoes the bliss of finally giving in to longing and desire. I realize that my craving for Chase isn't going to go away on its own.

"Kelly, I better go try one of those pink pills!" I make up the lie on the spot and start to paddle away.

"Lates," she grumbles, clearly dissatisfied that I won't divulge the information she wants. I don't care about her right now. I just care about finding Chase. I close my eyes a moment and feel the music. It's so romantic and melodious. I bob my head and sing along. When I open my eyes, I see him. A shirtless Chase Swanson opening the sliding glass doors. He looks like a Greek god with the sun shining on his face and muscular chest. His black Persol sunglasses and swagger make him look like a movie star or a rock star. His naturally athletic build makes him look like a professional athlete. He could be mistaken for any of them. James Dean's cool, Tom Brady's body, and Johnny Cash's attitude. I can see Kelly's lustful eyes on him. I fumble with my swan and almost fall into the water when I realize that everyone is staring at me,... because Chase Swanson only notices me. He is walking only towards... *me*. I can feel the mood of his admirers shifting from hopeful anticipation to dismay and jealousy, but I don't care. I see only him. He is standing over me now like a dark angel that has been cast out of heaven.

Aquamarine

"Do you need some help?" he asks, but before I can answer, he already has his arms laced beneath me and is lifting me up off the swan.

"Thanks," I say sheepishly as his strong arms set me down softly on the concrete. I grin up at him through my lashes. The chemistry between us is palpable. The invisible sparks of curiosity and lust that are striking between us have silenced everyone in the pool. He chivalrously hands me a towel and the animosity from Kelly, and his other female (and a few male) fans, permeates the air. I can hear their annoyed murmurs, but they sound a thousand miles away. I shyly wrap myself in the towel. He takes me by the hand and leads me to an empty cabana. I can practically hear Kelly curse from the pool when we sit down, intimately close, on a chaise lounge together.

"Good afternoon, Mr. Swanson," a security guard says to him as he stands at attention in front of our cabana. "Here is your beach bag, Miss Walker." The guard hands me the bag that I had forgotten all about.

"Thank you, sir," I say as I take it. I turn to Chase and grin flirtatiously.

"I thought you weren't coming to this 'kid's' party," I say, using finger quotes when I say the word *kids*. He shrugs.

"I was bored."

"Oh..." I say, trying to hide my disappointment. He puts a finger under my chin to lift my face which unbeknownst to me has fallen. His billion-dollar smile is back in my line of sight. The boyish twinkle and charm have returned, and the moody, despondent Chase from the music lounge is nowhere to be found.

"Plus, you looked like you could use some help getting off that swan," he teases.

"Oh! Well, thanks for coming to my rescue!" I say, and turn crimson at the sound of my own voice. My friendly Midwestern accent sounds so nerdy and out of place here. I've been trying to cover it up, but when I drink, it just comes out. He raises an eyebrow at me.

"Oh! Uff da! Betcha did!" he says in a fake Midwest accent.

"Stop!" I say and shove him playfully.

"What? It's cute!" He chuckles and grabs my thigh.

"Oh, don't patronize me!" I say. "I've been trying to work on it. I've been watching 'The Californians' skit. You know that one? How does this sound?" I jokingly quote the Saturday Night Live skit with conviction; hearing my voice sound like a valley girl's cracks us both up.

Without missing a beat, Chase responds in his own exaggerated California accent, and tells me that he knows, "the

162

best way to get to Mulholland." I continue to giggle as I put my beach wrap on. When my head emerges from the fabric, I see that his smile has faded and he is staring contemplatively into the distance. My stomach sinks. Oh no... I've lost him again. After a pause, he looks at me and grins, and my body relaxes.

"Actually, I do know a short cut to Mulholland and it is a great day for a drive. There is a Porsche in the fleet that's calling my name. It's similar to the one I race in Europe. You want to get out of here?" he asks, giving me a look that conveys that this is not a request for me to go with him, its simply something that is going to happen. A Porsche, Chase Swanson, and I, together on Mulholland Drive? I wonder if I should pinch myself. Is this real life, or did I take a pill from the pharm bowl?

"Can I drive?" I ask, already knowing the answer is no. He laughs at my silly request.

"No." he states firmly.

"But why?" I ask flirtatiously.

"Well, for one, you're a little drunk, and two, I actually like my transmission," he says as he grabs my hand. "But, you can help me shift." He gives my hand a suggestive squeeze. I think about his hand on top of mine shifting his sports car and my stomach flutters.

"Fine," I say and drop my head again, but this time as a joke. I didn't know he was a race car driver. In fact, I don't really know a whole lot about this mysterious man.

163

"Race car driver..." I whisper to myself, relishing the moment. My eyelashes flutter as I realize I was just thinking out loud. Luckily, he doesn't appear to notice. He doesn't let go of my hand as he leads me assertively into the house. I walk behind him, feeling vindicated and full of pride. Sorry beautiful plastic people, the Prince of Bel Air picked me.

As we enter the empty foyer, he lets go of my hand and turns to face me. He takes off his sunglasses and looks into my eyes as if taking me in for the first time. The intensity in his gaze as he appraises my body is exhilarating. I shiver, and I can't tell if it's from the air conditioning penetrating my pool soaked clothing, or if it's from the way he is looking at me.

"We should probably get you out of those wet clothes," he finally says. My bikini is leaving a wet outline in my aquamarine colored dress. I meet his gaze and notice that his eyes are the exact same color as my dress, not quite blue, not quite green. His eyes are enchanting as they trace the wet curves of my body. "I don't want a wet seat in my Porsche..." he says. "Then again, maybe I do," he adds with a wicked smile. I've never felt butterflies this intensely before. My body feels as if it is made of warm putty as his magnetic eyes and assertive body language transfix me. I am being coaxed and bewitched and I'm under his spell.

"Sure, I can change. I will just borrow something of Michelle's," I respond and he simply nods. We walk in silence

164

towards the elevator. No more words are necessary. The silence is filled with sexual tension and anticipation. We both know what is going to happen as soon as we are alone together; all logic and inhibition will be lost. The inevitable succumbing to the chemistry, to the gravity that has been pulling us together will be too much. It will all end very badly for me, I know this, but I have never been more captivated by anyone. It is an irresistible desire that is deeper than pure animalistic lust and I have no choice; I must explore it further. The elevator dings to announce its arrival. I am temporarily free of his spell until the door closes and we are alone. The chemistry and sexual tension are dangerously intoxicating in this enclosed space. I shiver again.

"You cold?" he asks.

"Yeah, kind of," I reply, trying to avert his gaze. I know that if I stare back into those hypnotic eyes, I'll end up in his bedroom. I just can't go there with him yet. I want to take it slow. He leans in, wraps his strong arms around me and pulls me close. I slip my arms under his and squeeze his body tightly. As I push my hips into him, I feel his hardness. My breath quickens.

"Better?" he asks.

"Much..." I reply, in a trance. I forget everything about what I'm not supposed to do in this moment. I forget about Sierra, and Michelle's tantrum. I forget about how he's bad news. I feel drunk on him, from his charm, from his sudden interest in me. When we get to his sister's room, I realize he is also struggling to control his desires.

"I want to take you to my room," he says temptingly, "but I want to take you on that drive first. Meet me by the elevator in ten?" I nod, still feeling completely addicted to him as I shut the door to my best friend's room. As soon as it's closed, I bury my face into my palms, do a little happy dance and squeal. "Oh my God!!!" I yell into my hands. I cannot believe this is real life right now. I want Chase Swanson more than I've ever wanted anyone. I prance over to Michelle's closet to find something amazing to wear, but a moment after I begin searching through her clothes, an unwanted sense of reality begins creeping into me. I know deep down she wouldn't approve of me hanging out with Chase today. She wouldn't approve of me hooking up with her brother, or dating her brother, or doing anything with her brother. I check my phone.

"I'm going to the Hills with my new friends. Be back in the morning! Have fun! Call me if you want the password to get into any of the cabanas." Michelle's text reads.

She's having fun. I deserve to have some fun too, for once. I shake the feeling off and pull out one of her tight, expensive sundresses and pair of wedges. I go to the mirror. My skin looks sun kissed and smooth. I do a quick makeup job and spritz myself with her Chanel perfume.

"Maybe nothing will happen. Maybe it will just be a drive. I can resist him," I reassure my reflection as I apply edible lip gloss

166

from Victoria's Secret. "Then why are you applying the edible gloss, Liv?" I ask myself as I stare at my kissable lips in the mirror. "Fuck..." I mutter. "You're fucked," I say to my reflection. Chase and I left alone cannot be trusted, we can't control the sexual tension between us. When I see him waiting by the elevator looking unbelievably sexy, it seals the deal... I'm definitely fucked; there is no way in hell I can resist Chase Swanson.

"Nice dress," he says, as his aquamarine eyes appraise my body lustfully.

"Thanks," I reply, suddenly glad that I'm a little tipsy from the champagne. My nerves would be out of control without the soothing bubbles inside of me. He pushes the button to summon the elevator.

"I don't know how I am going to focus on the road!" He is still looking me up and down as the elevator doors open. "After you," he says, and grabs my ass as I step in front of him. I jump, startled. "Sorry, couldn't help myself," he says with a sly look, and I giggle at his shameless antics. "Mulholland is kind of a piece of shit these days. It's uneven and full of potholes, so I can't go as fast as I'd like, but we'll still have fun." The twinkle in his eyes, and his naughty smile tell me that the fun will include something more dangerous than the just the drive. I stare admiringly at his chest muscles, which are perfectly displayed beneath his black t-shirt, and at his strong, lean arms. My eyes wander, following the veins in his biceps down his rippling forearms, before settling on his large hands and long, thick fingers. I picture his hands guiding and controlling me, and it sends sexual electricity through every cell in my body. I look at his perfect lips. I want his mouth on mine. I want him... fuck... I want him so badly. As if reading my mind, he looks deeply into my eyes, his face filled with desire for me; his body language is unmistakable... he's going to kiss me.

He tilts his head to the side, and my head tilts instinctually to the other side. I close my eyes and our lips finally come together in the most deliciously perfect kiss. It feels like heaven. How could something wrong feel this right? It's like our mouths were meant for one another. They fit together like a puzzle. His soft, full lips part and my body vibrates with unadulterated desire. His powerful, masculine hands glide silently through my hair as his tongue introduces itself to mine. He tastes like sex, passion, and risk. This is the best kiss I have ever had, I think to myself, as if watching from above. The make out session quickly becomes passionately hot and raw as we both become aware that we love kissing each other. The lust between us is growing like a fire, and I desperately want to give into the sexual tension that has been building. I rub my aching body against his hardness. His lips tremble as he moans into my mouth. My wetness is increasing with each movement of my hips against him. I lightly bite his bottom lip. He is running his hands along my body as if it belongs to him, and in this moment, it does. The elevator door opens and breaks the spell. Chase's hands are shaking as he fumbles with the Porsche's key fob. Whoa... did I just make Mr. International Playboy, Chase Swanson, nervous? What is this alternate universe?

"Fuck," he mumbles, "That was so fucking hot...." He seems stunned over the effect I just had on him. The mind-blowing make out session appears to have taken him by surprise. "Weren't we supposed to go on a drive or something?" he asks with a silly half grin as he adjusts his pants.

"Oh yeah, that. We should probably do that..." I say, still dazed and utterly intoxicated by him. He seizes the moment and takes my hand, and we walk through his father's impressive collection of luxury cars and arrive at a little black Porsche with a large wing rising out of the back of it.

"It's a GT3," he says with rich kid ease. "It's my favorite toy... besides you, of course," he says, and makes penetrating eye contact that stops my retort in its tracks. A delightful shiver ripples slowly through me. He opens the passenger door and I drop gracefully into the black bucket seat. I squeeze my knees together and slide my wedges over the sill of the door. Michelle once taught me how to properly get in and out of a sports car in a short dress. He exaggeratedly bites his fist and walks over to the driver's side. "You look fucking hot in my car," he says devilishly as he gets in, "and that dress... you do know what happens to wrapping paper, right Liv?" He glances provocatively at me as he presses the Start button. The car roars to life. Its engine is gurgling and popping angrily as we leave the parking garage. We drive to the gate without speaking a word. Chase reaches over to grab a pair of gold

Ray Ban aviators from the glove box, and his hand brushes against my thigh as he does.

"Liv, you know you're hot as hell, right?" he asks offhandedly. "Because it seems like you have no idea, or maybe you're just a great faker. The humble game is cute and all, but you should probably start to own your hotness a little more."

"Oh, come on Chase! I'm not hot! I'm cute I guess, but these L.A. girls are so stunning, they make me feel invisible sometimes," I say and look down at my hands which I notice are tightly clasped.

"Are there beautiful girls in L.A.? Sure. But most of them suck! Almost all of them are bitchy and completely lame. They just aren't interesting," he explains and places his hand reassuringly on my leg as he deftly maneuvers the sports car along the twisty road.

"You know I know everything about you, right?"

"What? What do you mean?" I reply, legitimately confused.

"Let's see, Olivia Jean Walker from Kaneville, Illinois. You have no criminal record, not even a speeding ticket. Squeaky clean. After high school, you would drive to Chicago to volunteer at Children's Hospital. You got into UCLA on a scholarship. You're a straight A student, you're majoring in Psychology, and you want to be a psychologist, which I'm assuming, is how you ended up here in Los Angeles as a Bruin." He recites all of this to me as casually as if I'm a character in a book he once read. "They have the best

Psychology program in the country, good pick... smart girl." He glances at me approvingly. I feel the color draining from my face.

"Thanks..." I mumble, feeling violated and confused.

"I assumed you were crazy at first, you know, for being friends with my sister. But I can see now it's because you have a soft spot for the wicked ones, because you want to mend broken wings. Your heart is as gold as your eyes."

"How did you..."

"Liv, my dad is one of the most paranoid people on the planet. Did you really think he *wasn't* going to do an in depth investigation on a girl that is going to be living in his home?" he interjects with a haughty smirk on his face. I feel so incredibly violated, but then I remember that entering Swanson World means that you must give up all personal privacy. "You looked really cute with braces by the way," he teases, giving my leg a squeeze. I groan, burying my face in my hands. I think about how many times I've stared at photos of Chase; he never went through an awkward stage like everyone else. He gives me a compassionate glance. "And Liv..." I tense and brace myself for what I know he is going to say next. "I'm really sorry about your mom. That probably wasn't easy." He delivers the words powerfully and with heartfelt sympathy, and I feel tears starting to form.

"It's okay. That was a long time ago," I reply, choking on the words as I struggle to hold back the waterworks. He removes his hand from my leg and laces his fingers into mine.

"Cheer up, buttercup! We don't have to talk about that," he says, kissing my hand gently. I fight the tears away like I always do when someone brings up my mom. I focus instead on the moment, on him, on the road, and on the music that is playing through the Porsche's stereo. It sounds like we are listening to a song from the 1950's. I glance at the screen; it's "California Soul" by Marlena Shaw. I make a mental note to put this one on my California playlist.

"Cool song," I say, eager to change the subject.

"Yeah, Marlena has soul," he responds and turns it up. As I stare out at the legendary palm tree lined neighborhood streets of Beverly Hills, I think I understand what the writer of this song was trying to convey when they wrote this song. California really does have a soul. The palm trees look so friendly and welcoming. They sway effortlessly in the wind as if to say, 'You, yes you... You could make it here in Hollywood and live on this street! You could be the American Dream! The California Dream!'

Rodeo Drive is on my right and the historic pink Beverly Hills Hotel is to my left. I wonder what it would be like to live life as a Swanson... Liv Swanson... Ooh! I'm melting over the way that sounds. I feel like a giddy schoolgirl who is doodling her crushes' last name in her Trapper Keeper. I glance apprehensively at Chase to see if he can read my mind, but he is focused on driving. I safely enter the day dream and picture myself as Chase's wife.

'Good afternoon, Mrs. Swanson,' the Beverly Hills Hotel valet man says to me in my fantasy. He parks my luxury car so I can go shopping on Rodeo Drive. I have a black credit card with no limit and everyone I see is happy to see me. Afterwards, I meet Chase and all our famous friends for lunch by the pool at the iconic pink hotel. He gives me a big kiss to greet me, and tells me how beautiful I look. We have our lunch date here because photographs are prohibited. It's a safe haven; the lights from the cameras have been blinding us lately.

Chase honks his horn, pulling me out of my charming day dream.

"The fuck is this moron doing? Come on dude, pick it up!" he yells exasperatedly.

"Fucking tourists!" he growls to no one in particular as he passes the incompetent driver. I push the fantasy from my mind. Chase might be too dark and reckless to ever be anyone's husband.

As if on cue, he gives me sparkling elevator eyes.

"You want to help me shift?" he asks, as our speed increases.

"Sure!" He places his large tanned hand over mine, and guides it to the stick shift.

"Ok, let's go to third," he says as he pushes in the clutch and moves my hand to exactly the right spot. "Ah, here we are, the good part of Mulholland. I used to go on drives up this road to clear my head. Even at sixteen I knew everyone was fucking crazy." I picture 16-year-old Chase driving a sports car up

174

Mulholland, the wind in his hair, blissfully unaware that he would be sent away and disowned by his father within a year. "Ok now go to fourth." He guides my hand perfectly. I recognize one of my favorite songs and give Chase an enthusiastic grin. I wonder if he picked this one for me, or if this is just a charming coincidence.

"Free Fallin'" by Tom Petty & The Heartbreakers rings out from the stereo. He sings soulfully, and I start singing along with him.

"You like Tom Petty *and* The Beatles? A true music lover! I think you might be my dream girl!" he says coolly and I melt at the words 'dream girl.' He holds up a fake microphone to his mouth to sing into it, and I giggle, filled with joy at seeing him so happy. His voice has so much more light and contentment in it than it did when I caught him singing "Creep" by himself in the music lounge.

"Here's our part, Liv!" he says when the song gets to the bridge. He holds the fist microphone between us, and we sing about gliding down Mulholland, as we actually drive down Mulholland, and about falling in love. It's a surreal moment for me. I stop singing and watch him perform with his silly fist microphone for a few moments. Chase Swanson is one of a kind... he sparkles more than all of Hollywood, more than all the "stars" that live here. My body comes to life. I didn't know it was possible to feel this high from another person. I lay my head back on the seat and watch as he expertly pilots the car, one that I think may have been made for exactly this road and this moment. I look out at the

175

twisty, iconic curves and listen to the lyrics of the song and it dawns on me... I am gliding down Mulholland with a man that I could easily free fall into love with.

The Santa Monica Pier

Chase pulls over to a lookout point. He gets out of the car first and walks around to open my door. Chivalry is not dead; thank goodness for his Southern mother. He takes me by the hand and leads me to a barrier which he effortlessly hops over, looking like a rebel without a cause as he does it. He helps me over it, and I follow him to a secluded spot. He throws a blanket on the ground and I sit down next to him. I can't take my eyes off of the spectacular view of Los Angeles which is illuminated below us. Looking at the City of Angels from above is truly magical. It doesn't look as intimidating as it actually is. We are sitting side by side, staring down into the iconic city. Chase seems preoccupied with something. His brow is furrowed as if he is contemplating something very important.

"Liv... Can I ask you something?" he asks, never taking his eyes off of the city. I inhale sharply and my stomach does a little flip flop.

"Yeah..." I reply hesitantly. His somber disposition is unsettling and I brace myself.

"Have you ever been to the Santa Monica Pier?" I let out a sigh of relief and feel a silly grin spread across my face. That was definitely not what I was expecting.

"Yeah. I've been a couple times. Why?" I reply curiously. He shrugs.

"I don't know... I was just thinking it would be fun to go, sometime, with you. Would you want to do that?" he asks while absently twirling some of my hair with his finger. I can't tell if it is my imagination or not, but I think I just heard a hint of nervous boy energy in his voice. The light-hearted question is so adorable and unexpected, it is honestly the cutest, most charming thing I've ever been asked.

"I would love that...," I reply sincerely and am immediately rewarded with a million-watt Hollywood grin. I feel a drop of rain on my head.

"Oh no!" I yelp as one becomes several. I put my hands out to feel the increasing raindrops.

"June gloom," he replies, "don't worry about it." I wipe the rain from my face.

"Should we get back in the car?" I ask.

"Nope... I don't give a fuck about the rain," he says softly as he cups his hand behind my wet head. His glowing green eyes gaze deeply into mine and I feel my soul stir.

"How about we don't go anywhere," he whispers as he weaves his fingers into my hair and brings my face to meet his. He bites my bottom lip lightly, and I hungrily return to kissing the mouth that was made for mine. The warm rain glides sensually down our bodies, tracing every feature of his face, each curve of his chest. I run my hands along his soaked t-shirt, feeling the rippling suggestions of power and agility, and I trace my fingertips teasingly along his belt line. He moans and pushes my hand down to his erection. I run my hand along it through his jeans.

"Fuck," he growls and kisses me more forcefully. He slips his hand under my dress. "Oops." He flashes me a devilish grin, knowing his green eyed desires are about to be met. He tugs on my panties. "Why are you wearing these? Take them off." He watches intently as I slide them down my legs. "Good girl. I'm keeping these," he says, tossing them to the side. His fingers are now skillfully tracing my smooth wet pussy lips. My clit desperately yearns for his touch. He is teasing me, torturing me, letting his touch linger for a moment before taking it away. I gasp as he shoves two fingers all the way inside me.

"You're so wet, Liv," he says approvingly. My body aches over the way he says my name. "Such a pretty, tight pussy, just like I imagined," he whispers into my ear as he gently sucks my earlobe. He puts his other hand up my dress and begins to circle my clit. I moan uncontrollably.

"Don't stop!" I plead as I grind into his hand. "Oh God, please don't stop! Oh fuck it feels so good Chase!"

"That's right, baby... say my name," he purrs as he fingers me, in and out, slowly at first but now faster, while massaging my clit with his thumb, "I want to feel you cum all over my hand."

"Chase!" I cry out with urgency in my voice. He cups my entire pussy with his hand and I grind down into his palm, his fingers still firmly inside me. He yanks my strapless dress down with his other hand, and my braless boobs spring free. He lightly sucks one nipple and then the other. My eyes are practically rolling back in my head, and I am having trouble not screaming. I bite down hard on my lip. "That's it baby, go ahead and cum for me," he whispers as he sucks on an exposed nipple. I am tingling from head to toe. He gives me a kiss and as his tongue slips into my mouth, I can't take anymore. His taste sends me over the edge.

"Oh fuck! Chase! I'm going to cum!!" I moan into his mouth as my back arches and my whole body starts to tremble and shudder.

His perfect hands have complete control over my body and he loves it. I can't fight the release any longer. I whimper and moan as I feel the orgasm take over. The wetness is increasing with each tingle and burst of electricity that shoots through my body. I am breathless, moaning, and aching. My stomach pulsates, my body sets on fire, and I let go... and for a moment, nothing but pure, unadulterated pleasure exists. I have never experienced anything that compares to this.

"Holy shit...," I whisper after I catch my breath. I let out a little shocked giggle. It almost feels like I could cry I'm so thoroughly cleansed. I didn't realize how badly I needed release from another person's touch, or how badly I needed him to set me free; the liberation was so damned sweet. We hear the sound of an approaching car and people's voices. I frantically scramble to pull my dress up over my exposed breasts. He grabs the panties.

"I *am* keeping these!" he declares as he slips them into his pocket. "Fuck Liv, I need to adjust my dick," he whispers playfully and chuckles. I giggle. I can see his throbbing erection poking through his pants. He hides it as best as he can, and we casually climb back over the fence. I see the tourists and feel kind of guilty.

"Hello..." Chase mumbles to them. I giggle even more and run to his car. When I get back into the Porsche, I lay my head back against the bucket seat, my wet hair against the leather. I have never felt more relaxed, more satisfied, or more full of life.

"That was so fucking hot to watch. Better than any porn ever," he says as he closes the drivers door. I am starting to like his brutal honesty and shameless behavior... it's refreshing to be around someone who is always their authentic self. I can see how hard he is through his pants. I feel bad knowing he will ache if I don't return the favor.

"Do you want me to..." I start to ask and point.

"Just rub it over my pants. It's too difficult to get road head in a manual." He sounds like an experienced playboy that has gotten a lot of blow jobs in cars before. He turns the key with the fingers that were just inside of me, and the engine roars to life. I place my hand on his aching erection and start to rub it.

"Would that work? Like, will this get you off?" I ask him skeptically as I rub his boner over his pants.

"With you? Probably. Only one way to find out," he mutters slyly. He is having trouble focusing as he maneuvers down Mulholland while I rub and stroke his pulsating shaft. He keeps swerving and missing gear shifts. The Porsche growls and gurgles in defiance.

"Fuck. I can't take it," he hisses. He yanks the steering wheel and the car obeys, skidding to a stop in the gravel on the side of the road. "I need those sexy lips wrapped around my cock." He sounds deliciously assertive as he unbuttons his pants and pushes them down just enough to get the head of his dick out of his boxers. It's just as beautiful as the rest of him, and it's pulsating and desperate for my attention. I notice that there is a slick wetness glistening at the top of it, and gliding slowly down the sides. He expertly gathers the wet hair off of my face and neck, and wraps his hand into the makeshift ponytail he just made. I gasp, surprised by the aggressive gesture, but also incredibly turned on by it. Chase Swanson is exotic and unpredictable, and the good girl in me is totally mesmerized.

"Fuck that felt good. I've been wanting to pull your hair for a while now. In fact, I really want to pull your hair while I fuck you. I want to spank you and choke you and pull your head back with that long, sexy hair. I'm going to fuck you nice and hard Liv. Are you going to be a good girl for me and take it?"

"Yes..." I whisper, knowing he can see right through to my naughty side; the side I've repressed so often that even I'm not sure it is real. Being with him is changing me. Chase makes me feel uninhibited and dangerous, and yet safe at the same time.

"Lick that off!" he demands as he pushes my head down to his lap to satisfy his needs. I obediently lick the pre-cum off and then slowly swirl my tongue around the head of his dick. He moans and leans his head back. "Good girl...." he says. "Now lick the shaft." I obey and slide my wet tongue along the underside of his cock, all the way down to his balls and back up again. "I want to gag you with my cock and watch that makeup run down your pretty face..." I open my mouth wide to accommodate his girth. He forcefully shoves my head down onto it, and I impress myself by taking a man so deeply. He is controlling my head with the tight grip he has in my hair. His legs are shaking, and he moans each time his cock slides into my throat. I like watching him receive so much pleasure from me, from this sensuous act. "Fuck!" he groans. "Yes baby! Keep doing that! I want you to swallow my whole load, okay? Every drop, don't waste it and do *not* get any on my seats!"

"Uh huh," I manage to say with my lips wrapped around it. His breath is quickening, and he is thrusting rhythmically into my throat. I smile with satisfaction over the way his body is shaking.

"Oh, fuck... I'm going to cum!" he moans as his grip tightens in my hair. His legs tremble, his body quivers and his pulsating

183

shaft grows even larger. He finally reaches the point of no return and begins pumping surge after surge of thick, hot cum down my throat. He groans and arches out of his seat as the powerful sexual release overwhelms him. Breathing heavily, he continues to thrust for a few moments after his orgasm peaks. I let the rest of his ejaculation gather in my mouth until he's completely done and then I suck on the head to pull the last drops out and onto my tongue. I swallow it all in one big, satisfying gulp.

Michelle once told me that I am "never, ever to spit it out under any circumstances!"

"Thanks, baby," he says casually as he pulls his pants back up, "that was great." His eyes close as he takes a moment to catch his breath.

"Let's go," he finally says as he revs the engine. He smiles wickedly and throws the car into gear. The tires screech and claw against the pavement as he hits the throttle, but the car obeys his expert commands and straightens. It is under his control, just like I am.

Limitless Black Cards

Parties at the Swanson's mansion are notorious for being wildly outlandish. Michelle's parents are throwing a soiree this evening in the hopes of enticing some famous rappers to make the switch to the Swanson's label. Their bash is going to put yesterday's pool party to shame. I have yet to attend an event in the Swanson's swanky, infamous lounge, but I know that it takes up the entire fourth floor, and that it looks like a night club that you might see in New York or Las Vegas. Michelle and I aren't usually allowed to attend the Swanson's adult parties, but tonight, her parents are making an exception. As excited as I am for the party however, I am beyond excited to see Chase. My stomach has been nothing but butterflies since I woke up. I can't stop thinking about what happened yesterday.

Michelle ended up spending the night with that male model in Calabasas after they had new friend porno sex in the pool house. When Chase and I got back from our drive on Mulholland, he invited me back to his room, but I declined. I was afraid Michelle would come home unexpectedly and catch us. He gave me a swift kiss on the elevator as he dropped me off on the common floor.

"Bye baby," he said and spanked my butt. I tiptoed away, desperately wishing that I would have gone back to his room with him. I would finally get to see his photos in color and read what his trophies were for. But most importantly, I wanted to cuddle with him all night.

Michelle is sitting at the vanity opposite mine right now. I hesitantly glance over at her, hoping she didn't find out about my rendezvous with her brother. She hasn't said anything about it yet, nor has she mentioned her tantrum in the music lounge. We have been poked and prodded with brushes, curling irons and flat irons for the last two hours by her team of makeup artists and hair stylists in preparation for the party. My makeup girl is applying a dark brown lipstick to my lips.

"This is perfect for you! You have the coolest eyes! Are those like, gold?" she asks.

"Her eyes are amber!" Michelle rudely interjects. The girl is staring at me admiringly and I feel myself start to blush.

"Wow! You are absolutely gorgeous!" she squeals.

"Thank you!" I reply, beaming. Michelle rolls her eyes.

"OK, Lauren!" she says, glaring at the girl. "Do you want to eat her box or something?" The makeup artist mumbles 'sorry' and focuses on fiddling with the lipstick cap. Michelle seems angrier than usual today and it's a bit unsettling.

"So, Liv, I heard my brother tried to impress you with his driving skills yesterday..." she says to me while arranging lines of a pink powdery drug on her vanity with her Visa Black card. She slams the card menacingly into the table and gives me a stern look. My stomach drops.

"Yes," I say softly. "Michelle, I've been meaning to tell you," I cautiously begin to explain myself. She dismisses me with a casual wave of her hand.

"I knew he would like you," she says flatly, and I can't quite read her expression.

"Really?" I ask, trying to conceal my giddy grin.

"Believe me, there is no one I would want more to be my sister-in-law than you. Like I want the usual gold digging bitches he typically goes after to be part of our family? Fuck no!" She lowers a rolled up bill to the mysterious drug.

"Come to me!" she says to the pink powder and sniffs a line of it into her nose. "Oh fuck, YES!" she squeals as she throws her head back in pleasure. She wipes her nose carelessly. Her makeup artist frantically tries to fix the spot where she just smeared pink powder all over her face. Michelle pushes the girl's hand away. "Don't touch me!" she snaps. "I think we are done here," she says frostily and glares at them. The girls obediently start putting makeup into a large silver caboodle. "Why are you all still standing here? Get the fuck out!" Michelle yells. The makeup artists appear panic stricken as they scramble to gather the rest of their belongings and run out of the room.

"Nosy bitches," she mumbles, rolling her eyes. "Everyone wants to know my business. It's so fucking annoying!" She stretches

187

her arms slowly above her head. "They can all suck my dick!" Contempt drips from her voice as she flips off the empty room. She looks like an exotic jungle cat with her dark purple lips and intense blue eyes darting back and forth. I can't help but feel a little uneasy.

"OK, back to the topic at hand," she begins. I feel myself stiffen. "As your best friend, I have to warn you... I really don't think it's a good idea. I don't think Chase knows how to love, and you deserve better babe. I just don't want to see you get hurt," she says disingenuously. "He's a dick to girls, he only cares about himself. You should probably go for a nice guy like Kevin. You guys would be perfect for each other!" My stomach is twisting into knots over her words, over what I know is coming next.

"You guys *just* went on a drive yesterday, right?" she asks. I am willing my dry mouth to answer but nothing is coming out. She shakes her head no. "Never mind, don't answer that. I know you are way too smart to fall for his tricks. You wouldn't do that to me. You are too smart and you aren't a slut. *Right*, Liv?" she asks with narrowed eyes.

"Yeah..." I mumble. "It was just a drive..." I'm literally lying through my teeth.

"Good, let's keep it that way," she says sternly. "Now that we have that out the way, you ready to have some fun?" she shrieks as she offers the rolled up bill to me as if the most awkward conversation didn't just happen.

"No thanks," I respond quietly. She rolls her eyes.

"Whatever! More for me!" Line after line disappears into her nose. "This is the good shit! Pink Peruvian cocaine!" She dabs some on her gums and I nod as if I knew the whole time. To be honest, I am a little scared of cocaine, especially any that is pink. I don't mind maybe taking an Adderall if I have a big study session, but Michelle will eat those all day just for fun. She has no qualms about what she puts in her body. She takes a sip of champagne from a flute on her vanity; the rim of the glass traps the purple outline of her pouty mouth. I can't take my eyes off of her. I am both fascinated and admiringly afraid of Michelle Swanson. Is she mean spirited and rude? Absolutely. Am I crazy for being her best friend? Probably. But there is just something special about her. It might be her audacity and confidence that I respect, or it could be the fact that she is so perfectly broken. Or maybe... it is the idea of her that I love; the potential of who she could be.

She looks like a rock star right now sitting at her pristine white vanity, admiring the pink cocaine that she arranged into perfect little lines using her Black Card - the credit card with no limits, just like her. Her hair is slicked back, and she is wearing large gold hoop earrings and a red fur collar above a tight black dress. She looks absolutely stunning; I have never seen someone so glamorous. I watch her sway her head carelessly to "Bohemian Rhapsody" by Queen. The song takes me back to 'the incident.' Michelle near death, naked and face down on her bed; the foamy

189

vomit. I quickly look away. Suddenly, I can't look at her anymore. She is beginning to look like a demented princess to me, like a sick and mangled Barbie doll stuck in a fucked up doll house. I run my fingers anxiously through my hair and stare at myself in the mirror on the vanity. My brownish blonde locks are shiny and long. I look like a real California girl, even though I feel like a fraud. Michelle checks her gold Rolex Presidential.

"We should head up there soon," she says indifferently. I watch her saunter over to her full length mirror. She reapplies more purple lipstick, turns to the side, grabs her boobs and does a little butt shake. I stand up and walk over to her giant gold framed mirror when she's done; I'm shocked by who is staring back at me. Is this one of those funny mirrors that they have at the carnival? That can't possibly be me... I have never looked so alluring and thin. My Dior couture dress is tight and revealing. My skin is tan and smooth. My lips look extra pouty beneath the dark brown lipstick, and my amber eyes are big and gentle as I flutter the fake eyelashes they put on me. I turn to the side and look at my small waist, which makes my bottom look exaggeratedly toned. I doubt my friends and family back home would even recognize me now. My intense workouts with Michelle's trainer over the past year have certainly paid off, along with the meal plan we follow and all the yoga and Soul Cycle classes we attend. I sit down on the bed and realize that my hands are shaking, as I attempt to buckle the straps on the Tom Ford heels that are about to adorn my feet.

"You look so nervous, baby!" Michelle says gently, "Relax! I got you!" She gracefully drops to her knees and straps the shoes for me. "I know just what we need," she declares and stands up. She stretches her hand towards mine and I take it, following her obediently to the kitchenette. "Tequila!" she squeals. She opens an upper cabinet and pulls out a skull shaped glass bottle filled with an amber colored liquid and two shot glasses. I sit down on the red bar stool across from her. She bends over seductively to open her mini fridge and grabs two slices of lime out of it. "You will feel so much better! I promise!" she says reassuringly, as she pours the liquor into the shot glass. She hands me the glass and a lime. She licks the top of her hand like a kitten. "Meow!" she purrs, and bites her teeth together aggressively. I jump and she laughs wickedly. "See! You need this!" She shakes salt onto the spot she just licked and outstretches her salt covered hand as if I am an admirer who is supposed to kiss it. I stare at her hesitantly... "Lick it!" she demands and rolls her eyes at my hesitation. She reminds me of Chase right now with her assertive and bossy demeanor. I think about yesterday, his hand in my hair, his demands. I lick the salt and bravely toss back the liquor.

"Aieeee!" I squeal and quickly reach for the lime to quench the burning sensation of the tequila.

"Don't be a pussy!" Michelle downs her shot easily, without using a lime afterwards. She pours us another. "Cheers, bitch!" We clink our shot glasses together. I lick the salt off my own hand this

191

time, shoot the tequila, and bite down hard on the lime. I shudder as the tartness hits my mouth but I love the warmth the tequila is bringing me. It is sending tingles throughout my entire body, just like her brother does. I shift my hips on the bar stool as I think about it.

"Ready?" She takes another swig straight from the bottle and prances out of the bedroom with it.

The Rappers

I follow her, unsteady and a little drunk. We keep drinking from the bottle as the gold elevator climbs towards the fun that awaits us. I know we are getting close, as the bass from the rap music and the animated chatter of people socializing grows louder in our little button powered cube. The elevator dings and its doors open. I stare wide eyed at the scene before me. The party room is more amazing than I could ever have imagined. It really does look like a swanky Las Vegas nightclub. It's hard to believe that this is in someone's home, but then I remember, the Swanson's home isn't really a home at all.

The oversized room is beyond posh and dimly lit with red mood lighting. There is a black velvet stage with a chrome stripper pole in the center of it and an ornate wooden bar near the back wall, where a pair of bartenders that could easily be male models are handing drinks off to beautiful, barely dressed young women to deliver to Hollywood's finest. Several large glass panels have been opened in the wall like old time garage doors, uniting the rooftop deck overlooking the pool and the inside lounge area into one large space. It's a gorgeous evening and I can feel the balmy California summer air on my skin. There are gorgeous, famous people in designer couture everywhere I look. They are socializing on white leather couches which encircle tables with buckets of champagne on ice. Some have made their way outside onto the deck, others are on the dance floor.

"Juicy" by The Notorious B.I.G bounces from wall to wall, the deep bass penetrating throughout the room. One girl is attempting to spin on the stripper pole as her friend in a short black dress and spiky silver shoes laughs at her and takes a long swallow from a glow-in-the-dark bottle of Dom Pérignon. I watch with star struck admiration as Britney Spears greets Michelle's mom with a big hug and a heartfelt kiss on each cheek. Then I remember, they are both former Louisiana girls. Cara Delevingne waves coolly from across the room and Michelle squeals and runs to greet her. My heart stops when I finally spot Chase.

He is sitting on a white leather couch with his parents. He looks like he just stepped out of a magazine in his perfectly fitted black leather jacket and dark jeans. I watch him laugh over something one of his friends just said. He runs his fingers through his silky brown hair with perfect bad boy ease. We finally make eye contact and his face turns to stone. He purses his lips slightly as he taps his cigar in an ashtray. I can't tell if his expression is one of approval or horror over the way I'm dressed. I look down at the ground, suddenly feeling insecure. What if I am too dolled up? What if yesterday I was simply the flavor of the evening? He lifts his cigar from the ashtray with the same sexy hands that were all over my body yesterday. I watch the cigar touch his lips. Oh, that mouth, those soft perfect lips. I can't help but bite my own lip, as I think about the taste of his cum and the warmth as it slid down my throat. I can't believe that really happened.

My nerves are jumping. The cloud of smoke surrounding him finally clears, revealing glowing eyes which are lustfully appraising my body. Ok, that was most definitely a look of approval. I smile sweetly at him, and he gives me a devilish grin. I chide myself to be brave as I saunter over to where he is sitting. We don't take our eyes off each other the entire time. Chase whispers something to his friend who is sitting next to him, and the friend quickly moves away to a different seat.

"Sit down." He pats the spot next to him. I stumble drunkenly onto the couch and land halfway on his lap. "You alright?" he asks, amused.

"Yeah," I slur and climb out of his lap. I notice a couple of guys around Chase's age eyeing me curiously.

"Liv, this is my friend Alex," he says, and I shake his friend's hand.

"And this is Harrison," he says and points to his other friend who is sitting next to Alex .

"Hello!" I slur. "Harrison Ford!" I hold my hand up to give him a high five. His friend returns my high five unenthusiastically while eyeing the crowd. I feel dumb. That was dumb. Chase laughs and nudges my leg flirtatiously with his. I feel instantly relieved by his touch.

"Nice dress," he says, as his lips land on my ear. "I can't wait to get you out of it," he whispers seductively and his sexy mouth leaves traces of fire behind on my skin. I can feel wetness forming in my panties. I take the tumbler of dark liquor out of his hand, take a sip and try hard not to make a face when the strong, spicy liquid hits my tongue.

"Arghhh!" I groan, scrunching my face as my whole body shudders at the flavor. "It tastes like a campfire! Omg what is that?" I squeal, fanning my face. He chuckles.

"Lagavulin," he explains, "Scotch whisky. It's an acquired taste, maybe someday you will be man enough for it." I giggle and he places his hand on my thigh. He gives my leg a squeeze and discreetly walks his skilled fingers up my dress, pausing on my panty line. I fight the urge to moan.

"You're wet..." He sounds surprised. I nod bashfully. He breathes heavily into my ear. "Why are you wearing panties? You should take them off," he whispers as he rubs the wetness through my panties. "You're making me want to take you into the champagne room right now and fuck you nice and hard... to teach you a lesson for wearing panties." I am breathless and so turned on I could die. He continues rubbing my clit through the silk panties and I feel my nipples harden. I nervously scan the room for Michelle. I would be in deep shit if she was watching us. I find her over by the bar flirting with a man who looks like a pro football player. I watch her stomp her foot like an angry toddler and grab

196

his drink out of his hand. She pushes rudely through some party guests with the beverage in hand. I push Chase's hand off of me as she approaches the couch. He rolls his eyes and crosses his arms in annoyance. Michelle practically falls down on one of the rapper's laps sitting at the couch next to us.

"Croix! There you are! Mmmmm! I've been listening to your shit nonstop! Your voice is so sexy and smooth," she purrs to him over the music, "you should really sign with us!" She grabs his large hand and leans in closer to him. "I will make it worth your while," she whispers as she starts sucking his finger. He looks genuinely shocked.

"Liv, let's dance!" Michelle shouts as she gets up from the stunned rapper's lap. I follow her to the dance floor. I can feel Chase's eyes on me as I attempt to dance in my high heels. Michelle orders a shot of Fireball for us. We share it on the dance floor. This one goes down way smoother than the shots from earlier. "Liv, I think I know how to get Croix and Stallion to sign with us," she says in my ear, "it's going to be a win/win, but I need you to be willing to do some stuff." She smiles mischievously. I am too drunk to understand what she is talking about, so I just give her a knowing nod.

She stumbles onto the stage and as the DJ changes the music on cue, she begins spinning around and around on the stripper pole with practiced and enviable skill. The men in the room are transfixed with lust and admiration; most of the women

197

are giving her hateful, disapproving stares. She slips the straps off her dress and grinds seductively against the pole. Her focus is on the rappers, specifically on Croix. She hops off the stage and saunters over to him, maintaining eye contact the entire time. She puts her hands on his shoulders and straddles him, slowly wrapping her long legs around him. He appears to have gotten over his initial shock and looks dangerously pleased with her lap dance. She starts to grind, slowly and seductively, down into his lap. She runs her lips down his body, lingering on his zipper. She is halfway out of her dress now, rubbing her exposed cleavage in his face. I am frozen on the dance floor, speechless over her complete lack of inhibitions. She whispers something in the rapper's ear and he nods. I watch them walk into the champagne room hand in hand. I look to see if her parents noticed the lap dance or that she just lured the rapper off, but they are expressionless. Her dad is fixated on Emma and her mom is flirting brazenly with one of Chase's friends. I feel someone come up behind me and it makes me jump. I instantly relax when I hear his voice.

"Balcony. Now," Chase commands in my ear. I trail behind him like an eager puppy. A tall skinny girl who looks like a supermodel is smoking a cigarette next to us outside on the deck. She glares at me, and I feel instantly insecure.

"You look smoking hot in this dress," he says to me. I giggle nervously.

"Stop it..." It comes out as more a flirtation than a protest. I run my fingers through his soft dark hair and grab his cute butt with the other hand.

"Bad girl," he growls.

"Get a room," the irritated model mutters in a German accent and throws her cigarette off the side of the balcony. I hear it fizzle as it hits the pool. She storms off like an angry gazelle.

"She needs to eat a cheeseburger," Chase says and we both laugh. He leans over the side and stares down at the pool. He furrows his brow, looking conflicted. I rub his back reassuringly.

"What's wrong, Chase?" I ask gently.

"Liv, a good girl like you. You shouldn't be here," he says gravely without looking at me. I squint to see if I can read his expression, but he just looks blurred. I sway a little, and he steadies me. I run my hand along his stomach. It feels like the most natural thing in the world to touch him, to be intimate with him. I drunkenly reach for his face to kiss him, but much to my horror, he pushes me away.

"Not tonight," he says firmly. I cross my arms and pout. He sighs. "Trust me, I want to. I want to do everything with you. I want you so bad. My dick is rock hard right now," he says, clearly pained, "but not tonight... you're too fucked up." He squeezes my hand.

"Plus, I get the feeling that you might be a virgin," he prompts. "Am I right?" he asks. I feel my cheeks turn crimson and my head falls.

"Yes," I mumble.

"Hey now," he says gently as he lifts my chin. "I don't mind. I would love to be your first. I will be gentle, I promise," he coaxes. A wicked smile crosses his face, "But then, I'm going to need to really fuck you afterwards... nice and hard," he whispers into my ear as I giggle. "I want you to be sober so you can really feel it. I want you to feel every inch of me, and I want to feel all of you." I nod, hypnotized. "I'm going to make you cum so hard baby... make you scream my name." He puts his arms around my waist and pulls me to him. I can feel his hardness, and I rub around on it with my hips. He moans. "Stop that," he says and pushes me off of him. "Don't play with fire, princess." I hear a playful giggle come out of me as I ignore him. I open his leather jacket up and run my hands along his stomach. "I'm serious, Liv. I will fuck the hell out of you if you're not careful," he warns.

"That would be okay," I say as I trace circles with my fingertips under his shirt, just above his pants.

"Fuck!" he yells. I can feel myself being pulled to a private spot on the balcony behind an umbrella. "I told you to be careful," he mutters as he lingers over me. He grabs a handful of my hair and pulls on it harder than usual as he leans in to kiss me. I can taste his animal desire as his tongue slips into my mouth and his hands take control of my body. He slides them down my back and grabs my ass cheeks, giving my butt a firm spank. I run my hands along the ripples of his abs and absently trace my fingertips just inside his waist line. I start to rub his hardness over his pants.

"Such a naughty girl," he says as he pushes me against the wall. "You want it right now?" he asks. I nod eagerly. He lifts my dress up and my panties are now exposed. He looks deeply into my eyes and slides his fingertips in my hair, his other palm against my cheek. I close my eyes and purse my lips, but he stops and pulls away. I stare at him through heartbroken eyes.

"Why did you stop?" I ask, stunned and hurt. "What did I do wrong?"

"Shit," he says. My stomach twists in a knot.

The Phantom

"Baby, I've got to go," he says.

"No, Chase! Stay with me!" I hear myself whine as I grab at the lapels on his jacket.

"Sorry, babe, gotta go," he says and gives me a chaste peck on the lips. I hate the platonic feeling of the kiss he just gave me, so I reach for him and go in for a sloppy tongue kiss. He smiles and we are back to desperately kissing, grinding, and groping. "Mmmm, baby. You are so perfect. I want to stay, but I really have to go..." he whispers into my mouth as he bites my lip and pushes me off of him. I hear him mutter, "fuck!" under his breath as he throws his hands up while he's walking away. I adjust my dress and take a deep breath. That was ridiculously hot. He's ridiculously hot. I am so turned on that I feel like I could cum just from walking. I follow him inside and I see T.J. on the stage in front of a podium. He taps his champagne flute into the microphone. I casually linger next to Chase.

"Hey you," he says and grins. "You're just in time, my father is breaking out the nice shit tonight. That's a $20,000 bottle of champagne." He points to it. My mouth drops.

"Really?" I whisper. A scantily clad woman is standing next to Mr. Swanson holding a tray with the absurdly expensive Ace of Spades champagne on it.

"Good evening," his dad booms into the microphone, "thank you all for coming this evening." Everyone around me immediately falls silent. T.J. has an uncanny knack for commanding the attention of a room.

"Croix and Stallion," he says, turning towards where the rappers are sitting. "I would like to present this champagne to you tonight as a thank you for your contributions to the music industry. Your cognac smooth vocals and battle tested lyrics are artistic creations which are truly unparalleled." He picks up the bottle from the tray and holds it enticingly towards them. The rappers look thrilled. I see Michelle laying on the couch with them, smiling, and clapping wildly. She sits up and begins swaying back and forth so much that it's making me dizzy.

"Ugh. My sister is a mess right now," Chase says as he stares at his disheveled sister with disgust. Michelle abruptly stands up and starts to fall backwards, but the rappers catch her. She takes her heels off and throws them to the side and then stumbles onto the stage. I cringe when I see her under the lights. Makeup is smeared all over her face, her dress is falling down, her black bra is exposed, and her cleavage is dangerously displayed. Her dad is glaring at her through narrowed eyes. The silence in the room is deafening.

T.J puts his hand over the microphone to cover it, and I can see him mouth, "Michelle, go sit down!" She shakes her head no, her whole body swaying as she does it. She is next to the podium and attempts to pull the microphone towards her but her dad has a firm grip on it. She shoves him as hard as she can and manages to pull the microphone off the stand while as he stumbles backwards. The screech of it makes everybody groan and hold their ears. She places her mouth directly on it so her lips are touching it.

"Good evening, bitches and hoes," she says in a fake deep voice and tries to sound formal. "No! Fuck that!" She paces back and forth. "Swanson Music Group is the shit! If you think that we aren't. Just ask... anyone!" she slurs loudly. She pretends to give the microphone a blow job and giggles. I can hear the guests snickering and murmuring to one another. "Mic drop!" she says and dramatically drops it to the ground. Another shrill screech echoes through the room. T.J. is still holding the champagne and looking horrified.

"Dad, let me pop it for them!" she pleads. He shakes his head, and she attempts to grab the bottle of champagne from her father's hand. "Dad, trust me! Let me pop it, and then I will go get tag teamed. The Money Shot!" she squeals delightedly as she puts her hand up to the sky. "I know what I'm doing!" she snarls through gritted teeth. She is yanking at the bottle of champagne so hard it looks like she will topple over at any moment. I look around and see guests whispering and putting their hands over their mouths.

She finally manages to snatch the bottle from her dad's appalled grasp. T.J. makes one last attempt to grab the bottle back, but she giggles and runs off the stage with it. "Nope, not this time!" she says playfully and skips off balance towards the balcony.

"Poppin' bottles, bitches!" she shouts as she attempts to undo the cork. "Ugh," she groans. "Too much work! Over it..." Then, as if in slow motion, she drops the $20,000 bottle of champagne off the side of the balcony. Everyone gasps as it shatters on the ground below us. She puts her hand to her mouth sarcastically. "Oops!" she says mockingly. "This party blows!" she shouts and runs towards the exit. I instinctually attempt to go after my best friend, but Chase grabs me by the waist. I try and wriggle out of his firm grasp but I can't, he's too strong.

"No," he whispers calmly but assertively in my ear, "Michelle is a grown woman."

"Let me go!" I yell, still squirming.

"Absolutely not. Liv, do *not* get involved with that. Let her figure it out on her own." On some level, I know he is right, and my body stills in his arms.

Mr. Swanson clears his throat... "Sorry about that," he says into the microphone, "I am having another bottle from the wine cellar brought up here."

Suddenly, I hear something very odd coming from the pool. I furrow my brow as I listen closely. It sounds like someone is blasting carnival music from the outdoor sound system. Other guests hear it too, and curious people have already started to make their way to the deck. It is the most eerie music I have ever heard. Dark and creepy, straight out of a horror film about spooky clowns or demented doll houses. It sounds like something Danny Elfman would come up with for a Tim Burton movie about an evil plastic doll. Chase rolls his eyes.

"I know what this is about," Chase mumbles. "She needs to get the fuck over it..." He storms over to the deck and I follow him warily. He must be talking about Michelle... it has to be Michelle. Shit! I knew she wasn't done. My best friend loves to put on dramatic, histrionic shows, and I have a feeling that this one will be unlike any I have ever seen before.

The lights in and around the pool are already on, illuminating the night sky. But now a new source of light is being introduced. Headlights are bouncing off of the pool house walls from the guest parking lot. My stomach drops as I hear the jarring sound of screeching tires and metal scraping against metal.

"Oh my God..." I whisper, putting my hand over my mouth as I take in the sickening sight below me. Michelle is driving her dad's top down white Rolls Royce Phantom Drophead as if it is a bumper car at an amusement park. I watch as she runs into luxury car after luxury car in the guest parking lot like an unhinged maniac. She rams a red Ferrari over and over again. The Rolls Royce emblem on her car snaps off from the impact and falls to the ground. Furious party guests are shouting from the balcony, horrified by what is taking place. Michelle skids the Phantom around the fountain, scraping it along the way. She brings the mangled car to a complete stop, facing the pool, as she revs the engine over and over again.

"Oh shit!" her mom gasps. "Michelle, NO!" she yells in vain to her deranged daughter, but it's too late. I turn around and bury my face in Chase's chest. I can't watch. His body is stiff and angry, his fists clenched by his sides. I hear the sound of the car's powerful engine as she floors it. The tires screech against the pavement and then I hear the grotesque silence of airborne aluminum. I scream when I hear the monstrous tidal wave and the accompanying symphony of something large gurgling and sinking. Chase pushes me off of him and storms over to the edge of the balcony. I feel sick as I take in the horrific scene below me. The Rolls Royce is in the pool and sinking slowly to the bottom. Michelle is standing proudly on the bespoke leather seat.

"TA DAAA!" she yells up to the party guests as she does an exaggerated bow. I glance at Chase. His face is a tightly controlled mask but I can tell that he is livid. Veins are popping out of his neck. I take a quick peek at Mr. Swanson; he looks exactly like Chase right now; red faced, his jaw clenched tightly enough to crack teeth. Mrs. Swanson is beside herself and sobbing.

"Why?!" she wails to her friends standing nearby. Michelle has made her way onto the hood of the car and is dancing seductively to the carnival music.

"I'm a fucking goddess!" she shouts as she peels off what is left of her drenched designer dress. She tosses it to the side and is now in only her black lace panties and bra. She is twirling round and round on the hood of the car like a manic ballerina, her long hair flinging water with every spin. She does a ballet leap, and her feet smack the hood of the car hard when she lands; yet another sickening sound.

Croix the rapper is standing next to me and he lets out a low whistle.

"Damn... that bitch is cray! Glad I didn't hit that! She was trying, but I had to turn her down. I ain't about to mess with no psycho!" he says to Stallion.

"That mothafucka better buy me a new 'Rari!" Stallion growls under his breath. He turns to T.J. "Sir, if I was you, I would lock her ass up and throw away the damn key. She ain't right!" he exclaims, shaking his head. "Fuck this! I don't have time for this shit!" He storms off, his phone pressed to his ear, as T.J. stares at him through narrowed eyes.

"We will replace all the damaged cars, everyone. I'm so sorry for this inconvenience," he announces to the enraged party guests. T.J. marches to the edge of the balcony and stands directly above Michelle. The veins in his neck are popping just like Chase's.

"You ungrateful little bitch!!" he shouts down to his daughter, causing everyone to stop and gasp. He sounds like the abrasive former New Yorker that he is. Mrs. Swanson wipes her eyes and places an anxious hand on her husband's shoulder.

"T.J., please don't make a scene! Go easy on her! She's sick!!"

"No! I've had enough!" Mr. Swanson brushes his wife's hand away and directs his attention back to his daughter. "You are going to Aspen in the morning, you little fucking ingrate! I don't want to see your face again until you start acting like a human being!" Michelle puts her hand over her mouth, mockingly.

"Oh no! Not *Aspen*!" she yells and then scoffs. "It's better than being here at this lame ass party!" She swims to the edge of the pool and starts to climb out. "Do you honestly give a flying fuck if I *accidentally on purpose* drove this one into the pool *father*?!" she shrieks. "There's one in Aspen exactly like it, and you can buy another one tomorrow if you want to!" She stares at the car with a sick admiration. "It looks better in the pool anyways," she snorts pompously and then skips away like a lunatic. Don runs after her, followed by his team of security guards. When he tries to grab her, she spits in his face. "Don't touch me you fucking asshole! Why don't you tell my dad about how you make me give you blow jobs on the reg? Why don't you tell your wife?" she taunts him, and then I remember our conversation in the elevator when she told me she trades sexual favors for access to all the cars. She looks back up to the balcony, and we make eye contact. I freeze.

209

Her wild, vacant stare is absolutely terrifying. I gulp and look away as quickly as I can.

"Oh and Liv!" she yells sardonically. Too late... I cringe. "Have fun fucking my brother while I'm away! You're going to get your heart broken! He only cares about himself! Did you tell him you're a virgin yet, and that I touched your pussy before he did? She gets so wet doesn't she, brother?" she screams at us. I can feel everyone's eyes on me. My face grows hot and my lip starts to quiver. The tears are welling up in my eyes. A guard finally grabs her, and I can hear her shout, "get your fucking hands off of me asshole!!" My heart is pounding through my chest and my mouth is dry; I feel sick. I have to get out of here. I'm heading towards the exit as fast as I can walk, when I'm intercepted by a tall brunette.

"Not so fast," she hisses, her tone dripping with malice. She catches my arm and spins me around. I recognize her now... Sierra Villa. She was the one drinking the glow in the dark Dom earlier. Her long, glossy hair is sable black, yet somehow the look she is giving me is even darker. Her fake, over-injected lips glint beneath the lights as she purses them contemptuously. I try and pull my arm away but she tightens her grip, making me wince. "Listen carefully you little cunt. You were maybe the homecoming queen at a public high school? Maybe made runner up in a couple of pageants at the state fair? And now you think you're going to cut to the front of the line and live happily ever after with Chase Swanson?!? You're lying to yourself if you think he actually likes you. That he actually finds you intriguing. He's only interested in you because you're a virgin. That's *literally* the only reason. He's always wanted to fuck a virgin, like he thinks it will give him special powers or some shit. It's time to walk away little girl, you're way out of your league and you have no idea what you are getting yourself into." The venom in her voice is palpable.

"Sierra! Let her go!" Chase barks. Sierra drops my arm but continues to glare at me.

"He's mine, bitch," she whispers menacingly. I feel panic and hot tears. I have to get out of here. Sierra looks smug and vindicated as I run towards the exit.

"Liv, wait!" I hear Chase yell to me. I make eye contact with him at the stairwell but it doesn't even slow me down. I run down a flight of stairs only to trip on the last step before the landing. Mortified, I yank my heels off and hold them in my hand as I sprint down the rest of the stairs and the hallway to Michelle's room. I slam the door and climb into her bed, still in my dress. Tears are falling freely down my face now. I pull the covers over my head, wishing this was all just a dream; just a horrible nightmare. I hear a faint knock at the door.

"Liv... its Chase. Will you please open the door?" I lay still, praying he goes away.

Famous

I feel bile starting to rise and I sprint to the bathroom; the vomit burns as the liquor comes out of me. When I'm finally done, I wipe my mouth with toilet paper and curl up on the floor, sobbing softly into the bathroom rug. I'm so confused right now. I didn't know it was possible to feel this alone in a house full of people. I don't understand how things got so crazy, so incredibly fucked up. Whenever I'm sad, my mind inevitably drifts to thoughts of my mom. This time is no different. She always smelled like vanilla and cherries, like Michelle's bubble bath. I sit up and grab the soap so I can smell it. I wipe my eyes as I think about my mom's dimpled smile and her sweet laugh. I try not to think about her for too long though, because after I've thought of all of my favorite things about her, my mind always begins to conjure visions of her, bald and emaciated, lying in her hospital bed. I clutch the soap to my chest and fall asleep on the bathroom rug. When I open my eyes, many hours later, my head is throbbing and my body aches all over. I feel like I've been hit by a truck. I walk unsteadily to the sink and splash my face with cold water, groaning from the hangover as I take in my pale, makeup stained face in the mirror.

"Ugh," I whisper to my reflection. I force myself to wash my face, brush my teeth, and put on fresh makeup. I open the bathroom door cautiously, looking around to see if Michelle is in the room. She's nowhere to be found, yet I still tiptoe to her dresser as thought I might wake her. I open the pajama drawer and see a bondage nightie from a boutique called Dolls Kill sitting on top. How appropriate. I push it aside and select an Agent Provocateur white silk nightie and the accompanying white silk robe and slippers. My phone is still on the floor from the night before. I pick it up and press the home button; no texts, no calls. I open Instagram and type Michelle's name in. There is a picture of us from last night, right before she lost her mind. We look so plastic, so glamorous, in our tight, revealing dresses. The post has the lightning emoticon she added, and thousands of likes and comments from strangers...

"I would fuck you both... even tho you dumb bitchexs!" Instagram user @shadytits69 said.

"They are so plastic and fake! Stupid cunts!" @sarathebarbie387 wrote. Horrified, I throw my phone on the bed. I hate reading the cyber bully comments. Michelle has so many haters that she can't even keep up with blocking them all.

  I peek out her door; the coast is clear in the children's wing. I walk quickly over to the the elevator and feel relief wash over me as I step inside to take it to the common floor. I'm almost home free. But as the doors open, I spot T.J. and Emma sitting on a couch in front of the sliding glass door that I was planning on going through to get to the guest house. T.J. is sipping coffee and Emma

213

is plugging away on the iPad. I try and backtrack but it's too late. Mr. Swanson and I make eye contact. His face lights up and he smiles graciously at me.

"Olivia! There's my little money maker!" He stands and gives me a warm embrace. I freeze, mystified that he is actually speaking to me, let alone being so nice to me. "So, how did it go last night, with Croix and Stallion? I can't wait to see the show!" He has look of greedy admiration on his face as he rubs his hands together. He looks like a villain in a comic book. My head is still throbbing, and now my heart is pounding and my hands are starting to shake as I try and remember the details of last night.

"I... um... I don't know what you're talking about..." I mumble.

"Dad, she didn't do it." Startled, I spin around to see Chase standing behind me. I scan his expression to see if I can read what is going on, but he is pokerfaced. Mr. Swanson's eyes glaze over as he sits back down on the couch. He turns away from us in an immature display of defiance. With his back to me, he pulls out his iPhone and starts texting. Emma's iPad dings.

"Mr. Swanson would now like to offer you $50,000 to do the sex tape with the rappers," she reads from her iPad. I am immobilized with shock, fear, and disgust.

"Umm... I'm not a porn star." I'm stunned and hurt that they would even think that was a possibility. T.J. lets out a little chuckle, and he starts typing something in his phone again. Her iPad dings.

"$100,000 dollars," Emma reads from the screen impassively.

"Is he texting you??" I ask in disbelief. "From his iPhone to your iPad?!?" I piece it together and feel an overwhelming sense of disbelief. What in the actual fuck??

"Mr. Swanson, why won't you speak to me?" I ask him, but he refuses to acknowledge me. Emma takes her glasses off and rubs her eyes.

"Liv, you would be crazy to turn down this deal," she says and looks at me with massive bags under her once beautiful honey brown eyes. "How else are you going to become famous?" she asks.

"I don't want to be famous!" I object. T.J. and Emma scoff in unison.

"Please, spare me the holier than though, do-gooder bullshit, sweetheart," Emma says patronizingly. "I know what you want. You wouldn't be here if you didn't want it. But sometimes, you have to do a little dirty work at the bottom and pay your dues, to get to the top." She stares at me deeply, like she's giving me invaluable life advice. "Olivia Jean, you are in good hands with the Swanson's, we are experts in the entertainment industry! Our skills go far beyond music. We can make you a star!" she affirms, sounding like a used car salesperson. She gives me a professional grin, but her greedy eyes don't smile at all. A chill runs down my spine.

"I don't.. I um... can't." I'm struggling to find the words. "Emma, I'm sorry, but I really don't understand what is happening right now..." Emma's cold attention turns to Chase.

"You didn't do your job," she scolds, "and now, I have to take time out of our schedule to explain this to her! This is what happens when you fall for the help!" Clearly annoyed, she turns to me. "Last night at the party, you and Michelle were supposed to seduce the rappers, lure them into the champagne room and have any type of sexual contact with them in front of the hidden camera. It would be a sure way to get them to make the switch to our label. There is always leverage in a sex scandal, especially because they both have significant others that would not want to see that footage! Unfortunately, Michelle was not in a good frame of mind last night, so we need to start over," she explains uncaringly.

"No shit," Mr. Swanson scoffs. "My daughter is a liability *and* a fuck up!" I don't always stick up for myself, but I always stick up for my friends, especially for Michelle. I straighten and march bravely over to T.J., who still has his back to me.

"Mr. Swanson, I thought you were trying to protect your daughter from media scandals and the paparazzi? But, now you're fine with her doing a sex tape?! What is *wrong* with you?!? You're her father! What if it got leaked?" I demand, completely appalled

216

by his attitude. He finally turns and looks at me through dark, cold eyes.

"I don't want anyone to know that my daughter is a criminal, an alcoholic and a drug addict. Sex sells. Sloppy, drug addicted mess does not, as was evident last night," he says, in a callous way that positively enrages me.

"You are a sick man Mr. Swanson!" I berate him through gritted teeth. I can feel the anger giving me blind courage. "You can give Michelle all the cars, clothes, trips, and money you want, but it will never fill the void in her that YOU created!" He ignores me and turns his attention to Chase.

"We need to salvage this deal, son. Call Sierra Villa today, offer her a million dollars to do the sex tape, we will use it against Croix and Stallion, and then leak it before her next single comes out." He looks me up and down and smirks. "It will be better with Sierra anyways..." he says, directing his words at me. "And get this one out of my face, please, before I lose my temper," he commands. Chase puts his arm around me.

"Come on, Liv. Let's go," he says gently. I throw his arm off of me and take off running towards the only place I feel comfortable in this fucked up place. Tears are streaming down my face as I slam the French doors to the library and plop down in between the tigers. I put my head in my hands and sob uncontrollably.

"Liv?" I hear Chase's concerned voice above me. I look up at him through my tears.

"What do you want?" I ask angrily as I wipe my eyes.

"I came to check on you," he says quietly. He sits down next to me and puts an arm around me. I hastily remove it.

"Don't touch me!" I snap. He sighs and crosses his arms. "You were in on the thing with the rappers? What the fuck is wrong with you?!?"

"Liv, it's my job," he replies calmly, "sometimes I have to do fucked up shit."

"Even to me?" My bottom lip starts to tremble and a horrified expression splays across Chase's face.

"Shit... I feel like I just kicked a puppy." he mutters and looks down. He takes my hand and stares deeply into my eyes. "Liv... I'm *so* sorry," he says sincerely. "I forget that you're not used to this L.A. stuff yet. Let me explain what happened. My dad knew that Michelle would be too fucked up on the job, so he couldn't trust her to do it alone. It's actually a compliment that he wanted you involved, it means he thinks you're responsible and that you have star power. He really does like you, even if it doesn't seem like it." I frown and stare out the window. "It was my job to talk you into the thing with the rappers, get you to sign the contract, and compensate you. I didn't bother telling you, because I knew you wouldn't do it, and I think that Michelle, even in her fucked up state, knew it too. That's just my dad and his wishful thinking. He is too blinded by his success and his money to think straight. I was hoping Dante could fix him, but it might be a lost cause. He's still an asshole. A very rich and successful asshole, but still an asshole. I also think he really wanted to watch you having sex on camera since he can't fuck you himself. He feels the same way about you that I do..." My anger is dissipating. I feel myself being lulled by the timbre and gravel in his deep voice.

"Is Michelle okay? I ask and wipe my eyes.

"Yeah, she's fine," he says, "they basically tranquilized her and put her on the Gulfstream with Dante late last night. I think she just overdid it on the blow."

"To Aspen?" I ask.

"Yeah, she loves it there," he says, while absentmindedly playing with my hair.

"Well, then, how is that a punishment?" I'm genuinely confused.

"Punishment? No, my dad just doesn't want to send her to rehab or have the paparazzi stalk her. And they will, after the story from last night gets out. He stashes her there when things like this happen. It's basically an in-home rehab center, and she will do just fine with Dante, the spiritual douche," he explains, smirking.

"Speaking of Michelle... did you really hook up with her?"

"No. I mean... I don't think so," I reply, "she kind of taught me something in the bathtub, but nothing really happened."

"My sister says she's bisexual, but I think she might really end up with a girl. And I get the feeling that she loves you, you know, as more than a friend..." He raises an eyebrow at me.

"No, she doesn't!"

"Yes, she does, Liv," he says firmly. "Do you feel the same about her?" I shake my head slowly.

"No, I love her like a friend. I've never been with a girl. I only like men... what I mean is... I like you Chase." I stumble over the words as I stare longingly into his pretty blue eyes. He gives me a sparkly thousand-watt smile.

"I like you too, Liv." He kisses me on the forehead and my body completely melts. I wish I could have a recording of him saying those words so I could play it over and over again. Maybe Don in the security center will give it to me, although he probably got fired after Michelle sold him out.

Chase's grin turns mischievous. "But I would be down with a girl on girl threesome sometime," he says, "just NOT with my sister. This is Los Angeles, not Kentucky!" he jokes, and I giggle. He stands and extends his hand. I take it and he pulls me up. We walk hand in hand, in and out of the rows of bookcases. He stops abruptly at one and pulls a book down from a high shelf. This doesn't look like an ordinary book; it doesn't even have a name on the cover, or any paper inside of it.

220

The Sun King

"What is this book?" I ask curiously. He opens it and places his thumb on a fingerprint scanner. The entire bookcase shudders and creaks. I jump backwards and he laughs at me. The entire case is now moving towards us and then sideways, revealing a spiral staircase. Another secret passageway in the Swanson's crazy world. I follow him up the steps.

"Wow..." I marvel when I see it. His words, 'I know a place,' flash in my mind. This must be the secret room, the only one without cameras. I notice the plush red carpet first. Then I see speakers that are taller than Chase, on either side of a beautiful fireplace. Multi-patterned turquoise tiles trace its elegant arch. The center tile at the top of the arch is a black Dia de los Muertos skull. It's clearly female, based on the red lips and fiery hair. She comes to life as he presses a button on a remote, igniting the fire. Chase points for me to look up. The domed glass ceiling of the library is directly above us and I can see the sky.

"I told you this spot was special," he says as I hear the bookshelf rumbling below to shut us in. "This is the music listening room, babe." There is a large circular leather couch in the center with soft cashmere blankets in a variety of colors strewn haphazardly about it. I notice that there are more speakers behind the couch. They are white and futuristic looking.

"Those look like Storm Troopers," I blurt out. He chuckles.

"Ah, you're a Star Wars nerd, it all makes sense now," he jokes, giving me a flirty wink. I smile bashfully.

"Maybe...." I mumble. An elegant red vinyl record player sits atop a stack of McIntosh audio equipment. Next to it, there is a tall ladder attached to a wall of shelves, which are full of records and CD's. Chase climbs the ladder, making it look athletic and effortless. He sifts through the records much more carefully than the books. "No iPod dock in here, princess." I am beginning to love it when he calls me princess, even if it's usually condescending. I can't help but adore this bad boy and his tainted heart. He pulls the record he wants from the shelf and bounds down the ladder. I see the green apple as he removes it from the sleeve and places it on the record player.

"I love Abbey Road."

"Oh, fuck. You really might be my dream girl!" he murmurs as he places the needle onto the record. I can't stop my grin or my flushing cheeks. I love hearing the words 'dream girl' roll off his lips. He opens a drawer and pulls out a little vial of white powder. His dangerous smile fills the room as he taps some of the drug out onto the slowly spinning vinyl. "My dad taught me this move," he says as he snorts the cocaine off of the record. I bite my lip and stare at the ground. I hope he doesn't turn into a psycho like his sister when he does coke. "It's all good," he says, noticing my discomfort. "I never get coke dick!"

Chase closes his eyes and starts to move his head to the beat of "Come Together" by The Beatles. I've never heard a recording sound like this before. It is crystal clear, like we are listening to the live recording in Abbey Road studios. I can hear every detail, every nuance, every note and every layer; all the emotion and soul of the song is suspended in this enchanted room. I sit down on the edge of the couch and cross my legs tightly.

"Here," he prompts as he pulls a joint out of the drawer and hands it to me with a lighter.

"How many different drugs are in that chest of drawers?" I blurt out. He leans back, laughing.

"All of them!" he responds flippantly. I shake my head and grin. I take a hit and my body immediately starts to feel relaxed. I slip my robe off and he stares at me very closely as I do it. "Damn..." he whispers. "You look smoking hot in that white thing, kind of like a virgin," he winks, as he compliments the white silk.

"Something" plays next and Chase pulls me close to dance to the romantic song. I hope that he feels the same way about me as what is being expressed in the lyrics. We slow dance on top of the soft red carpet, and I nuzzle my face into his neck and take in his delicious smell.

"I've always wanted to go to Abbey Road studios," I say into his skin.

"I've been there, it's fucking incredible, I will take you sometime!"

"Chase... that would be amazing! Going to London is like my dream. Did you walk on the crosswalk on Abbey Road?" I ask.

"Of course! They have a dude that monitors it so you can walk across and take your own Abbey Road picture. There is a photo of Blaire and I mimicking the album cover in my room. Blaire dressed up in an all white suit for the picture!"

"If you don't mind me asking.... what is Blaire like?" I ask. "I've never met her."

"She's great, you would adore her."

We both start to laugh as the next song, "Maxwell Silver Hammer" reverberates through the giant speakers.

"Wow! You can seriously hear every detail through these speakers! Like, did Paul just chuckle a little bit?" I ask with an amused expression.

"Yeah, babe," he responds, "did you know that records are the most unfiltered and pure way to play songs? Digitals have to be compressed, so the details get lost and the sound quality is reduced. I'll take you on a date to Vacation Records off of Sunset sometime, then I'll let you go on a shopping spree on Melrose afterwards. We will devote a whole day to being L.A. grunge rockers!"

"Chase! That would be so much fun!" I plop down on the red carpet and he sits down next to me. "My dad and I used to have a dance to this song."

"What? To 'Maxwell Silver Hammer'?" he asks and furrows his brow. "This is a fucked up song!"

"I know!" I giggle and cover my embarrassed face with my hands. He puts his arm around me and I snuggle into him.

"So, was it like a slow dance or an interpretive dance?" he asks playfully.

"No!" I scrunch my nose in between giggles. "It was like this..." I pretend to slam my hand over his head like I'm hitting him with a hammer.

"That's pretty weird Liv, but I kinda like it." He grins and pulls me in tighter.

"My dad loves The Beatles, I've been saving up so I can take him to see Paul McCartney for his 50th birthday. I'm sure you probably know Paul personally." Chase smiles slyly, answering my question without saying a word. "Of course you do," I murmur. He shrugs nonchalantly.

"Babe, my dad is in the music industry," he says. "Paul is cool, like *really* cool! He's down to earth and does nice things for people. Kinda like you..." We lie down on the carpet together, side by side. Chase holds my hand as we stare up at the clouds through the glass dome in silence, letting the music take us away. It is as if all the pain and turmoil is being pulled from us and replaced with the melodies floating out from the speakers. I take another hit off the joint and blow the smoke into the air, and then pass it to him and watch his lips wrap around it. He looks unbelievably alluring as smoke slowly rises in front of his rugged, handsome face; the sexual tension between us is rising even faster. As I turn on my side, he turns to meet me. I run my fingers gently through his hair.

"Oh God, do that again!" he says with his eyes closed. I stroke his hair and then his face. His pouty lips look so kissable, his chiseled features so striking. He kisses me gently on the lips and then on the forehead and then on the lips again. I stare into his hypnotic eyes. Next to the fire, they look blue green like turquoise water, like the Caribbean. They flash and sparkle invitingly.

"Do you trust me?" he asks gently.

"Yes," I whisper, under the grip of his spell. "Sun King" is playing through the speakers. The dreamy song is beguiling me, melting me.

"Good girl. Hold your arms up," he demands. I stare into the aquamarine intensity that is staring back at me, and then obey. He lifts the white silk from my body and I feel every inch as it glides slowly over my rapidly hardening nipples. He removes his own shirt and then takes my hand and leads me to the leather couch. He pushes me down onto it. Naked and incredibly alive, I sink slowly into the luxurious cashmere blankets, watching him intently as he unbuttons his pants and slides them off. I've imagined this moment a thousand times, but nothing could've prepared me for the butterflies in my stomach right now and the feeling of my heart accelerating as he lowers himself onto me. I stroke his stubble as his big soft lips eagerly seek mine. I close my eyes and open my mouth to meet his tongue. The kiss quickly gives in to instinct, becoming intense and filled with lust. "Holy shit..." he mutters as he pulls away to catch his breath. "I want to fuck you nice and hard... so badly, but,.... not yet ...not this time," he says, breathing heavily against my neck.

"Close your eyes baby," he whispers and I obey. His lips trace and follow and kiss every contour of my body. Moments become months. I am so totally enveloped in this bliss. "Liv... look at me," he commands. I do as I am told. I'm rewarded with a rare glimpse of pure admiration in his glowing, electric eyes. I inhale sharply as he kisses my inner thigh. "You're so wet," he murmurs approvingly as he spreads my legs with his strong hands. Warm breath teases me through my panties as he slides his fingers inside the lace on the sides of my ass. My body feels like it's vibrating as he slowly slides them off of me. His silky soft hair caresses my skin as his tongue dances up between my legs to my pussy, gliding delicately up one side and then the other. When the tip of his tongue finally lands on the sweet spot, my eyes almost roll back in my head.

"Chase.." I whisper. "Oh.. fuck...." I moan, arching my back. He swirls his tongue slowly around my clit, just barely making any contact at all. I never knew anything could feel this good. It is

227

driving me wild. He reads my mind and begins sucking on it softly, still swirling his tongue, with light but constant connection now. "Ahhhhh!" I cry out in pleasure as he expertly sucks and twirls my clit in his mouth. Chase moans into my wetness, which turns me on even more. His full lips feel unbelievable. The point of no return is racing closer with each stroke of his tongue, and the intensity of the sensations is removing me from reality. My body starts to tremble and shake. I am losing control, being taken away from the earth. My heart is pounding. I'm breathing rapidly. My body is on fire. I feel the drop happening and I whimper breathlessly. "Oh my... oh *fuck*... ohhh *fuuuck*!!" I scream the words over and over again as I cum harder than I have ever imagined, into his beautiful mouth.

"Damn,... you are delicious," he says huskily as he slides back on top of me. I know what is coming next as his pulsating erection finds my slick pussy lips.

"Chase, do we need a condom?" I ask softly as he is about to stick it in.

"No babe, I'm good, I just got checked out, and obviously you're good too," he says. "You're on the pill, right?" I nod. He smiles and our eyes connect and hold, never breaking away. We pause like that for a moment, and then he slowly pushes it in. I inhale sharply when all of him is finally inside me. "You are beautiful, Olivia Jean," he whispers. He kisses me and our tongues intertwine. There is so much love and understanding flowing between us in this moment. He takes my hand and interlaces his fingers in mine. I didn't know he had this tender side to him. He is moving more carefully than I know he's used to, deliberately being more gentle with me.

"Are you doing okay?" he asks, his bright blue eyes and dilated pupils penetrating into my soul.

"Yeah, I'm good," I whisper. He moves in and out of me, slowly and purposefully.

"You're so wet and tight, I don't think I can last very long. You are so fucking amazing, so fucking sexy." He kisses me with more force and lightly bites my lip, I moan into his mouth, and his body starts to tremble. I push my hips up into him and swivel them. It kind of hurts to do this because his dick feels huge inside of me, but oh fuck, it feels so good at the same time. A perfect cocktail of pleasure and pain. I watch the veins swelling in his neck as he closes his eyes. He groans deeply as sensations of intense pleasure begin to overtake him. I pull his face to mine for a kiss and as my tongue slips into his mouth, his body starts to tremble and shudder. His mouth is open and his full lips are still pressed against mine as thrust after thrust pulses into me. I'm unbelievably turned on and I instinctively meet each thrust with my hips. I start to go over the edge of a second, more powerful orgasm, this one quite different than the last. I whimper and his grip on my hand tightens. I try and stay quiet but I can't... I scream his name as we cum together.

He is laying on top of me, relaxed and spent, a few involuntary final thrusts the only movement as his body empties completely into mine. He moans softly with each one and I run my fingers through his hair as he gently kisses my shoulder. We are naked, skin slick with sweat, our souls feeling connected as we stare into each others eyes. This is the first time a man has used my body like this... and I loved it. I could get used to this. I could get used to him.

Breitling for Bentley

Chase and I walk down the spiral staircase, through the hidden bookshelf door and back into the library.

"Do you want to get out of here?" he asks when we get to the French doors.

"Where?" I ask, with giddy girlishness in my voice.

"Anywhere," he vows and puts his arm around my waist. "Lets just run away together!" I giggle playfully. We walk down the hall feeling drunk on each other.

"Hi, babies!" I hear Michelle's mom say sweetly from an office near the library.

"Hey mom," Chase greets her at the doorway. She looks up from her computer and smiles. "We were just talking about going somewhere," he grabs my hand and looks deeply into my eyes, his blue irises almost magically magnetic. "Just Liv and I," he says, impassioned.

"Why don't ya'll go to Malibu?" Samantha suggests charmingly. "Liv hasn't seen the 'Bu house yet!" A huge grin spreads across my face at her suggestion. Wow! Malibu with Chase Swanson! That sounds incredible! And then I remember Michelle and the disaster from last night. I frown at the memory of her Rolls Royce meltdown.

"But, what about Michelle?" I ask and stare at the ground. Samantha gets up from her desk and walks over to me.

"Oh darlin', Michelle is in good hands. You deserve to have a good time! Don't you worry sweetheart!" she purrs as she puts her hands on my shoulders.

"Yeah, Liv, listen to my mom, Michelle is fine," Chase says, "let's go!" He tugs at my hand impatiently. Mrs. Swanson grins at me and places her hand on her heart.

"You two are so cute! Ya'll can take my white Bentley!" she offers. "I would say the Rolls, but it is being fetched out of the pool right now thanks to that wild, party animal daughter of mine!" she sighs. "She sure was messed up last night, wasn't she? Drunk as a skunk!" she drawls, shaking her head.

"Something like that, mom."

"Oh well!" she shrugs absently. "Have a good time!"

"Thank you, Mrs. Swanson!" I say sweetly.

"Call me Samantha, sugar!" she coos, giving me a Cover Girl smile.

"Thanks, Samantha!" I correct myself. I really, really adore her.

Chase and I go to separate rooms to get ready for our romantic getaway. I quickly pack an overnight bag in my guest bedroom and rush downstairs to meet him.

"Hey baby." Chase greets me with a kiss as soon as I step off the elevator in the parking garage. I can feel Oscar's curious eyes on us.

"Mr. Chase and Miss Olivia have fun in the Bentley!" Oscar says as he hands Chase the key fob. Oscar secretly gives me a thumbs up and I grin from ear to ear.

"Thanks, dude," Chase says to him, oblivious to our exchange. He places one hand on the small of my back and flashes Oscar the peace sign with his other as we walk to the Bentley section of the parking garage. Chase looks delicious as he places my overnight bag in the hatch of the luxury convertible.

"I haven't driven a British car in a long time. I prefer German engineering myself, but I'm willing to give this one a try," he declares, with the kind of arrogance that only a child of significant affluence could have. He opens the passenger door for me, and I am greeted with the most beautiful interior I have ever seen. It is Chanel lipstick red and the Bentley symbol is beautifully stitched into each headrest. Chase is wearing a baseball cap and a light blue shirt that make his eyes look extra blue. This is the first time I have seen him wearing anything but black. I study his capable hands as he pushes the Start button, specifically the one with the big gold watch on his wrist. The big V12 engine roars to life and I notice that his watch also has a Bentley emblem on it, but I don't quite make the connection.

233

"Hey, look! Your watch matches the steering wheel!" I blurt out, as we wait for the gate to open. I silently kick myself for the nerdy comment.

"This is a Breitling for Bentley, Liv," he informs me. "That's why they match." He grabs a hat off the dashboard.

"Here." He hands me his mom's purple Louisiana State University baseball cap. "I don't want you to get a sunburn." I smile at his thoughtfulness and put it on.

"LSU! Cool!" I marvel, without any cool at all. That's all you could come up with, Liv? I think to myself as I pull the purple cap down to cover my now burning face. I can see him trying not to laugh out of the corner of my eye.

"I'm in a country mood today," Chase says as we wait for the white gate to open. "You know my mom used to be a country singer," he reminds me as he picks a song on his iPhone. He plays "Colder Weather" by Zac Brown Band. The lyrics are sad, and every time Zac Brown sings about Colorado, I feel wretched thinking about Michelle alone in Colorado. I sigh loudly. He reaches for my hand and gives it a gentle kiss.

"Don't worry about Michelle. She'll be fine, babe." I feel hot tears starting to form. "Sorry... sorry.... wrong song," he apologizes. "I'll put on a more fun song."

"Thanks Chase," I reply, wiping my eyes. We settle into the drive to "Dirt Road Anthem" by Jason Aldean. Chase turns off of

Sunset onto Hilgard. He is driving the same route that I take to get to school.

"You're not going to take Sunset to the 1?" I ask curiously. He gives me a relaxed smile.

"Just wanted to take the scenic route."

"Wow! Chase Swanson, you're an anomaly! Not taking the fastest route possible; what kind of Los Angeleno are you?!" I ask jokingly.

"The kind that wants to take my girl on a scenic drive. I've got nothing but time," he says with a wink, which makes me swoon inside. We turn onto Wilshire and slide into bumper to bumper traffic, but Chase just gives me a grin and turns the music up.

"How funny to be blasting country music in Los Angeles!" I shout over the stereo. "It feels so wrong!"

"The West needs some Southern spice, baby!" he shouts back and turns it up even more. He sings to me and I grin admiringly at him. I can feel the curious stares of strangers penetrating the white Bentley. Someone even snaps a photo of us; I pull my LSU hat further down to hide my face. When we finally arrive at Pacific Coast Highway, Chase puts his hand on my leg. His touch sends a ripple of electricity up my spine.

"Hey Liv... you recognize that pier?" he asks coyly as he points to the Santa Monica Pier. "I *might* kiss you on that Ferris Wheel someday."

"I would love that, Chase..." As he kisses my hand, it hits me... I never want to forget this moment. I have never had this connection with anyone before. I'm hyper aware of his every movement, I respond to his every touch, I melt with every glance and every smile. It feels right, all of it. Time is standing still. His scent is mixing with the aroma of California, and I inhale the two intoxicating fragrances deeply. A feeling of hopeful excitement washes over me as we drive with the beach next to us the entire way to the 'Bu.

The blue water shimmers like Chase's eyes as it splashes invitingly against the coastline to my left. *'Malibu: 27 Miles of Scenic Beauty.'* The sign comes into my line of sight and after a couple of turns, Chase slows the big Bentley and pulls into the driveway of a predictably gorgeous beachfront home. Like T.J. would ever have something that wasn't picture perfect. This home instantly feels far more peaceful than the Bel Air mansion. It is airy and sophisticated, modern in design, with endless glass and multiple balconies. If a house could talk, it would promise you tranquility and relaxation. We enter the house through the garage and I follow Chase up the glass staircase to the master bedroom. He drops our bags to the floor and pushes a small button near the door. The tall floor to ceiling glass wall begins to slide away until there is nothing left between us and the large balcony overlooking the ocean. The salt air fills the room, carrying the scent of bougainvillea with it. It is breathtaking. I walk towards the ocean and step out into the sunshine, drawn to the sound of waves crashing gently into the shoreline beneath us. As beautiful as this view is, the most stunning part is the tranquility. It's not like Newport or Hermosa where you are looking at a sea of people and activity the moment you step out the door. This balcony view is for our eyes only. No wonder so many overworked and stressed out people seek refuge in the 'Bu. I close my eyes and breathe in deeply. Chase comes up behind me and wraps his arms around me.

"Hi there," his deep voice whispers in my ear.

"Hi," I whisper back, filled love and excitement. We stand like this for several minutes, both of us silent and hypnotized by the waves. I start to realize just how tired I really am. My body is exhausted. I feel like L.A. has chewed me up and spit me out. I wonder how many people feel like this when they get away from it all. The plush patio lounge chair looks inviting. I reach back and grab Chase's hand to lead him to it. We lay down together and he wraps me up in his strong arms. I feel so warm and protected. My eyes are getting heavy as sleep begins to wash over me. I snuggle into his warm skin and fall asleep quickly. I wake up hours later, facing away from him, still wrapped in his arms. Our bodies are pressed tightly together. This must be what spooning is. I lift his arm off of my body and turn onto my other side to face him. I can't help but stare at him as he sleeps, peacefully intertwined with me. He is absolutely beautiful up close. I study his face, his dark eyelashes that flutter gently as he dreams, his full lips and the stubble that makes his boyish face look rugged and manly. I can't resist, I stroke his face gently. The stubble feels prickly against my hand. He opens his eyes and grins, and his straight white teeth light up the Malibu sky. The sun is setting over the ocean and the clouds look like pink cotton candy. I can't decide where to focus my attention as both are equally beautiful and alluring, but... Chase. Is. Gorgeous. He runs his fingertips through my hair, tugging on it playfully when he gets to the ends.

"You look cute after a nap."

"Thanks," I respond shyly, feeling self conscious. I wonder if I actually look cute, or if I really look like a rabid raccoon. I still haven't been able to get all the eye makeup off from last night. I lay on my back and wipe the corners of my eyes just in case.

"I could get used to this," he says and smiles, looking to the horizon.

"Me too," I say wistfully. If I could freeze time, I would never leave this moment. A pang of melancholy washes over me knowing this could never be my reality. He will eventually leave me. He will go back to his playboy lifestyle, and I will go back to school. We both know on some level that we are playing make believe right now, and that all good things must eventually come to an end.

The 'Bu

Chase pulls out his cell phone, makes one call, and dinner is on its way. It's so effortlessly easy to be a Swanson.

"We are going to be having dinner in the pool tonight. Why don't you get your swimsuit on," he says to me, "I will meet you in the hot tub." He stops at the doorway and gives me a playful, boyish grin. "Oh and Liv," he says. "You don't need your swim cap." I giggle as I remember the flirty exchange we had in the bowling alley. As soon as he shuts the door, I run to the bathroom. The smeared eye makeup situation isn't as bad as I thought. I clean up a little more from the corners of my eyes and pinch my cheeks. R&B music kicks on and the glass house comes to life. The walls reverberate around me like the engines vibrating in his sports cars. My body sways to the music as I apply a coat of waterproof mascara; the pulsating beat promising that everything will be sexy, fun and fast. I can't make out the words the low, sultry voice is singing, but I can feel the bass through the walls. I open my overnight bag and pull out the Beach Bunny black and white bandage swimsuit that Michelle bought me in Newport. It is by far my sexiest bikini. I slip out of my crop top and jean shorts and appraise my nude body in the full length mirror. My skin looks firm and California sun kissed. I run my hands across my flat stomach. I

239

feel ribs and oblique muscles. I turn to the side and push my butt out; it's a perfect S curve.

"You can do this, Liv," I reassure myself in the mirror while applying lip gloss. My nerves are jumping, and I wish I had something to calm them. I bet Chase is already downstairs drinking and smoking a joint. I slip on the swimsuit top and it puts my boobs on alert. They are sitting nice and high, exaggeratedly pushed up by the underwire. Yet another S curve meant to entice.

Michelle is always saying, "You have great tits! My doctor would barely have to do a thing!" I think about the day she barged in on me while I was in the shower - she had been drinking all day. "Liv, will you just admit your tits are fake?!?" she demanded while grabbing them aggressively. I also think about the champagne tub when she squeezed my boobs as if I was a science experiment. She really has no boundaries. Suddenly, I feel uncomfortable. I slip on my swimsuit bottoms and wince at the memory of last night. Michelle's meltdown, her wild vacant stare, her cruel words; I don't know how it is going to be between us now. If she finds out about Chase and I being on this trip together, she will lose her mind. Maybe it won't be so bad, maybe she will come back from Aspen a new woman! I picture her dressed like my hippie roommate, which makes me giggle. OK, so that's not going to happen. All I can do is hope that I'm not caught too badly in the crossfire of the meltdown that will inevitably ensue.

I apply one last layer of gloss and throw on a robe. I feel bold, sexy and confident as I float down the stairs and prance towards the sliding glass doors. Common's enchanting poetry is spilling from the speakers, his melodies seducing the waves just before they crash against the shoreline. The glow of the infinity pool pursues the Malibu night sky as I walk towards the hot tub. I watch Chase bobbing his head to the music and mouthing the words. He looks unbelievably alluring. As he takes a sip from his crystal tumbler of dark liquor and runs his carefree fingers through his silky brown hair, I realize I'm standing before Hollywood royalty. It makes me feel small and insecure. I nervously slip out of my robe and he finally catches sight of me. His eyes sparkle mischievously.

"Nice suit." The boyish grin beneath those dangerous aquamarines shines brighter than the ocean in the sun behind him. That smile,... holy shit. It has the same effect on me that the alcohol is having on him. I feel heat running through my body and it instantly soothes me. I am becoming addicted to his approval of me. I slowly make my way down the steps of the hot tub, attempting to look sexy, even though I don't feel it in front of Chase Swanson. He's 100% unicorn.

He also hasn't taken his eyes off of me. I slide into the water next to him and feel the jets pulsing against my back. The hot liquid makes my skin tingle, or maybe it's him.

"Aren't you going to pull your hair back? You don't want the water to mess it up," he suggests coyly as he lifts it off of my neck and gathers it into a ponytail for me. I nod, mesmerized. I toss my hair into a messy bun and tie it up with the band around my wrist. "You missed a piece," he says, sensually lifting a strand off of my face. He kisses my neck with just the right amount of force and gentleness. I tilt my head back, accepting his lips against my throat. He kisses me softly on the neck and breathes heavily into my ear. His breath feels incredible on my skin as he lightly bites my earlobe. "I remember the first time I laid eyes on you. I wanted to fuck you right then and there," he whispers. "When I heard you were going to be living in my house for the summer, I was stoked." He bites my bottom lip and kisses me forcefully on the mouth, his tongue moving in sync with mine. I moan and he pulls away. "And that blow job you gave me in my Porsche... damn." I bite my lip thinking about that hot liquid in my mouth and how much I liked it. I close my eyes, and he kisses my neck again. "And that dress you were wearing last night. Fuck... just the sight of you in it made my dick hard. I was hard all night. I wanted to fuck you on the balcony. I couldn't stop thinking about you in that dress. That's why I knocked on the door. I wanted to take you to my room and have my way with you." He starts massaging my tits. "Nice... and... hard," he growls.

"Uh huh," I purr. I'm so turned on by his words that I'm starting to wonder if his voice could make me cum.

"This morning was great, but I was being nice. I don't want to be nice anymore. I want you to put on a show for me. Turn around." His voice is low and self-assured. He grabs my waist and his hands glide down my back, eventually making their way to my ass. He cups it and pushes me to where he wants me, facing directly at the jet. At first I feel it on my thigh. "Move a little this way," he says, guiding my body to where he wants me. He finds exactly the right spot and my back arches from the pleasure.

"Ohhh!" I moan as the jet sends endless rippling waves between my legs.

"You've never done this before?" he asks, amused. His hands move from my ass to my tits and he sloppily massages them. He pushes his hardness against me and breathes into my ear.

"No, I've never done this," I reply, but I'm thinking back to that time in high school when I almost did. I was at my friend Gwen's house, we had just finished track practice.

"Liv, let's get in my hot tub! I have something to show you," she said with a naughty grin. We changed into swimsuits and slid into the hot tub. She instructed me to sit next to her. Her hands disappeared beneath the surface for a moment as she removed her bikini bottom. She bit her lip and gave me a look I'll never forget, and then turned around and slowly rode the jet's current to orgasm. Afterwards, she suggested I do it too. I remember feeling very shy and telling her no, but it turned me on so much to watch her moan and swivel her hips into the jet that I went home and

243

tried to masturbate. I touched everywhere but the spot I needed to touch. I think about Michelle teaching me how to masturbate properly and realize how strange and fucked up it is that I'm with her brother, doing the exact same thing right now.

I snap back to reality. Chase is controlling my hips with his hands and pushing them in and out of the jet's delicious turbulence. I am so turned on I could die.

"Mmm... time to watch you cum," he says. All my senses are heightened. I can feel his stubble on my neck, the liquor on his breath. I know the music is still playing, but I can't make anything out. It doesn't even sound like English anymore. The erotic sensations are overwhelming all of my other senses. He has a very firm grip on my ass, and is holding me directly in front of the jet now. I groan as I start to feel the build up.

"Oh my... fuck..." I cry out, "Oh fuck!" My body is letting go with each pulse.

"Yes Liv," he whispers into my ear. The sound of my name on his lips sends me over the edge. "Cum for me, baby." He grips my ass even harder. Electricity courses through my body as the orgasm runs over me.

I hear myself scream; a primal composition of release. My body is shaking and convulsing. When he knows I'm good and done, he spins me around and kisses me. A sloppy kiss filled with promises of naughty, wicked things to come.

Hotel California

The doorbell rings.

"Food's here," he announces while stepping out of the hot tub. "Hopefully this chubby goes away by the time I get to the door!" He looks down and attempts to adjust himself in his swim trunks. I giggle admiringly. A feeling of satisfaction soothes me as I hop up onto the edge of the hot tub, leaving my legs dangling in the water. I lean back and take in the sparkling night sky. I haven't seen this view in ages. The smog over L.A. usually obstructs it, making the stars look more like rusty diamonds; if you can see them at all. Yet another sinister trick by the City of Angels to make you feel extra isolated and alone, I think glumly. Just then I see a shooting star. I sigh, transported back to a memory of my parents sitting together on the porch of our little house.

"Mommy look! A shooting star! Daddy? Did you see it?" I asked, running towards them.

"I did see it! Make a wish, sweetheart," my dad replied, with outstretched arms. I remember closing my eyes as tightly as I could.

"I wish the sickness would leave mommy alone!" My mom ran inside sobbing.

"It'll be alright Livvie Jean," my dad said, hugging me tightly. Suddenly I feel homesick and sad, filled with a melancholy that makes me ache to the core. My poor sweet dad. I think of him crying at my mom's funeral, and of lonely nights where I desperately wanted someone to talk to, so I would pretend to talk to my mom. I remember being unable to get my father's attention at the dinner table. I can still see him sitting there, just staring into space. "DAD!" I shouted at him. I snap back to the present at the sight of Chase walking towards me, a team of waiters trailing behind him.

"Hey, you ok, Liv?" Concern flashes in his eyes.

"Um... yeah," I answer, smiling meekly. I push the memories aside and vow not to think about any of that. Not tonight. Not with Chase.

"Would you care to join me for dinner, Miss Walker?" he asks romantically as he offers an outstretched arm.

"But of course, Mr. Swanson," I reply, grateful to be saved from my trip down memory lane. He pulls me up by the hand, and I follow him to the pool. He gives me a dangerous smile. Oh no, the boyish charm is in full force.

"CANNONBALL!" he yells and jumps in, his knees to his chest. I squeal as the warm water splashes me, and he throws his head back in laughter.

I dive into the water to join him and he splashes me playfully when my head emerges. I splash him back, and we wrestle in the pool like best friends. He grabs me by the waist as if to play some more, but then suddenly, his mood changes. We lock eyes and he slowly pushes me up against the edge of the pool. He holds his gaze for a moment and then leans in to kiss me. My wet lips part and our tongues circle and explore ravenously. I didn't realize how desperate I was for his kiss, or how hungry I am for him. I can't get enough of him. I love the way he tastes. I love the way his body feels pressed against mine. We are sealed in this kiss under the sparkly Malibu stars. The moonlight creates a spellbinding glow in the pool around us and I think to myself, it doesn't get any better than this. Suddenly, a man clears his throat to get our attention, breaking the spell. I jump, surprised. Chase looks irritated at the interruption.

"Ahem... will you be needing anything else this evening, Mr. Swanson?" the man asks hesitantly. I look up and see a waiter, and suddenly remember that we aren't alone. All the platters have been dutifully set down at this point. I was so wrapped up in Chase that I hadn't even noticed.

"Looks great, thanks," Chase murmurs dismissively. The waiter scurries away. Chase dried his hands on a towel and pops a piece of sushi into his mouth. "Mmm, this is delicious!" He picks up a piece of salmon nigiri from the beautifully arranged sushi platter. "Open your mouth," he prompts. I obey and he places it on my tongue. Oh my god he wasn't kidding. It's amazing! By far, the most delicious, decadent piece of fish I have ever tasted.

"It's like butter!" he declares, popping another piece into his mouth. He continues to feed me sushi and I gladly accept each piece. The second tray is filled with an enticing array of truffles and chocolate covered strawberries. The smallest of the platters, I can smell before I see it. A skunk? I think, amused. Nope, no skunk, just a large bud of very crystalized marijuana and a pack of rolling papers. On the final tray is a bottle of pink champagne, resting casually in an expensive looking ice bucket. Chase lifts the dripping bottle, popping the cork with his thumb in one fluid motion. Champagne erupts, running over the veins in his hand. He pauses a moment to let it subside before slowly pouring the pretty liquid into the accompanying flutes. He feeds me chocolate strawberries and truffles. I can taste the champagne on his fingers. We toast to Malibu and to starlight kisses and I can feel myself relaxing a little more deeply with every sip. I study Chase as he rolls a joint. It's surprisingly erotic to watch. His hands expertly manipulate and break the plant, spreading it from the center out to the edges, before rolling it up and twisting it to his satisfaction. He stares back at me as he licks the paper.

"I want to play you a song," he says when he's finished. He wipes his hands on a towel and presses something on an iPad. I know from the first note which song he has picked. The familiar haunting guitar intro from "Hotel California" penetrates the night air. This particular piece of music pierces me on a cellular level. "These are Bowers and Wilkins Nautilus speakers. They'll make you

248

feel like The Eagles are right here, playing for us." I actually wonder if he has ever had a private concert from The Eagles. The thought is preposterous... or maybe it isn't. He lights the joint and takes a long drag, and then closes his eyes. His head sways back and forth to the music as he slowly exhales the smoke into the warm night air. The effect is hauntingly sensual. I have chills running up and down my spine... a little from the music, but mostly from him. He doesn't notice. He looks spellbound, as if the music is putting him in a trance.

"Do you hear the guitars layering on top of each other? 12 strings... that's pure gold right there. Don Felder came up with this guitar lick while he was here in the 'Bu. This place inspires people," he says as he hits the side of the pool twice at the *bom bom* part. I jump in surprise. He grabs my hand and pulls me to him.

"Dance with me," he says. We wrap our arms around one another, pressing our bodies together. We stare into each other's souls as we dance, each liking what we see. The balmy California air and the warm summer water envelopes us like a favorite blanket. I can taste the hormones on his breath mixing with the alcohol and marijuana as he sings along softly, spinning and twirling me, the water splashing wildly around us while we dance under the glittering night sky. He pulls me to him and sings sweetly into my ear. I bite my lip over the lyric he just sang. Is he talking about me; am I his girl with the candle? Am I his emancipation from the confusing and fucked up prison of dysfunction that he lives in? I picture him in Europe on his own and I wonder if he ever felt lonely, or if he was simply relieved to not have to deal with it all.

It feels like I am outside of my body right now, watching this picturesque scene. Looking at the excess and the decadence of it all; extravagant platters filled with drugs and expensive food. Literally, pink champagne on ice. The Malibu dream house, the $250,000 car in the driveway that was selected from the hundreds of millions of dollars of luxury automobiles waiting back in Bel Air. Chase's entire life is catered by self-indulgence and fantastic escapes from reality. I'm just a visitor, a tourist here...

Just Two Plastics Living In A Plastic City

In a pool beneath the shimmering glow of the moon, two beautifully conflicted souls find connection. They are intertwined, each finding comfort and solace within the other, if only for this moment. She is quiet and unassuming, and although she doesn't yet know it, she has been slowly, artfully, imperceptibly painted into the canvas of the California Dream. He on the other hand, has only ever known a life of luxury and ease. The dream within the Dream. Their bodies move effortlessly to the music. The girl drips sexuality, just as she has been taught to do her entire life. The boy, bravado and masculine strength. He never reveals the things that lay hidden just beneath the surface. His feelings, his emotions, his fears; always trying to shatter the walls he has so carefully constructed. When they begin to whisper too loudly, he silences them with sex, drugs and risk. They are a perfect pair, blissfully unaware that they are actually plastic and have been modified, molded and reconstructed; over and over, again and again.

Plasticity: the capacity of an organism to be easily shaped and molded; altered to fit into its environment. Chase and Liv: two plastics living in a plastic city.

The City of Angels has beckoned and enticed since the time of the Gold Rush. She makes alluring promises of wealth, beauty and fame. The lucky ones, the ones who achieve the impossible, are asked to stay. They are adorned with glitter and stardust; the gleam from the silver screen transfixes and they become addicts of the accolades, the admiration; they have no choice but to stay. They smile brilliantly into the voracious carnival of camera flashes as it slowly blinds them. They float from fix to fix with stars in their eyes, increasingly disillusioned but never really understanding why. Only at night, as the sun sets over the Hollywood Hills, will the Angel appear before the lucky ones. It is then that she blows away the sparkles and the glitter to expose the ugly, bitter truth.

"Welcome to Plastic City!" the Angel cackles, "where everything is fake and nothing is as it seems! Once you enter Plastic City, you can never leave! Any attempt at escape is futile! You will always belong to me, to Hollywood....to *us*." The Angel fades away, leaving the lucky ones to their disenchantment, their disillusionment. And suddenly, they don't feel so lucky anymore; the glitter doesn't shine as brightly and the stardust seems dim and rusted now.

They begin to wonder if they accidentally ended up north of the Bay, in the wrong part of California. Are they somehow trapped in Alcatraz, sentenced to a hopeless world of false promises and meaningless lies, steadily rotting and going mad? As time goes on, the plastic prison walls close in around them, an endless din of echoes whispering, *amnesty is never granted*. The dust slowly settles and mingles with the glitter until it is all one and the same. The camera bulbs that once flattered, now blind and disorient. The plastic smiles and lying eyes that once sparkled and beguiled, now encircle and enslave. The luck of the draw is all out of clover, and the formerly stacked decks are now stacked only with jokers. Fame and fortune have become a calamity. Eventually, the silver screen fades to black and the magical gleam from their starlight transforms into a dim flickering twinkle. Plastic City is ruthless, but it doesn't matter; the sun will always set in the West, gold will always charm and mesmerize, and fame and fortune will always be the seductive sirens' song.

Lucky

Chase and I finish eating and down the rest of the champagne. I am feeling deliciously loose and relaxed. He hops out of the pool and I follow suit.

"Lets take a shower," he says. He strips down confidently. His bubble butt looks so cute walking away from me. I glance around nervously, wondering if any neighbors can see us. "Relax, no one cares!" he says, reading my hesitation accurately. He turns the outdoor rain shower on. The cascade of water is running down his perfect body in the most sensuous way. I bite my lip as I watch him close his eyes and run his fingers through his wet hair.

"Come here," he demands. I walk towards him as if I were metal and he was a magnet. "Stand right there. You are so hot Liv... fuck. Take off that swimsuit top." I obey him and remove it. His eyes are glowing intensely. "And now the bottoms." I look him in the eyes and slowly slip them off. I am no longer worried about the neighbors; all I can see is him.

"Come here." He grabs my hips and pulls me to him. Our lips meet. Our tongues dance in anticipation. He spins me around so I'm under the water. His fingertips trace small circles along my neck and breasts and then slowly make their way down my stomach. I feel my breath catch when he reaches my wetness. His finger begins to circle softly, around and around. He is teasing me, avoiding the spot I desperately want him to touch. "I want to taste you again," he says devilishly. He drops to his knees and immediately finds the sweet spot with his tongue. My fingers wrap into his hair. Warm water is running down my naked body as I throw my head back, overwhelmed with pleasure. He is sucking and licking, tortuously slowly. It feels so good it hurts and I try not to scream. I look down at him, and his eyes flicker with naughtiness. He puts his finger in his mouth to wet it and sticks it inside me.

"Oh... oh... SHIT!" The combination of his tongue and finger are too much and I start to feel the familiar build up. It doesn't take long.

"Chase!!" I cry out as I cum hard into his sexy mouth. My pussy tightens and convulses around his finger, covering his hand with my wetness. He stands and kisses me sloppily.

"See how good you taste?" he growls. He reaches under my ass with both hands and lifts me up, wrapping my legs around his waist. "My turn," he says greedily as he pushes me against the wall. He slides me all the way down onto his hard erect cock, literally taking my breath away. I recover, breathing heavily and moaning as he controls me, his hips thrusting rhythmically and powerfully. "Fuck baby... you're perfect, you're all I need," he says as he lightly bites my lip. His tempo begins to increase. I am being shoved harder into the wall with each thrust. He sticks the finger that was just inside me, into my mouth. I wrap my lips around it and suck on it. "Oh fuck Liv!" he groans as he goes over the edge.

"Oh shit! Oh my God! CHASE!" I scream. I feel his cum filling me up with each thrust. He moans and buries his face into my neck as he pulls me in tightly to him, the muscles in his shoulders ripple and tremble as he completely empties inside of me. When he is done, he lets go of my legs, and I feel like an angel falling from the sky.

"That was great... I needed that," he says casually as he massages my boobs. "I like how nipped out you get!" He bites down on a nipple as he says it. "Your boobs are filthy! I should wash them!" he jokes as he squirts soap on my chest and massages them with a wicked smile on his face.

We drunkenly make our way upstairs. Naked and drunk, we fall into the large comfy bed and snuggle under the king sized down comforter together. He rolls over on his back and starts singing while looking at the ceiling and twirling his hand. I giggle at the randomness when I hear the lyrics of the song he's singing.

"Were you just singing 'Lucky' by Britney Spears?" I ask, amused.

"Yeah, I can do whatever I want. I'm the one that wrote it."

"Chase, *you* wrote 'Lucky'??'" I ask in disbelief. "We were just kids when that song came out!"

"Yeah, I was young, my dad had to help with some of it." I study his face and realize he is dead serious.

"Wait...you wrote 'Lucky'?" The song by Britney Spears?" I ask skeptically.

"Yeah," he says offhandedly, like it's not a big deal that he wrote one of the most famous pop songs in history for the Princess of Pop, at oh, about the age of seven.

"Seriously?" I ask. He nods with a silly smile, and then snorts and bursts out laughing.

"Liv, I'm fucking with you! God, you are so gullible! No! I didn't fucking write that song! Max Martin, Rami Yacoub and Alexander Kronlund wrote it!" He is laughing so hard that tears are streaming down his face.

"You jerk!" I shove him. "I totally believed you!"

"I was probably in the studio when Britney recorded it, but come on, I was just a kid! Maybe Max Martin could write that song as a child but not me!" I tilt my head.

"Who?" I ask.

"Livvie, you don't know Max Martin..." he says. I shake my head no. "Do you like pop music?" he asks.

"Yes, of course!"

"Well, you can thank him for most of your favorite pop songs over the last two plus decades. He's ridiculously talented, like fucking brilliant. He's the reason I started writing music," he explains.

"Wow Chase! I had no idea you write! Do you still?"

"Yeah, a little, I'll show you tomorrow. I have to go to the studio, you can come with." I feel the alcohol giving me a false sense of bravery.

"Why did you get sent to military school?" I blurt out. Chase sighs heavily.

"Liv, it's a long story. I don't really want to talk about it."

"Ok, but wasn't it because you were a trouble maker and then you crashed your dad's Ferrari...?" I immediately regret my words.

"Is *that* what Michelle told you?" He rolls his eyes and snatches a white pill from the nightstand. "My sister is a fucking psycho Liv." He pops the pill into his mouth and chews it. "Michelle was the one driving! Not me! I covered for her. I had no idea she was pregnant!" My mouth drops.

"Michelle was pregnant?!" I ask, shocked. He nods as he reaches for another pill off the nightstand.

"Yeah, she lost the baby because of the crash. One of my dad's biggest client's knocked her up. A bunch of gullible fucks believe that Michelle got pregnant at her all-girls boarding school in London," he says, chewing more pills. "The truth is that she was in Bel Air when this pervert came over for a meeting with my dad. That piece of shit took it upon himself to bang my fifteen-year-old little sister afterwards. Fucked up, isn't it?"

"Yeah, that's really fucked up," I reply quietly.

258

"She confessed to me that it was his baby, so I beat the shit out of him. It doesn't look good if you get in a fight with one of your dad's biggest clients - a fight that you instigated - and then you crash his multi-million dollar vintage Ferrari into the living room all in one evening," he says scowling. "That shitbag was married and still fucked my teenage sister. I never told anyone why I did it, because I didn't want his wife and kids to have to find out."

"That's crazy... I'm so sorry, Chase," I whisper as I stroke his face.

"It's okay babe. I was a pretty bad kid. Maybe not bad enough to get sent away and disowned, but I get it. I've had a great life. Don't feel bad for me, I'm one of the lucky ones," he says. He grins sleepily, yawns, and kisses my forehead. His eyelids look heavy as the effects of the pills he just downed takes over.

"Goodnight baby...." he slurs.

"Goodnight Chase." Happiness fills me to the core as he pulls me in close to cuddle. I snuggle in, feeling the warmth from his skin as I melt into the bed with my new favorite Swanson.

The next morning, I wake to the sound of waves crashing into the sand and the pitter patter of light rain against the rooftop. Chase is not in bed. I glance at my phone... 9am. I yawn and shuffle sleepily into the oversized bathroom and slip into the luxurious white robe that is hanging from a hook on the wall. I'm secretly relieved he's not in the room so I'll have time to brush my teeth and throw on a coat of mascara and lip gloss. 'Oh, I woke up like this,' I think and smile slyly at myself in the mirror.

I walk down the glass steps and find Chase sitting at the kitchen table. He looks absolutely delicious wearing nothing but boxers and a messy bed head. I can't wait to run my fingers through that hair. There's an open notebook on the table. His eyes are closed and he looks lost in thought. He has a pen pressed against his lips, and his brow is furrowed with focus. I glance nervously at his notebook. I mostly see scribbles and crossed out words, but I think I can make out a line, "...diamonds through my lucky eyes, not knowing this will be my last goodbye..." He lifts his head and smiles warmly when he sees me, but his eyes are sad.

"Good morning, gorgeous," he says softly and pulls me onto his lap. "Do you want some coffee? There's some from Coffee Bean over there if you want it."

"I'm okay, thank you." My stomach is already jumping with nerves. I don't think I can handle any extra stimulation. The table is full of fresh fruit, toast, waffles and freshly made scrambled eggs.

"Help yourself to whatever. I'll be outside, I just have to finish something."

"Thanks," I say softly. I run my fingers through his hair; it feels amazing to finally get my hands in it. He closes his eyes and smiles. His hair is slightly wet and he smells like the ocean. He smells like California.

"Did you just go swimming?" I ask curiously.

"I just got in from surfing," he explains, "the waves were killer this morning. I needed something to shake my hangover." I wish I had seen him surf. I bet his back muscles looked amazing as he paddled out to catch the waves. I imagine surfing is effortless for him, just like everything else in his world.

"I would've loved to watch you surf!" I blurt out. He grins, the boyish twinkle flickering back on in his eyes.

"Another time, babe." He starts to stand and I instinctively hop off of his lap. "I'll be right back, promise," he says, and gives me a quick kiss. I sigh playfully as he walks away, bending over unnecessarily in my robe to retrieve a plate as I turn my head and flash bedroom eyes his way. He marches right back over with an affectionate grin across his face. "Okay, one more..." he says, cupping my head in his hands as he gives me another delicious kiss.

"One more," I demand. We kiss again and again. He smiles dreamily with his eyes closed.

"Baby, you're perfect," he whispers, his eyes still shut. He pulls away. "But, I have to get some work done before we go." Chase leaves the sliding glass doors open so I can hear the waves crashing along the beach while I attempt to eat breakfast. I haven't really been hungry lately; this incessant state of pleasure and pain I've been in has made it difficult to eat. I'm not interested in food. The only thing I crave is Chase.

I go upstairs, apply my favorite bronzer, and slip into a bright blue sundress and wedges. The bronzer reminds me of this time we were at Michelle's parent's house. We were on the couch in her bedroom. I was watching her play what was apparently quite the intense game of Call of Duty. She was talking shit through her headset to an eleven year old boy from Denver, when suddenly, an excited expression came across her face as if she'd just remembered something important. She sprang up from the couch, yanked off her headset and pushed it at me along with the controller. I stared at the electronics, confused as to what I supposed to do with them.

I could hear the little boy yelling through the headset, "you're going down bitch!" I dropped it on the coffee table like it had a spider on it. Michelle came skipping back towards me holding a Chanel bag. She always likes to keep shopping bags from places she visits so she can use them to wrap gifts. This one said Rue de

Cambon, so I assumed it was from a recent shopping spree in Paris. She stared at me earnestly, her blue eyes wide with concern.

"Livvie, I'm seriously worried about you! You keep putting junk on your skin, you're going to give yourself cancer or something! Here, I got you some products to try!" She shoved the bag at me. It was full of all natural creams and lotions. "Girl, you are going to love the bronzer in there! I have it on right now!" She twirled with the ease of a ballerina. "Isn't my skin pretty?"

"Yes, very!" I always admired her tan sparkly skin.

"I look like a Bond Girl! I would *totally* fuck James Bond... but only Sean Connery and it would have to be in his Aston!" She squealed and started loudly humming the 007 theme song and sliding her back along the wall, while making a finger gun with both hands. She peeked around the corner, pretending to be nervous as she did the sign of the cross, took a deep breath and pointed her finger gun into the other room. "Bang Bang!" she yelled as she shot the bad spy.

Afterwards she suggested in her naughtiest voice that we take one of her dad's Aston's out and drive it to Santa Monica. We blasted the James Bond theme song the entire way there. We rode the rollercoaster at the Santa Monica Pier and I remember being surprised by her astonished expressions. When I asked her about it, she told me it was her first time ever on a rollercoaster. I didn't understand how that could be possible. I remember thinking, *but*

263

Michelle is an L.A. native and the Santa Monica Pier is one of the most iconic things in Los Angeles...

"Haven't you lived in Southern California your whole life?" I asked her, astounded. "How have you never been to the Santa Monica Pier?"

"I don't know," she responded sadly and shrugged her shoulders. She looked uncharacteristically small and dejected as she spoke. "My parents always said it was a dangerous place that was full of peasants... but it's actually not." Sun kissed vanilla ice cream dripped onto her sundress and she didn't even bother to wipe it off. "Thanks for taking me here today Liv, I had such a great time!" She kissed my cheek with her sticky ice cream lips and I dipped a napkin in some water to wipe the ice cream off of her pretty pink dress.

Snow Globe

Chase is out by the pool, sitting under an oversized umbrella. He is looking out towards the horizon and writing meditatively in a notebook. Rain drops are falling softly all around him. He looks serene, and I desperately want to be next to him... I desperately want to be a part of his picturesque world.

"Chase..." I say softly by the door. He turns to face me.

"Damn," he whispers as his eyes take me in. He closes his notebook, stands and walks towards me. I step outside and feel the raindrops tap gently against my skin. "You just got dressed, and I already want to get you naked." He kisses my forehead. "Are you wearing Hawaiian Tropic?" he asks. "You smell good."

"It's just my lotion," I answer and shrug, thankful for the luscious liquid gold on my skin right now.

"You're delicious, baby doll, hottest California girl I've ever seen!" he says as he pulls me in for a rainy embrace. My adoring heart melts. He checks his watch with his arm still around me, his oversized gold Breitling replaced with a square black watch that says B&R on it. The new watch matches the black v-neck shirt that he always wears. He's in soft gray sweatpants, his boxers poking out of the top of them and resting perfectly against his oblique muscles. "We have to get to the studio, I'll have to undress you

265

later." I feel him tracing my body with hungry eyes. I take his hand and we walk together towards the front door. I see through the window that the white Bentley in the driveway is gone, but in its place is a gloss black Audi R8.

"Has that Audi been here the whole time?" I ask.

"Nah," he says, grabbing the key fob out of a basket, "when I saw it was raining, I made a call to have another car brought over here... no need for a convertible today." He strides confidently towards the R8 and we both hop in. Like his Porsche, this car is also a manual. I admire his hands as he throws it in reverse. It is arousing to watch him expertly shift the car, making it growl with each gear change. He drives fast and smooth, just like he makes love. My body fills with sexual desire and I squirm in my seat.

"You alright, there?" he asks and gives me a sideways grin. He messes with his phone and the music of Taylor Swift fills the car.

Tickled by this discovery I ask, "Chase, you like TSwift?"

"I saw Taylor perform at the Formula 1 in Austin, Texas not too long ago. I heard this song and liked it. I complimented her on it afterwards while we were hanging out backstage. She said my boy Max Martin and this other guy Johan Schuster were co-writers on it," he explains with an impressive amount of ease as he tells me another insider story. I would squeal and lose my mind if I got to hang out with Taylor Swift backstage and would be even more star struck than I was the time I squeaked instead of spoke to

266

Emma Watson. He attempts to sing the song in a high pitched voice.

"You sound great, Chase!" I lie.

"This shit is out of my range!" he protests. "You sing, Liv." I sing a line and try not to sound too much like a dying animal.

"You've got pipes!"

"Oh, stop! No I don't!" I giggle.

"No, you really do! Your voice is very clean. It's pretty and soothing, I might need to get you a record deal." He smiles sweetly.

We make our way towards downtown Los Angeles and I slouch in my seat when I see the smog. It makes me wish we were still back in the crystal clear sanctuary of the 'Bu. The security guard smiles and waves as he opens the gate to the studio parking lot. Chase parks in the spot designated for him. 'Reserved for Chase Swanson,' the sign says.

"We're going to go through a back door," he says, pulling a key from his pocket. He unlocks a door, swings it open and motions for me to step inside. As I do, I'm greeted by a rich scent of wood. The floor, walls, and the ceiling are all a dark hardwood. There are three supple leather chairs sitting in front of a panel filled with thousands of buttons and switches; two Apple computer monitors sit on the desk. Speakers of varying sizes hang above the control panel and a large baby blue speaker sits off to the side, on the floor. Behind it all is a rectangular glass pane that allows the production magicians to see the musical talent. I glance through the glass and see a studio microphone, a plush red leather chair, and a black Les Paul guitar sitting on a stand. Chase sits down in one of the chairs in front of the controllers. I sit in the one next to him and turn my chair to face him. His lips are pressed tightly together and his face is unreadable as he holds the notebook in his hand.

"I thought about what song I wanted to play for you today," he finally says. I nod encouragingly and grab his hand. "This is one I started writing while I was living in Europe. I was on a ski trip in Chamonix, France. It was getting close to Christmas, and I knew it was going to be another year of not seeing my family." I can hear a piercing sadness in his voice, and I give his hand a reassuring squeeze. "One of my buddies was supposed to be with us in France, but he decided to go to St. Moritz, Switzerland instead... better powder..." Chase takes a deep breath and furrows his brow.

"My friend..." he begins and his voice breaks slightly. "...died in an avalanche that day." I gasp and put my hand over my mouth.

"Oh my God! Chase! I'm so sorry!" I stammer. I can feel his pain as though it's my own. He closes his eyes, and I see his long dark lashes trembling.

"It broke my fucking heart," he says, struggling to speak. "At this point in my life, my friends were the only family I had. This guy opened his home to me when no one else would. He was from a small town in Italy... he was hilarious, and as authentic as they come." Chase smiles fondly at the memory of his friend. "Liv... Enzo had a family. He had a wife and little kids. They lost their father that day... three days before Christmas," he says. I blink my tears away as I wipe a single tear from Chase's cheek. He clears his throat and shakes off the feelings. "It was just a very somber reminder that life is fragile, that the snow is your friend... until it's not."

"Yeah..." I reply softly.

"On Christmas Eve, my friends and I had an après ski party at Chambre Neuff in Enzo's honor. Afterwards, as I walked back to my chalet, it started snowing. The snow was blanketing me in this quaint French village and it looked like a scene from a snow globe. I was the idiot walking home alone in my clunky ski boots, ruining this picturesque scene for everyone. I pictured a happy, normal family looking at me in a snow globe on their mantel and wondering who I was, and why I was all alone on Christmas day. It made me feel sad and angry. The wind was blowing lightly, making the snowflakes dance around me. They sparkled like diamonds... kind of like your skin right now," he says, awakening from his trance.

He kisses my shoulder and continues, "It's almost as if the snowflakes were dancing just for me, but instead of thinking it was beautiful and nice, it made me mad... like they were taunting me.

'My friend died because of you,' I said to the snowflakes like a drunken fool. 'Fuck you guys. You're just as bad as all the fake

L.A. douchebags and assholes!' When I got back to my place, I pulled out my guitar and notebook and started writing. I hadn't written in years, but I knew I needed to put my anger and sadness somewhere. I haven't finished the song yet, but I want to play you what I have so far."

"Is the song about your friend?" I ask hesitantly.

"No not really. Parts of it maybe. I really don't know yet." He grabs a pair of oversized studio headphones from a stand and hands them to me.

"Here, put these on." I place them on my ears and watch him walk into the recording studio. He puts his own set of headphones on and picks the guitar up from the stand.

"Can you hear me, Liv?" he asks.

"Yep, loud and clear!" I say and give him the thumbs up.

He takes a deep breath and starts strumming the guitar. It's an enchanting, almost Spanish kind of melody; it sounds like a lullaby. He places his lips to the microphone and begins:

In the space between heartbeats
Then the sky comes softly floating down
Shaken and still un-shattered somehow
Too alone to be alone right now
Footsteps vanish leaving only moments of proof
I'm no longer feeling or believing
Seen too many diamonds to turn around now

Who could know this was our final farewell

Runaway crystals deeply buried in dreams
Heartache and loss never stolen by thieves
Love and pain often bear the same fruit
Hyena smiles twinkle and lie but still lead to the truth

Like him, the song isn't bound by ordinary rules. It isn't bubble gum pop hastily manufactured with the sole purpose of making money; it has more depth, more feels. His eyes close and I can feel the transition happening as he belts out the next part.

It's a snow globe world, baby
You're out there somewhere waiting
While I'm still here shit faced debating
And the sun it shines so brightly on you now
Burning shadows into the love we've created
It's so cold yet you're still so amazing to me
Standing there watching over me
Watching, wondering, fading...

His voice is smoky and smooth and I am glued to my seat, completely riveted as I watch him bare his soul to me. I wonder if he wrote some of these lyrics this morning. Am I the one that invaded his crystal world? I feel goose bumps forming on my skin as I contemplate it.

A million plastic smiles and enchanters tricks
Cheshire tears drown out the saddest goodbyes
And the diamonds never stop scheming
Even as rings grow old and wise....

Suddenly, he removes his headphones and sets the guitar back on the stand. He sits down in the red leather chair and his shoulders slump. I quickly remove my headphones and rush into the recording room. He looks up at me with tears in his eyes; my heart shatters.

"Sorry," he mumbles when he sees me entering the room. He wipes his eyes and stares at the floor.

"Chase... no..." I rush to him. "Babe, you don't need to apologize for feeling sad. Losing someone you care about is never easy," I say as softly as I can, as I sit down next to him and stroke his back.

"I miss my friend. He was a good dude. He didn't deserve to die." He crosses his arms and leans back. "It should have been me..."

"No, baby, shhh... don't say that," I whisper as I try not to cry. I stroke his hair to soothe him. "Baby, I'm so sorry you lost your friend, but you have to remember... it wasn't your fault." He nods and visibly softens. The anger and sadness appear to be dissipating from his body as he relaxes into my gentle touch. "I loved the song, Chase. You're amazing... thank you for playing it for me." He puts his arm around me. I kiss his hand and rest my head against him.

"You're welcome, baby. Glad you liked it," he says, kissing my head. As I stare into his sad eyes, I realize that I desperately want to take his pain away. I want to turn his sad green eyes into blue islands of happiness. He places his hands protectively on my cheeks, the tips of his fingers in my hair; he keeps his hands like this for a few beats. It's a protective and loving gesture and I know in that moment that I would do anything for him.

Red Leather

I kiss the stubble on his cheek and I can feel him smile as my lips glide over to his neck. I nibble softly on his earlobe and breathe seductively into his ear.

"I'm going to make it all better, baby," I whisper as I run my fingernails along his stomach, just above his belt line. I can see his stomach rising and falling rapidly as my body language shifts to pure seduction.

"Oh yeah?" he asks tauntingly and stares into my eyes. "What are you going to do?" Suddenly, I have an overwhelming desire to be a bad girl for him, and I know exactly how I'll take his pain away.

"Baby," I whisper, low and sultry. "I want to taste it... all of it," I exhale sexuality as I moan into his ear. "Every. Last. Drop." He looks stunned and I realize that even I'm a little surprised at my lack of inhibitions.

"Fuck..." he mutters, his lust filled eyes flashing with desire. My lips find his lips and they instantly lock. It's a desperate, passionate kiss. It feels like I'm kissing his pain away, and it makes me feel needed and loved. I grind my hips desperately into his lap and he groans. I can feel his hardness pulsing through his pants, aching for my touch. Chase needs a release, an escape, and I will be the one to give it to him. He grips my body with an animal desire and it makes me want to be his toy, his muse, his everything.

He slips the straps of my sundress off of my shoulders and pulls it down to the edge of my very erect nipples, but doesn't completely remove it. I help him pull his shirt off and toss it to the side. I take in his six pack and strong chest, his picture perfect face and his full lips that are currently covered in my gloss. He looks vulnerable and sexy with his messy hair and impassioned eyes. Chase Swanson is an absolute work of art. I can't believe he's mine right now. He kisses me gently all around my neck and breasts. I kiss his mouth and work my way down, kissing each ripple of his abdomen. I stop at his belt line and look up at him seductively through my lashes.

"Oh God, Liv. You are so sweet. You're perfect," he whispers, with a passion I've never heard before in his voice.

"I'm going to show you how bad I want you, Chase," I say and yank at his pants. He eagerly assists me with pulling them down. His beautiful cock springs free from the tight boxers. I stare admiringly at the absolutely perfect rock hard erection pulsating deliciously before me. The tip of it is touching his stomach muscles. I can see his heartbeat in the veins that run along it and there is silky wetness glistening on the head. Crystal clear liquid is leaking slowly from the tip, down the long thick shaft, all the way to his balls.

"Poor baby... you really were turned on!" I say as I begin slowly stroking it with my hand, rubbing the slick wetness all over the rest of the head and shaft.

"Ohhhh!" he moans and leans his head back. "Fuck Liv!" he growls as I begin to stroke it with rhythm. "Every time I think about you it makes my dick so goddamned hard... you're so fucking sexy! I can't get enough of you!" I beam up at him. "I want to see that sexy mouth wrapped around my cock." I run my tongue teasingly up his balls and along his shaft.

"Mmmm delicious," I whisper. He groans and grips the sides of the chair. I reach the head with my tongue and wickedly circle the tip. I maintain eye contact with him the entire time. His radiant green eyes flash wildly.

"Oh, Jesus..." Chase says. "That feels so fucking good!" He starts to aggressively gather my hair but I push his hand away.

"Nope, not this time." I pull my hair into a tight ponytail and tie it up with the band around my wrist. "Keep your hands to yourself, Chase Swanson!" I say bossily with a seductive wink. "You let me do all the work." His expression flickers with a mixture of shock, lust and approval. I part my lips a little as I lower them to his cock. I kiss the tip and pause for a beat as our eyes lock, but then I let the pulsating head part my lips fully before I slide them all the way down to the bottom of his long, thick, glistening shaft. I gag a little but I don't care.

"Ohhhh!" he moans, "Oh fuck yes!" He throws his head back, surrendering to the pleasure. I continue to deep throat him, swallowing the head of his cock over and over until I can feel his heart begin beating faster, then I go in for the kill. I wrap my hand around his shaft just beneath my lips, squeezing his cock lightly between my thumb and index finger. My wet grip chases my wetter lips and warm tongue, up and down his shaft, rotating my hand rhythmically at the same time, just like Michelle taught me to do. As I wait for the finale I keep thinking about how I can't wait to ride him after I swallow his cum. I moan as I think about it, and he responds by thrusting involuntarily into my mouth. I can tell he's desperately fighting the urge to cum, so I slow down a little to make the moment and his pleasure last.

"Oh fuck, Liv!!!!" he cries out. "Keep doing that! Just like that! Oh fuuuck!...." I know he is at the point of no return when his legs start to flex and his moans suddenly get louder. His whole body is shaking and trembling and he's gripping the seat so tightly that I can see veins all over his arms. I begin to suck his cock faster and more aggressively until finally, he goes over the edge. Pulse after pulse of hot liquid shoots down my throat. When it starts to subside, I let the rest of it gather in my mouth so I can swallow it in one big gulp. I give it one final lick and suck for good measure and then lick my lips as his body shudders one last time and relaxes.

"Holy shit…" he says with an extremely satisfied grin on his face. I stand up feeling quite pleased with myself. "You are officially a pro!" he declares and I feel an embarrassing surge of pride. He pulls me to him by my hips and puts his hand up my dress.

"No panties!" he declares greedily. "Good girl!" His experienced fingertip finds the exact spot that needs his touch and he circles it slowly, making me gasp. He looks at me with devious intent and I feel electricity coursing through my body. "You ready to go for a ride?" he asks. I nod eagerly and climb onto his lap. I encourage him with bedroom eyes as he guides his erect cock into me. I slide down onto it and gasp for the second time when I reach the bottom.

I ride up and down slowly at first, swiveling my hips in unhurried, sensual circles. I rock back and forth with it all the way inside me, my wet clit grazing his stomach with every forward grind. I moan and thrust into him a little harder each time.

"Chase!! Oh my God!! This feels so good!!!!" I scream, the sensations quickly overcoming me.

"Yes baby, use my cock to cum!" he hisses. My body has never felt this alive. My eyes are practically rolling back in my head as my pussy tightens around his girth. I whimper and moan and cry out. I am losing all control. The build up feels like it has been going on for hours; it is the most intense and powerful thing I have ever experienced. "I want you to cum all over my dick," Chase says huskily.

"Yes, baby, yes!!!" I scream. He moans and grips my ass tightly. I feel his shaft growing even thicker and harder as he starts to cum again and I finally lose all control. The most intensely exquisite orgasm consumes me completely. For one long moment, we exist only together, in pure, perfect harmony. Time stops and restarts again and I'm resting my head on his chest, still breathing hard.

"That was amazing," he says quietly.

"I know," I reply breathlessly, "incredible..." As I gather myself, I look around and take in the recording studio, I can't help but think about all the famous artists who have graced these walls. Who were their muses? What sort o f pain inspired them to write beautiful poetry that translated into powerful music? The greatest songs ever written have come from one of two things: heartbreak or love.

Chase and I, at this moment, are a love song. If the magic between us was translated into music, it would be a Grammy winning, multi-platinum, number one on the Billboards, hit song.

The 101

We walk together into the lobby of the studio. It's just as beautiful as the recording room, with beautiful red leather couches, dark hardwood floors, and expansive curved ceilings. Hung along the walls are pictures of T.J. with the great artists of yesterday and today. I see him as a young man, smiling proudly with his arms around the members of The Eagles. He looks at ease with everyone in the band. No wonder Chase likes The Eagles so much. In another, T.J. is standing with Lionel Richie, a huge smile across his face which makes his eyes twinkle like Chase's. As time progresses though, the sparkle in his eyes dims and his smile looks more plastic, as if it is painted on. He is in a picture with Drake, looking stiff, overworked and tired. He looks like a shadow of his former self. In some of the very recent pictures, he isn't smiling at all. I get chills looking at his cold and unmoved face in a picture with Nicki Minaj.

"What happened to you T.J.?" I whisper to no one. Chase is talking to the receptionist, a leggy girl who is hardly dressed in revealing black leather. She is wearing dark blue lipstick and has a silver nose ring. The gothic girl hands him some papers and a zip drive while purposely making her cleavage spill over the desk. I triumph as I watch him take the things impassively, oblivious to her flirty smile and silicone breasts splayed across the glass table.

"Liv, you ready?" he asks. Miss Goth receptionist looks me up and down and gives me an icy stare. Her dark lips purse with contempt as she glares. I'm guessing she is another who has fallen ill with Chase fever. I wonder if she saw what happened in the studio, and I don't know why, but some small part of me hopes she did.

'Bitch, he's mine,' I think as I protectively wrap my hand around Chase's. I return her frosty glare, and I can practically hear her hissing as we exit the studio. Chase is walking briskly in front of me and makes firm, precise movements with each step. My narrowed eyes are locked onto him as I think about that gothic girl with the crush on him. I skid to an abrupt halt and cross my arms.

"That girl was certainly flirty with you..." I remark, unable to hide the jealousy in my voice.

"Who?" he asks disinterestedly.

"The gothic girl. Your slutty receptionist!"

"Oh. Tiffany?" he shrugs and arches a brow. "I already fucked her. I thought she was going to be fun and naughty in bed, into S&M and shit, but she wasn't. She wanted candles and romance, and that's not my style." It takes all my focus to regain control of my expressions. It sounds like fucking locker room talk. How inconsiderate to talk to a girl you are sleeping with this way. "I don't make love, I fuck," he declares confidently and spanks my

281

ass. He charges ahead towards the car, and I follow behind him feeling sick to my stomach. We get to the R8 and Chase hops in without opening the passenger door for me like he usually does. I open it myself and collapse into the bucket seat in a confused stupor. I jump when he slams his door shut. He stares mindlessly out the window.

"We have to go back to Bel Air," he finally says without looking at me.

"What? Why?" I ask and bite my lip in trepidation.

"You're expected in Aspen tonight. The Citation is waiting for you at LAX, Michelle needs you." He rolls his eyes and snatches his phone from the center console.

"Aspen?" My face betrays my emotions. "I thought we were going back to Malibu?"

"Liv, you need to help my sister in her healing process. It's required. She wants you to stay for a week. Besides, I have to work tonight, so we would have had to leave Malibu today anyways," he explains dismissively. I stare wide eyed at the man who somehow just transformed into T.J. Swanson.

"I understand..." I'm trying not to cry. His face softens when he notices my bottom lip quivering. I wipe a tear from my cheekbone.

"Cheer up girl, it won't be so bad! The Citation is still a really great airplane!" My eyes widen and I fight the urge to stamp my feet against the R8's custom red floor lining.

"What?" I ask through gritted teeth.

"It's not the biggest of the jets, but you'll still like it!" he declares, giving me a stiff smile as he messes with his phone.

"Chase, are you serious?" I ask, throwing up my hands in disbelief. He cocks his head and gives me a sideways glance as though he just caught me in a lie.

"That's not why you're upset?" he asks flatly, suspicion clouding his voice. I shake my head no and cross my arms angrily. "Then tell me what the fuck your problem is?" I feel like I just got the wind knocked out of me.

"Don't speak to me like that!" I yell and he rolls his eyes. "My fucking problem is that I wanted to spend more time with you in Malibu, you inconsiderate asshole!" I'm shouting through tears now. "You honestly thought I was upset over not being able to take a bigger jet? Like some sort of spoiled brat? I've never even been on a private plane before, Chase! Do you even know me at all?!" He ignores me as he stares at his phone.

"There's a Sig Alert on the 101. I really don't want to deal with traffic..." he yawns indifferently. "I think I'm going to take the helicopter instead," he says.

"Seriously?" I stammer.

"Liv, if you're not comfortable with it, you can take an Uber. I don't really want you to drive my car." Superiority drips from his voice. I step out of the car in a daze. So this must be the real Chase Swanson; the conceited, arrogant, insensitive Chase... the pompous, condescending asshole I was warned about.

"Um... I'll go with you," I reply quietly as I follow him back to the studio.

"Do you have any weed?" he asks with a gleam of devilishness.

"No." This is so ridiculous that I am starting to wonder if Chase is trolling me right now.

"Damn. You should really keep some in your purse for me. I wanted to blaze up a joint on the chopper, do you have any pills?" I shake my head no and gulp.

"That sucks," he says with aloof blue eyes. A shiver runs down my spine. We step back into the cool air of the recording studio. Miss Goth receptionist is gone now. I hated her judgmental eyes and dark lips, and I really hate thinking about her and Chase together. She probably left to go poke holes in a voodoo doll.

I follow him to the elevator. The doors open quickly. The inside of the elevator is covered in pictures of rock stars. "Keep on Loving You" by REO Speedwagon is playing softly through the walls. I watch as he presses the gold button for the 13th floor. He lingers above me and his eyes flicker with excitement. As I try and catch my breath, he places a hand in my hair and leans in to kiss me.

"No!" I protest, pushing him off of me. "You're such an asshole!" He smiles wickedly and pushes me against the wall, my back hitting a picture of Pink Floyd in the process. His lips press heavily against mine and as soon as I taste him, it's all over. I can't resist him. We kiss each other greedily. Our hands are clawing at each others bodies. He yanks my dress down.

"Your nipples are rock hard, baby doll!" he says and sucks on one.

"Are there cameras in here?" I ask nervously.

"Yeah, there are cameras *everywhere*," he says and spreads his hands wide. He flips one off as he continues to kiss me. When the doors open, I quickly adjust my dress. The Los Angeles wind messes his brown silky hair. He runs his fingers through it, and I bite my lip in admiration. I look around for a pilot, but we are the only ones up here.

"You can fly this?" I ask, surprised. He gives me a sly smile in response. Of course he can...

"Ready?" He leads me to a gorgeous silver helicopter sitting on a helipad. As he opens the door for me, the matte black letters: SWAN are now facing away, and SON is what's left on display. How ironic. I step inside and sit down. He climbs in and pulls the seatbelt across my lap, clicking the two straps on either side into the latch. He places a Bose headset over my ears and then one over his. My nerves are jumping as I watch him pushing buttons and flipping switches without hesitation. The helicopter blades above us start spinning, slowly at first but then more rapidly, with greater and greater force. Chase leans his muscular neck to look out the window as he announces what sounds like nonsense into his headset - I can only make out "Bel Air." The butterflies in my stomach move down my body. He pulls back on the lever, and the helicopter lifts off the ground with ease. I can see the bad boy who went to military school right now; he looks like an Air Force pilot. I smile at him with stars in my eyes. He winks coolly at me above a sideways grin.

"Liv! Look at that traffic down there!" he says into his headset and points. I see the claustrophobic bumper to bumper mess that is the 101 and smile, delighted that I am up here with a Hollywood royal and not down there suffering with the mortals. "My dad was trying to pay the government to speed up the construction on the 101 because he was sick of the traffic. They said no, so he bought helicopters instead," he says as he maneuvers the chopper, "it's how he commutes to and from the office now."

"Wow!" I respond into my headset, even though at this point, this should not shock me. Minutes later, I feel myself sigh as we hover above their unwelcoming mansion. It is the same image of it that can be seen online. One of the security guards is in a long golf cart, waiting for us on the ground. He waves up to us, shielding his face as the wind from the descending helicopter buffets the foliage. Once it's safely on the landing pad, Chase shuts the chopper down and unbuckles his seatbelt. He pulls off his headset, and I remove mine as well.

"Did you have fun?" he asks as he leans over to unbuckle me.

"Yes! That was amazing!" I say, still feeling the adrenaline rush from the ride, and from him.

"Someone brought your bag to Bel Air from Malibu, so don't worry about that," he says. He opens my door and I take his hand to get down. "You'd better go pack. The driver is expecting you in an hour to take you to LAX," he says to me as we walk to the golf cart.

"Why can't you drive me to the airport?" I ask him, beginning to feel used and hurt.

"Liv, I told you, I have to work!" he snaps and I flinch. He composes himself. "I will come say goodbye," he says as if correcting himself. I try not to cry as we are driven through the garden and towards the guest house. I get dropped off first.

"Thank you," I mumble to the driver. "Bye Chase," I say. He is distracted by his phone and gives me a half ass, dismissive military salute in response.

"Drive me to the parking garage," he orders the security guard, as he climbs into the front seat of the golf cart.

"10-4, Mr. Swanson," the man says obediently and drives away. The sound of the electric engine humming across the courtyard as Chase and his silver spoon are driven to the parking garage is all I'm left with as I walk dejectedly into the guest house.

287

Miami Blue

I open my empty suitcase and stare blankly. What do people even wear in Colorado? I remember Chase saying something about hiking and yoga, so I pull out some workout clothes and tennis shoes. I finish packing as quickly as possible and throw on an oversized Chicago Blackhawks t-shirt over leggings. I pile my hair into a messy bun and walk outside to the waiting black Range Rover that is idling in the courtyard. I feel like crying from happiness when I see that Chase is actually waiting by the fountain... he stayed true to his word. I wheel my suitcase towards the car and notice that he is holding shopping bags. He places them on the ground and casually flips his baseball cap backwards while smiling brightly at me. I bite my lip again, despite all efforts not to. Damn, he looks good in a backwards hat. Even though he can be a pompous asshole sometimes, the compassionate side of him keeps me coming back for more. I think about how gentle he was with my body and mind as he took my virginity. The sweet memories of Malibu flash brightly in my mind. I can't help it... I run to him.

"Chase, I'm going to miss you," I whimper, all the contempt I felt towards him earlier now gone. I kiss his pouty lips, savoring his addictive taste.

"I know, baby. I would miss me too," he jokes and winks. "Maybe I will make a surprise visit in a couple days. I do need to make a weed run." He looks me up and down and I cringe when I see a look of disapproval cross his face. "You can't fly on our jet dressed like that." The matter-of-fact way in which he says it cuts me like a knife. "Liv, you have to remember that you're representing the Swanson's. Once you get to Aspen, you can dress down, but I would advise you to do so only if you are hiking or you're alone in the Starwood estate. You can't show up to the Caribou Club looking like a slob!" My head drops in shame. Chase is so bossy and controlling! It's infuriating! But at the same time, his brazen audacity and assertiveness make me feel something indescribable. It's kind of like the unconditional love a puppy feels towards its owner. Much like the puppy, my only drive is to please him. I just want him to love me. I crave his approval like a drug and when I fail him, it's devastating. I don't even know how to handle his raw intensity; it's so intimidating. He is simultaneously the deepest breath of fresh air I've ever had, and the shallowest.

"I'm... sorry... I wasn't sure what to wear...." I stammer, feeling red faced and embarrassed.

"You need to change. Lift your arms up," he demands. I look around the courtyard and see a man sitting in the driver seat of the Range Rover.

"But, I don't want to undress here, Chase!" I say anxiously. "There is a man right there!" I point to the car. Chase rolls his eyes.

"Stop being a prude," he says impatiently. "That man has seen it before." I stare into Chase's hypnotic eyes which are shimmering blue like the ocean right now. Much to my horror, I feel my arms rising shamelessly above my head. He pulls the shirt from my body, and I am now standing in the courtyard in only a black bra and leggings. I instinctually slip my tennis shoes off my feet and he yanks my leggings down. I slide them off when they land at my ankles. He reaches into one of the shopping bags and pulls out a couture Chanel little black dress. It's very chic and elegant, straight off the runway.

"Chase, that's gorgeous! Wow! Thank you!" I say, thrilled by his thoughtfulness. He shrugs.

"I called the stylist and told her your sizes. She picked it out," he explains apathetically. "I took the initiative because I knew you wouldn't wear the proper thing tonight."

"Oh..." I say, feeling mortally wounded.

"Put it on," he prompts as he hands me the dress. He watches me intently as I slip it on. His eyes flash with approval and a rush of joy runs through me, like a junkie finally getting a hit. "Much better, babe!" He steps around behind me to zip the dress and I feel his breath on my neck as he does it. I shiver despite the warm California summer air. He reaches into the next bag and tosses me a classic black Chanel purse on a rose gold chain without looking where he is throwing it. I catch it before it hits the ground. I start to place things from my inferior purse into it. Next, he hands me a Jimmy Choo shopping bag. I pull out the shoe box and find a sophisticated pair of gold stilettos adorned with rhinestones. He takes the shoes from my grasp and places them on the concrete. As soon as my feet slide into them, I feel like a Duchess. "One last thing," he says, pulling out a red velvet Cartier box. When the jewelry box opens, I gasp. Displayed in the elegant velvet is a double strand of stark white iridescent pearls.

"Chase!" I feel punch-drunk and weak in the knees. "I don't know if I can accept these gifts..."

"Of course you can," he says evenly, "money is no object." His lips land intoxicatingly on my ear. "You're worth every swipe of my titanium Centurion. If you were mine, I would dress you to my liking and turn you into my little sex doll. I will give you *everything* your pretty heart desires, so long as you are an obedient toy for me to use," he whispers. I lose my breath. He reaches around me from behind, holding the necklace, and fastens the clasp. The pearls adorn my neck beautifully. I look down and admire them. The bottom strand is resting just above the curve of my breasts. He removes the rubber band from my messy bun and my hair tumbles down my bare back in a luxurious cascade. "Such a hot little thing... my little vixen," he murmurs under his breath while brushing out my hair with his fingertips. The feeling of his hands in my hair is exquisite. My body is tingling from my new Cartier pearls all the way to my Jimmy Choo's. The love and adoration I feel for Chase Swanson in this moment is overwhelming. I turn around to face him and stare deeply into his eyes. They remind me of one of Mrs. Swanson's cars, a pretty little Porsche 911 painted Miami Blue. Chase is penetrating my soul with his own intoxicating Miami Blues. A surge of animal heat rushes through my body. It feels as though liquid adrenaline has been injected directly into my bloodstream.

Like the Porsche, he is as dangerous as he is stunning. He leans in for a kiss and I happily accept his lips on my mouth. When I part my lips in anticipation for a make out session, his tongue never meets mine. Instead, I feel the transfer of two small round and pungent pills. I flinch when I taste the bitterness.

"Yuck! What did you just put into my mouth?" I ask as I taste the powder of a pharmaceutical drug.

"Your first time on a private jet might be a little intimidating and I want you to feel comfortable," he says, justifying the violation.

"I need some water!" I announce desperately. He opens the backseat door of the Range Rover for me.

"There is a bottle of water in the cup holder," he says and points to it. I grab it and frantically open the lid to drink it. "Relax Liv. I just gave you a couple of benzos. They aren't going to kill you. Don't be such a nerd, you'll be okay," he says condescendingly as he pats me on the butt and gives me a quick kiss. "See you in Aspen, princess," he promises as he buckles me in.

"Bye Chase..." I mutter, more bitingly than I mean to as he shuts the door. I watch him walk into the house. His arrogant, carefree strut makes me feel foolish and used all over again. I have this sick feeling in my stomach that he was just manipulating me, distracting me with lavish gifts so I wouldn't see his true nature. A strategic move straight out of his womanizer playbook. I feel like I just naively laid all my money down at a sports book in Vegas, knowing full well that I was betting everything I had on the wrong horse and did it anyways. I just gave the biggest player I've ever known, Chase Swanson, all I had... and now he's finished with me. I was simply the flavor of the week, nothing more.

Cloud 9

As we head south on the 405 towards LAX, anxiety penetrates to my core. I'm going to be reunited with Michelle in few short hours. What if she knows about Chase and I being in Malibu together? I stare out the window, holding my new Chanel purse tightly, when I see the giant LAX sign looming up ahead.

"Do I need to go through security?" I ask my driver curiously from the backseat.

"No ma'am," he responds and smiles kindly at me from the rearview mirror. He presses the call button at the gate.

"Tail number, please," the man at the gate requests.

"N113C," the driver reads off of a sheet and the man nods approvingly. The gate opens to reveal the magnificent private jet stables of LAX. We drive slowly onto the tarmac. I look around at the impressive portfolio of sleek aircraft waiting devotedly for their masters. All of them brazenly promising speed, luxury and cachet to the ones fortunate enough to possess them. I know which one is Mr. Swanson's immediately because *SWANSON* is splashed in gold along the side of it. My driver gets out first and walks briskly to open my door. A man is already busy retrieving my luggage from the back of the Range Rover and placing it into the rear of the plane. The front hatch is open and a narrow set of fold out stairs patiently awaits me. I'm welcomed onboard by the co-pilot who takes my hand to assist me as I step into the plane. I glance around nervously and wonder where I am supposed to sit. There are eight empty seats, all upholstered in pristine white leather. The pilot, sensing the fact that I am out of my element, takes a break from his preflight checklist and smiles at me kindly.

"Don't worry about a thing, kiddo, we're expecting a smooth ride. We'll get you to Aspen safe and sound. Why don't you take a seat right there and relax?" he suggests and points to a seat. He reminds me of my dad, and I feel instantly calmed by his presence.

"Thank you, Captain," I say and smile warmly at him. I am starting to feel the effects of the pills Chase gave me. I recline my seat and stare mindlessly out the window. My body feels strangely detached.

The last thing I remember is being pinned to my seat as the plane made a steep ascent out of Los Angeles, the lights of the city becoming one big blur. I dreamt of Chase, of his kisses, his messy hair, his smile... oh God, that smile.... he was in the seat next to me. I straddled him and kissed him hungrily.

"Good evening, Miss Walker," I hear a man say in my dream. My eyes blink heavily as I come to. I look around the empty private jet without comprehending. It takes me a moment to realize where I am and that the pilot is speaking to me through the speakers on the airplane. "We are making our final descent into

Aspen, Colorado. We sincerely hoped you enjoyed your flight with us on Swanson Air. We ask that you sit back, relax, and enjoy a song selected just for you by Mr. Swanson himself." I groan and roll onto my side, covering my face with my hands. Really T.J.? You make your pilots call it Swanson Air and you advertise your music on chartered flights? Did he forget that it's only me on this plane ride, and he doesn't need to impress me, or is this standard protocol?

I sit upright when I hear the first lyric. "Die a Happy Man" by Thomas Rhett is playing through the private jet's top end sound system. I put my hand to my heart as I think of Malibu, the R&B music, the bottle of wine, dancing in the pool; of the amazing night we had together. Tears of happiness are welling up in my eyes. Holy shit... the pilot meant Mr. *Chase* Swanson picked this song for me, not *T.J.* Swanson. The feeling of the plane descending into the Aspen Airport makes my stomach float, but I am too focused on the song to be scared or nervous over the feeling of falling. When Thomas Rhett sings about driving a sports car up the coast of California, I put my hand over my mouth and let out a little squeal.

"Aww!" I exclaim. Chase Swanson is full of surprises! This is such an unexpected and romantic gesture. *Wow! Maybe Chase actually likes me*! I think enthusiastically as we touch down on the runway.

I snap back to reality when I look out the window and see a yellow Ferrari parked on the tarmac. Oh fuck, that's Michelle's car... Chase is Michelle's brother. I can't think of him anymore! I quickly delete any text threads or photos I have with him from my phone as the plane taxis to a stop. I look out the window and stare guiltily at her car. A stunning woman with long jet black hair is leaning casually against the Ferrari..

"Welcome to Aspen, kiddo! Have a good time!" the pilot says to me as I walk woozily up the aisle towards the hatch.

"Thank you, sir," I attempt to say back to him, but the words all blur together. I still feel so strange from the pills. I step out into the crisp, starlit mountain air and start down the stairs. Michelle's face lights up when she sees me. Her blonde hair is now black as night. My mouth drops.

"Liv!! LIV!! Hi baby!!" yells Michelle excitedly. She is wearing a long, tight black halter dress, and her eyes look extra blue in contrast to the crimson red lipstick beneath them. She runs over to me and gives me a huge hug and kiss on the lips, leaving a lot of cherry flavor behind.

"Michelle!!" I say, returning her hug. "Wow! Your hair... it's black!" I run my fingers through it. It feels different than her normal hair. She pulls the wig to the side, and I see her bald head. I gasp.

"I know! Crazy, right?" she squeals and laughs. "Oh my God, I'm so happy you're here! I have so much to tell you! Where to begin?" she purrs as she slips her long legs into the driver's seat of the car. I drop into the passenger seat and shut the lightweight door. The interior is exquisite Italian luxury with its fine stitching and carbon fiber accents. "Dante and I went on a Peyote journey when I first got here. It was incredible and such an eye opening experience! We went hiking, and at the top of the mountain he read me Edgar Allen Poe poems. I tried to dye my hair black to be like The Raven, but I was so fucked up, I must have accidently shaved it! Oops!" She shrugs carelessly. "I had one of my people get me some wigs. They are so fun! I have a pink one!" She giggles. "Pink hair! Can you believe it? Do you like it?"

"I do. You look beautiful, Michelle..." I say and mean it. We are at a stop light and she leans over and kisses me again, but this time her tongue slips into my mouth.

"I love you," she whispers and pulls away. Whoa. Her kiss reminds me of Chase's but a little sweeter and softer. Her lipstick tastes like cherries and vanilla.

"I like that lipstick you're wearing. What is that?" I ask, trying to sound cool about the fact that my best friend just kissed me the way I finished kissing her brother merely hours ago, among many other indecent deeds. She would freak and possibly kill me if she knew that.

"It's a local brand. I am only using natural products and eating raw and vegan. I'm on a cleanse right now. My life is so pure here! I have a raw food chef at the house. She is also a drink

298

mixologist... her drinks will get you fucked up girl! She used to work at a popular restaurant in New York but now she works for me," Michelle says arrogantly as she almost hits a car before making a sharp turn onto Cemetery Lane. The angry driver lays on the horn. "Oh, shut up, peasant!" she yells out the window. I try to disappear into my seat.

She is driving the Ferrari way too fast into a hairpin turn on the twisty road. I anxiously grip my seat, preparing for the inevitable tumble off the side of the mountain, but she quickly pulls up on the hand brake. The sports car growls and skids obediently. She squeals with delight as the car snaps back into the right trajectory. "I've been working on that!" she says and claps wildly. Her aggressive driving is exhilarating yet terrifying. She reaches over and slides her hand up my dress. She deftly moves my panties to the side and starts to rub her finger around. Her bright blue eyes, which look extra blue in contrast to her red lips and raven hair, sparkle with amusement.

"Michelle, can you please focus on the road?" I beg and she laughs and pulls her hand away.

"Whatever you want..." she says seductively as she puts the finger that was just up my dress, into her mouth. She circles her finger around her big red lips as her blue eyes flash wildly. "Delicious..." she purrs. I stare mortified out the window. We get to the gate and she checks in with the guard. After we drive through the gate, we go even further up the mountain road towards what appears to be a lodge at a ski resort.

"Um, is this your house?" I ask, puzzled.

"Duh! Where else would we be?" she giggles. My mouth drops. Her Colorado home is unbelievable, like the love child of the Bel Air mansion and a gigantic log cabin.

"I don't know, like, the ski resort..." I mumble, embarrassed.

"The ski resorts are that way," she says, pointing across the valley. "You're adorable, Liv! Why would we go skiing right now? There's no snow, dummy!" She puts her finger to her lips as if in thought. "Oooh, but we can probably still ski at A-Basin. I'll make a call. Even if they're closed for the season, they'll make an exception for me. We can ski in our bikinis!" she explains with joy in her voice, as she presses the garage door opener on the visor. The huge oak door raises to reveal more of the Swanson's luxury vehicles. These are mostly SUVs, but as promised, there is an exact duplicate of the white Rolls Royce Phantom she drowned in the pool in Bel Air. I wonder if this is the car the Swanson's take to their black tie events in Aspen.

"Look, Liv! The Phantom lives!" she squeals, pointing to it. "The driver picked Dante and I up in it after my hike slash peyote trip gone wrong! I was hallucinating so hard I thought it was the one from Bel Air and totally freaked, but it was so great because Dante totally calmed me down and helped me heal my pain from that night!" She smiles comfortingly at me. I shudder at the thought of that evening. I stare at the impeccable Phantom, amazed at the thought of a bald, drug induced young woman climbing into the back of it along with a handsome Rastafarian after a hike. The dirt from the trek and any remnants of her blonde hair probably got all over the seats of the $450k car, but it's no big deal because it's Swanson World.

A Place Called Aspen

"Michelle, your house is unbelievable!" I say, changing the subject. "I can't wait to see it!"

"Thanks babe! I love it here!" she says as her long legs swing out of the low slung Italian sports car. I hop out and grab my suitcase from the little trunk and follow her into the house. It's even more impressive on the inside than it is on the outside. I'm greeted by expansive arched ceilings crisscrossed with aged timber, weathered barn wood floors, a huge stone fireplace and hearth, and expensive leather couches and cozy blankets for curling up and taking in the impressive views through the oversized glass windows. It screams luxurious Colorado mountain ambiance. Michelle starts to walk towards the staircase and then pauses, her hand resting on the intricate iron railing for a moment. She turns to me.

"Make yourself at home babe. Zoey, my raw chef, will cook you whatever you want for dinner so long as it's vegan and not tainted by heat. Anyways, that drive got me really hot and bothered, so I need to take care of something right now," she says and giggles. "Dante and I have been doing a lot of tantric shit. Oh, and this orgasmic meditation thing. It's incredible! We have a couple of special guests who are also staying at the house. I've been exploring this other side of me, it's helping to channel my sexual energy," she says and her eyes flicker with excitement. "If you're feeling wild, come check it out. We will be upstairs, third bedroom on the right. Just follow the moaning," she says, making eye contact with a mischievous twinkle. She turns promptly and struts up the stairs.

I plop down on a couch and stare out the enormous windows. I can see the outline of the Rocky Mountains under the moonlight. The ridges and jagged edges of the various peaks look stunning, even at night. I pull my phone out as soon as I'm sure Michelle isn't returning, to see if Chase wrote me. I sigh. Nothing from the elusive Mr. Swanson.

"Hey Chase, thanks for the song! That meant a lot. Miss you already." I write and send.

I start aimlessly perusing my social media apps. As I scroll through my Twitter feed, I'm suddenly paralyzed with horror over a post from Us Magazine. It's a picture of Chase with his arm around Sierra Villa, on the red carpet outside of The Beverly Hills Hotel. I see the link to read the article and I feel physically ill.

"Welcome, Miss Walker!" says a woman, snapping me out of my despair. She is dressed in tie-dyed pants and a long loose tunic, and her neck is adorned with colorful beads. "I'm Zoey, Miss Swanson's personal chef and raw food expert. Can I make you anything special for dinner tonight, or will you be okay with the raw, vegan kale Caesar salad? The kale is from the farmer's market. It's locally grown!" she explains enthusiastically.

"Um... the salad sounds great, thank you," I reply, trying to conceal my panic at what I just saw. As soon as she is gone, I frantically unlock my phone and click on the link. My mouth instantly goes dry.

"Sierra Villa Debuts Her Hit Single 'Triangle Vision' At Launch Party." I see the date. The article is from this evening... the event is going on right now. That's what Chase meant when he said he 'had to work.' I scroll down and read print that makes me sick to my stomach.

'Sierra is looking hotter than ever in a custom Alexander McQueen gown as she and beau Chase Swanson, son of renowned music producer T.J. Swanson, arrive at the debut party for her new album.

"I'm so happy I signed with Swanson Music Group! They are the absolute best! Chase is T.J.'s protégé and he's just as brilliant and talented as his father! He's also very easy on the eyes!" says Villa admiringly of Swanson, who have been an item since early June.'

Zoey returns with a tray of drinks. She looks at me with concern flashing in her kind eyes.

"My sweet girl! You look like you've seen a ghost! Are you alright?" she asks as she rushes to my side.

"I.... um, maybe..." I say, feeling speechless.

"Here, my love, try this. I hope these will make you feel better. They are homemade kombuchas. They have been fermenting for a very long time, so don't be surprised if you feel a little transcendental afterwards. It is just the soul of the SCOBY asking you to play. The cleansing properties on these are out of this world. Please, let me watch you enjoy." She gently places her hand on my shoulder. I pick one up and take a sip. It's actually not bad, a little sweet and sour, with a somewhat strange aftertaste.

"I like it. Thank you." I say, still reeling.

"Of course!" she replies, "I will be right back with your salad!" A few minutes later, I'm onto my third kombucha and the anger keeps intensifying. It finally makes me brave enough to text him.

"How is the party? What the fuck Chase?" I write. I quickly erase it when I see Zoey walking towards me with the plate in hand. She sets it down on the table next to me.

"Olivia... I don't mean to be nosy, but... are you having boy troubles?" she probes gently. I nod and try not to cry. "Oh sweetheart! I had a feeling! I am a medium, a psychic. I can sense these things. Would you mind if I did a reading?" she asks.

"Okay, sure," I reply. She takes a seat on the ottoman across from me and stares deeply into my eyes as if staring into my soul. Her intense eye contact is kind of making me uncomfortable. I shyly look away.

"I can see that your pain is caused by a very confused young man," she says gently. "Is that correct?"

"Yes..." I whisper. "It is." She closes her eyes and takes a deep breath.

"It seems you have fallen madly in love with this broken soul... Yes?" she asks. I can feel tears welling up in my eyes.

"I'm... I'm not sure, Zoey..." I say, choked up.

"You are a beautiful and strong girl. I sense that in you. You experienced a great loss and suffered immeasurable pain from it. You are searching for a great love to replace it, but what you don't realize yet is that the love of your life is actually you Olivia! All the love you need is here..." she says, mindfully placing her hand on her heart. "Passion and longing for another human is volatile and fragile, and can quickly change from bliss to sorrow, and sorrow to bliss." she explains as if in a trance, her eyes closed tightly. My skin fills with goose bumps. "Take these experiences with this dark angel and these feelings with you on your journey. Learn from them, but know that they are not all that exist in this world..." I take a deep breath of courage.

"Zoey, does this boy care about me?" I ask quietly. She scans my face astutely.

"Sweetheart, this boy doesn't even care about himself. I'm picking up on dark energy. Poor baby. He lives in a black cloud of self-loathing. A relationship with him will be difficult. It will not be impossible, but it will be challenging. But my dear, if anyone can heal him, it's you."

"Thank you, Zoey," I reply graciously through tears. I adore this quirky and ultra spiritual hippie lady right now. She smiles kindly.

"I will be right back with dessert, sweetheart," she says as she walks out of the room. I jump when my phone dings.

"Send me a pic." Chase's text says. My nerves jump as I unlock my phone.

"What kind of pic?" I write back, even though I know what kind of picture he wants. In a classic 'fuckboy' way, I was just asked to send him a nude during his drunk evening with another girl. I can see the dot dot appearing and disappearing at the bottom indicating he is typing and erasing. My phone dings.

"I'm fucked up," the text says. My stomach is twisting into knots. Does he mean right now or as a person?

"How is the party? How is Sierra??" I bravely write and send. Zoey is back to clear my plate. She hands me a single piece of chocolate.

"Is this dessert?" I ask, disappointed.

"Yes, my dear," Zoey responds. How boring! Poor Michelle, no wonder why she is so skinny! "This is a piece of raw dark chocolate that contains something very special. It contains the beautiful and sacred THC. I would start with half to see how you do," she explains as she hands it to me on a small plate. I so badly want the escape that THC brings me, and so I pop the whole thing in my mouth.

"Wow, you are a brave girl! The THC content in that piece was 20mg! You should feel the effects in thirty minutes to an hour. Do not be alarmed! It is just the marijuana asking you to play. She is a beautiful plant and she means no harm. Namaste and cheers!" she says and walks away.

"Thank you, Zoey. Namaste," I murmur. I wrap myself in the soft cashmere blanket on the couch next to me. My phone dings and I frantically reach for it.

"Chase is at the party I'm at right now.... with Sierra!!" Kelly Rose's text says with about 10 different sad emoticons and broken hearts. I feel like throwing my phone into the fireplace. Fuck Kelly! Fuck Sierra! In fact, fuck Chase! I toss my phone to the end of the couch, thrust my middle finger into the air towards it in an act of defiance and make my way up the grand staircase. As I get to the top of the stairs, I am already starting to feel disoriented and confused. This house is gigantic, with like ten, maybe fifteen rooms. It feels like I keep walking past the same room over and over again, like I'm in The Twilight Zone. I see an open door and hear a man's voice from inside a room. His voice sounds strained and pleading.

"Please, mistress! *Please*! Let me cum! You've been teasing me for hours now! I don't want to be tied up anymore!" I stop dead in my tracks. Whoa. Um... what? The outside of the door is marked *"SNOW BUNNY ROOM"* with a *"Caution"* sign below it. I crack the door open and peek curiously inside. The room is lit with red light and sultry music is playing. I see whips, floggers and x-rated toys on shelves, and then I see Michelle. She is wearing a spiky black choker and her perfect body is covered in a skin tight leather body suit, but her perky breasts and smooth vagina are exposed. She is wearing knee high Christian Louboutin black boots. She looks like an X-rated version of Cat Woman. I have never seen her as bold and as dangerous as she is right now, antagonistically waving a whip over a very attractive and very naked man who is currently tied to a table. He looks like a male model with his chiseled jaw, six pack abs and bright green eyes, which are beautifully contrasted by his dark, untamed hair. "Mistress, may I please have my release??" he begs, his voice sounding strained and urgent.

"NO!" she yells and whips his chest. "Do you want me to put you back in the cock cage?" she asks angrily. He groans.

"No, please, not that!! But mistress, when may I have my release?" he implores.

"When I say you can!" she snaps as she rubs her breasts slowly up and down his body.

"Oh, fuck, please keep doing that...." he says urgently. "You are absolutely exquisite. I worship you!"

"Shut up, sub!" she yells, standing with her hands on her hips in a wide stance in front of him. She pulls out some oil and starts rubbing her exposed breasts with it. She puts her own nipple in her mouth to tease him. He moans from lust and desire.

"Oh fuck! You are so fucking hot, it's ridiculous... please, please let me cum!" he pleads. She squeezes her boobs together and runs her oiled breasts along his shaft. His body starts to shake. "I don't think I can take it any longer..." he says, pained. She grabs the head of his dick and squeezes it hard.

"Not yet...." she says through gritted teeth.

"Aaahhhh!" he screams. "Please mistress Michelle!! Please!!!" he yells. She finally grabs his desperate cock and strokes her oiled hand slowly, expertly, up and down his engorged shaft until I witness an orgasm unlike anything I've ever seen before. His whole body is convulsing, and he is screaming with pleasure. When the trembling finally subsides, he lays his head back and exhales slowly. "Oh Mistress... that was incredible! I held out so much longer than I ever have before! I will never forget the first time you controlled me. I came the second you touched it! Mistress, you are the sexiest woman I have ever laid eyes upon!" he fawns. She smiles, a genuine sparkly Chase-like smile and then deliberately straddles his face. He obediently begins pleasuring her with his tongue and moaning with every lick, "Mmmm, you taste like vanilla!" he exclaims, his voice muffled.

"You like that, sub?" she barks as she rides his face. Her hips are gliding back and forth slowly, her hands firmly laced into his dark locks. His tongue soon finds the magic rhythm and she begins grinding faster and more desperately in response. Her long black hair touches her ass as she throws her head back. "Oh fuuuck! I'm going to cum!" she nearly screams. She arches wildly, her perfectly erect nipples straining towards the ceiling as wave after wave of orgasm crashes through her. When she finally takes a breath, she rewards him by spinning around into 69. Still breathing heavily, she runs her full red lips and glistening wet tongue slowly up and down his throbbing shaft before sliding her experienced mouth over the head of his dick and sucking it all the way down to his large shaved balls. She deep throats his cock repeatedly, again and again, staring into my eyes through her long black lashes as she does it. I might as well be hypnotized; I can't look away. The man's legs start to tremble and he begins breathing rapidly. Michelle is performing like a pro, still staring me in the eyes, and then I hear her let out a whimper as her body starts to shudder. She covers his face with wetness as she climbs towards another orgasm.

"Don't stop licking you little bitch! I need to cum again!" she shrieks. She rides his face desperately now, her hips sliding back and forth over his willing mouth. I watch her back arch again as she screams out in pleasure. He begins to cum without her even touching his throbbing erection. Rope after rope of cum squirts wildly all over his stomach and Michele's tits. I think it has been a solid five minutes of orgasm between the two of them. I don't think I've ever been this horny and the effects of the THC are making it extra pronounced.

Snow Bunny

"Did you enjoy the show?" she asks me when she is finished.

"Er um - yes..." I reply. She unties the man from the table.

"Sub, go clean yourself up.... fucking filthy animal!" she growls and spanks him on the butt with the whip. He smiles a relieved and satisfied smile.

"Yes mistress. Thank you queen!" he says obediently as he walks towards the bathroom. Michelle looks at me and laughs.

"See what I mean? It's just so much fun!" she squeals.

"That was excellent, Michelle! I very much enjoyed the show!" Dante says from a nearby chair as he takes a bong hit. He approaches her, and I can see he is very aroused; his penis is erect and and sticking out above his waistband.

"Oh, poor baby..." she says and strokes it over his pants. He moans and closes his eyes in pleasure. "Do you need some assistance with that? Would you like me to page Marissa?" she asks him in a sultry tone.

"Yes, please!" he says urgently. She walks over to the intercom.

"Marissa. Please report to the Snow Bunny room," she says into it and smiles naughtily. She walks over to me and lingers above me.

"Listen Liv, I know I came on a little strong in the car earlier and I'm sorry for that. I don't want to make you uncomfortable. This is why Dante is helping me channel my sexual energy in a different way so I don't act out like that. I don't want to lose a friend over my behavior. I should warn you, things are about to get a little wild. You are welcome to stay, but I would advise you to go. You are my innocent angel and I just can't corrupt you!"

"It's okay!" I slur and start to giggle for no reason.

"How's that edible treating you?" she asks and raises an eyebrow.

"I feel amazing..." I respond from my self-induced La La Land.

"Good! Glad you are enjoying yourself! I love you! Thank you for being here and for being a good friend," she says keenly. I can't help but feel a pang of guilt as she says it, but the marijuana and the alcohol are numbing my feelings enough for me to feel vindicated in my actions with her brother.

"I love you too, Shells!" I say sweetly. I can hear the twinge of remorse in my own voice but she doesn't appear to notice. She only notices her boy toy. He has appeared out of the bathroom, wearing nothing but a towel. He runs his fingers through his shiny black hair and it looks like a scene out of a modeling shoot. I know I am not brave enough to stay so I regretfully shuffle away.

I'm wandering aimlessly, looking for my bedroom, when I pass a gorgeous petite brunette in the hallway. She is wearing a sexy black French maid outfit that leaves little to the imagination. It displays her stunning curves perfectly. Her long shiny hair glistens under the lights, and huge hazel eyes sparkle at me under blunt cut bangs. She gives me a flirtatious smile as she floats past, her oversized breasts looking extra impressive on her tiny dancer's body, as they spill out of a dress that can hardly contain them. Another gorgeous fantasy person brought to life in Michelle's mad world of erotic indulgence.

"Hey you," she says seductively to me. "Are you coming to the Snow Bunny room? I would love to please you." She grabs my hand and gently runs her fingertips along my palm. "I'm Marissa," she says coyly. Her Chanel Coco Mademoiselle perfume fills my nostrils. I can't stop staring at her, she's a total knock out.

I don't know if I let Marissa take me by the hand and lead me back, or if I wandered in here myself, but somehow I'm back in the Snow Bunny room. I watch Michelle reapplying crimson red lipstick in the mirror.

"Liv! I'm so glad you came back," she says to me from the mirror. "Marissa is a professional. Designed to please!" Marissa is smiling at me, flirting with me, batting her long black lashes from her huge hazel eyes. Is she a sex robot? She can't possibly be real, this girl is a work of art, she is so drop-dead gorgeous! She looks like a Playboy centerfold and I suddenly realize that she probably is. I'm still turned on from watching Michelle and the male model guy. I just need to cum and I don't care how or who does it. I desperately need a release and an escape from the hurricane of Chase that is taking place in my mind.

"Oh.. okay, um, yes please..." I murmur. Michelle claps excitedly. Marissa saunters closer and flashes perfect bedroom eyes at me. She pulls my panties down and drops promptly to her knees. She spreads my wet lips and licks me slowly from the bottom to the top. I moan and throw my head back as she swirls her tongue softly around my clit. Michelle wasn't kidding. Women are better at this than men. Her lips are glossed and pouty, she has a soft and delicate touch and knows exactly how to please me. Her tongue is taking over my world and she is not ignoring any part of me. She is sucking on my clit and twirling it expertly in her mouth.

Michelle watches, fascinated as Marissa slides two fingers into me, still sucking my clit and circling it with her magical tongue. I cry out in pleasure as my body goes over the top and releases powerfully, tingles and electrical bursts rippling from my head to my toes. I shudder and moan uncontrollably, and cum quickly. Michelle grabs the girl's hand.

"Marissa, that was so hot! I loved it!" she says. She leans in and softly kisses Marissa's wet mouth, savoring the kiss for a long moment before their tongues begin to intertwine and explore.

"Liv, you taste amazing!" Michelle says naughtily in the middle of her make out session. She stands and helps Marissa up. She aggressively pulls off her dress. Marissa, the sex goddess, is now wearing just a lace choker and heels. The girl's body is equally as impressive as Michelle's, except she is very petite. Michelle drops to her knees and practically buries her face in Marissa's vagina, licking and sucking with reckless abandon.

Marissa delicately 'ooohs' and 'ahhhhs' and whimpers in ecstasy. She grabs Michelle's hair and pulls her face deeper into her crotch. A nude Dante walks over and she reaches up for his throbbing cock and puts it into her mouth. This is one of the craziest and most exhilarating things I have ever seen in my life. The orgy taking place before my eyes has given me an insatiable need to cum again. I have no choice; I have to satisfy myself. I go over the edge the instant my finger finds my clit. Like Michelle, I'm also multi-orgasmic, I just never knew it until now.

Feeling sexually enlightened and still a little disoriented, I stumble out of the Snow Bunny room. I wander the halls aimlessly in just a t-shirt and panties. I don't even remember changing out of my black Chanel dress. Where the fuck is my room? I finally spot my suitcase in one of the bedrooms, sitting near a California king bed covered in fresh white linens. The bed looks so inviting and I'm so tired and so very stoned. I fall asleep on top of the comforter and wake up to intense sun shining in through a skylight. I look around frantically trying to place where I am or how I got there and I can't remember. I panic, still under the grip of heavy sleep. I see my suitcase and feel calmness soothe me as I regain awareness and dream world morphs into reality. Aspen... Michelle... I think about the Snow Bunny room. I have no idea if that was a dream or if it actually happened. I slowly get up, feeling woozy and heavy. I stare at my black panties and bite my lip with pleasure as I begin to recall everything about last night.

I slip on some pajamas, brush my teeth and wash the makeup off my face from yesterday. I apply the luxurious face lotion that is on the vanity in the bathroom. My skin feels extra dry in Colorado. When I open the bedroom door, I am immediately greeted with music. All the Swanson's homes are set up to live and breathe music; music is their lifeline. The Beatles, "Michelle" reverberates throughout the Aspen home. I walk down the stairs to find a smiling Dante with a joint in hand, and a cloud of smoke filling the living room.

"Good morning, O-livia!" he says cheerfully. I like the way my full name sounds in his Jamaican accent. I've missed hearing people call me Olivia. "Michelle is just finishing up her morning meditation. She is outside, next to the flower bed. Today we are working on self-love. You may join her in her final moments of meditation if you wish. Just do so gently and mindfully," he says. I can't take him seriously. I almost can't even look at him as the image of last night pops in my head.

"Ok, sure." I shrug and head for the back door. I step into the sunshine and it feels like the sun is sitting on top of me, because it kind of is. Most of Colorado sits a mile closer to the sky than California and the altitude is even higher in Aspen. The mountain view from Michelle's backyard is spectacular. "Wow..." I whisper, gently stunned by the beautiful colors and the raw jagged beauty of the Rocky Mountains.

Namaste Space

I spot Michelle by the flower bed, looking picture perfect as usual. The flowers are all different, many vibrant colors, and she is sitting in the grass next to them in lotus position. Her tan, toned legs are escaping her very short black shorts and her slender body is postured perfectly. I watch her toned stomach rise and fall slowly with each breath. She is wearing a black Lulu Lemon sports bra made with twisted fabric that covers her upper back. Her raven black hair is thrown into a messy bun and a colorful scarf is draped around her head. I can't tell if her eyes are closed or just barely open under her Tom Ford 'Samantha' sunglasses. Her pouty lips are adorned with the same red lipstick that she was wearing last night and it occurs to me that she looks like a Hollywood movie star of yesteryear. I don't think I've ever seen someone so effortlessly glamorous. I approach her as quietly and cautiously as I can, but she still sighs with aggravation.

"Liv, can you sit to the right of me?" she snaps bossily. I comply and scoot to her right, and start to sit down. "No, that's not going to work. Can you sit facing me?" I shuffle back in front of her. "Fuck, that's definitely not going to work. I don't mean to be a bitch, but you are really fucking up my namaste space right now. Can you just go?" I hear Dante quickly approaching.

"Michelle! No!" he scolds. "Your words are unkind. You are not spreading love right now, you are spreading hate. Now apologize to your friend and hug her sincerely."

"Ugh, fine. I'm sorry I used hateful words Liv. The light and dark in me honors the light and dark in you. Namaste," she says, sounding like a spoiled child as she gives me a cold half hug. Dante pushes us closer together.

"Tighter embrace. That's right, girls. Feel the love! Love one another. We are all one. The healing power of a hug and human touch is divine. Free love, baby!" he croons as he wraps his arms around both of us. I adore Dante in this moment. Despite what I witnessed last night, his intentions are pure. He has a very calming presence and knowing eyes. If there is such a thing as an after life, his is definitely a soul that has lived a thousand lives. He puts his arms around both of us and guides us inside.

"Are you ready for breakfast, girls?" he asks. "Your green juice and warm lemon water awaits you!"

"Zoey!! JUICE!!" Michelle yells into the kitchen. "NOW!" She snaps her fingers. Dante's brows knit in a frown.

"Michelle, did that feel good in your soul to boss Zoey around like that?" he asks. "Do you think that felt good to Zoey? Let's try that again." He places his hand on the top of her head and closes his eyes.

"Excuse me, Zoey. Would you mind bringing us the juice, please? Thank you so much," Michelle says politely, changing her tone. Wow, this guy is good. We drink our lemon water and green juice in silence at the breakfast nook. Michelle is staring into space and sipping absently. My head is still throbbing. I'm exhausted. After breakfast, I retrieve my phone from the couch, pleasantly surprised that it still has a little battery left.

"I'm kind of hung over... I need to go rest for a bit," I announce, desperate to look at my phone in private. Dante hands me a joint.

"Here you go, love. The magical cure." I thank him and head upstairs. Once I get to my room, I lock the door and slide into bed. I quickly light my joint and anxiously look for texts from Chase. The first one is from 2 AM this morning.

"I had to come to the party babe. Nothing happened. Strictly business." The next text says, *"Liv, come on."* The final one, *"Babeee...!"* My palms grow sweaty as I remember the party and Sierra, his asshole behavior, and yet... I can't resist. I need to hear his voice. I go to the C's in my phone and press "Chase."

"Hey," he answers sleepily after a few rings.

"Did I wake you?" I ask.

"Yeah, but that's okay," he says. "What's up?"

"Not much...." I respond softly. "What are you doing?" I can practically hear his mischievous grin through the phone.

"Just in bed. Wishing you were here next to me," he responds charmingly. I successfully manage to resist his sorcery and muster my courage. I can't let him get away with his shitty behavior.

"Chase, we need to talk," I say assertively. I hear his heavy sigh through the phone.

"Baby, I told you, last night was strictly business. Sierra has nothing on you..." he says. "I only want you." The tender timbre in his voice is making my anger dissipate. I picture his messy bed head and sleepy blue-green eyes and a lightning strike of longing shoots through my body.

"Is your hair messy right now?" I ask coyly.

"Not sure, why don't we switch to FaceTime so you can find out," he says, with a slight hint of naughtiness in his voice. My phone starts to ring a different tone. *"FaceTime call from Chase Swanson"* pops up, I answer it eagerly. He looks so damned cute on my phone screen with his messy hair and twinkling eyes. Chase is definitely my kryptonite.

"Hi princess," he says, and I can't help but flash the biggest grin I think I've ever given anyone. I am filled with so much adoration I could die.

"Hi!" I manage through the grin. "It *is* messy!" I stare at his bed head and desperately wish I could run my fingers through it, but I don't dare tell him that. "Chase, I want you to be here..." I say and exaggeratedly push my bottom lip out in a pout, just like I've seen Michelle do so many times before.

"Me too," he says. "I would do naughty things to you," he promises wickedly and I giggle. "Let me see what you're wearing." He gives me his signature smile – the one that works like a spell, making me obey his every command. I scan my body with the phone to show him my pajamas.

"Nothing sexy..." I say shyly. "What are you wearing?" I ask.

"Birthday suit," he says and shows me.

"Damn..." I whisper. He is staring at me intensely through the screen.

"Take off your clothes. I want to see that sexy body of yours," he demands and I obey. I remove everything but my panties. "Oh, come on! Don't do that to me. Take those off too!" I slide them off as slowly down as I can manage. "Such a bad girl! You're going to get punished for that next time!" he says in response to my torturously slow removal of my undies. "Are you wet?" he asks.

"Yes, very," I say breathlessly.

"Rub your pussy for me and show me," he commands. I place my fingertips on it and move the phone so he can see. "Fuck..." he whispers. He closes in on his throbbing erection and on him stroking it. I let out a soft moan. It feels so much more sensitive than I'm used to; it must be the marijuana. Every fiber of my being is reacting with pleasure.

"I wish you were here. I would let you use me as your toy," I say, surprised by the boldness of my statement.

"Oh fuck! When did you get so naughty?" he asks and gives me a sly smile. The picture is getting muffled and shaky, and I can tell he is having an orgasm. I join him, and his moans send me instantly over the edge. We smile at each other for a brief moment through the phone. "I need to go take a shower. I'm covered in cum..." he says. "Wish you were here to help me clean it off!"

"No! Don't go. Stay on with me... I'm lonely!" I hear myself whine. Liv, get it together, be cool, I scold myself.

"Sorry, princess, gotta go!" he says quickly. He beams with friendly, boyish charm.

"Okay fine, bye," I reply feeling very annoyed. I click the goodbye button and throw my phone to the other side of the bed as a feeling of apathy swallows me whole. I curl up in a ball and melt into the bed. I think about his smile, the way his fingertips feel on my skin, his smell, the way his hand fits in mine like it was made for it. Calmness envelopes over me like a warm summer breeze and I feel my body relax. Man, I've got it bad. I am completely under his spell. He is becoming... no scratch that; he is my favorite thing to think about. Just the thought of him makes me happy and positive about life. I literally crave him like a drug. What did you do to me Chase and how did you do it? I eventually drift off and wake a few hours later to Michelle paging me on the intercom.

"Liv! Oh Liv! Paging Liv!! Get your cute butt down here!" Michelle's voice booms into my room. I reluctantly open my eyes

324

and look around for the intercom. I finally spot it and walk over to it to press the button.

"Be right down," I mumble into it. I pull out a short skirt, tight top and flip flops from my suitcase. Just then my phone dings.

"Come to the St. Regis..." the text from Chase says.

My heart skips a beat.

"What? Where?" I respond.

"The one in Aspen. I'm on the way. Be there in 2 hours. I need to fuck you," he writes back with the purple devil emoticon.

I glower at the text. I wish it said something like, *"I need to see you, I miss you!"* But at this point, I will take what I can get. I'm a fool for him and I know it. I walk down the stairs wishing it was the other way around.

"Hey girrrllll!" Michelle greets me in a fake Southern accent and giggles hysterically. She is wearing a Dolly Parton wig and dancing to country music in cowboy boots and a hat. It is the most authentic version of Michelle I think I've ever seen.

"I love your boots!" I gush, admiring the glittering crystal eagles on them.

"Thanks! I got them in town at Kemo Sabe! Real Swarovski crystals!" she responds brightly.

We get paged for lunch and walk to the table together. Michelle is babbling excitedly about something but my mind is elsewhere. Lunch is a green vegetable soup and raw crackers with cashew cheese. The soup looks like baby food and tastes just as bad as it looks. It is disappointingly bland and boring. I look around for any sort of salt or seasoning on the table but I can't find any.

"Excuse me, Zoey?" I whisper. She walks over to me. "May I please have some salt?" I don't want these beautiful people sitting around the table to think I am some big corn-fed Midwestern girl. My stomach growls as Zoey walks out of the room and I realize I am starving. I don't think I've ever been this hungry in my life. I desperately want a hamburger, or a steak, or some pizza. My dad used to make the best hamburgers, with beef fresh from our farm. I've lost fifteen pounds off of my already small frame since moving to Los Angeles and probably even more lately. Zoey comes back with a jar of pink salt.

"Himalayan pink crystal salt, love," she informs me brightly. I happily dash some into my bland green soup. I pass it to Michelle.

"No thanks," she says unenthusiastically. I doubt any of the other people at the table need it either. I'm sure they are used to this kind of eating. Michelle's beautiful companions from last night have joined us for lunch. Marissa and the male model guy - I have no idea what his name is. I watch them absentmindedly sip their soup in silence and can't help but wonder if I'm sitting at a table with two high priced escorts.

You Don't Own Me

"Liv, I need you to go to the dispensary in town and pick up some weed. We're having a party on Friday and I want to stock the bud bar," Michelle says to me.

"Um, don't you have to be twenty one to buy marijuana?" I ask hesitantly.

"Go visit my friend, he's staying at the Sky hotel," she explains. "His name is Tanner Gold. I'll text you his number. He'll hook it up. The keys to the 'Rari are hanging up over there," she says casually.

"No problem!" I almost squeal, as I grab the red key fob attached to a Fendi keychain. "Wait, what kind of weed should I get?" I ask, still confused as to how this whole legal marijuana thing works.

"Liv, I'm not your fucking babysitter! Figure it out!" she snaps, in a classic Michelle flip to the dark side kind of way. I shrink at her cutting tone.

"Michelle!" Dante reprimands, as if scolding a child. "No..." he whispers and then stares deeply into her eyes.

Seemingly hypnotized, she says, "Sorry, Liv.... just ask for a variety of different strains."

"Okay," I reply softly. "Do you mind if I explore Aspen for a little bit?" I'm trying to sound as casual as possible. "I really want to check out that Kemo Sabe store!" She smiles condescendingly before responding.

"No offense, Liv, but I don't think you can afford a whole lot at Kemo Sabe. Take my Black Card, sweets. It's in a black velvet holder in my snakeskin Ralph Lauren bag over on the couch," she says. "And you can put whatever you want on my tab at Dior."

"Wow Michelle!" I say graciously. "Thank you!"

"No problem!" she replies insincerely. "Well, off to have some fun!" She grabs her beautiful companions by the hands and they disappear up the stairs, presumably to partake in another round of erotic delights in the Snow Bunny S&M room.

As soon as I get into the safe confines of the car. I text Chase, *"I'm coming into town on a marijuana run..."* I write and anxiously await his response.

"You're coming to the St. Regis first, right?" he replies quickly.

"Yeah. Can you help me get the weed?" I ask.

"For sure. Mary Jane is my thing. (sly face emoticon) But first we have business to attend to." My stomach tingles with desire as I press the Start button on the Ferrari. The car emits a low growl as it comes to life; the vibration from the car spreads through every inch of me; I could get used to these luxury cars. I enter the St. Regis into the map on my phone, and a moment later

the beautiful yellow sports car is guiding me to him like a magnet. I could care less about the weed or the dispensary; he is the only drug I want.

I'm having a blast driving down twisty Cemetery Lane in this unbelievably fun car. It is light, nimble and athletic, perfectly constructed for fun and excitement. And dripping with sex appeal... just like Chase. I can't get to the hotel fast enough. I pull into the valet and the engine's snarl echoes angrily within the brick enclosure. Everyone is staring and I wonder insecurely why everyone is looking at me. And then I remember, I'm in a bright yellow and very loud Ferrari. A guy in a polo shirt runs over to open the driver's side door.

"Good afternoon, Miss Swanson," he says without actually looking at me. He takes me in as I step out of the car. "Oh! Sorry about that ma'am. A regular here has the same car! Honest mistake!"

"Is it Michelle?" I ask, but I already know the answer.

"Yeah, exactly! Is she a friend of yours?" he asks curiously.

"Yes... this is her car. I'm just running errands for her," I admit, feeling oddly guilt ridden.

"Oh gotcha! Michelle's brother just arrived at the St. Regis, I assumed she was coming to see him," he says innocently and I feel an overwhelming sense of shame that it's me that's here to see him and not her.

"We will keep the car right out front for you," he says devotedly as he gets into the driver seat.

"Thanks." I mumble as I pull my phone from my purse.

"*I'm here,*" I write.

"*Be right down,*" he responds.

I wait in the lobby near the fireplace for Chase to come get me. I scan the glamorous and swanky room. A woman wearing fur is sitting across from me holding a French Bulldog in her arms. She is cooing and kissing it on the mouth over and over again. It's a bit odd that she is dressed in head to toe fur in the middle of June. There are people sitting at the bar sipping drinks, despite it being early afternoon. Chic couches and leather chairs encircle tables that face a piano. The place screams old money. I go weak in the knees when I see him coming towards me. He's wearing a sports coat and tie and has a huge grin on his face. I assume he dressed up for the private plane ride like he made me do. He looks like a rich East Coast kid right now.

"Hi there!" he says and hugs me. The rush I feel from his touch is unbelievable. I feel like a junky finally getting a hit. He's wearing a spicy cologne and smells amazing.

"Hi," I whisper and give him a kiss. Our mouths part and our tongues meet. With sexual tension and hormones dancing between us, the kiss turns into a full on frenzied make-out session, and then I remember we are standing in the middle of the St. Regis hotel lobby. I pull away and look around embarrassed, but no one seemed to notice or care about our indecent public display of affection. The rules must be different here, like they are in Los Angeles. Aspen, another dreamland catering to the debauchery and indulgences of the super rich.

"Upstairs," he orders, staring lustfully at me with those penetrating eyes. His lips are now covered in my lip gloss and I feel like I've claimed him, which gives me a second rush; another hit of my favorite drug. As we walk in silence past the reception area, I notice a pretty girl at the concierge desk glaring at me with envy in her eyes. I can almost hear her mouth 'bitch.' I subconsciously tighten my grip on Chase's hand.

When we get to the gold elevators, Chase presses the button and pulls me to him. We start to kiss each other again, feverishly and desperately. The elevator doors open and we step inside, kissing even more passionately now that we are alone. He has me pressed against the wall and we are both breathing heavily. I grind my hips into him and he moans into my mouth. The elevator slows and then dings as the doors open. We stumble out into the foyer, the chandelier above casting a beautiful amber light around us. We walk down the hallway together, aware of nothing but our intense lust for one another, until we arrive at a door with no other doors around it. He slides his key card into a reader that says 'Presidential Suite.' Of course he has this room... only the best for Mr. Swanson.

We enter the room and he shoves me against the nearest wall. Our lips lock and our tongues come together in a wet, erotic kiss. It feels like my world is spinning out of control. I'm going mad in my desire and am so lost in my lust and passion for him that I can't even piece together where anything is. I have no idea where the bed is nor do I care. I fumble with his belt buckle with shaking hands and he reaches down and yanks it loose. We pull his pants down together. He lifts my skirt up and pushes my panties to the side.

"Liv, what the fuck? With the panties?" he snaps. "Stop wearing them when you're around me!"

"Sorry..." I mumble. I strip them off and jump up to wrap my legs around his waist. He looks dangerously pleased, as he enters me harder than he ever has before.

"Ohhh... shit!" I whimper. He is already thrusting in and out powerfully, pushing me harder against the wall with each stroke.

"You've been a very bad girl," he growls, biting my neck like a vampire. "I'm going to teach you a lesson." He pulls out and drops my legs. I stare at him with confusion in my eyes. He removes his tie and wraps it around my eyes. "Bend over," he commands as he ties the back of it over my hair. I turn around and obediently bend at the waist, arching my back.

"That's it, such a good girl for me..." he whispers as he runs his fingers along my arched back and wraps his other hand tightly around my neck. He gives me a hard spank on the ass. I wince from

332

the pain but I also like it. It's exhilarating to let him have complete control of me. "You are mine! Do you understand?" he asks sternly as he grabs a fistful of my hair and wraps his hand in it, yanking my head backwards. I gasp. "I asked you a question!"

"Yes, baby!" I stammer, "I'm yours!"

"Yes, sir," he corrects me as he shoves his throbbing erection back inside me. I inhale sharply.

"Yes, sir," I say breathlessly.

"That's right, be a good girl and take this cock. I own you, Liv," he hisses. He gives me another aggressive spank on the butt. I bite my lip from the pain. He thrusts in and out hard and fast, his hand wrapped around my neck. It is honestly the most liberating sexual experience of my life. I moan and arch my back even more. "Oh baby! Yes! You're so fucking sexy!" he says, his voice strained.

"Oh fuck, Chase!" I scream, "Fuck me harder!" He thrusts harder and faster in response. "Baby! Use the tie to choke me!" I suggest, lost in the moment.

"Don't tell me what to do! I'm the one in control right now!" he says and squeezes my neck even harder. He sticks a finger in my mouth and I suck and bite down on it as he orgasms. He moans, breathing heavily as he empties completely inside of me. When he's finished, he abruptly pulls out.

"That was nice," he says dispassionately as if I'm a stranger.

Womanizer

I stand up, my legs feeling wobbly. What just happened? Confused, I follow him into the bathroom to clean up.

"Should we go to the dispensary now?" I ask him from the mirror. "I wanted to check out Aspen a little bit. Michelle told me about this cool store called Kemo Sabe, it's a cowboy store!" He checks his black and rose gold Rolex disinterestedly.

"You don't really have time for that now," he says, "Michelle will know something's up. I had someone get the weed for you. It's in the car." He stares at me from the bathroom mirror with bored blue eyes. "You should probably go," he says dismissively, his tone cockier than usual. I watch his arrogant demeanor as he runs his fingers through his hair and admires himself in the mirror and suddenly, I feel used and stupid. His smug expression makes me want to cry.

"Are you coming to your Aspen house tonight?" I ask, trying to hide my disgust with him.

"Liv, you know I can't do that," he says condescendingly. "I'm going to The Sky Hotel for a pool party. Then, I'm off to Chicago." He gives me a grin from the mirror. I cross my arms and glare at him.

"Oh..." I reply coldly as I think about how he promised me a trip to see my dad, I wonder if he even remembers that. "I thought we were going to Chicago together. Is that not happening anymore?" I ask. He ignores me as he picks up his phone from the bathroom counter. I see on the screen that he has a missed call from Sierra and I feel like I was just shot in the heart. His phone starts vibrating and ringing in his hand.

"I have to take this," he says, sounding preoccupied. He waves goodbye without looking at me as he answers his phone.

"Bye Chase..." I mumble, trying not to cry as I walk towards the door stunned and hurt. I am hoping he will at least open the door for me or walk me downstairs, but he doesn't. I can hear him on the phone when I get to the door.

"No, Sierra! I told you we are not re-mastering that song! It is perfectly fine. Who is the expert? You or me?" I hear him yell into the phone. "That's right, baby! Me! I'm the boss!" I slam the door behind me. He calls her baby too? The anger is filling my body like an out of control wildfire as I walk rapidly down the hall to wait for the elevator, alone.

Fucking. Asshole. I think bitterly as I ride it to the lobby. I stomp angrily through the hotel. I can see the pretty concierge girl smirking at me. She knows exactly what just happened. He will probably fuck her too I think, and another wave of anger rushes over me. I rudely shove some cash towards the valet guy without looking at him. He was so nice to me before, but I am so clouded by my anger that I can't even be cordial. What is happening to me? He looks nervous as he hands me the key fob to the stupid 'Rari. I thought Ferraris were supposed to make people happy? I drive aggressively out of the ritzy brick valet area of the St. Regis, the car clawing at the pavement in response to my angered touch. I am so mad at myself. I have zero self control when it comes to Chase Swanson.

I turn up "Womanizer" by Britney Spears and skid the car around a curve on the mountain road. Chase is the definition of a womanizer. I am just the flavor of the week and convenient for him right now. I think about him and Sierra and about all the girls who will soon be rubbing up against him at the Aspen pool party. It sends a wave of nausea through my body. As I wait for the gate to the Starwood neighborhood to open, I pull out my phone.

"You call Sierra baby too?? WTF?" I bravely write the biting text to Chase. He writes back as the gate opens.

"What are you talking about?" he responds.

"I heard you. And then you don't even have the decency to walk me out! That's fucked up! It's the least you could do after using me!" I write.

My phone dings as I'm pulling into the garage.

"Relax," is all it says. I feel like smashing my phone on the ground. I walk inside to find an empty house. I plop down on the couch feeling used, sore, and upset. Why did I get involved with Chase Swanson? How could I have been so stupid? There is grave

danger in falling for the bad boys, in losing a little bit of yourself to give to them. All I do is give and give to him and to his family, and they treat me like their property. T.J. is blatantly disrespectful, Samantha is in an alcohol and drug induced La La Land, so it is difficult to say if her kindness towards me is even genuine, and Michelle is rude and inconsiderate. What if Chase is the worst combination of all of them?

I hope to God that Blaire Swanson is actually normal, but I honestly don't know if it's possible to come out of the Swanson household unscathed. They are so fucked up. The money and the glitz and glamour has somehow twisted them into shells of human beings, into plastic versions of who they were supposed to be. I am starting to realize that all of the bitter and cliché truths about money are gospel. All that glitters is not gold, money doesn't buy happiness, and like P Diddy and Mase lyricize, "mo' money, mo' problems." It all seems so relevant to me right now.

I think about Pip in *Great Expectations*. He thought that becoming a gentleman would make him happy, but in reality, it made him feel alone, homesick, and sad. The only woman he ever loved was a sick and twisted person who received pleasure from his pain. I think about the part in the book where Estella makes him cry when she first meets him; she is cold and unmoved by his agony. A shiver runs down my spine.

In a world where everything is free and there is nothing left to fight for, apathy consumes and twists the most fortunate into unfeeling, self-indulgent plastics. The arrogance of knowing that they can have anything they want has made their moral compass spin out of control. How could I have been so foolish as to fall for a Swanson? And worst of all, how am I ever going to get over this? There is no one who will ever compare to him. I wrap myself despondently in a blanket and stare out the window, trying to keep my face as stony and still as the Rocky Mountains.

The Phone Bomb

The following days are a blur. The days blend into the nights and the loneliness and hurt stick to me like glue. Every day is the same day. Michelle and I do yoga and meditate, we eat raw food, indulge in spa treatments, and get driven around Aspen in the Rolls Royce by her driver. We finally mixed it up yesterday and went on a hike in an area called Maroon Bells. It was incredible! The air was thin at that altitude, but the beauty of the mountains made me forget about how hard I was breathing. Michelle and I took pictures on her pink polaroid camera with a beautiful alpine lake behind us because Dante had taken our phones for the week. And yes, of course we climbed back into the Rolls, mud, sweat and all after the hike, because... Swanson World.

I have no idea if Chase has written or called; and not knowing is not making it any easier. Each day that passes takes me further away from the sweet memories of him and I together, so I try to focus only on the present. Nothing more has happened in the Snow Bunny room. Dante thinks that Michelle is cured of her sexual addiction, for the moment at least. She has been working hard on expressing her sexual energy in healthier ways. She really is acting more and more normal by the day. I on the other hand, am slipping into an emotional abyss of pain and anger. It's almost like we are switching places. We haven't discussed her meltdown at the party, or anything about Chase and I. Dante says she isn't ready for that and I don't think I am either. Sunday is the day that we will have to sit down face to face to discuss the drama, in our 'truth therapy session.' I am dreading it. I go back to Los Angeles on Monday morning, but I wish I was leaving right after the 'truth session.' Michelle is not going to like the truth.

It takes every ounce of my willpower not to think about Chase Swanson 24/7. It doesn't help that I'm spending all my time with his sister. Michelle's eyes twinkle just like his when she smiles, she makes the same facial expressions, and worst of all, she has his casually cruel attitude with hints of sweetness that keep you coming back for more. I cry sometimes when I think about Chase's eyes, because no matter what his mood or eye color is in that moment, they are always passionate when he looks at me. I guess I would consider myself lucky, if he wasn't so dangerous. I did not want to be his next victim, but somewhere along the way, I got swept up in it all. I got swept up in *him*.

Today is the day we celebrate Michelle's successful week of cleansing and "sobriety." We took the Rolls into town and rode the gondola to the top of Aspen. Michelle seemed uncharacteristically sad and pensive as we took in the spectacular view of the mountains across from us.

"I have a lot of really good memories here..." she whispered and looked as if she might cry. "Liv, will you come ski with me this winter?" she asked.

"I will have to learn, but yes, I would love that!" I replied, hoping it would lift her spirits.

"We can start you off over at Buttermilk. There aren't any green runs here on Ajax. Plus, we can go over to Aspen Highlands afterwards. There is a restaurant and bar at the top called Cloud 9, that will literally put you on Cloud 9!" she explained enthusiastically. Successfully cheered up, Michelle insisted we take the gondola back down and go to Prada to buy matching bags. Afterwards, she helped me pick a suede skirt from Ralph Lauren and a tight, white top from Alexander Wang that zips up the front, to wear to the party tonight. She thanked me for being with her all week and gave me a huge hug. We have the top down and the sun feels splendid against my skin. The clean and crisp Colorado air is heavenly. I am going to miss it when I am back to the land of smog.

"Great job this week, girls, here are your phones," Dante says, handing them to us from the front seat of the Phantom.

"Thanks," I mumble nervously as I take it. My phone is dead so I won't have to check it next to Michelle, but I doubt she would even notice. She is already scrolling, texting and posting like a junkie who desperately needed a hit. We continue like this up Cemetery Lane for the next few miles.

When we get to the Starwood gate, I am surprised to see that there is a line to get in. Michelle's party has already started. The hostess, Miss Swanson, is fashionably late per usual. When we enter their Aspen mansion, I am greeted by a cloud of marijuana smoke and an oversized living room full of carefree, happy people. They are chatting animatedly, holding drinks and passing around a variety of pipes, bongs and joints, bowls of pills and little platters of cocaine. I'm still in my sweats so I quickly make my way upstairs to get ready for the party. I plug my phone into the charger next to my bed, and step into the bathroom to put my makeup on, anxiously glancing back at my phone in the mirror as if it were a bomb about to go off. When I finally see the Apple symbol appear on the screen, I practically dive for it. I type in my password and wait. My face falls... nothing, absolutely nothing. The last text from Chase is the one that says, *"Relax."* There are no missed calls, no new texts, no new anything... my worst fear has been confirmed. Chase Swanson has officially ghosted. I feel my eyes welling up with tears.

"FUCKING ASSHOLE!" I shout at the phone between sobs and throw it at a pillow. I stomp back to the bathroom, pick up a glass and throw the water at my reflection in the mirror. "You are so stupid, Olivia!" I shout through the tears. I stomp back to the phone and pick it up. Filled with rage, I run to the balcony and throw the phone as far as I can. The sound of it shattering against the pavement fills me with a sense of satisfaction. I think about how confused I was by Michelle throwing the expensive bottle of champagne off the balcony; I get it now.

"Bye Chase...." I say and close the door.

Ice Princess, Ballerina

"There you are!" Michelle shrieks when she sees me coming down the grand staircase. She taps her champagne glass loudly with a knife. "Everyone! This is Liv! She is my best friend, so everyone be nice to her!" she yells at the party guests. "And, Liv, this is... everyone," she says, gesturing with her hands. Introductions accomplished, she walks away from me to talk to someone else. Michelle is wearing a white corset with black sequins and a puffy white skirt that almost looks like a tutu, and a platinum blonde wig, her natural hair color, which she has pinned up in a tight bun. Her pouty mouth is enhanced with hot pink lipstick. She looks eerily like a ballerina as she prances gracefully around the party, from one group of guests to another. I sigh when I see her giggling with Paris Hilton and dancing to Paris' song "Nothing In This World." They look like a dream team from the silver screen, and I suddenly feel unworthy. That is the kind of friend Michelle should have, not some nobody who fucked her brother behind her back.

As I socialize with the party goers throughout the night, I realize that Aspen is filled with an eclectic blend of people from all walks of life. Locals and transplants, new money and old money, professional skiers and snowboarders in Burton and North Face attire, and of course, preppy trust funders from the South who remind me of Hunter the fucked up Southern Prince. The last group in particular, are instantly recognizable. Predictably clad in polo shirts and khakis, with names like Prescott and Foster, all smiling at you from under what Michelle calls "fox hunt bangs." I have conversations with celebrities, because they will actually talk to you here, with wealthy older men who haven't quite given up the party lifestyle yet, with their exceedingly confident and over-privileged sons, and with a variety of fantastically well heeled South Americans, Mexicans, Russians, Arabs, etc. It is quite the peculiar blend of human beings.

Suddenly, the room erupts in cheers and celebration as Bob Marley's voice comes over the speakers. He sings melodically about the government and ganja in his soothing Jamaican accent. Everyone applauds enthusiastically. The cloud of marijuana smoke in the room begins shimmering and thickening in approval.

Michelle looks authentically happy as she dances to the high energy Montmartre remix of Bob Marley's famous song, "Is This Love." Her white ballerina skirt is bouncing and twirling in sync to the rhythm of the music. Her body moves a lot like her brother's when she dances. I think about slow dancing with him in the ballroom under the magical chandelier to "Imagine," and my girl brain puts him in a tuxedo and me in a wedding dress. I sigh wistfully. Bob Marley croons romantically about love and I feel like

I could cry again. I will never know if it was love, Bob, I will never be lucky enough to know.

I drag myself over to the bud bar and take a hit off of a joint. A group of rich kids are singing karaoke to "Don't Stop Believin'" on the stage nearby. I feel a sense of bitterness wash over me, like they are mocking me, mocking every small town girl. I know it's completely irrational, because no one here knows anything about me. I blend in perfectly in my short suede skirt, cleavage revealing top, and knee high Chanel boots, but I can't shake the feeling that I don't belong. I march out of the room towards the real bar, the one with liquor behind it.

"Can I have a Fireball shot?" I ask the bartender.

"Um, we don't have that. We have a single malt scotch, The Macallan, aged 30 years, which I'm guessing is much older than you," he says with a friendly smile as he pours some over a single large ice cube.

"Whatever," I mumble and toss it down my throat. The bartender gives me a horrified look.

"Miss, that drink was for sipping! This is a $4,000 bottle of scotch! It is very rare. You should enjoy it as you slowly sip and observe how the flavor changes as the ice melts," he explains with wide, appalled eyes.

"You're not the boss of me!" I retort. "I will have another," I demand. He mutters something under his breath and shakes his head as he pours me a second. "Look at me sip!" I say sarcastically as I take an exaggeratedly delicate sip. "Is that to your liking, Mr. Bartender?" I ask mockingly. I hear a man chuckle behind me. Chase? I spin around, disappointed when it isn't him.

"I love a bossy American girl! It ees very sexy!" the stranger says to me in a thick French accent. He is about my size and has an attractive face.

"Oh yeah?" I ask, meeting his flirtatious tone.

"I am Dash Deschamps," he says formally and holds his hand out.

"I'm Liv. Nice to meet you," I say, extending my hand.

"The pleasure is all mine," he charms and kisses my hand.

"Are you here with anyone?" he asks.

"Nope," I respond and take another swig of my drink.

"How is this possible? A beautiful treasure like you has the boys going crazy!" he says, doubling down on the flirtatiousness. "If I saw you at one of my races. I would say for you to be le flag girl!"

"Are you a race car driver?" I ask. He scoffs.

"I am Dash Deschamps, I own the team," he explains and rolls his eyes at my ignorance.

"I'm sorry!" I say through playful giggles. He smiles at me but there is something in his smile that makes me feel uneasy.

"I will forgive you, but you must come to Monaco with me sometime. We can stay on my yacht!" he says.

"Okay, yeah, that would be fun," I reply carelessly and shrug.

"Please, is it possible to get you a drink?" he asks smoothly in his French accent as I finish my scotch.

"Sure!" I respond and bat my lashes. I am about to be wine and dined by a French guy! Ooh la la! What was his name? Champ? Dish? Whatever, I don't really care, I just want someone to help me forget about Chase Swanson for the evening. As I stand and wait for my drink from the Frenchman, I start to feel bad that I had such an attitude with the bartender. Perhaps I should go apologize to him. I am not sure where this temper is coming from lately.

Dash or Cash Champ or whatever is walking towards me with a drink in hand, a glass of champagne of course. I half listen to him tell me about the champagne and where it is from and how angry it makes him when Americans think they are the makers of champagne.

"It is le French who make the Champagne, the Italians make the cheap Prosecco, Spaniards make Cava, and Americans make the sparkling wine. There can only be one Champagne. Just like there can only be one Dash!" he says arrogantly. "Do you like it?" he asks. I nod halfheartedly as I down it. He smiles strangely at me. I feel uncomfortable around him, but I don't know why, so I ignore the feeling and fake a bright smile. I am still having trouble deciphering between disingenuous and authentic people. It is all one big mind fuck. The conversation with him is forced and awkward, not at all like the rapport I have with Chase. I have this strong urge to smack the smug look off his face, but I am getting too woozy to even make out his features anymore. I am starting to feel super disoriented and dizzy.

"Do you need to sit down?" he asks as he steadies me. "Please, follow me," he says, linking his arm in mine. A feeling of apprehension hits me as he leads me to a porch swing far away from the rest of the party goers.

"No. I want to be in the party...." I slur as I plop down. He ignores me and sits next to me on the swing. He has an oddly firm grip on my arm.

"You are very pretty, Liz," he says, stroking my face. I recoil from his touch.

"It's Liv!" I shout. He puts his mouth against mine, forcefully, and shoves his hand up my skirt. "No!" I yell and push his hand off of me. He tries again, but this time he grabs me by the neck. "STOP!!" I yell louder, hoping someone from inside will hear me. He puts his hand over my mouth.

"Shhh. Most women would kill to have a chance weeth Dash," he says. I try and move his hand away from my mouth, but I am too faint and confused to even figure out where his hands are or what he is doing. Through my blurry eyes, I see someone grab the man's hands off of me. I squint in confusion; is that a ballerina? I watch her slip her heels off. She tosses them to the side. The

349

mysterious ballerina removes her dangly earrings. She hands them to Paris Hilton.

"She said no!" the ballerina snaps coldly. "You don't know the word 'no' in your country?" she asks the man who is violating me.

"No," he responds pompously. The ballerina slaps him. Everyone around her gasps. He looks stunned and holds his face. "Snooty American bitch. This is why I hate Americans! No class," he hisses at her. She glares at him.

"America is the only reason you aren't speaking German right now you fucking asshole," she hisses. I hear a ripple of 'ooohs' and 'ahhhs' over her witty comeback.

"'Merica" shouts one of the Southern boys and the girl next to him hoots. The ballerina turns to me, and then I remember... Michelle... Michelle is the ballerina.

"Liv, you don't look so good. Are you alright?" she asks, concern flashing in her big blue eyes. I mumble incoherently and almost fall out of the porch swing. Her eyes turn to a frosty blue. The ballerina has transformed into the Ice Princess.

"Did you put something in her drink?" Michelle asks him through gritted teeth. He stands but doesn't respond. She grabs him by the shirt and gets in his face. "You fucking creep!" she yells. Everyone gasps when he spits in her face. Time stands still for a moment. "Motherfucker," she hisses. There's a blur of motion and then the swing jerks violently, nearly unseating me. It takes me a moment to realize that the ballerina ice princess has kicked him in the head with such shocking speed that he has been knocked backwards onto the swing. She immediately yanks him back off of it by his hair. He staggers forward, holding his mouth with both hands, bleeding, and squealing in French. She is quite a bit taller, and apparently stronger than he is. Even though she's thin, Michelle is exceptionally athletic. The veins in her forearms are popping as she drags him towards the pool, still gripping him by the hair. When they get there, she allows him to stand up straight just long enough to knee him as hard as she can in the balls. He shrieks and doubles over in pain. She takes a long step back and promptly soccer kicks him in the face, which sends him flying backwards into the pool. Even in my fog, I remember that she's friends with Donald Cerrone, the famous UFC fighter. He probably taught her how to do all of that. "How's it feel now asshole?!?" she asks when his bloodied head emerges. The backyard erupts in claps and cheers. She turns back to the crowd and does a graceful ballerina bow. "Thank you very much!" she says. "Now, get this fucking rapist out of my party!" she yells to her security detail. Everyone applauds as the two large security guards jump in the water and drag Dash roughly from the pool. A third man pins the Frenchman's wrist behind his back as they escort him away. Paris Hilton hands Michelle her earrings with a smile of admiration. At the same time, one of the ridiculously good looking Southern boys kneels and puts her heels back on her feet.

351

"You're a goddess!" he gushes in his Southern drawl.

"Thanks, doll," she responds. She saunters over to me as though she's floating.

"Liv, let's get you to bed."

"Ok. Michelle…. ballerina ice…. Princess. Wow," I mumble unintelligibly. "Thank you for my rescue!" I can hear myself slurring as Dante scoops me up. He carries me upstairs in his arms as if I'm an Aztec princess.

"Are you an angel?" I ask the ballerina ice princess who is gliding up the stairs in front of me in her sparkly heels. She giggles and tucks a strand of blonde hair behind her ear.
The last thing I remember is the strong ballerina stroking my hair soothingly in bed.

"Nooo..." I groan, holding my head. I have never had a hangover like this in my life. I look around through slits of bloodshot eyes, desperate for water. I see a glass on the nightstand, next to some pills and a can of coconut water. I swallow the pills without knowing or caring what they are, and as much of the coconut water as I can manage and then crawl back under the covers to die.

I have no idea how much time has passed when I finally wake up. I get out of bed against my will and make my way groggily down the hallway and then the stairs. All remnants from last night's party have vanished; the house has been magically restored to a pristine condition.

Michelle is sitting alone on a couch near the fireplace. A fire is burning in spite of the warm summer air outside. Her eyes are closed and her head is swaying softly to the rhythm of "Amber" by 311. She looks just like her brother right now. They must feel music in the same way, I think as I admire her from the staircase. She looks stunning and regal in a flowing dark purple print Roberto Cavalli dress. Princess Michelle, adorned in purple, the color of royalty. No, scratch that... Queen Michelle. The black wig is back and beneath it she is wearing purple lipstick that matches the dress. When she sees me, her face lights up.

"Good morning, doll!" she says cheerfully. I rub my sleepy eyes and walk over to her, and crumble next to her on the couch. "How are you feeling?" she asks.

"Horrible," I groan as I hold my throbbing head.

"Liv, do you remember what happened last night?" I close my eyes and try and jog my memory. It is coming back to me in bits and pieces, in hazy flashes. Dash. Feeling scared. Michelle punching him.

"Yes! You beat up a French guy! Holy shit! Michelle, you're a badass!" I stare admiringly. She grins and shrugs.

"Fuck that guy! I can't believe he told you he owned a Formula 1 team, what a fucking liar! And, he was planning on doing bad things to you. We're lucky someone heard you yelling!"

"Thanks for rescuing me! You're a rock star, Michelle Swanson!" I do a bow down motion to her, ignoring the pounding in my head.

"Girl! Stop it! You're going to make me blush!" she replies, giggling. She pauses and stares intently at me with a sparkle in her eyes.

"Liv, did you know that your energy is amber?" she asks. "This song reminds me of you... I mean, you have those amazing amber eyes and you have the kindest soul. Your heart is as gold as your eyes." I smile but sigh on the inside, thinking about how

354

Chase gave me the exact same compliment. I don't feel right accepting her undying praise. I have to tell her the whole truth, I have to tell her about how I lied to her, about what I did with her brother. I inhale sharply.

"Michelle, I have to tell you something..."

She holds her hand up to stop me. "I already know, you confessed everything last night when I tucked you in." I stiffen but she smiles softly. "I understand. I get it. All I've ever wanted is for you to be happy. That's why I molded you, that's why I was hard on you. It came from a place of love, Liv. I know my love is a little twisted and perverse babe... I'm fucked up." Her lip starts to quiver.

"No, no, hey... don't cry. You're not fucked up, Michelle. You're just a victim of your circumstances. I've always seen the good in you," I gently squeeze her hand and wipe the tears from her face. She squeezes my hand back and looks at me intensely.

"Liv, my brother is waiting for you in Chicago. You need to go to him."

"Really?" I ask dreamily.

"Yes... He promised you a trip to see your dad after giving you the first edition of *Great Expectations* as a gift, right?" She gives me a knowing smile.

"Wait, you knew the whole time?" I ask, perplexed. "About everything?"

"I knew about the gift because I saw it on the security camera footage. After you told me the rest of the story, I called my brother and yelled at him for being a dick. I even made him cry a little bit. He feels really bad about the way he treated you. Chase is really, REALLY into you! I don't think I've ever seen him this smitten with anyone! I know my brother, and I think he got spooked over his feelings for you, so he pushed you away before you could push him away." I feel a strangely familiar sensation, and I realize that it's a glimmer of hope.

"Michelle, I like him so much... I think I might be in love with him," I say it so softly that its barely a whisper. "I can't get over him. I miss him...." I can't believe I *finally* admitted it to my best friend. I look to her to read her reaction but she is staring vacantly into space. Her eyelashes flutter and her eyes suddenly widen like she is having some sort of grand epiphany.

"Miss Havisham!" she blurts out, her blue eyes electric with recognition.

"What?" I ask and furrow my brow.

"I am Miss Havisham," she announces, sounding slightly devastated. She looks at me with determination in her face. "I know what I need to do. Liv, I need to find *her*...."

"Michelle, what are you talking about? Find who?" I ask, my head tilting in curiosity.

"I can't go back to L.A. I'm staying here in Colorado. I can't go back to that place," she continues, her big eyes still wide and full of trepidation. "It's toxic..." she whispers.

"What, no? You have to come back! What about school?" I ask, panicked and saddened that she won't be there with me anymore. She stares resolutely out the window.

"I'll probably just take a couple classes at CU Boulder. You will do just fine without me girl, probably better. Just promise you will come visit me." She gives me a toothy grin. It is one of the most calm, peaceful, and genuine smiles that I have ever seen.

"Of course I will visit! As long as I can drive the 'Rari again!" I declare and wink.

"Totally! Vroom, vroom!" She kisses me on the forehead. "Lets get you ready for the ball, princess!"

We half run upstairs to her bedroom. She rummages through the top drawer of her dresser and pulls out a piece of lingerie. It's crimson red with roses sewn into it... it looks deliciously exotic, like it was custom made for a rock star.

"Okay, put this on first. It goes with the red lace panties and the black tights," she says and tosses them to me. She grabs a flirty short red dress from a hanger in the closet and a pair of classic Christian Louboutin heels from her shoe wall. I watch her stuff makeup and perfume into a white Hermès Birkin purse. She hands me the bag. "It's yours, all of it..." She looks relieved and at peace.

357

"Michelle, are you sure?" I ask hesitantly. "I don't think I can accept all of this."

"Dude! It's just stuff. I don't give a fuck about stuff anymore. You can have whatever you want from my closet at home too. But promise me one thing..." she says as she fastens a rose gold Rolex onto my wrist.

"What's that?" I ask.

"I want letters about where you wore it and what you did in it. How you *felt* wearing it. The memories attached to the stuff are far more important to me now," she explains as she hands me a leather bound notebook. "I prefer hand written letters." She writes her Aspen address on the first page of the book. "The first letter should be about how you felt walking up the stairs of the Gulfstream in this sexy red dress! I want details! Did it blow in the wind? Did you choose the nude lipstick or the classic red Chanel?" She smiles deeply and I remember why I love her.

"I will write you from the plane, I promise," I reply sincerely.

"I packed you a bag for Chicago. It's already in the car. I'll send the bag you packed for Aspen back to Bel Air," she says.

"Thank you Michelle. Thank you so much..." I say and mean it with all my soul. We walk downstairs together in silence. My Louboutin heels leave red tracers of confidence behind me as I follow her towards the door. We step outside together into the warm Colorado sun.

"Ah! It's so fucking bright here!" she exclaims. "Hang on..." She runs inside the house. When she comes back, her wig has been removed and she is wearing a pair of plastic yellow sunglasses with the words Veuve Clicquot on the sides. She hands me her Tom Ford sunglasses.

"Your Samantha glasses?" I ask, stunned. She smiles warmly.

"Wear them and think of me," she says.

"I will... I will think of you by the flower bed!" I respond. I feel tears welling up in my eyes.

"Stop! Don't cry! Your makeup is perfect!" she scolds. I nod and take a deep breath.

"Those are cool glasses!" I compliment, fighting back tears.

"I love them too!" she says as she touches the sides. "I love my Tom Ford sunglasses too, but Liv, they were ordered by my stylist. They came in the mail in a mountain of other stuff. These sunglasses are not fancy, they're plastic and cheap,... actually, they were free! But the memory of that day comes back to me when I wear them. I got them from a champagne tent at the top of Aspen Mountain when I was with *her*," Michelle says and puts her hand to her heart.

"Michelle, who are you talking about? Who is she?" I ask curiously.

"I'll explain everything in my first letter to you," she says and pulls me in for a kiss. It's a platonic kiss, not ill-intentioned or hyper sexualized, but rather, a soulful kiss that goes beyond anything sexual... finally.

"Bye Olivia," she says, and I sparkle when she calls me by my full name.

"Be good, Queen Michelle," I respond. She beams at me as I gingerly step into the backseat of the Rolls Royce. Michelle displays the peace sign as she holds both arms out into the crisp mountain air. Her billion-dollar smile is splashed across her face as she turns her gaze to the sky with a look of satisfaction and relief. She looks like Richard Nixon on the helicopter pad after he resigned as President and left the White House. Like him, she has been freed from her life of deceit. She has chosen to resign from the confines of her personal prison walls; her life sentence as a plastic in L.A. as been commuted. Still beaming, she stares blissfully into the sky, her bald head naked beneath the sun. She shines brighter than the sunrise on a Colorado summer morning. A calmness surrounds her as her long purple dress blows in the wind, leaving positive electromagnetic energies of peace and love with each movement it makes.

I feel tears roll down my cheeks at the sight of her. This is far better than the macabre Rolls Royce in the pool scene. I will never forget this moment. I love this demented and conflicted princess and I always will. I pull out the compact with Marilyn Monroe shining brightly on the cover from the purse that she gave me. I snap it open and wipe away the makeup that I ruined with my tears. I take a deep and cleansing breath and pull out my red Chanel lipstick.

"I picked the red one, Michelle. It's the color of confidence."

The Gulfstream

The Rolls Royce pulls slowly onto the tarmac. My eyes find the Swanson's plane immediately. The gold undercarriage is mesmerizing and impossible to miss. I feel bad for the lesser aircraft that have the misfortune of being parked next to it. The private jet stable in Aspen is as competitive as it gets, but there's always one aircraft that is the alpha.

I think about the day I met Chase and the instant spark between us. It's hard to believe how much our relationship has evolved since then. I never would have imagined in my wildest dreams that I would be here right now, about to climb onto his jet to go be with him. *G550* is splashed boldly across the tail of the plane. The jet's perfect curvature and long wing span suggest that it is a machine built for power and speed. The angular lines scream glamour, sophistication, and world class engineering. The Gulfstream is flirting with me, prancing and strutting, promising the world. The allure of glamour + adventure is bewitching and my heart skips a beat knowing that this beautiful bird will soon be soaring gracefully into the endless sky, to carry me home.

My luggage has been retrieved and placed into the back of the plane. This time around, I am far more confident about how this whole flying private thing works. I step out of the Rolls Royce, feeling like a princess as my red bottoms touch the tarmac. My red dress lifts in the wind. I feel like Marilyn Monroe as I bashfully push my dress down to cover my red lace panties which are being exposed to the men working nearby. They watch me with admiring eyes. I strut in my Louboutins towards the long sleek jet. I feel like a celebrity, like Hollywood royalty as I walk with all eyes upon me. I hear the sound of the Phantom's powerful engine as it slowly glides away, disappearing like the apparition that it is, or maybe I am the apparition... I feel like a phantom invading a dream realm. My legs move in slow motion across the tarmac. The stairs drop like a needle onto a song and my heels make click clack noises up every step. I am stunned when I see the inside of the plane; it might be more impressive than the exterior. The ceiling and sides of the interior are wrapped in immaculately quilted black leather. The seats are a decadent Ferrari red. There are several darkly glossed mahogany tables offering golden buckets of champagne on ice and baskets filled with treats. I forget it all in an instant when I see him sitting on a couch off to the side. The Gulfstream can seat at least fifteen people, maybe more, but it is just *him* waiting devotedly for *me*, Olivia Jean Walker from nowhere, Illinois. Chase Swanson is here to fly *me* to Chicago. It is so surreal, it's hard to fathom. My stomach tingles as I watch him take a pull from the beer bottle in his hand. He is wearing jumbo B&W headphones and bobbing his head to the music that is pulsing through them.

"Chase?!" I shout, hoping he can hear me over the music. We make eye contact and he chokes on the beer he just swallowed. He looks a little embarrassed as he coughs and sets the bottle down on the table next to him.

"Damn," he whispers, visibly tracing my body with his eyes. I notice that his eye color is dead neutral right now, not quite blue, not quite green.

"I thought you were already in Chicago?" I give him my own thousand-watt smile. I pull off my Tom Ford sunglasses and flip my hair confidently off my shoulder. His mouth drops.

"Nice dress..." he barely manages to say.

"Thanks," I reply with a grin.

"I was there, but... I wanted to fly with you," he answers, stumbling over his words. My long legs propel me to his hesitant body on the couch. I lean down, staring into his eyes for a moment.. and then I kiss him, smearing red lipstick all over his lips. Our tongues embrace and quickly remember how to explore and excite each other. I revel in his scent and his taste. I run my fingers through his hair. That messy hair, I've missed it so much. He leans back into the couch.

"Wow...." he whispers and shakes his head, looking pleased. "You're mine?" He pulls me effortlessly onto his lap.

"That's one possibility..." I reply coyly. I am swept away as I remember how much I love to kiss him, to feel him, to taste him. I grind back and forth, kissing his neck and his deliciously sexy

364

mouth. My red lace panties are instantly wet from rubbing against his hardness. He is moaning and his hands are exploring my body. The pilot announces that it is time for take off and requests that we buckle up because the ascent out of Aspen will be bumpy. I hop off his lap and walk to one of the red leather chairs. I start to buckle the seatbelt and he smirks at me.

"Come back here," he demands and pats the seat next to him.

"I can sit on that during take off?" I ask, astonished. He grins and points to the seat belts that are attached to the couch.

"Of course," he says. I sit down and he reaches around me and secures me. "Are you ready for the ride of your life?" His mouth and neck are covered in my red lipstick, and I can't wait to leave traces of it on the forbidden parts of him. I stare longingly at the erection straining against his pants.

"I should ask you the same thing," I say provocatively, in a sultry tone that I hardly recognize as my own. He raises a fascinated eyebrow at me. I drag my fingertips lightly along his hard on, tempting and teasing him over his pants.

He takes a deep breath and bites his lip. I give him my best bedroom eyes as I tease and tug at his belt buckle. When I pull my hands away, his gleaming green eyes burn with a desire more powerful than the jet engines currently thrumming against the fuselage, fully engaged and ready to thrust the Gulfstream into the air in one powerful rush of energy. There is something mystical about flight. What was once only a fantasy, an insurmountable barrier, now empowers us to explore the world in hours instead of months, or even years. I am sitting here in one of the most magnificent, innovative pieces of machinery ever designed; a pinnacle in the art of aviation, and I can't help but feel pity for my ancestors who had to suffer in covered wagons for months at a time, some not even making it to their final destination. How vastly different... I catch myself. Liv, stop being a nerd! I chastise myself and shake all thoughts of the Oregon Trail and covered wagons from my head. I bat my lashes at Chase and attempt to reclaim my newfound racy and seductive persona.

"I love this jet," Chase announces, thankfully interrupting my not so sexy stream of thoughts. "... almost as much as I love you in this red dress," he says huskily. The intensity in his tone snaps me completely back to the present. My body is on high alert. I get chills from the exquisite feeling of his mouth against my skin as he glides his lips to my ear. He lightly sucks my earlobe, allowing his mouth to linger for a moment. "This Gulfstream is the big boy. It's the daddy, the boss... like me. I'm the boss of you, right baby?" he asks, and it's more a declaration than a question.

"Mmm hmm...." I purr, nodding obediently.

"It has Rolls Royce engines, that's what gives it power and thrust, like I'm about to give you," he says as he slides his hand up my leg and begins tracing the wet lace. I desperately want him to touch me fully, to release me from this agony. "Did you know that they made the wingspan wider in this version for a more comfortable ride?" he asks as he pulls my panties to the side. I bite my lip. "I'm not going to give you a comfortable ride though, I'm going to be rough with you," he growls. His eyes are absolutely glowing green now. He pauses to admire the cleavage that is spilling out of my tight red dress, as his skilled fingertip lingers on my clit, causing little lightning bolts of ecstasy to surge through my body. He tugs at my panties, snapping the elastic against my inner thigh. I slip them off quickly without him having to ask and he rewards me with a sly smile. "Good girl. I'm keeping these," he says, tossing my panties behind him as he pulls me in for a deep kiss. His hand is beyond fluent and it takes all of my focus not to immediately orgasm as he fingers me while massaging my clit with his thumb. All of the things he already has going for him and oh btw, he's also the pussy whisperer. Life isn't fair sometimes. I bite his lip and moan, "Oh my god... oh fuck, Chase!" I whimper, overwhelmed with erotic sensations. "I missed you baby.... I missed you so much!"

"I missed you too, babe," Chase whispers and kisses me gently. The pleasure is escalating deliciously, perfectly in sync with the big jet which is rising swiftly into the fading crimson sky. Chase is like the plane to me. Powerful, luxurious, and one-of-a kind. I can't resist his hypnotic charm, his masculine presence, or his indifferent demeanor. He has complete control over me. The plane bounces a little as it rises and it only intensifies what he is doing to me.

"Oh fuck, turbulence is amazing!" I groan through strained lips.

"For real," he whispers in my ear. "But unless you want to get spanked, you're going to hold out until this plane reaches cruising altitude."

"I don't know if I can make it!" I whimper and he moves his hand down to my thigh in response. "No, please!" I beg, pushing his hand back up my skirt. "Don't stop!" He teases his fingers casually around my wetness, but purposely not on the spot that is desperately aching for his attention. I have never felt torture like this before. Chase however, clearly enjoys it. The plane finally hits the peak of its climb and so do I. He gives me me a naughty smile and shoves two fingers inside of me while his other hand massages my clit. I push my hips into his hands, crying out as I go over the edge. Wave after wave of orgasm surges through me. My legs are still trembling after I lay my head back onto the red leather and attempt to catch my breath. I need to level out, like the plane is so gracefully doing right now. Chase has other plans. He eagerly unbuckles my seat belt and I tear at the belt buckle on his pants as he frees me. I can hear Ariana Grande sensually singing "Dangerous Woman" through the plane's sound system. She is coaxing me to do naughty things to him. I want his pants off now. I unbutton them and pull them down to his ankles. I hear his belt buckle hit the floor, and I smile at the sight of his large cock pulsating, straining, desperate for my touch. I kneel between his legs and run my tongue slowly and teasingly over his balls and up his luscious shaft, lingering at the top while I watch him seductively through my lashes, knowing I'm leaving traces of Chanel red lipstick behind. He moans and lays his head back against the leather. I kiss my way up to his chest and slide my cleavage gently along his shaft, but I'm not ready to give him what he wants yet. I lay on my back across the mahogany table and spread my legs open to tease him, giving him a full view as I cross and uncross my legs to the beat of the music.

"Jesus, Liv. Where did you learn this stuff?" he asks, stunned. I give him my own wicked grin, and open my legs even wider for him. I slide my middle finger inside myself. "Fuck… you're so hot…" he whispers, and I notice that his voice doesn't sound as stern and commanding as it usually does. I am melting him with sexual desire and bringing him under my control for once. I stand up in my heels and saunter over to him. I stick the finger that was just inside me into his mouth and he grins and bites down on it. "Delicious,… now turn around and bend over," he demands. I shake my head no and smile as I slip a strap off of my shoulder, I remove the other strap slowly and slide the red dress down to the floor. I step out of it and stand in front of him in just my red corset and heels. "Wow…" he says with wide eyes. "Oh my God, you are so fucking sexy! Please take that thing off so I can see your tits…"

he begs. I trace my red lips with my finger and drag it lightly down my throat and into my cleavage. I push my finger in and out of my boobs which are pushed up dramatically by the corset's underwire. He is watching me with a hunger I have never seen before and it makes me feel powerful and seductive. I turn away, arch my back and spank my firm ass cheek.

I spin back around and sit on his lap, grinding against him to the beat of the music, but only for a moment. As I move away he tries to grab me to pull me back onto his lap but I stand up defiantly and strut away from him. I look back over my shoulder with dangerous bedroom eyes and bite my bottom lip to tease him. I throw my head back and my hair cascades down my bare skin. My hips move to the music as I unhook the corset. I turn around to face him as I slowly peel it off, freeing my breasts one at a time. He is spellbound and I am now completely naked in front of him except for the heels. His eyes are glowing with lust. I take my sweet time straddling him, enjoying that his cock is throbbing and straining to reach me. When I finally feel his warm erection pulsing between my legs, I push my boobs into his face and slide slowly down the shaft. Even though I'm really wet, I have to swivel my hips around to work it in. He moans loudly as he cups my ass.

"Fuck, you're so tight!" he hisses.

"I'm going to give you the ride of your life," I whisper into his ear. I slide up and down slowly, grinding my hips into him each time as I reach the bottom. I can tell he is fighting the urge to cum, and so am I. I slide all the way down on it, until I feel his balls smash against my ass. This makes me even hotter and my hips instinctively begin rocking back and forth into the base of his thick shaft, milking his cock as I pull him deeper inside of me. I orgasm almost immediately. I feel myself tighten around him as I cum with him fully in me, and I can tell its driving him wild. When I'm finished, I slowly glide up his shaft again.

"Holy shit... yes!" he yells. I suddenly stop at the top and lift my hips off of it. "No, Liv! Oh fuck.... please don't stop! I need to cum!" he begs.

"Karma," I whisper. I stare into his eyes and slowly slide back down onto it, much to his delight, and then slide up and all the way off of it again. He groans with frustration. I tease him like this until I know he can't take it anymore and he is about to explode. I start riding up and down his dick to the tempo of the song. He grips the red leather so hard he might tear it. I run my fingers through his hair and suck on his neck. "Poor baby, do you need to fill me up with your cum?" I ask, my voice low and sultry. His eyes are slits of pure lust. I start riding him harder and faster, my boobs bouncing and hitting him in the face, as my wet pussy slides all the way down to his balls with every stroke. He only makes it through a few moments of this and then his hands clench my ass like a lion taking down a zebra and he orgasms harder than I thought possible. His back arches powerfully, lifting us both off of the couch as I lace my fingers tightly into his hair and bite down hard on his bottom lip. The intensity quickly builds to a crescendo and his entire body ripples with release as he pumps wave after wave of warm cum into me. His orgasm is the hottest thing I've ever experienced and I feel myself going over the edge for a third time. I don't fight it. Moments later, we're both sweaty and satisfied as I lay against him.

"Holy shit..." is all I can manage to say as I kiss his cheek.

"Damn..." he whispers and kisses my shoulder. "Hottest plane ride of my life! Definitely my favorite mile high experience!" he says casually. I cringe. I think about all the other women he has had on private jets. About how many times he has joined the mile-high club. I can feel intense bitterness creeping over me. He kisses my neck sweetly.

"God, I love you," he says carelessly. I hate the casual tone in which he just said those powerful three little words that every girl so desperately wants to hear... words that I so desperately wanted to hear. I glare at him.

"You don't love me, you love what I can do for you," I snap, and the cold, cutting tone in my voice makes him grimace. He looks like I just slapped him as I stand up and snatch my red dress from the floor, holding it against my body as I stride to the bathroom. I lock the door behind me and try to calm my breathing. I study my angry amber eyes in the mirror. Since when did I get so jaded, so distrustful? I fight the anger, clean myself up and put the dress back on. When I finally come out of the bathroom, Chase is dead asleep, tranquilized by his own cum coma. Yet another unfair advantage men have. We don't get those, we just get to lay awake all night, wracked with angst, thinking about what just occurred and whether the sex really meant anything or if we were just used. I pick up his half empty beer bottle from the mahogany table next to him and sit on one of the red leather seats across from him. I take a sip and take him in. He really is stunning. The beer is lukewarm at this point but I don't care, the alcohol is soothing me. I look at the bottle - Stella. Such a pretty name, it reminds me of Estella from *Great Expectations*. Poor Estella, incapable of love and never able to be vulnerable. What a tragic way to go through life. I sigh and open the Birkin bag Michelle gave me. I pull out the leather bound notebook and flip it open to begin writing her a letter, but the page isn't blank... and it's in Michelle's hand writing.

   "I am what you designed me to be. I am your blade. You cannot now complain if you also feel the hurt." - "'Great Expectations.'" Next to the quote is a doodle of a rose in what looks like a snow globe. It's beautiful. I squint closely. The rose is black and has writing in a petal. Another *Great Expectations* quote: *"My heart is as cold as ice."* A shiver runs down my spine, and I realize I am gripping the beer bottle so tightly my knuckles are white. I set the bottle down and turn to the next page; my stomach drops harder than the Gulfstream, which is just beginning its descent into Chicago O'Hare.

Truth Journal: *6/11*

"This fucking truth journal is the dumbest shit ever, but I'll play along. I've been home for a day, and everyone is just as dysfunctional as they were when I left. My dad is still an egotistical asshole, despite all the hippy dippy spirit quest bullshit he's been doing. I was trying to figure out how to kill myself with an ice cube during his speech about chakras and mindfulness while his spiritual healer, Dante, or whatever this latest clown of the week is named, was kissing his ass. Such a douchebag. I kept catching him eye fucking my sister, which made me want to strangle him. Mom is still a raging alcoholic with a pill problem. She's been crying and laughing and downing handfuls of pills with scotch and wine.

I have to admit, it's pretty emasculating to move back home at 25, especially under the same roof as my raging narcissist father, but I have to play their fucking game if I'm going to take over Swanson Music Group some day. Its a little ridiculous that I have to prove myself to him, especially since there's not really anyone to compete with for it. Certainly not Michelle - I love her but she's out of her damn mind. And I know there was a lot of whispering about me coming home - reckless, crazy Chase Swanson back in Bel Air oh no!... but I'm not actually crazy like they say I am. I was just a rich kid with too much money, privilege and freedom, and I liked being the "bad boy" so I played it up. Sure, I did a lot of stupid shit, but the thing that got me sent to military school wasn't my fault, and an over reaction if you ask me. Michelle was the one driving the Ferrari. I covered for her because she's my little sister, and I'm protective of her to a fault. Had I known it would have landed me in a military school and disowned by my father, I would have made her bite the bullet on that one. I still can't believe she never fessed up, even after I got sent away. What a little bitch. My sister is selfish and entitled and always has been. The only saving grace in the whole evening, was that hot little thing she brought for me."

I rub my sweaty palms against my dress as I realize that Chase is about to talk about the first time we met. My mouth is dry. I flip to the next page and feel a wave of nausea.

"I really like my sisters latest project. Watching her half dressed friend, Liz or Liv, whatever, made the lame conversation around me a little more bearable. I should look her up to see if she's a cheerleader at UCLA. She has that prissy good girl thing going on. Well done Michelle - I really enjoyed the view. I am going to need to fuck her at some point while I'm here so don't think about cock blocking me, you owe me and you know it, so stand down... ;) She was sitting on the couch across from me in a short little skirt, politely listening to my dad go on and on about himself. I kept trying to see what color her panties were each *time she crossed and uncrossed her legs. Her nipples were rock hard from the air conditioner, but it might have been from me - she seemed pretty smitten. I'm used to that reaction. My dick started to twitch while I was watching her though, and then she bites her lip and gives me this seductive look and it tried to climb out of my pants! It was kinda surprising. I've been with supermodels and had trouble getting it up and this little college girl makes me rock hard over a look?*

To be honest though, she had really pretty eyes and a gorgeous face and her body was amazing. Quite the gem. I especially liked her pouty mouth all greased up in that same lip shit that my sister wears. I can't wait to get her lips wrapped around my cock. She was smiling sweetly at everyone and kept running her fingers through her hair. I want to pull her hair. When she finally spoke more than two words, I heard a Midwest accent. That explains why she is so sweet and polished, she's not an L.A. bitch. She has that good girl thing going on, naïve and unassuming, sexy but doesn't know it yet. Those are my favorite kind of girls. The ones I like to corrupt. I hope she's a virgin. I've always wanted to fuck a virgin. There aren't many virgins left in L.A.

At one point, she noticed me checking her out and rolled her eyes. She probably saw my boner as I adjusted it. She had a look of alarm, like I kicked her puppy or something. Not quite the reaction I was hoping for but okay.... Who am I kidding? She probably has some nice boyfriend that cries when they have sex and writes her poetry.

My mom tried to move the party to the pool. My dad in his asshole tone told her no, that he and Emma had work to do. Oh, like Emma sucking you off? That bitchy Swedish assistant of his. She still looks good - scratch that, she's still hot. She has been working for my dad forever. I remember jerking off to her from age 13 on. She's a petite little spinner, like 5'1" which is why she is always wearing those heels.

Emma, that whore, I hope she remembers the pool party. She walked in on me while I was jerking off in the bathroom. She had just gotten new fake tits and they were spilling out of her tiny bikini and I couldn't take it. I had to go rub one out. When she caught me, I was embarrassed at first, and then I realized she was drunk and liked it. Like really liked it.

'Need some help with that?' she asked and then grabbed my dick before I even answered and looked me right in the eyes with this super naughty, almost wild look. 'I can be very discreet...' she said then dropped to her knees and opened a little bullet of coke on her necklace.

'First I'm going to blow this...' she said, as she tapped out a long thick rail onto my 17-year-old cock and then blows the whole thing in one pass.

'Now what else should I blow...' she asked with a wicked smile and then started deep throating me like she was going to

win a prize. *Still the best blow job of my life. That was a month before I got sent to military school. Part of me wonders if my father found out and it factored into his decision to tell me to fuck off forever. I think he might be in love with Emma. He doesn't appear to love my mom or really anyone for that matter. Probably the closest thing he has ever felt like love is towards Emma. Whatever, my mom is happy with her boyfriend, who happens to be my best friend. I was furious at first, but I'm not anymore, I just want her to be happy. I also made a vow to myself to never get married. Monogamy is a joke.*

Speaking of not being monogamous, I'm so horny right now... I should hit up that struggling pop star Sierra. She texted me a picture of her tits earlier. She will take care of me... L.A. girls will do anything for fame.

I turn the page with a shaking hand.

"I saw my sister and her friend out by the pool. She looked really hot sipping champagne. I liked the way she brought the flute to her lips. Confession - I'm rock hard in my room right now, and it's not from Sierra. I didn't even call her. Sierra is hot too, but fuck, I can't get that other girl out of my mind. I started leaking pre cum just thinking about her so I used it for lube and jerked off. Came in like a minute - shot the first four or five ropes over my head - thinking about Michelle's friend and her long legs in that short skirt with those perfect perky tits. I have a lot to teach a little girl like that."

I hastily shut the notebook. What the fuck did I just read? My face falls as a shockwave runs through my body. I remember Michelle and Chase talking about a 'truth journal' while we were in the bowling alley. Why would she give this to me? Is this some sort of sick joke?

I try and act normal when I see Chase wake up as the wheels hit the runway. He glances over at me and gives me a sexy smile.

"Why are you over there?" he asks in his effortlessly flirty tone, the tone that is just so Chase. I can't fake it. I can't return the smile. I feel disdain. I feel bitterness. My worst fear was just confirmed. I was just a conquest. He stares at me intently with concern flashing in his eyes which have returned to a blue-green. "Liv, are you okay, baby?"

"Don't call me baby," I respond sharply. He unbuckles, stretches out, and yawns.

"Can I get your bag for you?" he asks, ignoring my confrontational spirit.

"No. I can get it," I say coldly and snatch it from the ground. There is a blacked out Escalade waiting for us on the tarmac. I walk as fast as I can to it in my heels. He is tipping the line guys who are placing our luggage in the back of the SUV. When he is done, he casually slips into the backseat of the Escalade next to me. His scent drifts towards me. He smells like sex, like passion, like risk; like Chase. He moves his hand towards my thigh and I quickly push it away.

"What the fuck, Liv?" he asks, startled.

"It's Olivia... Not Liv. Not *Liz*, either," I hiss and glare at him. His whole body deflates as a look of recognition splays across his face.

"You started reading it, didn't you?" he asks.

"This?" I shout and pull the leather bound notebook from my purse. I wave it in his face. "Yeah, I did! You're sick! This is sick! Why would you guys want me to read that?" I scream at him.

"I just want to be an open book, for once," he says as he looks out the window at the Chicago skyline.

"What do you want from me, Chase?" I ask angrily.

"I want you," he says quietly. I roll my eyes.

"We're done. It's over," I say evenly and cruelly. I stare out the window and watch all the familiarity of Chicago pass me by as we sit in silence. I feel numb even when I see Navy Pier in the distance and think of my mother. I think about the day we went there together. I kissed her on the cheek as I thanked her for taking me. She gave me the sweetest smile. It was the same smile that she gave me right before she took her last breath. She died when I was a teenager. It wasn't fair. I watched her lose to cancer for eight fucking years. I spent my childhood caring for her. I wasn't on private planes flying from Chicago to London and living a sheltered and charmed life like Chase Swanson. We are definitely from different worlds. I will never have it easy like him. The Prince of Bel Air never was and never will be my other. He doesn't belong to me. This life doesn't belong to me.

Chicago Penthouse

The Escalade is driving towards Navy Pier, and I cross my arms bitterly as it pulls into the parking lot.

"What are we doing here?" I ask Chase coldly.

"You told me you would go with me to the Pier..." he says quietly.

"I said I would go to the *Santa Monica* Pier with you and that's not going to happen, ever." I scoff. "Also, if you haven't noticed, Navy Pier is closed. Great job, Chase," I retort frostily. I can see the driver giving me that *"what a bitch"* look from the rearview mirror but I don't care.

"Liv. Please. I planned something. Will you just give me a chance?" he asks and looks as if he might cry. I scowl at him.

"I thought for sure you would take me to the *fabulous* Swanson Chicago Penthouse on the 95th floor in the tallest building in all of Chicago so you can wine and dine and use me some more for your sick pleasure!" I snap. He sighs in defeat and I feel vindicated by his pain. He reaches into a black leather duffle bag near his feet. His hands are shaking as he pulls something out of it.

"I got you something.... I don't really know how to wrap," Chase says as he hands me a box wrapped sloppily in newspaper. Much to my dismay, a little smile starts to form on my face over his

382

horrible wrapping job. "The newspaper is from Kaneville... your town," he says as he turns on the dome light. I stare, stunned at the pictures of my high school.

"*Kaneland High School. Mr. Keefe Earns Teacher of the Year Award.*" I read the title of an article and start to cry. The nostalgia is crushing, and I feel homesick and sad.

"Mr. Keefe was my favorite..." I whisper, fighting back tears. I know that if I start crying, I'll never be able to stop. "And this was my favorite restaurant," I mumble, looking at the owners of the diner I went to with my mom.

"Will you please open the gift?" Chase pleads. I unwrap carefully so I don't rip the newspaper; I want to keep it. I pull out a turquoise box. Chase carefully folds the newspaper for me and tucks it into my purse as I pop the lid off the box and feel around through gold tissue paper. At the bottom I find something smooth and round. I pull it out curiously. It's a snow globe. The scene inside of it looks like a quaint European village.

"That's Chamonix, France," he says softly. There is a man in a red ski suit, his skis and poles planted in the snow next to him. Across from him is a girl in a white ski jacket with a fur hood and matching white ski pants. They're facing each other and holding hands. She is smiling wholeheartedly, but not at him. Her head is facing upwards, like she is staring at me. I gasp when I see the color of her eyes; they are amber. She looks just like me! The boy in the ski gear is staring and smiling at her in adoration. His aquamarine eyes are sparkling. "And..... that's us..." Chase mumbles. Transfixed, I shake the snow globe and stare wide eyed as I watch the fake snow flakes and flecks of gold come to life and surround the picturesque scene that he had created for me. "Real 24 Karat gold," he mutters and clears his throat nervously. "Let me show you the best part." He reaches for it carefully from my now frozen hands. He flips it over and winds the handle on the bottom. A lullaby version of "All You Need Is Love" fills the silence. It is magical. I can't help myself as I place my hand over my heart and tears well up in my eyes. Chase shakes the snow globe again and I watch, transfixed, as the crystals of snow and the flecks of gold dance to the music.

"Chase, this was the song that my dad and I picked for the memorial video at my mom's funeral," I can barely breathe. "How did you..." The tears are streaming down my face at such a rapid rate that I can barely speak or keep up with wiping them away.

"Also, I finished Snow Globe," he says and hands me a folder. I take it and see his sheet music and his lyrics. "You should probably know that you have been my muse the entire time." He sighs. "Read from here on," he says, pointing.

Invited inside to explore by your fire
Mirrors on walls catching flickers of flames
But entitled eyes see only entitled liars
And reflections that blind will burn the same way

I'm trapped here in this snow globe world baby
No more shaking this glass must be shattered
You've waited so patiently waiting to save me
These diamonds don't love me they just want to bury me

Lake Shore Drive

"Oh wow... Chase. Oh my God...." I try to speak but I can't find the words. My racing mind is interrupted by the sound of a car pulling up next to us in the empty parking lot. I recognize it immediately. It's my dad's old truck. My daddy, Jesse Walker, who I have completely ignored for an entire year is here to meet me at Navy Pier. I didn't even visit him over the holidays. The sweetest man alive and I picked the Swanson's instead. I watch him step out of the car in his faded blue jeans and white button down. I grin when I see he is wearing a bowtie and a sports coat. My dad never dresses up. He is holding a single red rose. He straightens his bowtie as he nervously looks around. The love and pain I feel at this moment is the most intense combination I have ever felt; a speedball of emotion. I am no longer numb. I ache for him. I miss him. I miss him so much. I open the car door as quickly as I can, toss my heels to the side and run to him.

"Daddy!" I squeal and hug him tightly.

"Livvie Jean!" He pulls me to him. "Sweetheart, you are skin and bones!" he says with concern in his eyes. "Let me make you a big meal when we get home. And your hair, it's different!" He runs his fingers through it and I hug him tightly. I take in his scent. It brings me feelings of comfort and familiarity. The emotions overwhelm me. He wipes my eyes tenderly, "Don't cry sweetheart," he says gently as he kisses my forehead. "That nice friend of yours set up something very special for us." He takes my hand and leads me to the entryway to Navy Pier. I stand hand in hand with him at the bottom of the staircase.

"That Chase Swanson is a very sweet boy," he says. "He stayed at our home last week for a few days. Everyone in town loved him!" My mouth drops.

"What?!? He did?" I ask in disbelief. He nods as he stares with an excited smile at the entryway to the Pier.

There are large speakers, a microphone and a guitar set up underneath the Navy Pier sign. I see a man walking to the microphone. No... way... I hardly believe what I'm seeing. I gasp, and my hand goes to my mouth to try and muffle my squeal. My dad's grin is so wide it could light up all of Navy Pier! Hell, it could light up all of Chicago.

"Good evening Jesse and Olivia Walker," Paul McCartney says in his smooth British accent. "Thank you for coming tonight! Chase informed me that Abbey Road is Olivia's favorite album. I would like to play you two a very special song. I know what it's like to lose someone who you love. Losing John and George was rather difficult, but memory lives on in song. George Harrison wrote this song, and I think of him fondly every time I perform it. And remember, the sun will always come out tomorrow," he purrs into the microphone as he picks up the guitar and begins to pick the notes to the familiar tune. Tears are streaming down my face and I feel like the wind has been knocked out of me. More lights turn on revealing the Chicago Symphony Orchestra behind Paul McCartney. Playing together as one, they give us the most magical performance of "Here Comes the Sun" that I could have ever imagined. I have goosebumps from head to toe. I look around and suddenly realize that this is a private concert, just for us. Navy Pier has been completely blocked off by security guards and police officers. My dad takes my hand and wraps his arm around my waist as we dance together beneath the lights. I squeal with delight when he twirls me, my red dress dancing in the Illinois summer wind. I see Chase watching with his arms crossed. He looks satisfied and yet conflicted. I beam at him and mouth, *"thank you!"* He smiles back at me with the most genuine, authentic, magnetic smile I think I've ever seen. It conveys a thousand promises and a thousand lies and I will take the lies with the truths just to see it every single day. I love those twinkling bad boy blue-green eyes. I love that dark angel. I love that haunted soul. I blow him a kiss. He stands upright and gives me a stern and professional military salute.

Then, I watch in horror as he climbs into the back of the SUV and closes the door. My heart stops as I watch it leave the parking lot. He left all of my stuff outside by my dad's car. I see the turquoise box and the music sheets blowing in the wind.

"But... I wanted him to kiss me on the Ferris Wheel..." I whisper as Paul McCartney croons the lyrics to "Something" into the microphone.

To be continued...

BIO

Sloane Carter has a phenomenal imagination and the gift of creating addictively seductive storylines, leaving readers desperate for more. She lives in Colorado with her Boston terrier, her unusually sexy husband, (who also happens to be an amazing editor and sounding board), and their two teenage sons.

Made in the USA
Las Vegas, NV
02 February 2021